Includes Bonus Story of
Lucy's Quilt
by JOYCE LIVINGSTON

The House on Windridge

TRACIE PETERSON

BARBOUR BOOKS
An Imprint of Barbour Publishing, Inc.

The House on Windridge ©1998 by Barbour Publishing, Inc.
Lucy's Quilt ©2002 by Joyce Livingston

Print ISBN 978-1-63409-778-9

eBook Editions:
Adobe Digital Edition (.epub) 978-1-63409-874-8
Kindle and MobiPocket Edition (.prc) 978-1-63409-875-5

All scripture quotations are taken from the King James Version of the Bible.

This book is a work of fiction. Names, characters, places, and incidents are either products of the author's imagination or used fictitiously. Any similarity to actual people, organizations, and/or events is purely coincidental.

Published by Barbour Books, an imprint of Barbour Publishing, Inc., P.O. Box 719, Uhrichsville, OH 44683, www.barbourbooks.com

Our mission is to publish and distribute inspirational products offering exceptional value and biblical encouragement to the masses.

ecpa Member of the
Evangelical Christian
Publishers Association

Printed in the United States of America

Prologue

The pathetic cries of a newborn continued to split the otherwise heavy silence of the day long after the sheet had been pulled up to cover the infant's dead mother. The baby's hunger and misery seemed to feed her wails, despite the housekeeper's attempts to soothe and comfort the distraught child.

Gus Gussop had already borne the pain of hearing the housekeeper tell him his wife was dead. Now he faced the hopelessness of trying to satisfy a newborn—his wife's departing gift. Running his hands through his chestnut hair, Gus felt pain more acute than any he'd ever known. The tightening in his chest gave him cause to wonder if his heart had suddenly attacked him. He prayed it would be so and that he might join his beloved Naomi in eternal rest.

The baby's high-pitched cries intensified, causing Gus to storm from the room. "Find some way to shut her up!" he bellowed over his shoulder.

Slamming the door to the bedroom he'd shared with Naomi, Gus made his way downstairs to the front door. But he'd no sooner reached it than he heard the approaching footsteps of his good friend and ranch foreman, Buck Marcus.

"I'm deeply sorry for you, Gus," came Buck's apologetic voice.

"What do you want?"

"You can't be going out there now," Buck reminded. "Did you forget we're in the midst of a blizzard? Ain't no visibility for miles, and you'd surely freeze to death before you made it ten feet."

"Well, maybe I want to freeze to death," Gus answered flatly, turning to scowl at the red-haired Buck. "Leave me be."

Buck nodded at the order and took his leave, but when Gus turned back to the massive front door, he knew the man was right. For a few minutes, all Gus could do was stare at the highly ornate oak door—stare and remember. He'd paid a handsome sum to have the door designed with stained glass and detailed woodcarving. Naomi had been so very fond of pretty things, and this door, this entire house for that matter, had been Gus's gift to her for having a good nature about moving to the Flint Hills from her beloved home in New York City.

He turned and looked up at the beautifully crafted oak staircase. Wood came at a premium in Kansas. For that matter, with a nation at war against itself, everything came at a premium. But Gus had found ways around the inconvenience of war. The beautifully grained oak had been meticulously ordered and delivered over a two-year period, all in order to give his wife the best. The wood floors and heavy paneling in the library had been equally difficult to come by, but Gus had successfully managed each and every problem until he had exactly what he wanted for his impressive ranch house.

The house itself had been designed out of native limestone and stood atop the hill Gus had affectionately named "Windridge." They said the wind in Kansas was the reason that trees seldom stayed in place long enough to grow into anything worth noting. And while Gus had made his home on Windridge, or rather on the side of this massive hill, he was of the opinion that this was true. For miles around, they were lucky to find a single stubborn hedge tree or cottonwood. The rolling Flint Hills stretched out as far as the eye could see, and the only thing it was good for was grazing cattle.

Gus had built his empire, constructed his castle, married his queen, and now it all seemed to have been in vain. She was dead. Naomi had died in the house he had gifted her with upon their marriage, died giving birth to their only child.

"What do I do now?" Gus questioned aloud, looking up the stairs.

At least the baby had quieted. He had never once considered Naomi might die in childbirth. She seemed such a healthy, vital woman that to imagine her dead over something women did every day seemed preposterous. After all, they were only an hour away from Cottonwood Falls, and should there be any need for a doctor, Gus knew it would be easy enough to get one. But on the last day of the year, a blizzard had set in, making travel impossible. The storm had now raged for over twenty-four hours, and snow piled in drifts as high as the eaves on the house. The stylish circular porch was covered in ice and snow, and no one dared to set foot outside without a rope secured to him to guide him back to safety.

A line had been tied from the house to the barn and to the bunkhouse, but other than checking on the livestock, which had been crammed into every possible free spot in the barn, the men were ordered to stay inside, out of danger. This he could order and see performed to his specifications. But Naomi's labor was another matter entirely. It had begun in the midst of the storm and was so mild at first that Katie, their housekeeper, had thought it to be a false labor. But then Naomi's water broke, and Katie informed him that there would be no stopping the birth. The child simply would not wait until the storm abated.

Things went well for a time. Katie had attended many area birthings due to her experience growing up with a midwife for a mother. It didn't seem they had anything to worry about. But then the baby came breech, and Katie said the cord seemed caught up on something. She fought and worked her way through the birthing, praying aloud from time to time that she could save both mother and child. Standing at Naomi's side, offering what assistance he could, Gus had heard the prayers, but they didn't register. He still refused to believe that anything could mar the happiness he had shared together with Naomi.

But as the hours passed and he watched his wife grow weaker, he knew those prayers were very necessary. There seemed to be nothing Katie could do to ease Naomi's suffering. She instructed the young mother-to-be, and Naomi heeded her, performing whatever task she was told to do. Katie had her out of the bed at one point to squat in order to push the child down. But nothing seemed to work the way it should, and Katie soon began saying things that Gus didn't want to hear.

"We may lose the baby," she had told him. "We may lose them both."

Gus had gone to the door then, just as he had a few minutes ago. He had planned to fight his way through the storm to the doctor's, if necessary. But one look outside, and Gus had known there was no hope of leaving Windridge. He prayed the storm would abate. Prayed his child might be born safely. But never did he pray that Naomi might not die. It was unthinkable that such a thing could happen. It simply didn't fit Gus's plans.

But the unthinkable did happen.

Shortly before midnight, Jessica Gussop arrived as a New Year's Eve baby. She cried out in protest as Katie lifted her from her mother's body. She cried in protest when Katie cut the cord, and she cried in protest when Naomi, after holding the child and kissing her tiny head, had died.

He could still see the look in Naomi's eyes. She knew she wasn't going to make it. She smiled weakly at Gus, told him she loved him— that she would always love him. Then she whispered Jessica's name and closed her eyes.

Gus shook his head, trying to force the horrible scene from his mind. It just couldn't be true. They were all mistaken. He would go back upstairs now, and Naomi would sit up in bed and call his name.

He reached for the banister.

It was possible. They could be wrong.

Sorrow washed over him, and he knew without a doubt there had been no error in judgment. Her presence was gone from Windridge. There was nothing upstairs for him now. Naomi's body was there, but not the lighthearted laughter, not the sweet spirit he had fallen in love with.

She would never sit up. She would never call his name.

He turned and walked away from the staircase and passed through large double doors that slid open to usher him into the walnut-paneled library. This had been his refuge and sanctuary whenever the events of the day proved to be too much. Now, it only echoed the sounds of his heavy steps as he crossed to the desk where he did his book work.

She was gone. There was nothing left. Nothing to hope for. Nothing to live for.

He pulled open a drawer and saw the revolver that lay inside. He could join her. He could settle it all with one single bullet. The idea appealed to him in a way that went against all that he believed. He had shared a Christian faith with Naomi, had served as an elder in the church at Cottonwood Falls, and had always remembered to give God the glory for all that he'd been blessed with. To kill himself would directly violate God's law but to live violated his own sensibilities.

Gus heard the cry again and knew that before he could settle his own affairs, he would first have to do something about the baby. Jessica. Naomi had called her Jessica, and Jessica she would stay. He hadn't cared much for the name—had teased Naomi, in fact, about calling any daughter of his by such a fancy name. Bible names were good enough for the Gussop family. But then Naomi had reminded him that Jessica came from the masculine root of Jesse—the father of King David. So it was to be Jessica for a girl and Jesse for a boy. Gus had liked that idea. He'd liked it even more when Naomi, the granddaughter of a highly respected preacher in New York City, told him that Jesse meant "the Lord exists" and she liked very much to think that God would prove His existence through the life of this child.

"I see His existence, all right," Gus muttered. "The Lord giveth and the Lord taketh away." He refused to finish Job's ancient proclamation by blessing the name of the Lord.

"I can't raise a baby without a mother," Gus said emphatically. He slammed his hands down on the desk, then sent the contents flying with a wide sweep of his arm. "I can't do it! Do You understand!" he bellowed, "I won't do it!"

He shook his fist at the ceiling. "You can't expect me to do it without her. You can't be that cruel. You may give, and You may take away, but You can't expect me to be happy about it—to go about my business as if nothing has happened."

Silence. Even Jessica's cry had quieted. Gus looked down at the mess he'd made and slammed the desk drawer shut. First, he would see to the child. There would no doubt be someone who would take her and raise her to adulthood. Especially given the fact that upon his death, Jessica would inherit everything he owned. That would make her an attractive package to prospective parents. But who should he approach on the matter?

Katie, his housekeeper, was hardly the one to saddle with such a responsibility. At twenty-five, the thing that most amused Katie was Buck, and even though the man was thirteen years her senior, a May wedding was already in the works. No, it wouldn't be right to put Jessica off on Katie and Buck. Buck had been a friend to him long enough that Gus knew the man wanted no part of owning a big spread of his own. He'd told Gus on more than one occasion that if he died tomorrow he would be happy being Gus's hired man and friend.

Gus considered neighbors and friends in town, but no one struck him as having the right combination of requirements for raising his child. And those requirements were very important to him. Just because he didn't feel capable of seeing to the needs of his daughter didn't mean he wouldn't take those needs into consideration while choosing her guardian.

After several torturous days of thinking through all the possibilities, Gus had eliminated all names except one. Harriet Nelson. Harriet was the maiden aunt of his deceased wife. The woman had practically raised Naomi, and as far as Gus was concerned, she made the perfect choice for raising Naomi's daughter. But Harriet lived in New York City, and exchanging letters or even telegrams would take days—maybe months. Gus didn't like the idea, but it seemed his only recourse.

Then, too, Jessica was too young and sickly to travel. Katie had tried to find a proper source of nourishment for the child and had finally come up with sweetening and watering down canned milk. At least the poor babe could stomach the solution. Which was more than could be said for the other dozen concoctions that had been tried.

Taking pen in hand, Gus began the letter to Harriet. He explained the death of Naomi first, offering Harriet his condolences in recognition of her position as adoptive mother to his wife. Then he told her of Jessica. He described the child who'd been born with her mother's dark brown eyes, despite the fact that Katie had never heard of any infant being born with other than blue eyes. She also had her mother's dark brown hair, although there wasn't much of it. He described her as a good baby, telling of the trial and error in finding something to feed her. Then he concluded the letter by expressing his desire that Harriet take over the rearing of his daughter. He made no pretense about the issue.

> *I find that I am ill-equipped to care for an infant on a prairie ranch. The housekeeper has done a fine job, but with her own upcoming wedding, I hardly can rely on her for such assistance in the future.*
>
> *Harriet, you are the only one to whom I would entrust this job. The reflection of your ability was clearly displayed in Naomi's character. I know you would raise the child to be a good Christian and to occupy herself with godly service. I know, too, that Jessica would be loved and pampered. Please understand, I am well aware of my own responsibilities. I would, of course, provide financially for the child and yield to your authority on matters concerning her schooling.*
>
> *Please do not refuse me on this matter, Harriet. I know you planned a different life for Naomi, and apparently your choice would have been wiser. A Kansas cowboy and a prairie ranch were unworthy of a woman such as your niece, but I recognize my own limitations and would go so far as to say this is a matter of life and death. I would appreciate your speedy response on the matter.*
>
>

Ever Your Faithful Servant,
Joseph Gussop
>

He reread the letter several times before finally sealing it in an envelope and penning the New York address on the outside.

There, he thought. *The job is done. I have only to mail this letter and receive her response and then—then I can put this all behind me.*

Buck came in about that time. "Boss, we've been looking things over as best we can. Looks like most of the stock survived."

Gus nodded. He had little desire to talk about the ranch or his responsibilities.

"There's something else I need to discuss with you," Buck said hesitantly.

"Then speak up," Gus replied, seeing Buck's apprehension. It wasn't like the man to skirt around an issue.

"It has to do with her."

Gus felt the wind go out from him. For days the only way he'd managed to get through the hours was to avoid thinking about her. It was one thing to mention her in a letter to Harriet, but another thing to consider what was to be done in the aftermath of her death. In fact, he had no idea what had already been done in the way of preparing her for her burial. He'd simply refused to have any part of it.

"All right," he finally answered.

"Well," Buck began slowly, "I built her, ah. . ." He faltered. "I mean, well, that is to say—"

"You built her a coffin?" Gus questioned irritably.

Buck nodded. "Yes sir. We took her out like you asked. But Gus, the ground is too froze up for burial."

Gus growled and pounded his fists on the desk. "I don't care if you have to blow a hole in the ground with dynamite. I want her buried today." Buck nodded and without another word took off in the direction from which he'd come.

Several hours later, Gus heard and felt the explosion that signaled the use of dynamite. It rattled the windows and caused the baby to howl up a fit, but Gus knew instinctively that it would also resolve the problem. They would bury her today. Buck would say the words, given their inability to have the preacher ride out from town, and they would put her body into the ground.

Gus tried to think of everything analytically. First he would see to

Naomi. Then he would see to Jessica's care. Then he would take care of himself.

~

Two weeks after the little funeral, Gus was finally able to post his letter to Harriet in Cottonwood Falls. And two months after that, with a strangely warm March whipping up one of the first thunderstorms of the season, Gus rode back from town, reading the missive he'd received from New York City.

> *Of course, you must realize I am hardly the young woman I was when Naomi was small, but I would be honored to raise Jessica for as long as time permits.*

He breathed a sigh of relief. She had agreed to take the child. He continued reading.

> *However, I do have my own requirements to see to such an arrangement. First, I desire final say over her upbringing. As you pointed out, you are hardly aware of her needs. I want no interference, no monthly visits, no constant trips back and forth between the desolate American desert and New York. I want the child to know proper society and schooling before she is exposed to the barbaric plains of Kansas. I also believe it will diminish any sense of loss in the child. In other words, if she is constantly looking toward her next trip to Kansas, she may well be unruly and unwilling to focus on her life here.*

Well, Gus thought, *that certainly wasn't a problem.* He wouldn't be around, but of course, he couldn't tell Harriet that.

> *Secondly, I have devised the figures that I believe constitute the proper amount of money necessary to care properly for a child in New York City. She will be a child of social standing, and, therefore, the cost is higher than you might otherwise believe necessary.*

11

*If you will note the second page of this letter, however, you will see
I have detailed the information for you.*

Gus looked at the page and noted that Harriet had indeed outlined the cost for food, clothing, schooling, supplies, toys, furniture, and a nanny to assist Harriet. It all seemed perfectly reasonable, even if it was a pricey figure. *Still,* he thought, *it didn't matter.* He wouldn't be around to argue or protest Harriet's judgment. He turned back to the first page of the letter and continued to read.

*If these things meet with your approval, then I will expect to receive
the child whenever you deem yourself capable of delivering her.*

Gus breathed a sigh of relief. It was all falling into place.

Once he'd arrived at Windridge, Gus called Katie and Buck into the library and explained the situation.

"I'm sending Jessica to her mother's aunt in New York City," he said flatly, without a hint of emotion in his voice. His emotions were dead. Dead and cold, just as she was.

Katie spoke first. "What? How can you do this? I'm perfectly happy to bring her up for you, Mr. Gussop."

"Katie," he replied, "you and Buck are about to begin your lives together. There's no need to be saddling you with a ready-made family."

"But we don't mind," Katie insisted.

"Honestly, boss," Buck added, and Gus would have sworn there were tears in his eyes.

"This is how it's going to be," Gus stated, leaving no room for further protest. "The Flint Hills is no place to raise a child. The desolation and isolation would be cruel. There'll be no other children for her to grow up with, and the responsibilities of this ranch are enough to keep you both running from day to night. That is, unless you'd rather not stay on with me." Gus watched their expressions of sorrow turned to disbelief.

"Of course we'll stay on with you," Katie replied.

"Absolutely, boss. We're here to do our job but more important, we're here because we're friends."

Gus nodded. He would leave them both a hefty chunk of money upon his death. They were faithful and loyal, and a man didn't often find friends such as these.

"I have a favor to ask," he finally said. "I need Katie to take Jessica to New York. You can go along, too, Buck. Act as her escort. Miss Nelson is expecting the child, and the sooner we get started on it, the better. I'll go with you into town, and we'll purchase train tickets. I'll also draw out a substantial sum of money from the bank, and that will be your traveling money. I'll wire another substantial amount directly to Miss Nelson's bank account, so there will be no need for you to worry about carrying it with you. Will you do this for me?"

Katie broke down and started to cry, and Buck put his arm around her. "Hardly seems like the kind of thing we could refuse," he told Gus. "But I can't leave Windridge right now. You know full well there's too much work to be done. Those Texas steers will be coming our way in another month or two, and that last storm took out a whole section of fence. Not to mention the fact that we're breaking six new stock horses. I can't take the time away and stay on top of this as well."

"It'll be here when you get back," Gus assured him.

"No sir," Buck said emphatically. "Katie's ma and brother can go along with her. If you'll pay their ticket instead of mine, I'd be much obliged."

Gus didn't like the idea but nodded in agreement. "If that's the way you want it," he told Buck.

"It is."

⌣

And so it was nearly a week later that Gus watched the carriage disappear down the long, winding Windridge drive. He felt strangely calm as he watched them go. He knew he'd done the right thing. The very best thing for all parties concerned. Jessica would grow up never knowing either parent, but she would be loved and cared for just as Naomi would have wanted.

With a solemnity that matched the weight of the moment, Gus turned and stared at the house he'd created. Three stories of native limestone made a proud sentinel against the open prairie sky. It was her house—her home. She had loved it, and he had loved her. The memories were painful, and for the first time since she had died, Gus allowed himself to cry.

At first, it was just a trickle of tears, and then a full rush of hot liquid poured from his eyes. He couldn't have stopped it if he'd tried, and so instead of trying, he simply made his way to the library and closed the door behind him. He thought for a moment to lock it but decided against it. Someone would have to come in and take care of the mess, and there was no sense in having them have to bust down the door and ruin the house in order to do so. The house would one day belong to Jessica, just as it had belonged to her mother. He wanted to keep it neat and orderly for her. He wanted to offer her at least this much of himself.

He took a seat at his desk and pulled out his handkerchief. Wiping away the tears, Gus took out a piece of paper and began to pen a note of explanation for Buck. He'd already seen to his will when he'd gone into Cottonwood Falls for the train tickets. Everything would go to Jessica, with the exception of five thousand dollars, which was to be shared equally between Buck and Katie.

But this letter was an apology. An apology for not having been stronger. An apology for the problems he would now heap on his dearest friend.

I can't go on without her. The pain of losing her is too much to bear alone. If you can see your way to staying on and keeping up the ranch on Jessica's behalf, I would count it as my final earthly blessing. I have also arranged for you to be paid handsomely for the job. I just want you to know there was absolutely nothing you could have done to prevent this. I did what I had to do.

He signed the letter and left it to sit in the middle of his desk. He didn't want Buck to have a bit of trouble locating it. Then with a final glance around the room, Gus reached into the desk drawer and pulled out his revolver.

A knock on the library door caused him to quickly hide the gun back in its drawer. "Come in," he called.

Buck moseyed into the room as though nothing sorrowful had ever come to them. He held a pot of coffee in one hand and two cups in the other. "Thought you could use this just about now."

"I'm not thirsty," Gus replied.

"Well, then, use it to warm yourself."

"Ain't cold either."

Buck put the coffee down on top of the note Gus had just finished writing. He stared hard at Gus for a moment, then put the cups down and took a seat. "I can't let you do it, Gus," he said so softly that Gus had to strain to hear him. "I ain't gonna let you die."

Gus stared at him in stunned surprise. "What are you talking about?"

"I know what you're doing, and that's why I didn't go with Katie," Buck said, quite frankly. "I know you've been putting your affairs in order, and I know why."

Gus said nothing. He couldn't figure out how in the world Buck had known him well enough to expect this action.

"See, I know what it is to lose someone you love. You probably don't know this, but I was married a long time ago. I am, after all, thirteen years Katie's senior. Anyway, my wife died. Died in childbirth, along with our son."

Gus shook his head. "I didn't know that."

Buck nodded. "Well, it happened, and I would have followed her into the grave but for the ministerings of my ma. She knew how heartbroken I was. Sarah—that was my wife's name—and I had been childhood sweethearts. We'd grown up side by side, and we'd always figured on marrying. My ma knew it would be like putting a part of myself in that grave, and she refused to leave me alone for even a moment's time. And that's what I intend to do for you." He shifted back in the chair and crossed his leg to fumble with his boot for a moment.

"See, I know you intend to kill yourself, Gus. But it isn't the answer."

"I suppose you know what the answer is," Gus replied sarcastically. He wanted Buck to storm out of the room and leave him be. He didn't care if Buck hated him or called him names; he just wanted to forget everything and go to be with his Naomi.

"I do know," Buck replied. "God will give you the strength to get through this. You may not think so, but He will. I'm going to stay with you, pray with you, eat with you, and I'll even sleep at the foot of your bed if it keeps you alive."

Gus gave up all pretense. "I don't want to live. You should understand that."

"I do. But you're needed here on earth. You have a little girl who needs you. You have friends who need you."

"I don't want to be needed."

Again Buck nodded. "Neither did I, but I had no choice, and neither do you. Do you really want to leave that little girl with the guilt that she somehow caused her ma's and pa's deaths? It's bad enough that she'll have to live with the guilt of her mother dying, but hopefully, some kind person will teach her that it wasn't her fault. But if you put a bullet through your head, she'll be convinced it was her fault."

"That's stupid. It wouldn't have anything to do with her," Gus answered.

"You and I might know that, but she won't. And Gus, there won't be a single person in this world who'll be able to convince her otherwise."

Gus realized the truth in what Buck said. He felt his eyes grow warm with tears. "It hurts so bad to lose Naomi—to face a lifetime without her."

Buck nodded. "I know, and that's why we aren't going to face a lifetime. We're just gonna take one day at a time. I'll help you get through this, but you've got to be willing to try. For Jessica's sake, if for no other."

Gus thought about it for a moment. He didn't have the strength to do what Buck suggested, but neither did he want to burden his child—her child—with the idea that she was responsible for his death. "I just don't know, Buck. When I think about the years to come—and I know that she won't be there—it just isn't something I want to deal with."

"I understand. But like I said, we don't have to think about the years to come. We only have to get through today," Buck replied. "And we'll let tomorrow take care of itself."

In that moment Gus chose life over death. His heart was irreparably broken, but logic won over emotions. One day at a time, Buck said, was all he had to face. Just one day. If life proved to be too much today, he could always end it tomorrow.

Chapter 1

October 1890

Jessica Albright wrapped her arms around her nine-month-old son and frowned at the dark-skinned porter. He held her small traveling bag and held out his arms to further assist her departure from the train.

"If it pleases ya, ma'am," he said with a sincere smile, "I kin hold da baby and hand him down to ya."

"No," Jessica replied emphatically. "No one is taking him."

The porter shrugged and then held up his hand. "I kin go ahead of ya. Then iffen you fall, ya'll fall against me." He smiled broadly and jumped down the steep steps ahead of her.

Jessica had no choice but to follow. She gripped the baby firmly against her breast and made her way off the train. The nine-month-old howled at the injustice of being held so tightly, and Jessica could only jostle him around and try her best to cajole him back into a decent temperament.

"Oh Ryan, neither of us is happy with the arrangements," she said, glancing from her son's angry face to the crowd gathered around the depot platform.

"Miss Jessica," a voice sounded from behind her.

Whirling around, Jessica met the smiling face of a snowy-haired man. "Hello, Buck. Thank you for coming after us. I'm sorry for having to put you out."

"Wasn't any other way you were going to get there, short of hiring someone in town to bring you out. Besides, Katie would skin me alive if I refused. This your little guy?" he asked, nodding at the angry baby.

Ryan continued to howl, and Jessica grew rather embarrassed from the stares. She felt so inadequate at being a mother. Where her friends in the city had spoken of natural feelings and abilities regarding their children, Jessica felt all thumbs and left feet. "Could we just be on our way, Buck?"

Buck looked at her sympathetically. "Sure, sure. Let me claim your baggage, and we'll be ready to head out."

"This here bag belongs to the missus," the porter announced. Buck took up the bag, but Jessica quickly shifted the baby and reached out for it. "It has our personal things." Buck nodded and let her take it without protest.

"I'll go for the rest." He ambled off in the direction of the baggage car, and Jessica felt a sense of desertion. What if he forgot about her? What would she do then? She had very little money with her and even less ambition to figure out how to arrange transportation to her father's Windridge Ranch. No, she thought, it was her ranch now. Her father had died, and there was nothing more to be said about the situation. Still, she'd only been here on three other occasions, and the last time was over five years ago. She'd never know which way to go if she had to figure a way home for herself.

Ryan finally cried himself out and fell asleep, but not until his slobbers and tears had drenched the front of Jessica's plum-colored traveling suit. She couldn't do anything about it now, she realized. Aunt Harriet had always said that a lady was known by her appearance. Was her attire in order? Was her carriage and walk upright and graceful? Jessica felt neither properly ordered, nor upright and graceful. She felt hot and tired and dirty and discouraged.

"Here we are. This all you brought?" Buck asked, one huge trunk hoisted on his back, a smaller trunk tucked under one arm, and a carpetbag dangling from his hand. He turned to include the young boy who followed after him with two additional suitcases.

"Yes," Jessica replied. "That's everything."

Buck never condemned her for the multiple bags, never questioned why she'd needed to bring so much. Buck always seemed accepting of whatever came his way. Jessica didn't know the man half as well as she would have liked to, but Buck was the kind of man she knew would have made a wonderful father.

Buck stopped alongside a mammoth, stage-styled conveyance. Jessica watched, notably impressed, as Buck gently placed the trunk and bags up on the driver's floor, then paused to hand her and Ryan up into the carriage. She arranged a pallet for Ryan by taking his blanket and one of the carriage blankets and spreading them out on the well-cushioned leather seats, while overhead Buck secured the baggage on top.

The opulence and size of the carriage greatly impressed Jessica. No expense had been spared. In fact, it very much resembled an expensive stagecoach of sorts. The beautifully upholstered seats sported thick cushions, leaving Jessica with the desire to join Ryan in stretching out for her own nap. After four days on the most unaccommodating eastern trains, she found this a refreshing reprieve.

Blankets were positioned on a rack overhead, as well as a lantern and metal box that she presumed held other supplies. Outside, she heard Buck instruct the boy to hand up his cases, then figured he must have tipped the boy for his actions when she heard the child let out a hearty, "Thanks, Mr. Buck."

"You all settled in there?" Buck called out, sliding a window open from where he was on the driver's seat.

Jessica thought the window ingenious and nodded enthusiastically. "I'm ready. The baby is already sleeping comfortably."

"All right, then. We'll make for home. I know my Kate will be half beside herself for want of seeing you again."

Jessica smiled weakly and nodded. She could only wonder at what her reception might be when they learned she was coming to Windridge to stay.

Since Buck had pulled shut the slide on the window, Jessica felt herself amply alone and reached inside her purse to pull out a letter. She'd only received the missive a week ago, but already it was wrinkled and worn. Kate had written to tell her of her father's death. He'd suffered a heart attack, or so it was believed, and had fallen from his mount to his death. The doctor didn't believe he suffered overmuch, and Jessica had been grateful for that.

"We'd love to have you home, Jessie," the letter read. Kate was the only one who had ever called her Jessie. *"Windridge is never the same without you. Now with your father gone and what with the death of your own husband, we'd like to be a family to you. Please say you'll come for a visit."*

And she had come. She had telegraphed Kate before boarding the first available train, and now she was well on her way to Windridge.

But what would she do after that?

She stared out the window at the dead brown grass of the Flint Hills. She had felt fascinated the first time she'd laid eyes on the place at the age of twelve. Her aunt Harriet had figured it was time for Jessica to make a visit to the place of her birth; and sent west with a most severe nanny, Jessica had had her first taste of the prairie and rolling hills where thousands of cattle grazed.

And secretly, she had loved it. She loved the way she could stand atop Windridge when her nanny was otherwise preoccupied and let loose her hair ribbon and let the wind blow through her brown curls. She liked the feel of the warm Kansas sun on her face, even if it did bring her a heavy reprimand from her nanny. Freckled faces weren't considered a thing of beauty, not even for a child.

Now she looked across the vast openness and sighed. *I'm like that prairie,* she thought. *Lonely and open, vulnerable to whatever may come.* A hawk circled in the distance, and Jessica absently wondered what prey he might be seeking. It could possibly be a rabbit or a mouse, maybe even a wounded bird or some other sort of creature.

"Poor things," she whispered. Life on the prairie was hard. Often it came across as cruel and inhumane, but nevertheless, it continued. It went on and on whether people inhabited the land or died and were buried beneath its covering.

Jessica felt she could expect little more than this.

Her own life had taken so many different turns from that which she had expected. She had married against her father's wishes. But because he was a man who had never taken the time or trouble to be a real father to her, his hand-written letters of advice had held little sway with Jessica. After all, she scarcely knew her father. Harriet chose the man Jessica was to marry based on his social status and ability to conduct himself properly at social gatherings. It mattered very little that Jessica didn't love him. She was, Harriet pointed out, twenty-two years old. It was time to marry and take her place as a matron of society.

But society wasn't very accepting of you when you ran out of money. High society was even less forgiving.

It grieved Jessica to know Gus Gussop had been right in his long-distance judgment of Newman Albright. Gus had called him a dandy and a city boy. Called him worse than that, as Jessica recalled. And Newman had been all of those things.

Harriet had died shortly after Jessica's marriage. With her death came the inheritance of a fashionable house and a significant amount of money. Newman refused to move them into the Nelson place. Instead he insisted they sell the place and buy a less ostentatious home. Jessica quietly agreed, having been raised to respect her husband's wishes as law. What she didn't realize was that Newman had managed to get himself deep into debt through gambling and needed the sale of the house to clear his ledgers.

He robbed her of both the fortune left to her upon Harriet Nelson's death and her father's wedding gift of ten thousand dollars. A gift Newman never bothered to mention. She found out about these things after Newman had died. Of course, by that time they were living in poverty, and Newman's only explanation was that Jessica's father had cut them off without a dime, and their investments had gone sour.

Upon Newman's death, Jessica learned the truth about everything. Things she'd much rather have never known. Part of this came by way of her father's request. Gus had sent a telegram asking her to be honest with him about her financial situation. When Jessica had given the pitiful statements over to her father via a long, detailed letter, Gus had written back in a livid anger that seemed to leap off the page and stab at Jessica's heart.

"That blackguard has robbed you blind, Jessica. He has taken the ten

thousand dollars I wired to him, which was intended to go toward the pur-
chase of a lovely new home, and has apparently wasted it away elsewhere.
He's taken additional money, money he telegrammed requesting of me, and
apparently has lost the fortune given you by Harriet."

Jessica knew it was true. By the time Newman's death darkened her life, Jessica knew he had a gambling problem. A drinking problem. A fighting problem. And a multitude of other sins that had destroyed any possible hope of her loving him. He was a liar and a cheat and an adulterer, and Jessica could find no place in her heart to grieve his passing.

He had stumbled home one morning after an apparent night in the gutter not far from their poor excuse for a house. His nose was red, and his throat raw, and he bellowed and moaned about his condition until Jessica, then in her eighth month of pregnancy, had put him to bed and called for the doctor. Within three days, however, her husband was dead from pneumonia, and Jessica faced an uncertain future with a child not yet born.

It was at the funeral for Newman that Jessica realized the full truth of his affairs. Not one but three mistresses turned up to grieve their beloved Newman. None of the women had any idea about the others, and none knew Newman to have a wife and child. One particularly seasoned woman actually apologized to Jessica and later sent money that she explained Newman had given her for the rent. Jessica wanted to throw the money into the street but was too desperate to even consider such a matter. As a Christian woman of faith, she knew God had interceded on her behalf to provide this money. To throw it away would be to ignore God's answer to her prayers.

It had been painful to admit to her father that she was living from day to day in abject poverty, but even more painful to endure his response. He had raged about the injustice, but never once had he suggested she come home to live at Windridge. Jessica never even mentioned the baby to him. She was too afraid of what his reaction might be. Instead, she did as he asked, providing the information he sought on her finances. Then she followed his instructions when a letter came informing her that he'd hired a real estate agent to move her elsewhere and had set up an account of money in a New York City bank so that she might have whatever she needed. Such generosity had deeply touched her. But still, he never asked her to come home.

That broke her heart.

Then her life grew even more complicated when her best friend, Esmerelda Kappin, began to suggest Jessica give Ryan over to her for raising. Essie, as Jessica had once affectionately called her friend, was barren. She and her husband had tried every midwife remedy, every doctor's suggestion, and still they had no luck—no children. Essie took an interest in Ryan that Jessica didn't recognize as unhealthy until her friend began to suggest that Ryan preferred her care to Jessica's. Then Essie's very wealthy mother appeared on the doorstep to offer Jessica money in exchange for Ryan.

Of course, Jessica had been mortified and from that point on began guarding Ryan as though the devil himself were after the child. The Kappins grew more insistent, showing up at the most inopportune times to remind Jessica that she was alone in the world and that Ryan deserved a family with a mother and a father.

Jessica looked down at the sleeping boy. He did deserve a father, but that wasn't to be. She had no desire to remarry. Perhaps it was one of the reasons she'd decided to come to Windridge. Running Windridge would keep her busy enough to avoid loneliness and put plenty of distance between her and anyone who had the idea of stealing her son.

The prairie hills passed by the window, and from time to time a small grove of trees could be spotted. They usually indicated a spring or pond, creek or river, and because they were generally the exception and not the normal view, Jessica took note of these places and wondered if their gold and orange leaves hid from view some small homestead. Her father had once prided himself on having no neighbor closer than an hour's distance away, but Jessica knew that time had changed that course somewhat. Kate had written of a rancher whose property adjoined her father's only five miles to the south and another bound him on the west within the same distance. The latter was always after Gus to sell him a small portion of land that would allow him access to one of

Gus's many natural springs. But Gus always refused him, and the man was up in arms over his unneighborly attitude.

Jessica wondered at her father's severity in dealing with others. Kate told her it was because he'd never managed to deal with life properly after the death of Jessie's mother. But Jessica thought it might only be an excuse for being mean tempered.

Her conscience pricked her at this thought. She didn't know her father well enough to pass judgment on him. Her Christian convictions told her that judgment was best left to God, but her heart still questioned a father who would send away his only child and never suggest she return to him for anything more than a visit. With this thought overwhelming her mind, it was easy to fall asleep. She felt the exhaustion overtake her, and without giving it much of a fight, Jessica drifted into dreams.

～

Her first conscious thoughts were of a baby crying. Then her mind instantly awoke, and Jessica realized it was Ryan who cried. She sat up to find the nine-month-old trying to untangle himself from the blankets she'd so tightly secured him inside.

"Poor little boy," she cooed. Pulling him from the confines of his prison, Jessica immediately realized his wetness.

Looking out the window, Jessica wondered how much farther it was to the house. She hated to expose Ryan to a chill by changing him in the carriage. Wrapping a blanket around the boy, Jessica shifted seats and knocked at the little window slide. Within a flash, Buck slid it open.

"Something wrong?" he asked, glancing over his shoulder.

"How far to the house?" she questioned.

"We're just heading up the main drive. Should be there in five minutes. Is there something you need?"

Jessica shook her head. "No, thank you. I'm afraid the baby is drenched, and I just wondered whether to change him in here or wait. Now I know I can wait and not cause him overmuch discomfort."

"Kate will probably snatch him away from you anyway. That woman just loves babies."

Jessica cringed. What she didn't need to face was yet another woman seeking to steal her child.

"Sure wish you'd told us about him sooner. Kate would have come east in a flash to help you out and see the next generation of Gussops."

She didn't bother to correct Buck by pointing out that the baby was an Albright. She thought of him as a Gussop as well. Despite the fact they both carried the Albright name, Jessica considered both herself and her son to be Gussops.

Buck left the slide open in case Jessica wanted to say something more, but she held her silence. She was nearly home, and the thought was rather overwhelming. *Home.* The word conjured such conflicting emotions, and Jessica wasn't sure she wanted to dwell on such matters.

"Whoa!" Buck called out. The carriage slowed and finally stopped all together. Jessica looked out and found they were sitting in the wide circular drive of Windridge. The house stood at the end of a native stone walk, and it was evident that her father had sorely neglected the property in the last five years.

"Well, we're here, Ryan," she whispered against the baby's pudgy cheeks. "I don't know about you, but I'm rather frightened of the whole thing."

Ryan let out a squeal that sounded more delighted than frightened, and Jessica couldn't resist laughing.

Buck quickly came to help her down from the carriage, and just as he had predicted, Kate appeared to whisk them both inside.

"Oh my!" Kate remarked in absolute delight upon catching sight of Ryan. She reached arms out for the baby, but Jessica shook her head.

"He's soaking," she warned.

"Like that could stop me." Kate laughed and took the baby anyway.

Jessica felt a moment of panic, then forced herself to relax. *This is Kate,* she reminded herself. Kate, who had kept up correspondences over the years. Kate wouldn't try to steal her baby. Would she?

"What a beautiful boy!" Kate declared. "Come on. Let's get you in out of this wind and into a dry diaper."

Jessica glanced around and felt the breeze on her face. It invigorated and revived her. Somehow it seemed that city life had stifled her and drained her of all energy. Windridge had a way of awakening Jessica. It had begun with that first visit at twelve and continued with each subsequent trip home.

She finally looked back at Kate and found the woman was already ten feet ahead of her and heading up the stone steps to the porch. Drawing a deep breath, Jessica followed after the older woman, thinking to herself how very little Kate had changed. She now had a generous sprinkling of gray in her hair, and she wore small, circular, wire-rimmed glasses that gave her an almost scholarly appearance. But she was still the same old jolly Kate.

"You can see for yourself that the place has suffered miserably," Kate told her as they made their way into the house. "Your father wasn't himself for the last five years."

"Since my marriage," Jessica replied flatly, knowing full well that she had grieved him something terrible when she'd married Newman.

Kate stopped dead in her tracks. "Oh Jessie, I didn't mean it that way."

Jessica shrugged. "But it's true. I know it hurt him. I wish I could take it back, but I can't."

"Don't wish for things like that," Kate admonished. "You'd have to wish this little fellow away as well. Everything comes with a purpose, and God turns even our disobedience into glory for Himself."

Jessica smiled. How good it felt to hear someone speak about God. Most of her friends in New York were into mystic readings and psychic adventures. They believed in conjuring spirits of dead loved ones and held all-night parties in order to satisfy their ghoulish natures. Jessica could have no part in such matters, even if the likes of such things were sweeping the eastern cities in a rage of acceptance.

She'd been told by a friend that Essie had purchased a charm to make Ryan love her more than Jessica. It was all madness, or so it seemed. Playing at what most considered harmless enchantments and magic spells had left Jessica desperate to find new friends. Friends whose faith was steeped not in manipulating people to do what they wanted but in seeking God and learning what He wanted.

"Did I lose you?" Kate asked, turning suddenly inside the foyer.

"Not at all," Jessica replied. "I was only thinking of how wonderful it was to hear someone speak of God again. I'm afraid all manner of strangeness is going on in the city, and I've been rather alienated from good fellowship."

"You'll have to tell me all about it," Kate answered, and Jessica knew she truly meant it. Ryan began to fuss and pulled at Kate's glasses in irritated fashion. "Come on, little guy; let's get you changed."

Jessica felt a momentary panic as the baby continued to cry. She fought her desire to rip him from Kate's arms. It wasn't Kate's fault that Essie had treated Jessica so falsely. Swallowing her fear, Jessica followed Kate up the ornate wood stairs.

Focus on the house, she told herself. *Look at everything and remember how good it always felt to come here.*

Inside, the house looked much the same as it always had. Kate kept it in good fashion, always making it a comfortable home for all who passed through its doors. She was, for all intents and purposes, the mistress of Windridge, and she had done the place proud.

"We've created a nursery for you in here," Kate announced, sweeping through the open bedroom door. "Your room is in there." She pointed to open double doors across the room. "Of course, you have access through the hallway as well."

Jessica looked around her in stunned amazement. A beautiful crib stood in one corner, with a cheery fire blazing on the stone hearth on the opposite side of the room. A dresser and a changing table were positioned within easy access of one another, and a rocker had been placed upon one of Kate's homemade rag rugs, not far from the warmth of the fire. There was a shelf of toys, all suitable for a baby, and yet another long oval rag rug on the floor where a small wooden rocking horse had been left in welcome. *No doubt,* Jessica thought, *Buck made most of the furniture, including the rocking horse.*

"It's charming here," Jessica said, noting the thin blue stripe of the wallpaper. "But really you shouldn't have gone to so much trouble."

"It wasn't any trouble," Kate replied, taking Ryan to the changing table. "I had kind of hoped that if I filled the place with welcome, you just might stay on." She looked over her shoulder at Jessica, her expression filled with hope. "We'd really like it if you'd give up the East and come home to Windridge. Would you at least think about it?"

Jessica nodded. "I've already thought about it. I had kind of hoped that you'd let me stay."

Kate's face lit up with absolute joy. "Do you mean it? You've truly come home for good?"

Jessica nodded. "If you'll have me."

Kate threw up her arms and looked heavenward. "Thank You, God. What an answer to prayer." She looked back to Ryan, who was now gurgling and laughing at her antics. "You're both an answer to prayer."

~

Jessica found her own room much to her liking. Delicate rose-print wallpaper accented by dusty rose drapes and lacy cream-colored sheers made the room decidedly feminine. Kate had told her earlier that the room had been designed for Naomi, and in spite of the feminine overtones, Gus had left everything exactly as Naomi had arranged it.

The massive four-poster bed was Gus's only real contribution to the room. It seemed a bit much for one person, but Jessica realized it had belonged to her parents and had always been intended for two. A writing desk was positioned at the window, where the brilliant Kansas sunlight could filter into the room to give the writer all possible benefit. A six-drawer dresser with wide gown-drawers was positioned in one corner of the room, with a matching vanity table and huge oval mirror gracing the space in the opposite corner. A chaise lounge of mahogany wood and rose print was the final piece to add personality to the room. Jessica could imagine stretching out there to read a book on quiet winter evenings.

The room seemed much too large for one person. But Jessica was alone, and she intended to stay that way. There seemed no reason to bring another husband into her life. How could she ever trust someone to not take advantage of her? After all, she was now a propertied

29

woman—not just of a house, but of thousands of acres of prime grazing land. She would no doubt have suitors seeking to take their place as the master of Windridge. She would have to guard herself and her position.

But while she had no desire to bring a man to Windridge, she did want to bring people into her life. She wanted to share her faith and let folks see the light of God's love in her life. She didn't know exactly how she might accomplish this stuck out in the middle of the Flint Hills, but she intended to try.

After changing her clothes into a simple black skirt and burgundy print blouse, Jessica checked on Ryan and found him still asleep. His tiny lips were pursed, making soft sucking sounds as he dozed. She loved him so much. The terror that gripped her heart when she thought of losing him was enough to drive her mad. Surely God would help her to feel safe again.

Jessica left Ryan to sleep and made her way downstairs. Her mind overflowed with thoughts about how she would fit into this prairie home, and she was so engrossed in figuring things out that she didn't notice the man who watched her from just inside the front door.

When she did see him, she froze in place on the next to the last step. Her heart began to pound. Was this some ruffian cowboy who'd come to rob the place? She forced herself to stay calm.

"May I help you?" she asked coolly.

He stood fairly tall, a good five inches taller than her own statuesque five feet seven. He met her perusal of him with an amused grin that caused his thick bushy mustache to raise ever so slightly at the corners. His face, weathered and tanned from constant exposure to the elements, appeared friendly and open to Jessica's study.

"You must be Jessica," he drawled as though she should know him.

She bristled slightly, feeling his consuming gaze sizing her up. His cocoa brown eyes appeared not to miss a single detail. "I'm afraid you have me at a disadvantage," she finally managed.

"I'm Devon Carter, your father's foreman for these past five years."

Devon Carter. She thought of the name and wondered if anyone had ever mentioned him in their letters, but nothing came to mind.

Buck had always been foreman over Windridge, but she knew he was getting up in years and no doubt needed the extra help.

"I'm Jessica Albright."

His smile broadened. "Good to have you at Windridge. Heard tell you have a little one."

"Yes," she replied and nodded. "He's upstairs."

"Kate has done nothing but talk about you and the little guy for days," Devon said with a chuckle.

Jessica stepped down from the stairs and folded her hands. It seemed fairly certain she had nothing to fear from this man. "Is there something I can do for you, Mr. Carter?"

"Devon."

She eyed him for a moment before nodding and saying, "Devon."

"I just came up to the house to talk to Buck about the feed situation. You don't need to pay me any never mind."

"I see." But in truth she didn't. Was this man simply allowed free run of the house? Did he wander in and out at will?

"Oh, good," came the sound of Kate's voice from the stairs. "You've already met. Jessica, this man was a godsend to us. Your father took him on as a foreman when Buck said the workload was too much, and he's quickly made himself an institution around here."

Jessica turned to find Kate coming down the stairs with Ryan. The baby appeared perfectly content in her arms.

"You do go on, Katie," Devon countered affectionately. "Say, he's a right handsome fellow. It'll be good to have him around. Keep us all on our toes."

"I won't let you change the subject," Kate said, coming down the stairs with Ryan. "Gus thought of you as a son. You earned his respect quickly enough."

Jessica felt her nerves tighten. Her father had never treated her with much respect, nor, as far as she was concerned, had he thought of her as a daughter. How dare this stranger come into her home and earn a place that should have been hers?

She quickly reached for Ryan as soon as Kate joined them in the foyer. She didn't want to feel angry or hurt for a past that couldn't be changed, but it bothered her nevertheless. How could these two people act so nonchalant about it, knowing full well that she had suffered from the separation?

"What with the fact you've spent all your life in the city," Devon said.

Jessica stared up at him, not at all certain what had preceded that statement. "What?"

"I just told Devon that you plan to stay on at Windridge and take over your rightful place as mistress of the ranch," Kate replied.

Jessica looked at Kate for a moment while the real meaning of her words sunk in. It was true enough that her father had left her the ranch, but she'd not thought much about the fact that by moving in, she would become the mistress in charge.

"And I was just saying I hoped our simple way of doing things wouldn't cause you to grow unhappy and bored, what with the fact you've spent all your life in the city."

"I assure you, Mr. Carter," Jessica said rather stiffly, "that I will neither suffer boredom nor unhappiness due to the location. Other things may well come about to make me feel those things but not the address of my new home."

With that she set off with Ryan to explore the rest of the house. She felt an awkward silence fall behind her and knew, or rather sensed, that Devon and Kate were staring after her, but she didn't care. She wasn't prepared for the likes of Devon Carter. And she certainly wasn't prepared for her reaction to him.

Chapter 2

At thirty-two, Devon Carter was pretty much a self-made man. He held deep convictions on two things. One, that he loved Windridge and the Flint Hills as much as any man could ever love a place. And two, that his faith in God had been the only thing to sustain him over his long years of loneliness and misery.

He dusted off his jeans, wiped his boot tops on the back of each leg, and opened the back door to the kitchen without any announcement. He found Kate busy at work frying up breakfast and crossed the room to give her an affectionate peck on the cheek. Kate had become a second mother to him, and he saw no reason that their closeness should end now that Jessica Albright had come home to claim her fortune, if one could call it a fortune.

"Morning, Katie."

"Morning, Devon. Did you sleep well in the garden house?"

"It was good enough," he replied. "Don't know how you and Buck ever managed to keep warm enough out there, what with the drafts and such."

"We had each other," Katie said with a grin. "Besides, nobody's lived out there in twenty years. Gus had us move up to the house when the quiet got to be too much. We brought the kids and all, and he never once complained about the noise."

"Well, I'm going to have to do some repairs to it today if I'm going to have a better sleep tonight."

"Why don't you just tell Buck what you need? That would be simple work for him, and I don't want him overdoing it by following you over the prairie searching for strays. He just doesn't have it in him anymore."

"Now, Katie, you're selling me short again," Buck announced as he came in from the pantry.

"Just being sensible," Katie replied, pausing long enough to turn over a thick ham steak from where it browned in a cast-iron skillet.

"Well, sensible or not," Devon replied, "the work still needs to be done. You want the pleasure, Buck, or shall I do it?"

Buck laughed, watching Kate pull down her wire rims just far enough to look at him over the tops. "I'll take care of it. You just give me some ideas on where to start."

"Will do." Devon turned then to Kate. "Table set?"

"Nope, you go right ahead and do the honors. Buck and I will bring in the food."

Devon nodded and went into the pantry where the fine china and everyday dishes were displayed in orderly fashion. He took down three plates then remembered Jessica and Ryan, as if he hadn't thought of them all night long, and added one more. He grabbed silverware and saucers and decided to come back for the cups after seeing that he was juggling quite a load.

He'd just finished laying out the arrangement and filling the saucers with cups when Jessica and Ryan appeared. She stood casually in the doorway, baby on her hip, looking for all the world like a contented woman. Devon smiled.

"Breakfast is nearly on."

She looked rather surprised as she took sight of the table. "Who else will there be?"

"Well, there's Buck and Kate," he answered, then added, "and me. Plus you and Ryan. That makes five."

"Oh," she answered, and Devon immediately wondered if she had a problem with the arrangement.

"Something wrong?" he asked.

"I'm just not used to. . .well, that is to say. . . ," she fell silent and shifted Ryan to the other hip, where he found her long chestnut braid much easier to play with.

"Jessie," Kate called out as she brought in a huge platter of scrambled eggs, "my, but don't you look pretty. I like that you've left your hair down. Reminds me of when you were a little girl."

Devon watched Jessica blush as Kate continued. "Do you know, Devon, this girl would defy her nanny and sneak out of the house to get to the top of the ridge. Once she got there, she'd pull out all her ribbons and whatnots and let her hair go free to blow in the wind. Anytime she got away from us, we could be sure to find her there."

Devon grinned and cast a quick glance at Jessica, who was even now trying to help her son into the wooden high chair at the end of the table.

"Here, let me help," Devon said, pushing Jessica's hands away. He made a face at Ryan as he positioned the boy in the seat and brought the top down around him. Ryan immediately laughed and reached out chubby arms to touch Devon's mustache.

"No, Ryan!" Jessica declared, moving back in position to keep her son from touching the cowboy.

"It's all right, Jessica. He won't hurt anything," Devon replied.

She glared hard at him. "I'm his mother, Mr. Carter. It's my place to decide what is right for him."

Devon saw the unspoken fury in her eyes, but rather than angering him, it made him want to laugh. *Better not,* he told himself. *That would really infuriate her.*

He waited until Jessica took her seat at the right of the high chair before considering that he'd positioned himself at the left. He liked kids. Liked them very much and had, in fact, planned on having several by this time in life. But life often didn't work out the way a person planned.

Katie and Buck took their places, and Buck offered grace over the food. He also added thanksgiving for Jessica's return, before putting on a hearty "amen" and directing everyone to dig in. If Jessica noticed that Buck was the one in charge of the meal, she didn't say anything. She sat opposite Buck at the end of the table, while Katie sat at his right and Devon at her right. One entire side of the table sat empty except for the food platters, and Devon wondered if maybe he should have arranged things differently. He was about to speak when Buck voiced a question.

"How did you sleep last night, Jessica?"

She put down a forkful of fried potatoes and smiled. "Very well, thank you."

"I told him a person could get lost in that big old bed of your pa's," Katie said, "but you know Buck. He said we could always send out a search party to find you."

They all chuckled at this, and Devon wondered if maybe the tension of the morning had finally subsided.

"Ryan also slept very well. In fact, it was his first time to sleep through the night without waking up to. . ." She reddened and stopped in midsentence.

Kate seemed to understand her discomfort. "He's a big boy now. Have you started him eating something more substantial?"

Jessica shook her head. "No, in fact, this is his first time at the table."

She hadn't noticed, but Devon had put several pieces of egg on the high chair tray, and already Ryan was stuffing them into his mouth.

"Well, it looks as though he thinks highly of the idea," Buck said with a laugh.

Jessica looked down in confusion and noticed the baby reaching for a piece of buttered toast. "No, Ryan!"

"He's fine, Jessica," Devon assured her.

"Mr. Carter, I don't appreciate your interference with my child," Jessica said harshly. "He's my responsibility."

"Around here, folks pretty much try to help out where they can," Devon countered, meeting her haughty stare. "I figured since you're staying on, I'd try to do what I could to fill in for the absence of his pa. I'm sure Buck feels the same way."

Jessica appeared speechless. She stared openmouthed at Devon and then turned to Kate and Buck. "And you think this is acceptable behavior?"

Kate laughed. "We don't hold any formalities around here. Ryan will be greatly loved and maybe even spoiled a bit, but those are good things, not bad. The ranch is full of dangers as well as benefits. You'll appreciate that folks are willing to keep an eye open for him."

"No, I'm not sure I will," she replied quite frankly.

"Jessica, you shouldn't worry about these things," Kate told her.

Devon watched her reaction and tried to pretend he was unconcerned with her hostility. But in fact, he was offended that she should be so put out with him. He was, after all, only helping. Maybe it was her upbringing that caused her to be so mulish about things.

"I'd appreciate it if we could change the subject," Jessica interjected. "And, I'd appreciate it, Mr. Carter, if you would leave the raising of my son to me."

Devon swallowed back a short retort and let it go. There would no doubt be time enough to take issue over these things. He felt deep gratitude when Buck did as Jessica requested.

"Well, since you've decided to stay on, Jessica, there are a few things you need to be aware of."

"Such as?" The woman's eyes were wide with a mixture of what appeared to be fear and pure curiosity.

Buck looked at Kate for a moment, and after receiving her nod of approval, he began what Devon knew he dreaded more than anything.

"It has to do with the financial affairs of Windridge."

"I see." She busied herself with her food, and when Ryan cried for another piece of toast, she calmly buttered one and broke off a piece for him.

"Well, anyhow," Buck continued. "Windridge is not in a good state. Gus got into drinking these last few years. About the time you. . ." He fell silent.

"Married Newman," Jessica filled in for him.

"Yes, well, when you got married, other things started happening around here as well. Your pa suffered a mild heart attack, and we had a round of viruses that took the lives of most our herd one year. One thing after another took its toll, and before we knew it, Gus was running pretty short on cash. After that, he just stopped trying. Wouldn't even keep up his partnership with the Rocking W down in Texas."

Jessica dropped her fork. "What partnership?"

Kate leaned forward to explain. "Your pa had an agreement to purchase cattle from a ranch in Texas. It was easier to get them that way, fatten them up here all summer, then sell them off in the fall—usually for a good profit. That way, we didn't have to worry about keeping them through the winter."

"I suppose that makes sense," Jessica agreed.

"Well, for the last three years or so, Gus let things get so far out of control that he couldn't even afford to purchase the steers. Jeb Williams, owner of the Rocking W, offered to spot him the herd. He knew Gus was down on his luck and knew he was good for the money, but Gus refused. He became more and more reclusive, spending most of his time nearby, but doing little or nothing."

"So you're telling me that we're broke?" Jessica questioned.

"Pretty much so," Buck replied. "Devon can give you better details on the matter."

She looked to him, and Devon thought from her expression that it had cost her a great deal to put aside their differences to pose her question. "What exactly is the situation, Mr. Carter?"

"There's not much in the bank. It'll get us through another winter, if the winter isn't too bad. There's only minimal livestock—a dozen milk cows, about the same number of horses, and the place is in a state of disrepair. We've tried to keep up with things, but it takes money to do so. Come spring, we'll be in a world of hurt."

"But I see cattle on the hills," Jessica replied. "Kate, you even mentioned the hands would soon be driving the cattle to Cottonwood Falls."

"They aren't ours," Devon told her instead of allowing Kate to answer. "We leased out the pasture without telling Gus. He mostly stayed in his room those last few months, and if he noticed the herd, he didn't say anything. The lease money is what we have in the bank."

"What are we to do?" Jessica asked, turning her gaze back to Buck and Kate.

"Well, there's a neighbor, Joe Riley, who'd like to buy a parcel of land that joins his property. It has a spring on it, and he's been after your pa for all these years to let him buy it. Your pa just felt mean about it, I guess," Buck replied. "Never did fully understand why that man refused to sell one little spring, but that's behind us now, and I don't intend to speak ill of the dead. He probably won't be interested until spring, but it's worth asking about."

"Then I thought I'd go down to the Rocking W on your behalf," Devon said rather cautiously. "I know Jeb Williams from the cattle drives I've helped with before coming to Kansas. I think Jeb might be willing to extend the same offer to you that he offered to your father. We could purchase a small herd from him—on credit—and fatten them up for a profit come fall."

"Of course," Buck threw in, "there's always a risk. Viruses, weather, insects, and all other manner of complications. It could end up that we'd lose our shirts in the deal and be unable to pay Williams back."

Jessica nodded, appearing to consider the matter. "I have an idea for the place," she said, surprising them all. "Back East, there is quite an interest in ranching and the West. Many people have never known much but the city—especially those in higher social classes."

"And your point would be?" Devon asked.

"My point is that opening resort ranches has become quite popular. They offer an unusual respite for travelers who otherwise live their lives in big cities. I have a couple magazines upstairs that talk about this very thing."

"Dude ranches," Devon said in complete disgust. "Your pa would sooner you sell the place in total."

"My father isn't here," Jessica reminded him. "And it appears that even when he was, he wasn't much interested in what happened with the ranch. The place is mine now, and I intend to run it as such. I realize I have a lot to learn, but I'm offering one simple solution. People could come here and take their rest. We have miles of solitude to offer them. We could feature carriage rides, hunting, picnics, and horseback riding—we could show them how a ranch actually works, and we could fatten them up on Kate's cooking."

"You forget," Devon replied, "the place would have to be fixed up first. There's a lot that needs to be done in order to make this a model working ranch. And that, my dear Jessica, takes money."

She frowned at him. "I realize it would take something of an investment to get things started. I didn't say the plan was without challenges."

"A plan? So do you figure to just move forward with this plan? Didn't you think it might be important to get the advice of those who know the place?" Devon questioned.

Kate and Buck stared on as if helpless to interject a single word. Jessica slammed down her empty coffee cup and countered. "I am not stupid, Mr. Carter. I am simply offering the idea up as a possibility. That is all." She glanced to Kate. "I also believe it would be nice to open the ranch up to hurting souls. People who need the quiet to escape and heal from whatever woe they have to face. As Christians we can minister to these people and share the gospel of Christ."

"Now you're suggesting we turn this into some sort of revival grounds?" Devon asked.

"And what if I am? Are you a heathen, Mr. Carter?"

"No ma'am. I accepted Christ as my Savior a long time ago, but I never once felt called to be a minister."

"Neither have I called you to be one, Mr. Carter." She stressed the formality of his name, and Devon cringed inwardly.

Ryan pounded the tray with his hands and fussed for something more to eat or play with. Devon handed the baby a spoon without even realizing what he was doing. Jessica scowled at him and merely took the spoon out of Ryan's hands. This caused the baby to pucker up, and as his bottom lip quivered, he began to cry.

"Now, do you see what you've done?" she snapped at Devon.

"I didn't make him cry. You're the one who took his spoon away."

"Ohhh," she muttered and handed the spoon back to Ryan. "You and I are going to have to have a more private discussion of this matter, I can see."

"You name the time and place," Devon countered, feeling completely up to any challenge Jessica could offer.

"The point is," Buck finally interjected, "Windridge is going to need some help. Arguing about it isn't going to make improvements around here."

"I think if we sink our remaining capital into spring stock," Devon replied, "we could have enough to sell off next year and make a good profit. Beef sales are doing just fine. The immediate need is for us to build back our capital—not to spend it on frivolous ideas that might never come to be worth anything."

"I disagree," Jessica replied. "And since I now own Windridge and you are just the hired help, I believe I have the final say."

Gasps from Kate and Buck came at the words *hired help*, but Devon held his temper in check. "I may be the hired help, but I was hired because I knew ranching. Your father thought enough of my skills to honor me with his trust. I think that should say something for itself."

"It says plenty, and so does the rundown state of this ranch. If you are such a good foreman, Mr. Carter, why do I arrive to find the place in such a state?"

Kate put a hand on Devon's arm. "Jessie, you don't understand all that has happened. Devon had little say about matters of finance. He is a good foreman for the ranch, knows cattle and horses, and is handy with repairs, but he didn't have any say over the money. Your father was the one who made all the decisions—bad and good."

"And he's gone," Jessica said simply.

"Not if you just pick up where he left off," Devon proclaimed without thinking.

Jessica stared at him for a moment. "I resent that implication, Mr. Carter. And I would further add that if you don't like the way I intend to do things and if you think it impossible to take my orders seriously, then I'd suggest you find another place of employment."

"No, Jessie!" Kate declared. "You don't even know what you're saying. Now I want both of you to calm down and stop acting like children. A ranch takes a lot of people to see it through. We can work at this together and build it up, or we can destroy it. It's pretty much up to us."

Jessica seemed to take heed of Kate's words and fell silent.

Devon threw down his napkin and got up from the table. "I have work to do," he announced and stormed out of the room. *Aggravating woman*, he thought. *Thinks she can just come in and solve the problems of the world by forcing us all into her mold.* He slammed the kitchen door behind him as he made his way into the crisp October morning.

Glancing skyward, he prayed. *Lord, I don't know why this has to be so difficult. I figured her visit would be trying, what with her being a city gal and all, but I didn't figure on her turning this place into a dude ranch. I need some help here, Lord.* He looked out across the broken-down ranch and sighed. *And I need it real soon.*

Chapter 3

Winter moved in with a harshness that Jessica had not expected. Living near the top of a high ridge caused them to feel every breeze and gale that came across the prairie. It also made them vulnerable to the effects of that wind.

Jessica tried not to despair. She knew that any plans she had for the ranch would have to wait until spring, so she tried to busy herself around the house. Her friendship with Kate also blossomed as the women worked together. Kate gave Jessica her first lessons in canning, butchering, and quilting, and out of everything she learned, Jessica thought quilting to be the very best.

"I think quilting is the only way to make it through the long, lonely winters," Kate told her one afternoon. "I've passed many a winter this way."

Jessica stared at the quilt block in her lap and sighed. "I just wish I was a better seamstress. My stitches are so long and irregular. I'm sure I shall never be able to make anything useful."

"Nonsense. We all had to start somewhere. You do a fine job embroidering, and if you have a way with a needle, you can certainly learn to quilt."

"What do you do with all the quilts you make?" Jessica asked.

"I give them to family, use them here, or just stack them up in the storage room."

"I'll bet folks back East would pay good money to have a beautiful quilt like that one," she said, pointing to the quilt frame where Kate worked.

"This old flower basket pattern isn't that hard. Most folks could whip one up for themselves. Can't imagine they'd pay much of anything for my work."

"But they would. I have several friends in New York who would be very happy to purchase something like this. They don't sew—in fact, they're worse than me when it comes to putting in a stitch. They love beautiful things, and your quilts would definitely fall into that category," Jessica protested.

Kate stopped in her tracks. "You honestly think folks would pay good money to buy my quilts?"

"I do," Jessica replied enthusiastically. "Kate, if you were willing to part with some of your quilts, I could ship them back to my friends and see what kind of money they could raise. They could send the money, as well as some additional materials, and maybe if they talked to their friends and families, they would have orders for additional quilts."

"That might be one way we could raise some money for the ranch," Kate replied. "Of course, it wouldn't be like selling off a steer, but every little bit would help. Especially after so many years of waste."

Jessica paused and grew thoughtful. "Kate, what happened with my father? I mean, what caused him to start drinking?"

Kate stopped her work and looked sympathetically at Jessica. "I can't really say. I know he was never the same after Naomi died. He loved that woman more than he loved life. Buck feared he'd kill himself just in order to be with her. He just lost all desire to go on, and we did our best to keep him among the living."

"But he seemed so capable whenever I came to visit. And the ranch, I mean, it never looked like this."

Kate's expression took on a sorrow that immediately left Jessica feeling guilty.

"Your father had a number of things happen to put him into despair. The losses were just too much for him to bear."

"What kinds of losses?" Jessica dared the question, fearful of what the answer might be.

Kate pushed up her glasses and set her attention back on the quilting. "He lost a great deal of money, for one thing. I'm not really sure where it all went. I know he gave everyone a bonus, and when hard times came, we tried to give it back, but Gus wouldn't hear of it. Buck and I just gradually added it back into the purchases we took on for the ranch. Gus was always helping one friend or another out—never thinking that the money might not be there in the future.

"Then that summer, half the stock came down sick and died. That caused all kinds of problems. Drought came on us later that same summer, but we still had the freshwater springs, so we didn't suffer for water like most folks. Just when things seemed to be getting a little better, a late summer storm set the prairie on fire and burned most everything in its path. The bad thing was, it wasn't just one fire, but a series of fires, and the cattle and wild critters had no place to run. For some reason we'd neglected plowing fire strips—those are wide breaks in the prairie where we don't allow anything to grow. They can be very useful in containing fires because when they reach those places, the fires just sort of burn themselves out. But that year we just didn't see to it properly.

"The fire killed whole herds in some areas. We spent over forty-eight hours toting water up from the springs and watering down everything in sight and plowing wide strips around the main homestead. We were able to save the house and most all the outbuildings, but nothing else. The house smelled like smoke for months afterward. We lost so much that I thought Gus was going to up and sell it off for sure. But he wouldn't sell—felt it was too important to stay on."

"Why?"

Kate shook her head. She seemed reluctant to speak. "I think Gus worried about all of us. You, included."

"Worried? In what way?" Jessica couldn't imagine that this powerful figure she'd always known as her father would be worried about anything.

"He worried about whether we'd be cared for. He worried about Buck and me having a place to live. He worried about you back East with that money-grubbing social dandy." Kate stopped and threw Jessica an apologetic look. "Sorry. I shouldn't have said that."

Jessica sighed and shook her head. "Why not? It's the truth. Might as well tell it like it is."

Kate turned up the lantern a bit, then went back to work. "Well, he worried about you. He always feared that sending you back East wasn't the right thing to do, but you must understand that he felt so inadequate to deal with you."

"Is that why he sent me in the first place?" Jessica asked flatly.

Kate halted her work and pushed away from the quilt frame. "Jessie, I know we've never really talked about any of this, but with your father gone, I figure it's all right to talk about it now."

"Then please do," Jessica encouraged.

"Your father intended to send you off to your aunt, then kill himself."

"What?"

"You heard me. He totally broke down with Buck and told him he had no desire to live. Buck had been your father's friend long enough to realize that he would feel this way. He stayed with your father through the next months. Sometimes he even slept in the same room with Gus—on those nights that were particularly bad. Buck would make a pallet on the floor of Gus's room and keep watch over him until he fell asleep. Those were usually anniversaries. You know, her birthday, her death day, their wedding day. Those were the worst for Gus."

Jessica nodded. It was easy to imagine the pain and suffering that those simple reminders must have put upon her father. It seemed funny that where Newman was concerned, Jessica felt only relief. Sometimes it made her feel guilty, but most of the time she was just glad to be rid of him. She tried not to hate him, because hating him seemed to make it impossible to love Ryan in full. And she wasn't about to jeopardize her relationship with Ryan. He was all she had, and no one would take him from her.

"When you married," Kate began again, "your father feared for you. I remember him hiring a man back East to send him a report on Newman's background and financial status."

"He did what?" Jessica questioned.

"He hired a man to check into Newman Albright. The reports that came back weren't at all flattering."

"He knew about Newman?" Jessica questioned, completely

mortified that she'd not been able to hide the details of her married life from her father. She'd known that her father was aware of the gambling and the financial crisis Newman had heaped upon his family, but surely he didn't know about the mistresses and other problems.

"He knew it all. The women, the abuses, the baby. He made me promise to never say anything to you in my letters. It worried him sick sometimes. He used to talk to me about it—ask my advice. I told him if you felt like talking, you'd do it."

"But he never showed me any sign that he'd be open to my talking to him," Jessica replied angrily. "Even when he knew me to be widowed, he never asked me to come home."

"But you never gave any indication that you would have wanted to come home. You stopped visiting, even though you were old enough to make your own decisions. You up and married without even asking him what he thought—"

"Why should I have asked him?" Jessica interrupted. "He'd barely showed the slightest interest in my life."

"That's not true, Jessica. Your father had detailed monthly reports from your aunt Harriet. It was her rule that you not be allowed to come to Windridge before you reached twelve years of age."

"I didn't know that," Jessica replied, her anger somewhat abated. "I thought he didn't want me here. I mean, he's the one who sent me away."

"He sent you because he planned to end his life. Then when he finally had a reason to go on, you were well established with your aunt, and to force you to a life out here on the Kansas Flint Hills seemed cruel. Besides, he'd signed an agreement with Harriet. Your father, if nothing else, was a man of his word."

"Would he have really asked me to come here? If Aunt Harriet would have been willing, would my father have brought me home?"

Kate shrugged. "Who can say? We have no way of reliving the past to see what other choices we might have made. You have to stop worrying about what might have been and focus on what is. You have a fine son and a failing ranch. It's the future that needs your attention."

"I realize that, but sometimes the choices for the future find their basis in the past," Jessica replied.

"True. I guess I can see the sense in that."

"Well, you ladies are gonna freeze to death if you don't stoke up that fire," Buck said, coming into the room with an armload of firewood. "I just put more wood on the fire in the baby's room."

"Is Ryan still asleep?" Jessica questioned.

"Yup. He didn't even stir," Buck replied. He put several thick logs into the massive stone fireplace and took the poker to it in order to help the wood catch.

"He truly seems to like Windridge. He's slept through the night ever since our coming here," Jessica said.

"Well, he is a year old now," Kate reminded them.

"It's so hard to believe," Jessica said. "When I think we've been here at Windridge for almost four months, I can't imagine where the time has gone. It seems like just yesterday we were sitting down to our first breakfast together."

"It only seems that way because you've hardly spoken two words to Devon since then," Kate admonished.

Buck chuckled but knew better than to join in the conversation. He quickly exited the room after replacing the poker against the wall. Kate watched him leave before turning her attention back to Jessica.

"You really should work out your differences."

"He wants to run my life—and Ryan's."

"He just cares about you and the boy. He's good with Ryan, and Ryan really seems to love being with Devon. Why would you deprive the child of such a meaningful relationship? Devon's a good man."

"Yes, I suppose he is, but I cannot have Ryan getting close to someone who may well be gone tomorrow."

"Why would Devon be gone tomorrow? He loves Windridge—loves it as his own."

"But it isn't his. It's mine!" Jessica protested, knowing she sounded like a spoiled child arguing over toys. "Devon has interfered in my son's life, and he tries to manipulate and run mine. He tells me constantly how bad the finances are, but he never has suggestions as to how we could improve things. In fact, I'll bet he'd even laugh at our idea to sell quilts back East."

Kate smiled. "I kind of laughed at that idea myself, so don't hold that against Devon."

Jessica put her sewing aside and went to the fire. The warmth felt good to her. "I don't want to hold anything against anyone, Kate. I just want to be given due respect. I want Devon to realize that I love this place, too, and just because I didn't get a chance to grow up here doesn't mean I don't have Windridge's best interests in mind."

"So tell him that," Katie urged. "He's a reasonable man. He'll listen."

Jessica shook her head. "But what if he doesn't? What if he just wants to fight with me?"

Kate laughed. "What if you step out the door and the lion eats you?"

"What?"

"It's in the Bible. The foolish man refuses to go about his duty because he's afraid if he steps out of the house, a lion might eat him. There's a lot of things in life like that. We refuse to take steps forward because we're afraid something overwhelming will happen."

Jessica nodded. "I just don't know how to take that man. He's so, well, he's too confident of himself. He acts like he has all the answers, and nobody else can possibly have anything good to say."

Kate shook her head. "I've never known Devon to fit that description. He's confident—that much I'll give you. But honestly, Jessica, his confidence is in the Lord rather than himself."

The muffled sound of Ryan's cry came from upstairs. Jessica immediately went to the sitting room door and pulled it open. "I think someone is telling us his naptime is over."

"I think you are right," Kate laughed. "It's time for me to be putting supper together anyway. Those men are going to be hungry pretty soon, and I'm starting to feel a mite caved in myself."

Jessica, too, felt a slight gnawing of hunger. "What are we having tonight?"

"Roast," Kate replied. "Left over from last night, but tonight I'll fix it up in a stew with biscuits."

"Sounds wonderful."

With that, Jessica made her way upstairs. She had nearly reached the nursery door when Ryan's cries abated, and she could hear the sound of a male voice from within. She paused outside the door, wondering if Buck had gone to check the fire and had accidentally awakened the boy.

"There now, partner," came Devon's voice. "No sense in getting yourself all worked up. Ain't much good can come of it."

Jessica could hear Ryan's animated babble, as well as Devon moving around the room.

"Let's get you out of those wet clothes and into something more comfortable."

At this, Jessica could no longer stand idle. She burst through the door as though the house were on fire and stared daggers at Devon Carter. Her mind was flooded with thoughts of Essie Kappin trying to steal her son's loyalty by always insisting Jessica allow her to deal with the child whenever they were at the Kappins' for a visit.

"Just what do you think you're doing?" she protested. She came forward, grabbed Ryan out of Devon's arms, and maneuvered past him to the changing table. "Whatever possessed you to just allow yourself entry into my son's room?"

Ryan began to cry again, reaching around Jessica's tight hold toward where Devon stood rather stunned. Jessica hated that he was making such a scene. It was almost as if she were the monster having ripped him from the security of his parent, rather than the other way around.

"He was crying," Devon replied. "I figured he needed attention, and I was free for the moment."

Jessica plopped Ryan down on the changing table and set her mind on the job at hand rather than arguing with Devon. As soon as Ryan was changed and happily occupied on the rag rug with a toy, Jessica turned her full fury on Devon.

"I've told you before that I don't like having you interfere with my son."

Devon put his hands on his hips. His thick mustache twitched a bit as he frowned. "Jessica, this is a pretty isolated place. Don't you think we could agree to a truce of some sort?"

"No, I don't. I'm tired of telling you how I feel, only to have you ignore me." She hadn't noticed Ryan getting to his feet or the fact that he was walking, until he padded across the floor to Devon and took hold of his leg.

"Say, you did a right good job of that, little fellow," Devon said, clapping his hands.

Ryan laughed and let go to clap his own hands, only to smack down on his bottom. For a moment he looked startled, then he laughed again and got on his hands and knees as if to try the whole thing again.

Jessica, stunned that her son was walking, refused to allow him to make Devon the center of his attention. Devon was stealing her son away from her, and she could never allow that.

"If you don't mind," she said, snatching Ryan up protectively, "I'm needed downstairs to help with supper."

"I could watch him for you," Devon suggested.

Jessica could hardly believe he'd made the offer. He wasn't listening to her protests at all. Battling Ryan's squirming body, Jessica answered him as coolly as she dared. "You were hired to work the ranch, Mr. Carter, not the nursery." With that she left, refusing to give him a chance to reply. Oh, but the man could be infuriating.

Ryan began to cry, only furthering her frustration. One way or another, she would put an end to Devon's interference before he'd totally turned her son away from her. She would not have another situation on her hands where someone suggested her son was better off without her.

Chapter 4

Jessica spent the next two weeks feeling deeply convicted about her attitude and behavior toward Devon. Not only had he refused to share supper the night of their disagreement, but he had refused to share all subsequent meals from that night forward. Jessica knew the fault lay with her. She knew, too, that in order to deal with the matter and put things aright, she would have to be the one to do the apologizing.

She realized that Devon had meant only to be helpful, but her own insecurities regarding Ryan had caused her to act unforgivably bad. Sitting with her Bible in hand, Jessica felt hot tears trickle down her cheeks.

"I just don't want to lose Ryan's love, Lord," she whispered in the silence of her room. In the nursery Ryan already slept contentedly, but there would be no sleep for Jessica until she dealt with the matter at hand. Already she'd spent some fourteen restless nights, and her misery was rapidly catching up with her.

"I came here with such great expectations, Father," she began to pray again. "I thought there would be financial security and a place to belong. I have thought of the house on Windridge as my own special utopia since I was a small child. You know how I felt about it. You know I loved this place and always desired to be here. I just wanted everything to be perfect. I want to be perfect. The perfect mother. The perfect mistress of Windridge. But I fail and continue to fail no matter how hard I try."

She opened the Bible and found herself in the book of Colossians. "'Put on therefore, as the elect of God, holy and beloved, bowels of mercies, kindness, humbleness of mind, meekness, longsuffering,'" she read aloud. Glancing past the desk where her Bible lay, Jessica peered out into the darkness of the night. Only the shadowy glow of lamplight from the cottage where Devon stayed could be seen on this moonless night.

"I certainly haven't been merciful or kind where he is concerned. Neither have I been meek or longsuffering, and I come nowhere near to being humble of mind. But Father, I'm so afraid. I'm afraid of failing once again. I failed Harriet when I pleaded to come west. I failed when I married Newman. I failed even when I was born—taking the life of my mother and the joy of my father. If I fail here, then what is left to me?

"If I fail to be a good mother to Ryan, then someone will come along and take him from me. And if I fail to bring this ranch back into prosperity, then I might well lose the roof over my head. I want to make things perfect, but I feel so inadequate. My life has been so far removed from perfection, and now that I finally have some say over it, nothing seems to be going right." She sighed and added with an upward glance, "What do I do?"

She felt the turmoil intensify and continued to read from Colossians. " 'Forbearing one another, and forgiving one another, if any man have a quarrel against any: even as Christ forgave you, so also do ye. And above all these things put on charity, which is the bond of perfectness.' "

Jessica returned her gaze to the cottage. *I've not been forbearing or forgiving, and I certainly haven't put on charity. I've shown Devon Carter nothing but anger and resentment.* She thought of the close, affectionate manner in which Devon handled Ryan, and her heart ached. The situation tested every emotion within her. On one hand she feared Devon's involvement because of the Kappins. And on the other hand she feared Ryan's reaction to Devon's attention.

She couldn't provide Ryan with a father. Certainly not a father like Devon. Was it fair or right to allow the boy to grow close to Devon, when the man could pick up and go at any given moment? Kate said Devon would never do such a thing, but what if he grew tired of the failing ranch? What if he left them like so many of the other ranch hands had already done?

"Oh Father, what am I to do? How do I show this man charity instead of fear?" Then a thought came to mind, causing Jessica to feel even more at a loss. Devon seemed perfectly willing to answer her questions, to take time out of his schedule to work with her on matters—at least those times when she had allowed herself to ask and seek his help. But the relaxed nature of Devon—his considerate and generous spirit—made Jessica uncomfortable. Devon clearly represented the kind of man she would have chosen for herself had others not interfered with her life.

"If Harriet hadn't thrust me into her social circles, demanding I choose a husband from the men of leisure who haunted her doorstep, I might have known true happiness. I might even have come here and met Devon Carter long before joining my life to Newman; then Ryan would be his son, and I would be his wife."

The thought so startled Jessica that she slammed the Bible shut. *I can't allow myself to think that way,* she scolded. *There is nothing to be gained by it. I can't take back the past. I can't bring my dead mother and father to life and start over under their care instead of Aunt Harriet's. I can't remake my life.*

The light went out in the cottage, leaving Jessica to feel even more deserted. Somehow, knowing that Devon was awake made her feel less alone. As if taking this as her own cue to go to bed, Jessica made one more check on Ryan, then turned down the lamp and crawled into the massive bed. Scooting into the very middle, Jessica could extend both arms and never touch the sides of the bed. How empty it seemed. How empty her entire life seemed.

I'll try to do better, Lord, she prayed the promise. *I will humble myself and go to Devon and apologize for my attitude and actions. I will even be honest with him about the reasons. But please, just go before me and help me to say the right thing. Don't let me make a fool out of myself—again.*

⁓

The next morning dawned with a promise of spring. The air felt warm on Jessica's face as she made her way out to what Kate called the garden house. The ground gave off a rich, earthy smell that made Jessica want to plant something. Maybe she'd talk to Kate about restoring the flower garden that used to grow along this walk. Kate had spoken of the prairie flowers and the delicate splotches of color that graced the hills when springtime was upon them in full. Kate said it had been Naomi's favorite time of year.

Standing just outside the cottage, Jessica gave a brief prayer for courage. She wanted to speak to Devon before breakfast in hopes that he might join them and ease the tension that had engulfed the house since Jessica's last outburst. She also intended to follow through with her promise to God and humble herself before this handsome stranger.

Knocking lightly, Jessica tried to plan what she'd say. She had continued to wrestle with her conscience long into the night, but somewhere around two in the morning, she'd finally let go of her fears and given them over to God. It wouldn't be easy to face her mismatched emotions, but somehow she knew God would give her the grace to handle things day by day.

Devon opened the door, stared at her blankly for a moment, then smiled. "And to what do I owe the pleasure of a visit from the boss lady?"

Jessica swallowed hard and tried to think of each word before speaking. "I've come here to apologize."

Devon crossed his arms and leaned against the door frame. "Apologize?"

Jessica nodded. "That's right. My behavior toward you has been uncalled for. I've known it all along, but I'm hoping you will give me a chance to explain."

Devon's expression softened. "Why don't you come in and tell me all about it."

Jessica nodded. "All right."

She entered the cottage for the first time, amazed at the hominess of the front room. A native stone fireplace took up most of one wall, while a big picture window that looked out onto a small porch graced yet another. A narrow pine staircase took up the south side, while an open archway made up most of the remaining west wall. A large rag rug, no doubt put together by Kate, lay on the floor in front of the fireplace, and a couch, upholstered in a sort of brown tweed, stood awaiting them behind this.

"Might as well sit over here," Devon said, leading the way to the couch. "It's really the only warm spot in the house. Buck and I are trying to find materials to make repairs, but it's rather slow going."

"If there's anything I can do to help. . . ," Jessica offered, letting her voice trail off.

"That's all right. I think Buck and I can handle it," Devon countered. "So you were going to do some explaining."

Jessica nodded. She gazed into Devon's dark eyes and felt a wave of alarm wash over her. Maybe coming here wasn't a good idea, after all. She looked away and clasped her fingers tightly together. "I know I've treated you rather harshly."

"Rather harshly?" he questioned.

Jessica took a deep breath and let it out. "All right. I've treated you badly, and I'm sorry. There's a great deal in my life that makes it hard for me to trust people. Especially strangers. From the minute I stepped foot on Windridge, you seemed to be everywhere, and frankly, it made me uncomfortable."

"I can certainly understand," Devon replied. "That's kind of why I've been trying to keep my distance."

"Then there's Ryan," she continued uneasily. Devon was a man. What would he understand of her motherly insecurities? She looked up and found his expression fixed with a compassionate stare. Maybe he would understand. "Do you know my story, Mr. Carter? How I came to live back East rather than on Windridge?" He nodded. "Well, it's left me with a very real void in my life. I never knew my parents—never saw my father until I was twelve. Even when I came here to spend a few weeks that summer, I still didn't see him much. He probably felt as uncomfortable as I did. Neither one of us knew what to do with the other one."

She paused as if trying to sort out her words. She wanted Devon to understand why she resented his interference with Ryan, but it seemed important to set up the conflicts from her early days in order to make her present days more clear.

"I never felt love for my father," she admitted. "I think I was afraid to love him. I certainly didn't want to give him another chance to send me away or to reject that love. My aunt Harriet encouraged neither shows of emotion nor words of endearment, and so I never felt loved in her home. I've been taught most of my life to bury my emotions, or at best, to shut them off. I tell you this because I would like for you to understand my difficulty in being open with my feelings."

Devon chuckled. "I thought you made your feelings quite apparent. You don't like me or my interfering with Ryan."

"No, that's not it," Jessica replied, looking at the dying embers in the fireplace. "I love Windridge. It's the only thing that couldn't reject my love." Her voice trembled slightly under the emotion of the moment. "I don't want my pride to keep this ranch from becoming a success once again. I don't want my feelings from the past creeping into the future of this place, and I won't allow myself to cause the demise of Buck and Kate's happiness, nor of yours."

"You don't have the power to put an end to Buck and Kate's happiness. Nor can you destroy mine for that matter," Devon replied, seeming most emphatic. "As for the success of this ranch, well, maybe the time has come to put an end to Windridge. There are folks out there willing to buy. Maybe you'd be happier back East or even in town."

"No!" Jessica said, looking back to see Devon watching her reaction with apparent interest. "I don't want to sell. If I gave you that idea, then I know I've failed to say the right words. Look, I mentioned the idea of a resort ranch only because it seemed to be profitable. We're only an hour away from the train. We already have a perfectly suited stagecoach, though why my father ever purchased such an elaborate means of transportation, I'll never know."

Devon laughed. "Gus got it in trade, to tell you the truth. One of the locals ran a stage line for about two months. He went broke in a hurry and then took sick. When he saw he couldn't keep it up, he asked Gus to trade him for some good beef stock so his son could start a small ranch. Gus agreed, and there you have it."

"Well, that does explain it rather neatly," Jessica agreed. "But don't you see? I envision the healing power of this ranch will draw others to its doorstep, just as it has me."

"But honestly, Jessica," he said, his voice lowering and his expression growing intense, "part of Windridge's healing is the isolation. You bring in a bunch of city folks and suddenly it's not so very isolated anymore. Folks will come with their strange notions and ways of doing things, and soon you'll find that Windridge is nothing like it once was. I'd hate to see that happen."

Jessica felt a bit defeated. She honestly tried to see Devon's point. Maybe he knew what he was talking about. Maybe she was the real fool in the matter. She reached into her apron pocket and pulled out several folded pieces of paper. "These are the articles I mentioned to you awhile back. All I ask is that you take a look at them."

Devon reached out to take them, his fingers closing over hers for a brief moment. The current of emotions seemed to leap from Jessica to Devon, and for a time he looked at her as if he could read every detail of her soul. The longing, the loneliness, the fearfulness, and the insecurity—Jessica worried that if she didn't look away quickly, she'd soon reveal more about herself than she'd ever intended. She dropped her hold on the papers and pulled her hand back against her breast as though the touch had burned her fingers.

Devon seemed to understand her discomfort, but to what extent, Jessica couldn't tell. "I'll look these over," he promised, tucking them between the cushions of the couch.

"I appreciate that. I also have another favor to ask you."

"All right."

She lowered her head and stared at her lap. "I would very much appreciate your help with the Windridge accounts. I've looked at the books, but I'm still not sure what I'm looking at."

Devon chuckled. "I can't say that Gus was the best bookkeeper in the world. He knew his system but seldom wanted to share it with anyone else. It wasn't until about a year before he died that I knew we were in real trouble. After that, things just sort of went from bad to worse. But in answer to your question, I'll be glad to do what I can. I do know the workings of this ranch—very nearly as well as Buck. I think together we can give some strong consideration as to what is to be done."

Jessica nodded. "Thank you. I do appreciate it. I know I've not acted with Christian charity, and God has quite seriously brought it to my attention." She glanced up to find him studying her. Her heart skipped a beat when he grinned at her.

"He's had to bring it to my attention quite often as well—not because of your attitude," he said, pausing, "but because of my own."

Jessica got to her feet. The intimacy of the moment was rapidly becoming quite noticeable. "I hope this apology of mine will mean that you'll reconsider and share meals up at the house again. Kate hasn't been herself since you stopped coming up, and I know you're staying away because of the way I acted."

Devon walked with her to the door. "That's not exactly true," he told her. "I also stayed away because of the way I acted when I was around you."

Jessica turned to look at him—wondering at his meaning—afraid to know the truth. Instead of asking him to explain, she realized she'd omitted a very important matter. "There's one more thing, and it comes very hard for me."

"By all means, speak your mind."

Jessica looked at him for a moment. She felt down deep inside that she could trust this man. That his motives were pure and his actions were not intended for harm. What she wasn't sure of was whether or not she could accept that her child would have needs in his life that she would be unable to fill—needs that would require a man's thought, perspective, and guidance.

"It's about Ryan," she finally said.

"I see."

Devon took a step back and looked like he might say something, but Jessica hurried to continue. "I was wrong there as well." He raised a brow but said nothing, and Jessica realized she'd have to explain further. But how much should she say? Would it be appropriate to tell Devon about Esmerelda and her mother? Would it be appropriate to explain her deepest heartfelt fear that she might somehow lose Ryan to another?

She looked away, tears forming in her eyes. How could she explain? She scarcely understood the feelings she had. She felt so protective of Ryan, not only for him, but for fear she would once again be denied love.

"I'm sorry," she whispered. "It's very difficult for me to speak about it."

Devon's voice was low and filled with tenderness. "Jessica, I know you're still grieving your husband's passing and all. I wasn't trying to take his place."

Jessica laughed and turned to meet Devon with her tears flowing freely. "It isn't that. Believe me, it isn't that at all." Her voice sounded foreign in her own ears. It came out as a mixture of a laugh and a sob all at once. "I didn't love Newman Albright, and he certainly didn't love me. We married because he was chosen by my aunt Harriet. I often thought afterwards that for all she did to sing his charms and merits, Harriet should have married him herself."

Devon reached out and touched her tear-streaked cheek. "Then what is this all about?"

"I might never have loved my husband, but I would die rather than lose my son," she answered, quivering under the touch of his warm fingers.

"I still don't understand what that has to do with me."

He looked at her with such intensity, such longing to understand, that Jessica had to close her eyes to regain her composure. "The only reason," she began, her eyes still tightly closed, "that I didn't want you interfering with Ryan—"

"Yes? Go on," he encouraged when she fell silent.

"I don't want you replacing me in his life," she finally managed, but the tears came again. "He's all I have." Her voice came out like a whimper, and Jessica hated sounding like a lost child. She knew it was better to be honest and face humiliation than to lie and go on dealing with her conscience.

To her surprise, Devon put his arms around her and gently pulled her head to his shoulder. No one had ever done this for her. Not once. Not even Newman. The action seemed so intimate, so loving, that Jessica broke down and cried in deep, heart-wrenching sobs.

Devon did nothing but hold her. He let her cry, all the time keeping his arms tightly around her. He didn't say a word or try to force answers out of her. He just held her. Oh, but it felt wonderful! It felt like something Jessica had been searching for all of her life. Warm arms to comfort and assure her that the world outside would not break in to hurt her anymore. Without even realizing it, she had wrapped her own arms around Devon's waist and clung to him as though in letting go, she might well drown in a sea of emptiness.

After a few minutes, Jessica felt the weight of her emotions lift. Her tears subsided, and she fell silent. She knew it was quite uncalled for to be standing there alone with Devon, embracing him so familiarly, but she was quite hesitant to let go.

"Feel better?" he asked softly, reaching a hand up to smooth back her hair.

Jessica sniffed in a most unladylike way and nodded. "I think so." She let go of him and wiped her face with the edge of her apron. "I'm sorry about losing control that way."

"Don't be," Devon answered quite seriously. "You don't have to face the world by yourself, Jess."

The nickname warmed her, where only weeks ago it would have irritated her. "I know. I know. The Bible makes that clear, but sometimes it seems God is so far away."

"I wasn't talking about God." She looked up to see Devon's eyes narrow ever so slightly as he scrutinized her. "God is there for you," he agreed. "I wouldn't presume to say otherwise. But I meant that we're here for you, too. Katie, Buck, and me. We care about you, and we care about Ryan. And honestly, Jessica, I would never do anything to harm your child or to take him away from you. I do realize that there is more to this than you're telling me, but maybe one day you'll feel confident enough of our friendship to share it all. Until then, just know I care.

"We'll get through this, but we'll need to rely on one another. Ryan is starting to walk now, and there are plenty of dangers around the ranch. You'll wear yourself to the bone if you worry about having to watch him alone. Let us help you. We want to make your life easier, not harder, and certainly not more painful."

Jessica nodded. "I know that." She lowered her head and looked at the floor. What she would say next would come at considerable risk to her security. "Ryan seems so miserable without you around. I want you to feel free to play with him and be around him. I know he's already taken to you in a big way. I would even go so far as to say he loves you."

Devon reached out to touch Jessica's chin with his index finger. Lifting her face, he replied, "He loves you, too, Jessica. That won't change just because other people come into his life. It's been my experience, the more love the better. People need to be loved."

Jessica felt his words cut deep into her heart. If she didn't clear out now, she'd start crying all over again. "Thank you," she whispered quickly and hurried to the door. Throwing it open, she looked back over her shoulder. "I'm sure Kate has breakfast nearly ready. You will join us, won't you?"

"You bet. I'll be up to the house in a few minutes."

⁓

Devon watched Jessica walk up the path to the big stone house. He felt an overwhelming urge to run after her and declare his love for her. Funny, he thought, he'd fallen in love with her almost from the start. At least he thought it was love. He certainly knew that it was something powerful and strong. He thought about her constantly and worried that she would give up on the ranch before he had a chance to convince her to take his help.

He had money in the bank. Not a lot, but enough to help the ranch. He would just do as Buck and Kate had done and start purchasing things as they needed them, and he wouldn't let Jessica know about it. Of course, Buck would know, and so would Kate. But he knew they would keep his secret. Kate had told him of their scheme to sell quilts. Maybe he'd offer to take some to Kansas City when he went there to buy cattle. He could always add some extra dollars to the amount he actually managed to make.

It was easy enough to formulate an idea about bringing in more cattle and maybe a ranch hand or two, but it was harder to decide how he would help Jessica to work through her inability to trust. He longed to help her feel secure in the house on Windridge. He wanted her to know that her home would be here as long as she needed it. That he would be here, too, if only she would let him.

He thought of her fears of losing Ryan's love and realized rather quickly that with Jessica's very personal declarations of her life, he had become privy to the knowledge that she had never felt loved. Kate had loved her from the start and had said so on many occasions. But Kate had not been allowed to raise the baby of Naomi and Gus Gussop. A cold, unfeeling woman with social concerns had raised Jessica. The father Jessica had never known had no idea how to receive her or her needs when that unfeeling woman had finally allowed Jessica a visit home.

Even her husband hadn't married her out of love. And Devon found that particularly distressing considering his own growing feelings. He hadn't said anything about his interest in Jessica, primarily because he assumed she wouldn't be ready for such attentions. Now he realized she was not only ready for it, but she'd been ready for over twenty-seven years. She needed love. She needed the love of a good man.

He smiled and leaned against the doorjamb as Jessica disappeared through the back door of the house. "I'm a good man," he said aloud, a plan already formulating in his mind. His smile broadened. "In fact, I'm the only man for the job."

He looked up into the clear morning sky and felt the overwhelming urge to share his thoughts with God, "This was what You had in mind for me all along, wasn't it? I wouldn't have been happy with another woman, and that's why You didn't let me waste my life on Jane Jenkins."

He thought of the petite blond who'd appeared at the ranch less than two weeks before their wedding day to announce she was marrying someone else. At least she'd been good enough to bring back Devon's ring. The ring had belonged to his grandmother, and Jane knew how much it meant to him. She hadn't been totally without feeling.

"I can't stay out here in the middle of nowhere," she had told him that day so long ago. *"I hate Kansas and everything that goes with it. I want to see the world and live in a big city, and I've found someone who feels exactly like I do. I hope you'll forgive me like you said you would."*

Last Devon had heard, Jane was living just outside of Topeka. She had three kids, a cantankerous mother-in-law, and a husband who was seldom home due to his job as a traveling salesman. He felt sorry for her, knowing her dream had not been realized. At the time, her rejection had hurt him deeply; but as the months and years passed, Devon knew God had saved him from a miserable life.

"Thank You," he whispered. "Thank You for sending Jane out of my life and for bringing Jessica into it. Now, it's my prayer that You would show me how to help her. How to make her feel loved and safe."

He realized they would all be sitting down to breakfast soon, so he grabbed his hat and closed the door to the cottage. "It wouldn't hurt if You helped her to love me, too." He grinned and tapped his hat onto his head. "Wouldn't hurt at all."

Chapter 5

One of Jessica's greatest pleasures came from horseback riding. Buck had suggested it one glorious April day, and Jessica found it a perfect solution to those times when the house seemed too quiet and the day too long. Of course, with Ryan now getting into things, those times were few and far between, but nevertheless, Jessica found it a wonderful time. Riding out across the prairie hills, she could think about the days to come—and the days now gone. She could plan her future without anyone barging in on her thoughts, and she could pray.

It also became an exercise in trust. She forced herself to leave Ryan in Kate's care and trust that nothing would happen to threaten her relationship with her son. It wasn't easy, but Jessica knew instinctively that it was right.

Now, having ridden to the top of the ridge, Jessica stared out across the rolling Flint Hills and sighed. Flowers were just beginning to dot the prairie grasses. It reminded her of her mother. Kate had told her that this view had been Naomi's favorite because of the flowers and the contours of the hills and the glorious way the sunsets seemed to spill color across the western horizon.

Jessica wearied of the saddle and dismounted. "All right, boy, it's back to the barn for you."

The horse seemed to perfectly understand her, and with a snort and a whinny, he took off in the direction of the corrals and barn. By letting the horse go free, she found that he always made his way back to the stable and to Buck's tender care. The first time it had happened totally by mistake when Jessica had dismounted and let go of her reins. Buck had worried she'd been thrown, but Jessica had assured him as she came running down the hill to recapture her mount that she was fine. Buck had laughed; so had Devon; and when they'd shared the scene with Katie, she had laughed as well. Buck said the Windridge horses were so spoiled and pampered, they'd return to the barn every time, and after that, it just became the routine.

Today, the wind came from the south as it often did, but with it came a gentle scent of new life. Flowers bloomed sporadically across the prairie, and Jessica reveled in the addition of color to her otherwise rather drab world. The fields had greened up, much to the delight of the cattle who seemed rather tired of hay and dried dead grass. Even the house itself seemed to take on a more golden hue.

Jessica sighed and reached up to take off her bonnet. She let down her hair and shook it free, grateful to feel the wind through it one more time. Kate said her father had called this God's country, and Jessica could well understand why he felt that way. Just standing there, watching the cattle feed, seeing the occasional movement of a rabbit or the flight of birds overhead, Jessica felt her heart overflow with praise to God. His presence seemed to be everywhere at once.

The land was so wholly unspoiled. The city had a harshness to it that she'd once accused the prairie of having. Both could be ruthless in dealing with their tenants, but while the prairie did so from innocence, the city made its mark in snobbery, class strife, and confrontation.

In the city, Jessica seldom knew a moment when noise didn't dominate her day. The activities were enough to cause a person to go mad. And it seemed the poorer you were, the higher the level of clatter. Street vendors called out their wares from morning to night. Children—dirty urchins who had no real homes—raced up and down the streets begging money, food, shelter. Poverty brought its own sounds: the cries of the hungry, the street fighting of the angry, the con men with their schemes to make everyone rich overnight.

But always the needs of the children concerned Jessica. She had tried to do what she could, but there'd been so little, and she could hardly take away from her own child in order to provide for someone else's. When her father had started to provide for her once again, she had shared what she could with some of the others. Esmerelda had thought her quite mad. "Charity," she had told Jessica, "is better left to the truly rich." Essie thought Jessica's money could be much better spent on a new gown or toys for Ryan. It was easy now to see how harsh Essie could be when Jessica refused to play by her rules.

And there were so many rules. Not just Essie's but New York's rules as well. The rules of class—of not crossing boundaries, of staying where you belonged. Jessica had provided a dichotomy for her friends. She had been raised in the best social settings with Harriet Nelson and married a man who held rank among the well-to-do. But when their money was gone, so, too, were their friends. It seemed strange to suddenly find that she was never invited to parties or teas. Never visited by those she had once been bosom companions with. Essie had maintained a letter-writing campaign, but never once had the young woman come to visit after things had gone bad for Jessica. She hadn't even come to Newman's funeral.

But once Jessica's father stepped in to move her back to the proper neighborhood and reinstate her with financial resources, everyone flocked around. It was all as if Jessica had only been abroad for several years. In fact, Essie had once introduced her that way, telling the dinner guests that Jessica had enjoyed an extensive stay in Paris. It was true enough that she had done exactly that, but Essie failed to mention that Jessica had been thirteen years old at the time.

She let her gaze pan across the western horizon, while the waning sun touched her face with the slightest hint of warmth. She knew Aunt Harriet would have been appalled to find her in such a state, but to Jessica, it felt wonderful! She cherished the moment, just as she had when she'd been twelve.

"Thank You, Father," she whispered, raising her hands heavenward as if to stretch out and touch her fingertips to God.

"You make a mighty fetching picture up here like that," Devon said.

Jessica turned, surprised to see the overworked foreman making his way up the ridge. "I thought maybe you'd hightailed it back to civilization," she teased to ease her own embarrassment. "I've scarcely seen you in two weeks."

"There's been too much to do," Devon told her. "But you already know that. Kate told me you've been pretty busy yourself."

"Yes. We've finished up some quilts, and then Buck dug us up a garden patch."

"I saw that. Can't say this is good farm ground, but Kate's gardens generally survive. It's all that tender loving care she gives them." Devon took off his hat and wiped his brow with a handkerchief. "Feels good up here."

"Yes," Jessica agreed. Her hair whipped wildly in the breeze, and she felt a bit embarrassed to be found in such a state. It was one thing to know they could see her from down below the hilltop, but for Devon to be here with her made Jessica self-conscious.

She reached up and began trying to pull her hair back into order, but Devon came forward and stilled her efforts. "Don't do that. It looks so nice down."

Jessica laughed nervously and stepped away. "It's just something I do sometimes. Kind of silly, but it reminds me of when I was a little girl."

"Nothing silly about that."

"Maybe not," Jessica said, forcing herself to look away from Devon's attractive face to the start of a beautiful sunset. "The prairie used to make me lonely. I used to feel so small and insignificant in the middle of it all. The hills just go on and on forever. It reminds me of how I'm just one tiny speck in a very big world."

"What happened to change how you felt? I mean, you told me you wanted to stay here and never leave. Surely you wouldn't feel that way about a place that made you feel lonely and insignificant."

Devon had come to stand beside her again, but Jessica refused to look at him. "I never had many chances to visit here before getting married, but after the second visit, I had already decided that the prairie was growing on me. I went home to New York City and felt swallowed up whole. The lifestyle, the parties, the activities that never seemed to end—it all made me feel so forgotten."

"How so?" Devon questioned softly.

Jessica stopped toying with her hair and let it go free once again. "No one really ever talks to anyone there. You speak about the city, about the affairs of other people. You talk about the newest rages and the fashionable way to dress. You go to parties and dinners and present yourself to be seen with all the correct people, but you never, ever tell anyone how you feel about anything personal. It fit well with my upbringing, but I came to want more."

She finally looked at him. "I feel alive out here. I feel like I can breathe and stretch and let my hair blow in the wind and no one will rebuke me for it. I feel like I can talk to you and Buck and Kate, and you not only talk back, but you really listen."

"I can't imagine being any other way," Devon said. "But, as for the coldness of the big city, I do understand. I go to Kansas City once, sometimes twice a year for supplies and to sell off the cattle. I hate it there. No one seems to care if you live or die."

"I know," Jessica replied, admiring the way the sky had taken on a blend of orange, yellow, and pink. "And you certainly never get sunsets like these."

Devon laughed. "Nope."

"I know God brought me here for a reason. I know He has a purpose for my life, and I feel strongly that my purpose involves helping other people. That may sound silly to you, but I know God has a plan for me."

"It doesn't sound silly at all. I believe God has a plan for each of us."

"What kind of plan does He have for you, Devon?" she asked seriously, concentrating on his expression.

Devon shoved his hands into his pockets and stared to the west. "I don't guess I know in full."

"So tell me in part," she urged.

"I know God brought me to this ranch. It was a healing for me, so when you speak of it being a healing for other people, I guess I understand. I was once engaged to be married, but it didn't work out. Windridge saw me through some bad times. Now, however, I feel God has shown me the reason for that situation and the result."

"What reason?" Jessica questioned, truly wondering how Devon could speak so casually about losing the woman he apparently loved.

"I know God has someone else for me to marry. He's already picked her out."

"Oh," she replied, her answer sounding flat. She'd only recently allowed herself to think about Devon as something more than a ranch foreman. She'd actually given herself permission to consider what it might be like to fall in love and marry a man like Devon Carter. His words came as a shock and stung her effectively into silence.

"I don't like being alone. I see myself with a family of my own. Six or seven—boys, girls, it doesn't matter—and a fine spread to work. Ranches can be excellent places to bring up children."

He looked at her as if expecting her to comment, but Jessica had no idea what to say. His words only told her that one day he would go his way and leave her alone. Not only that but leave Ryan alone as well. A dull ache caused her to abruptly change the subject.

"I see Windridge surviving and becoming stronger. I think we have a lot to offer folks here. Have you had a chance to look over those articles I left with you?"

"I've looked them over. I have to say I'm not nearly as against the idea as I once was. It seems the ranch would mostly be open to the public during summer months, is that right?"

Jessica perked up at his positive attitude. "Yes. Yes, that's right. Late spring to early autumn might be the biggest stretch of time, but basically it would be summer."

"Ranches can be mighty busy during the summer," he commented.

"Yes, but that's part of the attraction. Folks from back East will come to see the workings of the ranch. You and your men would be able to go about your business, and the visitors would be able to observe you in action."

"They'd also want to ride and maybe even try their hand at what we do, at least that's what one of your clippings said," Devon countered.

"But only if we wanted it to be that way," Jessica replied. "It can be arranged however we see fit. No one makes the rules but us."

"I suppose it wouldn't be so bad if the rest of the year allowed us to get back to normal. The location does seem right for something like that. I suppose we could even fix one of the larger ponds with a deck and a place for fishing."

"What a good idea," Jessica replied. "Maybe swimming, too."

Devon nodded. "Hmmm, maybe. Might be a bit cold. Remember, those aren't hot springs." He appeared to be genuinely considering the matter. "And you see this as a ministry?"

Jessica felt herself grow slightly defensive. "I do. I see a great many things we can share with people. Kindness and love, mercy, tolerance— you name it. I know it would be a resort, and people would pay to come here and rest, but how we handled their stay would be evidence of Christ working in our lives. They would see how we dealt with problems and handled our daily lives."

"One of the articles talked about taking folks out camping under the stars to give them a taste of what the pioneers experienced when they went west in covered wagons. You thinking about doing that?" Devon asked.

Jessica considered the matter for a moment. "I think at first it would be to our benefit to just keep small. We could advertise it very nearly like a boarding home for vacationers. We could offer quiet summers. Maybe fishing, like you suggested, and horseback riding. We could build some nice chairs for the porch, and Kate and I could make cushions; folks could go through my father's library and pick out something to read and just relax on the porch. I just want to make a difference in people's lives."

Devon stepped closer. "You've made a difference in mine. You and Ryan both."

She looked into his warm brown eyes and saw a reflection of something she didn't understand. His words sounded important, yet he'd made it clear that God had someone already in mind for him to marry.

"I need to get back." She turned to leave, but Devon reached out to touch her arm. "I meant it, Jess. And I'm starting to think that maybe a resort wouldn't be a bad way to get the ranch back up and running.

Hopefully, this small herd we've taken on from the Rocking W will make us a tidy profit and allow us to get a bigger herd next year. You keep praying about it, and so will I."

Jessica nodded and hurried down the hill to the three-story stone house. She didn't know how to take Devon or his words. He always treated her kindly and always offered her honesty, but today only served to confuse her.

Quietly, she entered the house through the back door, hoping that she'd not have to deal with Kate. Kate would want to know how Jessica had spent her day. Kate would want to know what she and Devon had talked about. And there was little doubt in Jessica's mind that Kate would know they had talked. She'd probably observed them up on the ridge. Everyone would have seen them there. Buck. The ranch hands.

Jessica felt her face grow hot. She had very much enjoyed being with Devon, and she enjoyed their talks. But Devon had another woman in mind to marry, and Jessica knew the heartache of losing a man to another woman. She'd not interfere in Devon's relationships. She'd not ruin his chances at happiness with the woman of his dreams. The woman God had sent to him.

With a heavy heart, Jessica admitted to herself that she was gradually coming to care about Devon. She liked the way he moved, the way he talked. She loved how he played with Ryan and how Ryan's face lit up whenever Devon came into the room. Reluctantly, Jessica began to put her hair back up in a bun. "I'm being so childish and ridiculous," she muttered.

"Oh, so there you are. Guess who just woke up?" Kate asked, coming down the back stairs with Ryan in her arms.

Jessica had just secured the last hairpin in place. "How's Mama's boy?" Jessica asked, holding her arms out to Ryan.

"Mamamama," Ryan chattered. "Eat." He pulled at Jessica's collar, and she knew he wanted to nurse. She'd only managed to wean him a couple weeks earlier, but he nevertheless tried to coerce her into nursing him.

"Mama will take you to the kitchen and get you a big boy's cup,"

Jessica told him, gently tousling his nearly hairless head. "Do you suppose this child will ever grow hair?" she asked Kate.

"I've heard it said you were the same way," Kate said chuckling. "I think you finally achieved those glossy brown curls when you were nearly two."

"I hope he doesn't take too long," Jessica replied as she retraced her steps to the kitchen. She thought for a moment she was off the hook until Kate, pouring fresh cold milk into a cup for Ryan, asked, "So what did you and Devon have to talk about while you enjoyed that beautiful sunset?"

Jessica tried not to act in the leastwise concerned about the question. "We discussed the ranch. It consumes most of our talks. Devon is finally coming around to my way of thinking. He's not nearly so negative about turning this place into a resort ranch."

"I never thought you'd convince him, but he talked to Buck about it just yesterday. Buck said he actually had some good ideas about what they could do to make this place ready by next year."

"Next year? But Devon said nothing to me about next year. I figured I'd have to spend most of this one just convincing him to let me do it."

Ryan drank from the cup, finished the milk, then tried to pound the empty cup against the wall behind his mother. Jessica finally put him down on the floor and turned her attention back to Kate.

"Did he really say next summer?"

Kate smiled and pushed up her glasses. "He did. I take it that surprises you?"

"Indeed it does. He said only that he was starting to see some merit in the idea. I had no idea he was actually working toward a date."

"Well, he's found some extra capital to sink into the ranch. Then, too, we have the quilts to sell, and we can always busy ourselves to make more. Besides, Devon doesn't own this ranch—you do. If you want to turn it into a resort, you certainly don't need anyone's permission."

"Yes, but I want you all to be happy."

"Devon, too?" Kate grinned.

"Of course. You told me I needed to consider his thoughts on the

matter, and I have. I respect Devon's opinion. I know all of you understand the ranch better than I do, but nevertheless, I want to learn, and
I want to keep everyone's best interests at heart. I've been praying hard
about this, Kate. I'm not going to just jump in without thinking."

Kate reached out and gave Jessica a hug. "I knew you wouldn't. We
want you happy though, and if turning this place upside down would
do the trick, I have a feeling Devon would start working on plans to
figure a way."

Jessica said nothing but turned instead to see Ryan heading for the
stove. "No, Ryan! Hot!" she exclaimed and went quickly to move the
boy to another part of the kitchen.

"Why don't you and Ryan go out on the porch and spend some
time together?" Kate suggested. "I've already got supper well underway,
and there's no need to have you both in here underfoot."

Jessica laughed. "Just when I started thinking I had become needed
and useful."

Kate laughed. "Oh, you're needed and useful, all right. Maybe more
than you realize."

Jessica picked up the boy and made her way to the front door and
out onto the porch. The sky had turned deep lavender with hints of
even darker blues to the east. Night was still another hour or so away,
but already shadows fell across the hills and valleys. Jessica liked the
effect and wished fervently she could draw or paint. It seemed a shame
that something so lovely should go by unseen. This thought provoked
another. She could always advertise the ranch to artists. Mention the
beautiful scenery and lighting. Of course, many people would consider
the scenery boring and anything but beautiful. Perhaps that wouldn't be
a very productive thing to do. What if someone went home to complain
about the falsehood of her advertisement?

As Ryan played happily with Katie's flowerpots, Jessica allowed her
thoughts to go back to Devon. She couldn't help it. She didn't want to
care about him, at least not in the sense of falling in love and sharing a
life with him. She didn't like to think of the rejection that could come
in caring for someone, only to have them not care in return.

Still, if she couldn't have him in that capacity, then it was enough to have him here on the ranch full time. He made a good foreman, and she prayed he'd stay on for as long as she kept the ranch. A gray cloud descended over her thoughts. What if he married and brought his wife here to Windridge? Jessica shuddered. She'd not like that at all. And then with Ryan already so attached to Devon, it might create even greater problems. What if Ryan wanted to be with Devon instead of Jessica? What if Devon's new wife attracted Ryan's attention as well?

Jessica shook off the thoughts and tried to remain positive. "I can't be given over to thoughts of what if. There's plenty of other things to worry myself with."

Ryan babbled on and on about the flowerpots. Some words came out in clarity, and others were purely baby talk. Jessica found herself amazed to see how much the child had grown over the last few weeks. It seemed he'd almost aged overnight. She didn't like to think of him growing up and not needing her anymore. She didn't like to think about him becoming an adult and moving away. What would she do when he was gone? Who would love her, and whom would she love?

Devon's image came to mind, but Jessica shook her head sadly. "That's not going to happen," she told herself again. "He has other plans, and they don't include me."

Ryan perked up at this and toddled back to Jessica. He pounded the flats of his hands on her knees. "Me. Me. Me go. Me go."

Jessica looked down at him, feeling tears form in her eyes. "I know you will," she told him sadly. "One day, you will go."

Chapter 6

"If we convert those two sitting rooms at the back of the house," Kate said one evening after dinner, "we could have additional bedrooms for guests."

"True," Buck replied, looking to Jessica and Devon for their reactions.

"It might even work better if Ryan and I took those two rooms and let our rooms upstairs be used for guests," Jessica replied. "I mean, that way the entire second floor would be devoted to guests, and the third floor would still belong to you and Buck."

"Maybe it would be better to give the third floor to you and Ryan," Devon said thoughtfully. "After all, Kate needs to be close to the kitchen to get things started up in the morning, and Buck needs to be close to the barn and bunkhouse."

"I hadn't thought of it that way," Kate replied. "Those two rooms would be more than enough for Buck and me. In fact, one room would be enough."

"No, now I wouldn't feel right about it if you and Buck didn't have your own sitting room for privacy," Jessica said firmly. "Having a house full of strangers will be cause enough to need our own places of refuge."

"I could give you back the cottage," Devon offered. "If you and Buck think you'd be more comfortable there, I could move into the bunkhouse."

"Nonsense," Kate said shaking her head. "You've already moved once; you might as well stay put." Jessica wondered what she meant by this statement, but the conversation moved along so quickly that she never had a chance to ask.

"Katie and I would be happy just about any place you put us," Buck stated. "I think those two sitting rooms are just perfect for us. It would eliminate running up and down all those stairs, and what with my rheumatism acting up from time to time, that would be enough to motivate the move on my part."

"Buck, you should have told me you were having trouble," Jessica countered. "I would have seen to it that you and Kate were moved long ago had I known."

"The exercise does us good," Kate said. "But I agree with Buck and Devon. Moving us downstairs into those back rooms would be perfect. That way, you and Ryan can have the full run of the third floor. You can set things up differently or keep it the way we have it. Either way, Ryan will have more room to run around, and there's a door to keep him from heading down the stairs when you don't want him to get away from you."

Jessica laughed. "No doubt he'll figure doors out soon enough."

"I think we could safely conclude," Devon said, pointing to a rough drawing he'd made of the house, "that we could have six rooms to offer to guests. We could even offer the bunkhouse's extra beds if someone wanted to come out and truly experience the life of a ranch hand. Those articles Jessica brought from back East said that some folks actually pay money to be abused that way."

He grinned and poked Buck lightly in the ribs. "A drafty room, work from sunup to sundown, dirt and grit everywhere, and the smell of sweat and horses and cattle—yes sir, that's the kind of stuff I want to pay out good money to experience."

"You get to experience it for free," Jessica chided.

"But when we're back on our feet, I expect to be paid," Devon replied, looking at her in a way that made Jessica's pulse quicken. Oh, but he was handsome. She loved the way the summer sun had lightened his hair and tanned his face.

"I doubt that will happen for a while. Every dime we make is going to have to go back into making the ranch successful again."

"I wasn't necessarily talking about being paid in money," Devon said, his lips curling into a grin.

Buck snorted, and Kate turned away, but not before Jessica saw her smiling. They were all so conspiratorial in their teasing, and sometimes

Jessica felt oddly left out. She had come onto the scene after they were all good friends, and sometimes it made her feel very uncomfortable. Like they all knew a good joke and refused to tell her.

"Well, it's getting late," Buck said, getting up from his chair. "I suspect Katie and I should retire for the evening. You two going to church in the morning?"

"Planning on it. I figured to drive Jessica and Ryan. You two need a lift?"

"No," Buck answered. "I figure on preaching a bit myself. Those ranch hands of ours need to get some religion now and then. What with the fact that it'll soon be time to herd those prime steers of ours to market, I figure on giving them a couple of pointers on staying out of trouble."

Kate joined Buck, leaving Devon and Jessica alone in the front parlor. "See you both tomorrow. I figure on frying up a mess of chicken for the hands and for us as well. Anything else you're hungry for?"

Devon grinned. "How about some of your famous raspberry cream cake?"

Jessica threw Kate a quizzical look. "I don't think I've ever had that. Do you mean to tell me I've been here almost a year and never once had the opportunity to taste your 'famous raspberry cream cake'?"

Kate laughed. "It's only famous to Devon. But sure, I'll fix us up some. The raspberries came on real good this year. I'll bet those bushes down by the main springs are still bearing fruit."

"Maybe Jess and I could pick some for you after church tomorrow," Devon offered.

"Maybe you could just speak for yourself," Jessica added in mock ire.

"You two can work it out," Kate replied as Buck slipped his arm around her waist. "I'll see you tomorrow."

When they'd gone, Jessica turned back to find Devon still grinning at her. "What?"

"I don't know what you mean."

"You're looking at me oddly," Jessica replied. She liked the way he was looking at her but refused to allow herself to show it. Devon's weekly trips into Cottonwood Falls had convinced her that he had a girlfriend in town. She tried not to think about it, but it bothered her nevertheless.

Devon chuckled and got up from his chair. "How about a stroll to the ridge? The moon is full, and the air warm."

"I can't," Jessica replied nervously. She was desperately afraid of being alone for too long with Devon. Just thinking about the ride into town for church caused her stomach to do flips.

"Why not?"

"Well, I should stay close to the house in case Ryan needs me."

"Guess that makes sense. So how about just coming out on the porch with me? The upstairs windows are open. You'll be able to hear him if he cries."

Jessica realized that she'd either have to be rude and refuse or go along with the plan. "All right. Maybe for a little bit. Then I need to go to bed."

He nodded and allowed her to lead the way to the front door. Neither one said another word until they were out on the porch. Devon and Buck had made some wonderful chairs and a couple benches, and it was to one of the latter that Devon motioned Jessica to follow him.

Nervously licking her lips, Jessica joined Devon on the bench. She put herself at the far edge of the seat, hoping Devon would take the hint and sit at the opposite end. He didn't, however, choosing instead to position himself right in the middle of the bench.

"It's a fine night," he said. Suddenly he jumped up. "Say, wait here. I have a surprise."

Jessica couldn't imagine what he had in mind, but she obediently nodded and watched as he bounded down the porch steps and disappeared around the side of the house. When he returned, he was carrying a guitar.

"I didn't know you played," she said in complete surprise.

"I just got started last winter. I've been taking lessons in town from Old Mr. Wiedermeier. That man can pick up anything and make music with it."

Jessica smiled as she wondered if it was this, and not a woman, that had been taking Devon to town on Friday evenings. It made her heart a little lighter, and she suddenly found herself quite eager to hear Devon play.

He began tuning the strings, strumming one and then another, then comparing the two to each other. When he finally had all six in agreeable harmony, he began strumming out a melody that Jessica instantly recognized.

"Why that sounds like 'O Worship the King.'"

Devon laughed. "That's good. It's supposed to." He played a few more bars.

"Do you sing as well?"

"I don't know about how *well* I do it, but I do sing." He didn't wait for her to ask but instead began to harmonize with the guitar. Devon's rich baritone rang out against the stillness of the night and stirred Jessica's heart. How lovely to sit on the porch in the warmth of late summer and listen to Devon sing. She could easily picture herself doing this for many years to come. Seeing it in her mind, she imagined herself married to Devon with four or five children gathered round them. It made a pleasant image to carry in her heart.

"I don't think I've ever seen such a look of contentment on your face, Miss Jessica," Devon drawled.

Jessica realized she'd just been caught daydreaming. "I was just thinking about something."

Devon put the guitar aside and moved closer to Jessica. "I've been doing some thinking, too. There's something I want to say to you."

Just then, the sound of Ryan crying reached Jessica's ears. "Oh, that's Ryan. I guess I'd better go."

Devon looked at her with such an expression of frustration and disappointment that Jessica very nearly sat back down. But her own nervousness held her fast. "I'll see you in the morning," she paused as if trying to decide whether or not she should say the rest, "and we can talk on the way to church."

With that she hurried upstairs, anxious and curious about what Devon might have had to tell her. Perhaps she was wrong about his trips into town. Maybe there was more than just the guitar lesson. Maybe her earlier feelings of Devon meeting up with a lady friend were more on target than she wanted to imagine.

By the time she'd reached Ryan, he'd fallen back to sleep and lay contentedly sucking his thumb. Jessica tidied his covers, gently touched his cheek with her fingers, and went back to her own room.

"There's something I want to say to you," Devon had said. The words were still ringing in her ears.

What could he possibly need to say?

⁓

Devon knew nothing but frustration that Sunday morning. He'd barely slept a wink the night before, and now the horses were uncooperative as he tried to ready the buckboard wagon. He knew it wouldn't be nearly as comfortable for Jessica and Ryan, but there were supplies he'd been unable to bring home on Friday night, and he'd need this opportunity to get them safely home before he headed to Kansas City with the sale cattle.

He kept rethinking what he'd nearly said to Jessica the night before. It should have been simple. Jessica was a widow going on two years, and by her own declaration she'd never loved her husband. It seemed more than enough time to put the past behind her and deal with Devon's interests.

"Say, after church you might want to ask Joe Riley if he still wants to buy that acreage on the western boundaries of Windridge," Buck said as he came into the barn. He saw the difficulty Devon was having and immediately went to work to see the task completed.

"I'll do that," Devon said absentmindedly. "I'll ask Jessica if she's still of a mind to sell. You know how angry she gets when we try to question her."

"Still, she's a good-hearted woman," Buck replied.

"Yeah, I know that well enough," Devon muttered.

"You ain't gonna let that little gal get away from you, are you? There's plenty of fellows down at that church who'd give their right arms to be able to spend time with Jessie the way you do."

"For all the good it does."

"You feeling sorry for yourself, son?" Buck questioned. "That doesn't hardly seem like you."

"Not sure I even know what's like me anymore," Devon admitted. He took hold of the horses' harnesses and led the two matched geldings from the barn. "I wouldn't have been of a mind to turn this place into a dude ranch ten months ago, but look at me now."

"You just see the wisdom in it," Buck replied. "Besides, ranching and courting are two different things. I know you have feelings for Jessie. Why not just tell her and let the chips fall where they will?"

"I tried to say something last night, but—"

"Here we are," Jessica announced, coming down the steps with Kate and Ryan directly behind her. Jessica stashed a small bag of necessities behind the wagon seat, then beamed Devon a smile that nearly broke his heart. How could a woman look so pretty and not even realize what she did to a fellow? She had a face like an angel. Long dark lashes, delicately arched brows. A straight little nose that turned up ever so slightly at the end, and lips so full and red that Devon was hard-pressed not to steal a kiss.

"We're all ready. Say, why are we taking the buckboard?" Jessica asked, letting Buck help her up onto the seat. She reached down and lifted Ryan from Kate's arms.

"Devon's picking up some supplies that came in on Friday. He didn't have the wagon with him when he went into town Friday night, so he secured them at the train station until he could pick them up today."

"No doubt someone will frown on his toting home necessities on the Lord's Day," Kate murmured. "But if we don't get some flour and sugar soon, not to mention coffee, we'll have a mutiny on our hands."

"No one will think anything about it," Devon said, climbing up to sit beside Jessica. The buckboard seat was very narrow and pushed the two people very close together. Devon could smell her perfume. "If they have a problem with it, they can answer to me." With that he smacked the reins against the backs of the geldings.

The trip into town passed by before Devon and Jessica could get past discussing how they were going to renovate the house for their guests. Jessica had all manner of thoughts on the matter, and it seemed she and Kate had made some definite decisions. Each room would have a color theme with quilts and curtains to match. And guests would share breakfast together, which meant the extra extensions for the dining room table would have to be located and additional chairs ordered to match the existing ones.

Church hardly presented itself as a place to explain his feelings. Devon went through the motions of worship and even managed to focus his attention on the sermon, but over and over he thought of how he might share his feelings with Jessica. He was due to leave with the cattle in little more than two weeks, yet so much needed his attention, and very little time would be afforded him for quiet, romantic talks.

After church, Devon loaded up the ranch supplies while Jessica fed Ryan. Fussy and cantankerous from a day of being cooped up, Ryan seemed to do his level best to make life difficult for his mother. Jessica said he was teething, and she had it on Kate's authority that chewing a leather strap was the best thing to ease the pain. She'd brought one along just for this purpose and was trying to interest Ryan in chewing on it. Ryan just slapped at it and cried. Devon shook his head and finished securing two rolls of bailing wire before jumping up to take the reins.

"I imagine he'll be a whole lot happier when we get home," Devon suggested. He could see exasperation in Jessica's expression.

"I suppose you're right."

"You want me to hold him awhile?" he asked, seeing Ryan push and squirm while crying at the top of his lungs.

To his surprise, Jessica shrugged, then handed the boy over. Ryan instantly calmed and took notice of Devon's mustache. "Now, partner, we're going to have to have an understanding here. I'm driving this here wagon, and you're going to have to help me." He showed Ryan the leather reins, and immediately the boy put them in his mouth.

"No!" Jessica began, then shook her head and relaxed. "Oh, might as well let him. I found him eating dirt yesterday. Guess a little sweat and leather won't hurt."

Devon laughed. "It could be a whole lot worse." He called to the horses and started them for home while Ryan played with the extra bit of reins.

Jessica watched them both for several moments, and Devon could sense she felt troubled by the situation. They rode in silence for several miles while Devon battled within himself. The selfish side of him wanted to just get his feelings out in the open—to express how he felt about Jessica and the boy he held on his lap. But the more humanitarian side of him figured it was only right to find out what was troubling Jessica.

"You're mighty quiet. You going to tell me what it's all about?" Devon finally worked up the nerve to ask.

Jessica looked at him blankly for a moment. Then he noticed there were tears in her eyes. She shook her head, sniffled, and looked away.

Ryan's head began to nod, and Devon figured it the perfect excuse to draw her focus back to him. "I think someone's about to fall asleep. You want to take him back?"

Jessica smoothed the lines of her emerald-green suit and reached out for her son. Ryan went to her without protest, and Devon thought Jessica looked almost relieved. She cradled the boy in her arms, and Ryan willingly let her rock him back and forth. Within another mile or two, he'd fallen asleep without so much as a whimper.

Devon tried to figure out what Jessica's display of emotions had been about. He'd never been around women for very long. Even his mother and sister, who now lived a world away in Tyler, Texas, always kept to themselves when emotional outbursts were at hand. His mother had always said such things were not to be shared with their menfolk, but Devon disagreed. He worried about those times when his mother went off to cry alone. His father always seemed to be away working one ranch or another, always someone else's hired man. He seldom knew about his wife's tears or needs, and Devon determined it would be different with him—mostly because he knew how painful it was for his mother to bear such matters alone.

He could remember the time when his younger brother, Danny, had still been alive. Pa had gone off to work on the Double J Ranch, hoping to earn extra money before the winter set in. Danny had contracted whooping cough and died within a week of their father's departure.

His mother had borne the matter with utmost grace and confidence. Devon tried to be the man of the house for her, supporting her at the funeral, seeing to her needs afterwards. But she would have no part of sharing her pain with him, and it hurt Devon deeply to be left out. When their father had returned, his mother had simply said, "We are only four now." Nothing more was mentioned or discussed. At least not in front of Devon.

Unable to take the situation without pushing to understand, Devon looked over at Jessica. He watched her for a moment before saying, "Please tell me what's bothering you."

Jessica continued to stare straight ahead. Her expression suggested that she was strongly considering his request. Finally she answered. "It isn't worth troubling you with."

"How about letting me be the judge of that?"

They continued for nearly another ten minutes before Jessica finally answered. "I can't hope that you would understand. It has to do with being a mother."

"I suppose I can't understand what it is to be a mother," Devon agreed, "but I do understand when someone is hurting, and you are obviously in pain."

Jessica nestled Ryan closer to her in a protective manner, and instantly Devon realized that her mood had to do with her insecurities over the boy. He'd figured she'd outgrown her concerns, but apparently she still carried the weight of her fears with her.

"Are you still afraid of losing his affection?" Devon finally asked.

Jessica stiffened for a moment, then her shoulders slumped forward as if she'd just met her defeat. "You can't understand."

"I only held him to help calm him down. You looked so tired, and Ryan was obviously tired; I just figured it might help."

"It did help," she said, wiping at tears with her free hand. "It's just that he's all I have, Devon. If I can't be a good mother to him—if I can't make it work between us—then I might as well give up."

"Give up what? Motherhood? You can't take them back once they're here."

"But there are those who would take them from you," Jessica declared.

Devon felt confused. Who did she fear would take Ryan from her? "You don't mean to suggest that someone might come after Ryan, do you? Someone from back East? His grandparents? Is that it?"

Jessica shook her head. "Newman's family is all dead. They died when he was a teenager. His only brother died some years after that. He'd never married, and therefore Newman was the end of the line."

"Then who?"

Jessica still refused to look Devon in the face. "There was a friend in New York, Essie. She always offered to help me with Ryan. She always insisted on having us spend our days with her, and she never wanted me to lift a finger to care for Ryan. She made me uneasy, but I felt sorry for her. She was barren, you see."

Devon did indeed begin to get a clear picture of what must have taken place. "Go on," he urged.

Jessica ran her hand across Ryan's head. "One day she came to me with the idea of letting her and her husband adopt Ryan. She said it was impossible for me to give Ryan all he needed. She said she would make a better mother."

"She obviously didn't know you very well," Devon muttered.

Jessica turned and gave him a look of frantic gratitude. "She thought she did. I'm afraid I was rather harsh with her and sent her home with her suggestion completely refused. Two days later, her mother showed up on my doorstep. The woman was positively intimidating. She took one look at my home and condemned it. She said it would be a wonder if Ryan weren't dead by winter."

Devon clamped his teeth together in anger. He wanted to say something to counter the horrible insensitivity of the woman's actions, but he knew there was nothing he could do.

"She finally left, but then Essie showed up the next day and the next day and the day after that. Ryan adored her because she spoiled and pampered him. I began to fear that he loved her more than me, and when I sent her from my home for the last time, I had to forcibly remove

Ryan from her arms. He cried and cried, and Essie cried and declared it a sign that she should be his true mother. I told her to never come back, and I slammed the door on her. Three days later, the letter came announcing Father's death. It seemed like an answer from God, and yet I would have never wished my father dead. I'd just about decided to beg him to let me return to Windridge anyway."

"But Jess, she can't hurt you," Devon said, hoping his words would comfort her. "She's far enough away that she can't just drop in on you and make you miserable again. And Kate would never tolerate anyone storming into Windridge and threatening yours and Ryan's happiness. This Essie can't hurt you anymore."

Jessica said nothing for several moments. Then she shifted Ryan in her arms and looked at Devon with an expression of intense pain. "But you can."

Devon felt the wind go out from him. "What?" he barely managed to ask.

"Ryan adores you. He seeks you out, and he's drawn to you like flies to honey. I can't ignore that. I can't just look away and say it doesn't exist. Neither can I find it in myself to deny him."

"Why would you want to? You have nothing to fear from me. I'm completely devoted to the little guy. I wouldn't do anything to hurt him or you."

"Maybe not willingly," Jessica replied. She looked away, and Devon watched as she fixed her sight on the horizon where the house on Windridge was now coming into view.

Devon wanted to reassure her and thought for a moment about declaring his feelings for her, but it didn't seem right. Somehow he feared she would just presume he'd made it all up to comfort her. Feeling at a loss as to what he could say, Devon said nothing at all. He looked heavenward for a moment, whispered a prayer for guidance, then fixed his sight on the road ahead. Somehow, someway, God would show him what he was to do about Jessica and Ryan.

Chapter 7

D riving cattle had always been a loathsome chore to Devon. He didn't like the time spent with cantankerous animals on the dusty trail, and he certainly didn't care for being away from Windridge. Especially now. Leaving Jessica wouldn't be easy, and Devon tried to avoid thinking of how he would handle their good-bye.

The days passed too quickly to suit him, and before he knew it, Devon was giving instructions to the other four ranch hands, explaining how they would drive the cattle to Cottonwood Falls and from there board the train for Kansas City.

"I'll only need you as far as Cottonwood. You all get two weeks to settle any other business you have." He pointed to two of the cowhands. "Sam and Joe can take off after we get the livestock settled in the freight cars. Neil, you and Bob need to wait until the other two get back. Buck will handle the ranch until I return, which hopefully won't be any longer than two, maybe three weeks."

The men nodded, asked their questions, and waited for Devon to dismiss them to prepare for the drive. "We'll head out in fifteen minutes or so. Be ready."

The men moved off to collect their horses just as Buck ambled up. "Heard tell the Johnsons down Wichita way are working with a new breed," Buck said as Devon finished packing his bags. "You could go down that way before coming back here. You know, check it out and see if it would work for us."

"I suppose I could. But do you think that's the direction we want to go?" Devon questioned, not liking the idea of delaying his return to Windridge.

Buck shrugged. "It's just an idea. Heard they're getting an extra twenty to fifty pounds on the hoof. You can suit yourself though."

"I'll give it some consideration. Maybe I'll find the same thing in Kansas City. Most folks in these parts are going to end up at the livestock yards there anyway. It just might work out I can get the information there."

Buck nodded. "That sounds reasonable."

Kate appeared just then, Ryan toddling behind her. "I brought you some sandwiches to take with you. I know you don't have that long of a drive, but those animals can be mighty slow when they set their minds to be that way."

"Thanks, Katie," Devon said, taking the basket she'd packed. "If we don't need them, I'll take some of them to Kansas City."

"Eat my sandwiches instead of Mr. Harvey's fine railroad food?" Kate laughed. "I can't imagine anyone making that trade."

"Then you just don't realize what a good cook you are," Devon replied. About that time, Ryan wrapped his arms around Devon's leg and started chattering.

"Horsy! Horsy!"

Devon laughed. He often gave the boy a ride on his knee, and it was clear Ryan wasn't about to let him leave until he received his daily fun.

"Okay," he said, reaching down to lift Ryan into the air. He swept the boy high, listening to his giggles, then circled him down low. Finally he stepped over to a bale of hay and sat down to put Ryan on his knee. "Now tighten those legs," Devon instructed, squeezing Ryan's legs around his own. "A good rider knows how to use his legs."

"You keep an eye on him for a minute," Buck called out. "I'm going to walk a spell with Katie and tell her good-bye properly."

"Will do," Devon called out, "but you won't be gone for more than a few hours."

Buck laughed. "To Kate, that's an eternity."

Devon, too, chuckled and returned his attention to Ryan. "You know, you'll be a right fine rider one day. I'll take you out on the trails and teach you all there is to know about raising cattle. You'll know more than your ma or anyone else in these parts, 'cause I'm going to show you all the tricks."

Ryan giggled and squealed with delight as Devon bounced him up and down on his leg. The boy had easily taken a huge chunk of Devon's heart, while the other portion belonged to his mother. The only real problem was finding a way to tell her.

Devon had fully planned to discuss his feelings for Jessica before he left for Kansas City. But the opportunity never presented itself. Jessica had been overly busy under Kate's instruction, and when she wasn't working at quilting or sewing or any number of other things Kate deemed necessary to her ranch training, Jessica was busy with Ryan. She almost always retired early, not even giving Devon a chance to suggest a stroll on the ridge or a song or two on the porch. The only time she went into town was on Sunday, and that was usually with Buck and Kate at her side. Devon had no desire to make his confession of feelings a public issue. Even if Buck and Kate already presumed to know those feelings, Devon wanted to get Jessica's reaction first.

"Well Ryan, a fellow just never knows where he stands," Devon muttered.

Ryan seemed to understand and chattered off several strange words, along with his repertoire of completely understandable speech. "More horsy! Mama horsy."

Devon laughed. "I doubt Mama would appreciate the idea, son." The word *son* stuck in his throat. He wished he could call Ryan son. He thought of Jessica's worries that he would steal Ryan's affections, but in truth, Devon worried that Jessica would take Ryan from his life. He already cared too much about both of them, and the thought of losing either one was more than he wanted to contend with.

Lifting Ryan in his arms, Devon rubbed his fuzzy head. "You've got to grow some more hair, boy. You don't want to go through life bald." Ryan reached out and pulled at Devon's thick mustache. "Ah, a mustache man. Well, grow it there if you prefer," Devon teased, "but the head would be better for now."

He gently disentangled his mustache from Ryan's pudgy fingers, then gave the boy a couple of gentle tosses into the air. Ryan squealed once again, and the expression on his chubby face was enough to satisfy Devon.

"You take good care of your mama while I'm gone," Devon told him and hugged him close.

"Kate said you two were in here," called Jessica.

Devon looked up, almost embarrassed to have been caught speaking of her. He wondered how long she'd been watching. She looked to have been there for some time, given her casual stance by the open door.

"We were just having a talk," Devon said, putting Ryan down.

"Horsy, Mama," Ryan said, toddling off to Jessica's waiting arms.

She lifted Ryan and held him close and all the while watched Devon. "Are you about ready to go?"

"Yup," he said casually, taking down an extra coil of rope from the wall. "Everything's set. We have to give ourselves enough time to make the train."

Jessica nodded. "Well, I hope you won't have any trouble finding everything we need."

"I shouldn't," Devon replied, wishing they could get beyond the chitchat.

Ryan began squirming and calling for Devon. The boy had not yet mastered Devon's name, so when he called out, it sounded very much like "Da da."

"Unt Da da," Ryan fussed, straining at Jessica's hold. She put the boy down, not even attempting to fight Ryan's choice.

The boy hurried back to Devon, inspected the rope for a moment, then raised his arms up and bobbed up and down as if to encourage Devon to lift him.

"It's easy to see how much he loves you," Jessica said, her voice low and filled with emotion.

"I love him, too," Devon said, wondering how she would react to this. "He's a great little guy. It would be impossible *not* to love him."

Jessica nodded. "I just hope you take that love seriously."

"What do you mean?" Devon asked, wishing he could turn the conversation to thoughts of his feelings for Ryan's mother.

Jessica stepped closer and studied Devon before answering. "I just ask one thing of you, Devon Carter. Don't let Ryan get close to you unless you plan to be around to be his friend for a good long time. It'll be too hard for him otherwise."

At first, Devon wanted to reply with something flippant and teasing, but he could see in Jessica's eyes that she was dead serious. His heart softened, and he gave her a weak smile.

"I plan to be around for a very long time. I wouldn't dream of leaving Ryan without making sure he understood my reason for leaving. And since he'll be too small to understand much along those lines and will be for a good many years, I guess you'll both just be stuck with me."

"Just so you understand."

He rubbed the boy's head, kissed him lightly, and put him back on the ground. "I intend to always be here for Ryan," Devon stated firmly. He looked deep into Jessica's dark eyes—knowing the longing reflected there. He wanted more than anything to add that he would also be there for Jessica, but he could already hear Buck calling everyone to mount up.

"Guess you'd better go," Jessica whispered.

Devon took a step toward her, then stopped. There wasn't enough time to say what he wanted—needed—to say. "I suppose so," he finally murmured.

"You've got the list?" she questioned.

He nodded, almost afraid to say anything more.

"And you will be careful?"

Her voice was edged with concern, and Devon longed to put her worried mind at ease. He remembered that moment months ago when he'd held her while she cried. "It's a piece of cake," he replied. "The hard part is getting the critters to Cottonwood. After that, there's nothing to it but haggling the money." He grinned, hoping to put her at ease.

"I've heard about folks killed in stampedes," she countered. "And Kate says we're coming up to time for a tornado or two."

"We'll be careful," he promised, realizing that whether she spoke it in words or not, she cared about his well-being.

"You coming?" Buck asked as he poked his head into the doorway.

Devon caught his mischievous expression and sighed. "I'm coming."

Jessica had the distinct impression that had Buck not interfered, Devon might have said something very important. She sensed his desire to tell her something, but no matter how long she stood there in silence, he seemed unable to spit out the words. Of course she did no better. She had hoped to say that her concerns for Ryan were based on concerns she also felt for herself. She knew she was coming to depend too much on Devon. She also knew that she'd lost her heart to him, and that for the first and only time in her life, she was in love.

With this thought still weighing heavily on her heart, Jessica followed Devon from the barn, calling to Ryan as she moved back to the house. She picked the boy up and told him to wave good-bye to Devon.

"Unta go," Ryan began to whine. "Me go, too."

"No, Ryan," Jessica said. "You have to stay here. We can't go this time."

Ryan continued to fuss, and Katie tried to still him with a cookie that she kept in her apron pocket for just such occasions. Ryan contented himself with the treat, while Jessica found no such consolation.

I should have told him how I felt, she thought. But her feelings were so foreign and new to her that she wasn't sure what she would have said to him.

"I should be back by the end of November," Devon called to them, bringing his horse to a halt just beyond the porch. "Don't worry though if I'm later than that. It may take some time to secure the freighters and collect all the things you ladies have deemed necessary to running a good resort."

"Do you have the money?" Jessica asked.

"I'll pick up most of it in Cottonwood Falls. I have the deed papers for Joe Riley's piece of land, and that will allow me to take his money for the land and add to what we have in the bank." He glanced over his shoulder and saw that Buck was already positioning the ranch hands in preparation for moving the cattle from the corrals. "I'd best get over there and do my job." He turned the horse and started to leave.

"Devon!" Jessica called out. She knew her voice sounded desperate, but she couldn't help it.

He stopped, looked at her quite seriously, then grinned. "What?"

Jessica swallowed hard and tried to think of something neutral to say. "I'll be praying for you," she finally managed.

Devon's grin broadened. "Thanks. With that bunch," he said, motioning over his shoulder, "I'll need it." He took off before either Kate or Jessica could say another word.

"Wonder whether he means the men or the steers?" Kate teased.

"Probably both."

Jessica brushed cookie crumbs from Ryan's face and headed to the front door when Kate called out, "Looks like we have company."

Turning, Jessica could see the faint image of a black carriage making its way up the Windridge road. "Who could that be?"

Kate shrugged. "I don't know. I'll go put some tea on and set out some more cookies. It's been so long since anyone's come calling at Windridge, I might not even be able to find a serving plate."

Jessica laughed. "Don't you go running off when whoever it is finally arrives. I don't want to have to entertain on my own."

"Maybe we could set up things in the quilting room," Kate suggested and Jessica nodded.

"Sounds perfect. That way, we'll be busy, and if the conversation lags, we can talk about the quilts."

Kate nodded. "Why don't you put Ryan down for a nap in the back room? Then he'll be close at hand and yet out of harm's way."

Jessica nodded and followed Kate into the house, after sending one final glance south where Devon and the rest of the ranch hands were organizing the cattle on the trail. Giving Ryan a drink of milk while Kate fixed the tea, Jessica made her way into one of the two rooms that were being converted for Buck and Kate's use. It had been Kate's idea to put another bed in for Ryan. It seemed senseless to run up and down the stairs all day, and Jessica quickly saw the sense in it. Kate had even suggested that maybe Jessica and Ryan would one day prefer the privacy of the cottage once the guests overtook the house.

Jessica had quickly pointed out that Devon now occupied the place in question, but Kate had just shrugged and told her that God had a way of working those things out.

"But the way I'd like to see it worked out," Jessica told Ryan, "isn't likely to happen. Devon said God already has a wife picked out for him."

Ryan yawned and pulled at his ear. This was his routine signal that he was tired. Gently, she tucked him into bed and brushed his cheek with her fingertip. Ryan quickly realized she intended to leave him for a nap and decided he wanted no part of it. Jessica wasn't surprised at the display as he began kicking at the covers. Soon he was sitting up and fussing for her to take him.

"Ryan," she said in a stern voice. "You lie back down and go to sleep. When you get up, we'll go up to the ridge and see what we can see."

Ryan made no move to obey, so Jessica gently eased him back down and pulled the covers around him once again. "Now go to sleep and be a good boy."

"Goo boy," Ryan muttered in between his fussing.

"That's right," Jessica smiled. "You are a good boy, and Mama loves you."

She left him there to fuss and upon returning to the kitchen found that Kate had things well under control. "Is there anything you want me to do?" she questioned.

"No. Just relax."

Jessica looked out the side kitchen window, hoping to catch a glimpse of the cattle drive. She could just catch sight of the last two outriders, but Devon was nowhere in sight. She strained her eyes for some sign of his brown Stetson, but the hills hid him from view.

"You should have told him how you feel about him," Kate admonished. Jessica felt her face grow hot as she looked back to where Kate studied her. "It's pretty apparent."

"I didn't realize," Jessica admitted. "You don't suppose he knows, do you?" She realized her voice sounded high pitched, almost frightened.

"No, I don't suppose he does," Kate replied, turning back to putting cookies on the tray. "I think he's too wrapped up in his own feelings."

Jessica nodded. "I think you're probably right."

"Why don't you go check on our visitor? Ought to be up to the house by now."

Jessica did as Kate suggested, her heart heavy with thoughts of Devon being in love with another woman. When she opened the front door, she was surprised to find a smartly dressed woman making her way up the front steps of the porch.

The woman, looking to be in her late forties, carried herself with a regal air. Her golden-blond hair, although liberally sprinkled with gray, was carefully styled and pinned tightly beneath a beautiful bonnet of lavender silk.

"Good morning," Jessica said, trying her best to sound welcoming.

"Good morning to you," the woman replied. "I'm Gertrude Jenkins, and you must be Jessica Gussop."

"Albright. Jessica Albright. Gussop was my maiden name."

"Of course. I remember Gus having quite a spell when you married."

Jessica felt her defenses rise to the occasion. "We don't get many visitors here, Mrs. Jenkins. Won't you come in?"

The woman smiled. "I used to come here quite often, you know, before Gus died. After he died, I went on an extended European trip. Couldn't bear to stick around here with him gone, don't you know?"

Jessica couldn't figure the woman out. She'd never heard of Gertrude Jenkins, much less in any capacity that endeared her to her father. She ushered the woman into the house and, rather than stopping at the front parlor, led her down the hall to the room she and Kate used for quilting. Kate already sat sewing behind the quilting frame, while Jessica's work lay on the seat of the chair nearest to Kate. It looked for all intents and purposes that Jessica had only moments before left the work in order to answer the door.

"Well, if it isn't Gerty Jenkins," Kate said in greeting. "I heard tell you were back in the area." Jessica watched the exchange between the two women, feeling the immediate tension when Gertrude spotted Kate.

"Hello, Kate," came the crisp reply. She glanced around the room and sniffed. "Well, if this isn't quaint."

"We've been working on quilts. We were just going to have some tea and cookies," Jessica offered rather formally. "I do hope you can stay and partake with us?"

Gertrude glanced to the small table where the refreshments awaited their attention. "I'm certain I can. Especially after coming all this way."

"Gerty lives on the ranch directly south," Kate told Jessica. "It's her drive you pass by on the way to church."

Jessica smiled and nodded. "I remember Devon mentioning the drive leading to another ranch."

"Devon? Devon Carter?" Gertrude questioned. "Don't tell me he's still here at Windridge."

"Of course he is," Kate replied before Jessica could answer. "He was like a son to Gus, and Jessica has come to rely on him as well."

Gertrude eyed Jessica rather haughtily as she pulled white kid gloves from her hands. "I suppose it is difficult when you know nothing of ranching."

Jessica could immediately see that Gertrude had no intention of being a friend. But her reasons for visiting in the first place were still a mystery.

Ignoring the comment, Jessica motioned to a high-backed chair. "Won't you sit down? I'll pour the tea."

"Cream and sugar, please," Gertrude stated as she took her seat.

Jessica nodded and went to the task. "Would you care for some of Kate's sugar cookies? They're quite delicious."

"If you have no cakes, I suppose they'll have to do," the woman replied.

Jessica served her and then brought a cup of plain tea to Kate. She tried to question Kate with her expression, but Kate only smiled.

"I suppose I should have visited sooner," Gertrude continued before anyone else could take up the conversation, "but I've only returned last week. A year abroad has done me a world of good."

"This last year has done us a world of good as well," Kate replied, continuing with her stitches.

Jessica thought the response rather trite given Kate's usual friendliness, but she said nothing. Instead, she tried to draw out the reason for Gertrude's visit. "I'm pleased you have found the time to call upon us," Jessica began. "I don't believe we've had a single visitor in the past year."

"Well, it really is no wonder. The place is in an awful state of disrepair."

"Oh," Jessica said, looking first to Kate, then back to Gertrude, "you must not have had the opportunity to look around you. We've been making steady progress throughout the year. We are, in fact, moving ahead with plans to turn Windridge into something rather special."

"Well, it once was quite special," Gertrude said, flicking crumbs from her skirt onto the floor. "Do tell, what plans have you for the place?"

Jessica licked her lips and took the tiniest sip of tea to steady her nerves. "We're opening Windridge to the public. We are taking on guests next summer and becoming a working vacation ranch. A quiet respite from the city, if you will."

Gertrude appeared stunned. "Are you suggesting this place will become a spa—a resort? Here in Kansas?"

"Not only suggesting it, Gerty," Kate threw in, "but the plans are already in the works. Devon is bringing back the final touches in new furnishings and supplies."

"Was that him heading out with that scrawny herd?"

"Him and Buck and the others," Kate replied. "Only Devon is heading on to Kansas City. He figured we'd best keep the others here to keep an eye on things."

"Yes, but who will keep an eye on Devon Carter?"

Jessica perked up at this. "Whatever do you mean?"

"I simply mean, my dear," Gertrude began, "the man should not be trusted."

"Bah," Kate said in disgust. "Gus trusted him."

"Yes, and see where it got him."

"I don't think I understand," Jessica interjected, feeling the anger between the two women.

"Gerty is just showing her age." All eyes turned to Kate at this. "Gerty's daughter was once engaged to Devon, but she broke it off."

"She had to. There was simply no other choice under the circumstances," Gertrude said stiffly.

Jessica felt the tension mount. She silently wished Kate would stir the woman into another subject of conversation, but Gertrude remained fixed on her mark.

"Devon was seen with another woman in Cottonwood Falls. Of course, my poor Jane was devastated. They were barely two weeks away from their own wedding. It grieved her so much she stayed out the entire night and came home weeping in the wee hours of the morning."

Kate rolled her eyes, and Jessica was hard-pressed not to smile. Apparently Kate thought the story to be less than accurate, but Gertrude didn't seem to notice. "I was heartsick, and had her father still been alive, he would no doubt have gone to take Devon Carter to task for his behavior.

"Poor Jane cried until she was exhausted, then told me she had found Devon in the arms of another woman." Gertrude leaned closer. "He was kissing her, don't you know? Of course, Jane felt terribly misused. She was never herself after that and ran off with the first man who asked for her hand after Devon's terrible behavior."

"That wasn't exactly the story we heard," Kate muttered under her breath.

Gertrude glared at her but said nothing to support the idea that her version was anything but the honest facts of the matter.

"I simply wouldn't trust him out of sight, my dear. Gus and I discussed it on many an occasion, and while Gus felt the need to give the young man a chance, I always felt there was something rather shiftless about him."

"You let Jane get engaged to him," Kate threw out.

"Yes," Gertrude replied in a clipped tone, "but then every mother makes mistakes. I wanted Jane's happiness, and she was certain Devon Carter could give her everything she desired."

Jessica felt shaken and uncertain of herself. She wondered if the other woman Jane had found Devon with was the same one who now held his heart. "More tea?" she asked weakly.

"No, thank you," Gertrude replied, setting the cup and saucer aside. "I really should be going. I can see that you both have your hands full, and there's much that needs my attention at home. I do recall someone mentioning, however, that you have a child, Mrs. Albright."

"That's right. My Ryan is almost two. He's sleeping right now, or I'd give you a proper introduction. Perhaps Sunday at church?"

"Yes, perhaps so," Gertrude replied, getting to her feet. "I do suggest you heed my advice. Devon Carter is not all he appears to be, and if you have given him a large sum of money, it might well be the last time you see him or your funds." She glanced at Kate. "Good day, Kate. Mrs. Albright."

Jessica walked out with the haughty woman and paused on the porch. "Thank you for coming, Mrs. Jenkins."

"I felt I owed it to Gus. You know we were very close to an understanding. Had he lived, I'm certain I would be mistress of Windridge, and our ranches would join together to make a mighty empire."

Jessica did her best to show no signs of surprise at this announcement. She merely nodded and bid the woman good day.

Gertrude Jenkins climbed into her carriage and pulled on her gloves. "I suppose we will be seeing each other again soon. Don't forget what I said about Mr. Carter. It's not too late to send someone after him and change the course of events to come."

With that, she turned the horses and headed the buggy down the lane. Jessica watched for several moments, uncertain what to think or feel about the woman and her visit. Not only had Mrs. Jenkins discredited Devon, but she'd implied an intimacy with Jessica's father.

An intimacy that suggested marriage. Jessica found it impossible to believe and thought to question Kate about it, but it was clear the two women had nothing but disdain for each other.

With a sigh, Jessica decided it wasn't worth the bother. She trusted Devon to do what he said he would do. Closing the door behind her, Jessica decided to close out negative thoughts of her visitor. She had no reason to worry and refused to borrow the trouble that Gertrude Jenkins so expertly offered.

Chapter 8

The first week without Devon at Windridge left Jessica feeling listless and bored. Kate kept her occupied with canning and butchering, but at night Jessica had nothing to keep her from thinking about Devon. Not only that, but Ryan cried and called for him, leaving Jessica little doubt that her fears about Ryan's attachment to the cowboy were well founded.

Week two spent itself out with the return of Sam and Joe and the departure of Neil and Bob. Jessica worked with Kate to make lye soap. Kate told her there was no sense in paying out good money for store-bought soap when they had the hog fat and other ingredients on hand. Jessica hated the work but realized she was doing something important to keep Windridge up and running. Soap was a necessity of life—especially if you intended to keep guests.

By the third week, Jessica began to watch from her upstairs window for some sign of Devon's return. She mourned the loss along with her son and grew despondent and moody. Kate and Buck watched her with knowing smiles and tried their best to interest her in other things, but it was no use.

An early snow followed by a fierce ice storm caused Jessica to sink even lower. Now it was impossible to spend much time outside, and even horseback riding was curtailed. Making the hour journey into Cottonwood Falls was clearly out of the question, and so their boredom intensified.

Gertrude Jenkins's words kept intruding into Jessica's thoughts. She realized the older woman had planted seeds of doubt, and although Jessica was determined not to let them grow, Devon's delay seemed to bring about their germination. She wondered at Devon's past and why her father thought so highly of him. She wondered if Gertrude had

The House on Windridge

known something about Devon that no one else had knowledge of. Maybe Jane Jenkins had truly seen Devon betraying her.

Jessica hated even allowing such thoughts, but as November passed and December came upon them and still there was no word from Devon Carter, she began to fear the worst.

"Buck says it looks to be nice for a few days," Kate told Jessica one morning. "He doesn't see any reason why we can't go in and participate in the ladies' Christmas quilt party."

"I don't feel like going," Jessica told Kate.

"I know. Which is exactly why we're going."

Jessica looked up from where she was busy washing the breakfast dishes. Kate had that determined look that told Jessica clearly she'd brook no nonsense in the matter.

"What about Ryan?" she asked, casting a glance at her son. At almost two years of age, Ryan was into everything, and it was too cold for him to travel the long distance into Cottonwood Falls.

"Buck is going to take care of him," Kate told her firmly.

"Buck?"

"Absolutely. He handled our own boys well enough. There's no reason at Ryan's age that Buck can't see to his needs. I've already talked with him, and Buck thinks it's a good idea. He knows how worried you are and how hard the waiting has been. Besides, Devon might even come in on the train while we're in town."

It was this last thought that made up Jessica's mind. "All right, let's do it."

Kate grinned. "I thought you'd see things my way."

⌒

But three hours later, Jessica wasn't at all sure that they should have come. The location for the sewing party rotated each year through the various families in the church and this time was at Esther Hammel's house. The living room had been cleared of furniture with the exception of wooden-backed chairs, a couple worktables, and several quilting frames.

This was an annual event for the women of Cottonwood Falls, and everyone took their duties quite seriously. One person came to help Esther set up the frames and worktables, while another was in charge of organizing the refreshments. Someone else held the responsibility of making sure the word got out as to the place and time, and yet another lady arranged a group of women to help with the cleanup.

Everyone brought food to the party, and Jessica was rather relieved to find that this was the only requirement she had to meet. Esther said that being as it was her first year to join them, they would go rather easy on her.

The women gathered, taking their places around the various work areas. Jessica and Kate were in the process of piecing some quilt tops together, so they took seats at one of the worktables rather than at the frames. Esther Hammel, a petite woman with fiery blue eyes and a knotted bun of white hair, saw to it that everyone had all they needed in order to work before calling the women to order.

"First, we'll pray. Then we'll gab." Everyone smiled and nodded, while Esther bowed her head. "Father, we thank You for this beautiful day and for the fellowship of friends. Bless our work to better the lives of those around us. May we always bring You glory and honor. Amen."

Jessica murmured an amen, but her heart and mind were far from the prayer. She had hoped to see Devon by now. She had imagined how they would meet on the road to Cottonwood, and he would surprise her with a caravan of goods and supplies that would leave no one doubting his honesty and goodness. But they had met no one on the road between Windridge and Cottonwood.

Buck had instructed Sam to drive the massive stagelike carriage for the women. That way, they could enjoy the warmth and comfort of the plush furnishings. Sam had family in town and was only too happy to go home to his mother's cooking while waiting for Kate and Jessica. It was also rumored that his parents' neighbors had a fetching daughter who seemed to have an eye for Sam.

Jessica had instructed Sam to check on Devon at the railroad station, just in case there was some word from him. She'd also told him to pick up the Windridge mail and to check with the telegraph office, just in case some word had come in that they'd not yet received because of the weather. She could hardly sit still through the sewing for want of knowing whether Sam had found out anything about Devon.

"So when I finish with this quilt," Esther was telling the women gathered around her frame, "I intend to donate it to poor Sarah New-come. Her Elmer died two weeks ago, and they're dirt poor. She's got another baby coming in the spring, and those other three kids of hers don't have proper clothes or bedding. I figured this here quilt could keep all three of them warm."

"My Christmas project was to make and finish five baby blankets for the new mothers in the area," spoke another woman. "As soon as I get this last one quilted, I'll probably start on my spring projects."

The chatter continued until it came to Jessica and Kate's turn to speak. Kate seemed to understand Jessica's confusion and took charge. "Jessica and I have had many projects this year. The latest one, however, is to put together a number of quilts to give to the orphans' home in Topeka."

Jessica said nothing, realizing that Kate had indeed mentioned the project some weeks ago, but since that had occurred around the time of Devon's departure, she'd totally forgotten what they were working toward.

"The quilt tops we're working on today are for the girls." Kate held up her piece to reveal carefully ordered flower baskets. The colors were done up in lavender and pink calicos, with pieces of green and baskets of gold. "I think we'll have them put together by Christmas, but whether or not we'll be able to get them shipped north will depend on the weather."

At this the women made comments on the weather and how the early snow hampered one thing or another. The ice had been the worst, they all agreed, and for several minutes that topic held the conversation. Jessica sighed and worked to put together her pieces in an orderly fash-ion. There were only a few weeks left before Christmas. Devon should have been home already, and yet here she sat, with no word from him and no idea as to his welfare.

A knock on the front door sent Esther off to find out who had arrived and caused Jessica to hold her breath in anticipation that the visitor might be Devon. Disappointment engulfed her, however, as the visitor proved to be Gertrude Jenkins.

"Sorry for being so late," Gertrude announced. "I had so much to take care of this morning that I just couldn't seem to get it all accomplished." Her gaze fell upon Jessica and Kate, and her pasted smile faded. "Well, if I'd have known you were planning on coming to the party, we could have shared transportation." Her voice sounded accusatory, as though Kate and Jessica had committed some sort of heinous crime.

"Sorry about that, Gerty," Kate replied without missing a beat. "We figured you'd still be all worn out from your travels abroad."

Jessica nearly smiled at this. She knew how artfully Kate had maneuvered Gertrude into her favorite topic. There'd be little more retribution for their lack of notification once Gertrude focused on her journeys.

"Oh, I suppose I'm still young enough to bounce right back from such things. I do admit at first I was quite exhausted, but a few days of rest and I felt quite myself again." She allowed Esther to take the pie pan she still held and then swept out of her coat and gloves and handed them to Esther just as she returned from the refreshment table.

"We were just commenting on the weather and our projects," Esther told her after seeing to Gertrude's coat and gloves.

Gertrude removed her ornate wool bonnet and set it aside on the fireplace mantel. "We suffered terribly from the ice," she admitted. "But as for my project, well, I simply haven't started one. I thought I'd come here and help someone else with theirs."

"Good," said Esther. "You can help us quilt. I've already told the girls, but my Christmas project is for Sarah Newcome."

Gertrude's chin lifted ever so slightly, but she said nothing as she took her seat at the quilting frame. After several moments of silence, someone finally asked her about her time in Paris, and the conversation picked back up with a detailed soliloquy.

"Of course," Gertrude said, eyeing Jessica suspiciously, "I was quite happy to arrive in Kansas City and make my connection for home." Without pausing for breath she added, "Speaking of Kansas City, has Devon returned with your supplies?"

Jessica felt the wind go out of her. She didn't know what to say that wouldn't provoke a new topic of conversation centered around the possibility that Devon had deserted ranks. Apparently this dilemma showed on her face, because Gertrude nodded and continued.

"I thought not. I hadn't heard from any of my hands that he'd made it back into town. Well, I certainly hope for your sake that he's at least notified you as to what's keeping him."

"No, Gerty, Devon doesn't need to check in with us," Kate responded. "He's family, and we trust him to be making the right choices. He left here with a long list of things to accomplish, and we don't expect him to return until he's able to negotiate everything to the benefit of the ranch."

"Yes," Gertrude said, taking a stitch into the quilt, "but then, he left here with much more than a long list."

The other women in the room fell silent. Jessica felt as though all eyes had turned on her to learn the truth. Swallowing her fear and pride, Jessica looked blankly at Mrs. Jenkins. "Yes, he also left with about one hundred head of prime steers."

Gertrude, not to be toyed with, smiled. "Yes, I suppose he'll be selling those for you in Kansas City."

"That's right."

The tension in the room mounted as Gertrude replied, "I suppose he'll be taking the money in cash."

Kate laughed. "Well, I certainly hope he doesn't take it in trade."

The other women chuckled. They appeared to know how Gertrude could be, as evidenced by the way they remained so obviously cautious at the first sign of her attack on Devon.

"I realize you believe the man can do no wrong," Gertrude said, continuing to focus her attention on Esther's quilt, "but you all know how I feel about him. You know how he hurt my Jane."

Unintelligible murmurings were the only response to this statement. Esther seemed to understand the pain it caused Jessica to hear such things. She smiled sweetly, giving Jessica the first sign of support from someone other than Kate.

"I believe the Carters to have raised a fine son," Esther began. "I knew his mother and father most of my life. When his father died and his mother and sister moved to Texas, I allowed him to stay here until he took up the position at Windridge. He showed only kindness and godliness while living in this house."

Gertrude was clearly offended by this and put down her sewing to stare angrily at Esther. "Are you suggesting that his actions with my daughter were kind and godly? Kissing another woman while only weeks away from marriage to another? No, Devon Carter is a deceiver. I only hope that his long absence doesn't signal yet another fault in him—that of theft."

"Devon is no thief!" Jessica declared, realizing how angry the woman had made her. "He has a job to do, and he will take as long as he needs in order to do it properly."

Gertrude turned a cold smile on Jessica. "Believe what you will, my dear, but actions have always spoken louder than words."

Jessica gripped the edge of her material so tightly that her fingers ached from the tension. Kate patted her gently, and Esther took up the cause. "Gerty, you'd do well to keep from being overly judgmental. You know what the Good Book says about such matters."

Gertrude appeared unfazed. "I know it says not to cast your pearls before swine. That's exactly what this naive young woman has done if she has given her fortune over to Devon Carter. If she has any expectations other than to find herself devoid of the money given over to that fool, then she's more naive than I think."

"I suppose the *Christian* thing to do," Esther suggested, "would be to pray for Devon's safe return."

Jessica felt like a lightning bolt had hit her. In all her worry and concern over Devon's whereabouts, she'd sorely neglected the one thing she could do to aid him. Pray. She'd fretted—given herself over to all manner of wild imaginings, talked about his absence—and now fought about it as well. But she'd not really prayed. Furthermore, she'd promised Devon that she would pray for him, and other than a quickly rattled off request for his health and safety, she'd not given the matter another thought.

"That's an excellent idea," Kate said. "Christian women should be more given over to speaking to God about matters rather than judging them falsely."

Gertrude glared at her, but Kate seemed unmoved by the obvious hostility that was directed at her.

From that point on, the day moved rather quickly. Jessica found herself actually enjoying the company of the women, in spite of the rather frustrating beginning to their day.

Later that afternoon, Esther stopped Jessica and Kate as they were preparing to leave. "Don't pay any mind to Gerty," she admonished. "The woman has a bitter heart. First, her daughter disgraces herself the way she did, then Gus refused her advances. She isn't likely to be a good friend to you, Jessica."

Jessica wanted to ask Esther about her father and Gertrude but decided it would make better conversation on the trip home with Kate. "Thank you for all you did," Jessica said instead. "I do appreciate it."

"That's what we older women do best," Esther said, patting Jessica's arm. "We have the privilege of not caring what others think about us because we're old enough to realize that the truth is more important than opinions. You stick with Kate, and she'll help you through this."

"I will," Jessica promised, already feeling much better.

"And one other thing," Esther added. "Your pa put a lot of faith in Devon Carter, and I put a lot of faith in your pa. He wasn't without his mistakes—sending you away after Naomi died was probably his biggest one. But he had a good heart, and he was smart as a whip. He could judge horseflesh and humans like no one I've ever known. He trusted Devon for a reason." She paused and smiled. "The reason—Devon is worthy of trust. Plain and simple."

Jessica smiled and nodded. "Yes, he is."

Devon pulled up his coat collar in order to shield himself from the cold winter wind. It seemed the wind was worse in the city than in the Flint Hills. The tall buildings seemed to force the wind down narrow corridors and tunnels of roads and alleyways. He'd be glad to get home and knew he was long overdue. He'd thought to drop a postcard to Jessica and let her know about his delays, but always he figured he'd be leaving in a day or two at the most and would surely beat the thing to Windridge. What happened, however, was that one day turned into two and then into a week. And now Devon was clearly three weeks overdue and had sent no word to Jessica.

But there was a light at the end of the tunnel. Devon had finally managed to negotiate an order for the furniture needed at Windridge, and he'd arranged for the freighters to take the supplies out come spring. Then he'd taken it upon himself to telegraph his mother and ask her to speak on his behalf to Jeb Williams. This resulted in a telegram from Jeb himself stating he was more than happy to manage a deal between the Rocking W and Windridge. Devon felt as if he had the world by the tail. Everything was going better than he could have ever dreamed.

Now, as he made his way back to his hotel room, Devon decided the cold was a small price to pay. Tomorrow he would go to the train station, where he'd already made arrangements for those supplies he intended to take home with him, and board a train for home. How good it would be to see them all again. Especially Jessica and Ryan. He smiled at the thought of their birthday presents sitting back in his hotel room.

Kate had told him that both Jessica and Ryan shared their birthday with New Year's Eve. So along with baubles for Christmas, Devon had picked out toy soldiers for Ryan and a jewelry box for Jessica. He already imagined how he would place his grandmother's wedding ring inside the box and wait for her reaction when she realized that he was asking her to marry him. Turning down the alley where he always made his shortcut, Devon nearly laughed out loud. *She would be surprised to say the least,* he thought.

Halfway to the hotel, Devon felt the hair on the back of his neck prickle. He felt with certainty that someone had stepped into the alley behind him, but he didn't want to turn around and make a scene. He stepped up his pace but had gone no more than ten steps when a big burly man popped out from behind a stack of crates.

"I'll just be relieving you of your wallet," the man said in a surprisingly refined tone.

Devon felt a bit of relief, knowing that his wallet didn't contain much more than a few dollars. He'd secured his remaining money in the hotel safe, recognizing that it was foolish to walk about the city with large quantities of money.

He started to reach into his pocket just as the wind picked up. The gust came so strong that Devon's hat blew back off his head. He turned to catch it before it got away from him, but apparently the man who'd been following him took this as a sign of attack and struck Devon over the head.

Sinking to his knees, Devon fought for consciousness as the men began to beat him mercilessly. He thought of Jessica and how he wouldn't be leaving on the morning train. He thought of how worried she'd be when he didn't come back to Windridge. As his world went black, Devon Carter wondered if this was what it felt like to die.

Chapter 9

Christmas at Windridge came as a solemn affair. Jessica had no spirit for the holiday, and even Ryan moped about as though thoroughly discouraged at Devon having not returned. Kate and Buck had to admit that enough time had passed for Devon to have seen to all the responsibilities he'd gone to Kansas City in order to accomplish. They had very few words of encouragement for Jessica, and the house grew very quiet.

Jessica still tried to pray. She worried that Devon might lay ill somewhere in the city with no one to care for him. She fretted that he'd been unable to sell the cattle or that some other catastrophe had befallen him causing him to be unable to purchase the things they needed.

It was in a complete state of anxiety that Jessica decided to do a little cleaning. She started with Ryan's room, thoroughly scouring every nook and cranny in order to make certain it met with her approval. Then she started on her own room. She went through the closet, re-organizing her clothes and even managing to pull the feather tick and mattress from her bed in order to turn them. That was when she found her father's journal.

Surprised that a man like Gus Gussop had been given over to penning his thoughts onto paper, Jessica felt nervous about opening the book. She felt intrusive, almost as if she were committing some kind of sin. Her father had never shared any part of himself with her—at least not in the way Jessica had needed him to share.

Finding Ryan quite content to play in his room, Jessica took a seat near the fireplace and began to read.

"'It's hard enough to allow my thoughts to come to mind,'" she read aloud, "'but to put them to paper seems to give them life of their own.'"

These were the opening words of her father's journal. Eloquent speech for a rough-and-ready rancher who'd sent his only child away rather than be faced with raising her alone. Then Jessica had the startling realization that the words written here were to her mother.

Naomi, you should never have left me to face this alone. You knew I wouldn't be any good at it. You gave me a child, a beautiful daughter, and left me to live without you. How fair was that? I never had anything bad to say about you, with exception to this. You were wrong to go. Wrong to die and leave me here.

Jessica continued to read in silence, unable to speak aloud the words that followed.

She's beautiful, just like you. I can see it every time she comes to visit. I see you in the roundness of her face, the darkness of her brown eyes. I see you in her temperament when she gets a full head of steam up, and I hear you in her laughter. How I loved you, Naomi. How I love our little girl.

Jessica wiped away the tears that streamed down her face. Why couldn't he have told her these things? Why couldn't he have been honest with her and kept her at Windridge? The injustice of it all weighed heavily on her heart.

These long years have been like a death sentence to me, and the only reason I write these things now is that the doctor tells me I'll be joining you soon. What glory! To finally come home to you after all of these years. I know a man is supposed to look forward to heaven in order to be united with God, but forgive me, Lord, if I sin in this thought: It's Naomi I long to see.
  Twenty-seven years is a long time to live without the woman you love. Others have tried to fill the void, but there is no one but you, my beloved. I tried to take interest in other women, but they paled compared to you, and how fair would it have been to have

made another woman live here at Windridge in your shadow?

Jessica bit her lip to keep from sobbing out loud. Ryan would be very upset to see her cry, and with him just beyond the open doors of the nursery, she knew he'd hear her and come to investigate. The words of the journal opened an old wound that Jessica thought had healed with time. She felt the pain afresh, remembered the bitterness of leaving Windridge while her father watched from the porch—no wave, no kiss good-bye, no word.

She saw the devotion he held for her mother, believed that devotion extended in some strange way to herself, but also knew the emptiness her father had felt. An emptiness he imposed upon himself in order to be true to the memory of someone who had died nearly three decades ago.

It was never fair that I should have sent Jessica away from here.
Kate scolded me daily for weeks, even months, and finally she
stopped, seeing that I would not change my mind and bring the
child home. I wanted to. Once Buck helped me past the worst of it,
I wanted to bring Jess here to Windridge, but Harriet would have
no part of it. We'd signed an agreement, which she so firmly
reminded me of anytime I wrote to suggest doing otherwise.

Jessica startled at the realization that her father had tried to bring her back to her real home. She felt a growing anger at the knowledge that Aunt Harriet had kept her from such happiness. She thought of the years of strange girls' schools, where the loneliness threatened to eat her alive. She thought of her miserable youth and the parties and men who stood at Harriet's elbow, hoping to be chosen as a proper mate for Jessica. If only her father could have found a way to break the contract and bring her home. If only she had known that he desired her to be with him, she would have walked through fire to make it happen. She would have defied Harriet and all of her suitors in order to be back on Windridge permanently.

*Naomi, I never imagined you would leave me. I built an empire to
share with you. Built you a house on Windridge and planned a
lifetime of happiness here in God's country. When you went away,
you took all that with you. Took my hopes, my dreams, my future.
After that, there was no one. Not even Jessica, because Harriet
wouldn't allow her to be a part of my life.*

Jessica could no longer contain her sobs. She moaned sorrowfully at
the thought that her father had longed for her return.

*Then Jessica married. He was nothing, less than nothing. A
miserable worm handpicked by your aunt. I should have
remembered her choice of husbands for you and realized how far
I fell from the mark. How upset she was when you ran off with
a cowboy from Kansas. Jessica had no one to fight for her, and
she didn't have your strength of mind. She did what Harriet
told her to do and married that eastern dandy who did nothing
but bleed her dry.*

*Harriet died and left them a fortune, but Albright squan-
dered it on gambling and women. I had him watched, knew his
every move, but because Jess loved him, I did nothing. I couldn't
hurt her more by interfering where I wasn't wanted. Devon
Carter helped me to see that it was no longer my place to fret and
stew. Devon's a good man. He's a Christian and a finer son a
man could not ask to have. I consider him the son we never had.
He's there, just two doors down, whenever I need him.*

Jessica suddenly realized that Devon had lived in the house prior
to her coming to Windridge. She also realized, without having to ask
Kate for confirmation, that Devon had moved out of his own accord in
order to maintain the proprieties for Jessica and Ryan. She'd only been
coming for a visit as far as they had known. Her decision to stay had
caused Devon to have to move permanently from the house. It made
her feel bad to realize that she'd sent him off like the hired hand she'd

so often accused him of being.

I've given Devon a piece of his own land, some two thousand acres on the south side. I also gave him a bonus of five thousand dollars. I figured if Gertrude Jenkins and Newman Albright could bleed me for funds, I might as well leave money to those I love. Jess will get the house, of course, and all of what remains of Windridge. Although in truth, I've neglected it badly, Naomi.

Several things came immediately to mind. First of all, Gertrude had taken money from her father, and from the sounds of it, she'd taken quite a bit. Jessica had known about Newman's indiscretions from her father's letters, but Gertrude came as a surprise.

But the most important thing that Jessica realized was that Devon Carter had his own money and his own land. He didn't need Jessica's pittance. He had no reason to run from Windridge and Kansas. He could have quit his position many times over and headed over to his own land and started a new life, but instead he stayed at Windridge— with her.

Warmth spread over Jessica in this revelation. Devon hadn't run away, taking her last dime. No, the delay was for some reason other than his alleged dishonesty, and with that thought, Jessica really began to worry. Perhaps he *had* fallen ill. Or maybe someone had done him harm. The possibilities were endless.

Wasting no more time with the diary, Jessica lovingly tucked the book beneath her pillow and went in search of Kate. There were several questions burning in her mind, and Kate would be the only one except Buck who could answer them.

Kate was in the kitchen mixing a cake when Jessica came bounding down the back stairs.

"Kate, I want the truth about something," Jessica announced.

Kate turned and looked at Jessica over the rim of her glasses. "As if I've ever given you anything else."

Jessica smiled. "I know you've been honest with me. That's why I know I can come to you now."

Kate seemed to realize the importance of the matter and put the mixing bowl aside. "So what's on your mind?"

"Devon."

"Now why doesn't that surprise me?"

Jessica smiled. "Devon lived here in the house when my father was alive, didn't he?"

Kate nodded. "How'd you find that out?"

"My father kept a journal shortly before he died. He knew he was dying and wrote the words as if speaking to my mother."

"I never knew this," Kate said in complete surprise. "Where did you find this journal?"

"Under my mattress," Jessica replied and laughed. "Remember how you wanted to turn the mattress last spring, and we only turned the tick and said we'd see to the mattress come fall? Well, I finally remembered it and took it on my own initiative to resolve the matter. When I managed to pull the mattress off, there it was."

"Well, I'll be," Kate said in complete amazement. "If I'd just turned that mattress after Gus died, we'd have found it a whole lot sooner. Guess that's what I get for being a poor housekeeper."

Jessica shook her head. "Don't you see? This was exactly as God intended it. There was a hardness to me when I came to Windridge that would never have allowed me to deal with the words I read in that journal. God knew the time was right and knew, too, that I needed to read those words."

"What words?"

"My father talked of how he loved me," Jessica said, tears forming anew in her eyes. "He talked, too, of how he loved Devon as a son. How he gave Devon land and money. Devon is considerably better off than I figured, isn't he?"

Kate smiled. "I don't know how much he has left. He took a good deal of his own money and started using it to fix up Windridge."

"What?"

"He knew he couldn't just offer it to you, Jess. He knew you'd say no.

So he just started buying things that we needed. And he figured to add a good portion of his own funds to whatever the steers sold for and just tell you that he got a really good deal."

"And here I thought Devon was an honest man," Jessica said, wiping her eyes and smiling.

"He didn't want to hurt your feelings or spoil your dreams. Took a lot for him to accept the idea of a resort ranch, but he did it because he knew what it meant to you."

"I only wanted to make something of Windridge without relying on others for help. Guess that was my pride getting in the way of reality," Jessica admitted. "And to think I called Devon the hired help."

"That was pretty hard on him. Gus had treated him like a son, then you came along and relegated him to one of the hands."

Jessica shook her head. "Why didn't you tell me?"

"Devon made us promise we wouldn't. Made us promise we wouldn't say anything about any of it. As much as I love you, Jess, I couldn't betray that promise."

"Papa's diary also said that Gertrude Jenkins and my husband had bled him for money. What do you know about that?"

Kate thought for a moment. "I don't know too much about his dealings with Newman. I know your husband would send telegrams asking for money, telling of one emergency or another. Gus always sent whatever he asked for, knowing that even if Newman spent it on something other than what he claimed, it would at least keep you from suffering."

"It didn't keep me from suffering," Jessica replied. "But if Papa thought it did, then I'm glad."

"I think he knew the truth," Kate replied. "He knew about a lot we never gave him credit for. As for Gertrude, well, she thought she was going to talk Gus into marriage. She's a poor manager of that ranch of hers, and Gus lent her sum after sum, all in order to help her keep afloat. She finally deeded the ranch over to him, although no one was supposed to know that but she and Gus. That's part of the reason why she took off for Europe. She didn't want to face the retribution of listening to what folks would have to say when they learned she'd borrowed against the ranch until Gus owned the whole thing."

"Why wasn't I told about this?" Jessica asked.

Kate took a deep breath. "Because Devon arranged to buy the land from Gus, and when Gus died, Devon gave it back to Gertrude. It's the reason she hates him so much. He told her he knew he didn't owe her anything, but that he couldn't bear to see her suffer, especially if there was the slightest chance that he had somehow caused Jane to look elsewhere for her happiness. He also told her the truth about finding Jane in the arms of a traveling salesman. Told her how he confronted Jane, agreed to forget the whole matter, and still planned to marry her. It wasn't the story Gerty wanted to hear."

"I can well imagine."

"Anyway, Gus never knew. He probably figured Devon saw the merit of the property because it adjoined the land Gus had already given Devon."

Jessica wouldn't have thought it possible that she could love Devon more than she already did, but hearing of his generosity and giving to a woman who hated him made her realize how deeply she admired and loved Devon Carter.

"This changes everything," Jessica murmured, wishing silently that there might be a way to win Devon away from the woman he knew God had intended him to marry. *Perhaps that is the reason for his delay,* she thought for the first time. *Maybe he's gotten himself married.*

"Not really," Kate replied, interrupting Jessica's thoughts.

"What do you mean?" Jessica asked.

"You love him, and he loves you."

She shook her head sadly. "No, he told me there was someone he cared for. Someone God had chosen for him to marry."

Kate started laughing. "Silly woman, he meant you. He told Buck as much."

"What?" Jessica felt her chest tighten and her breathing quicken. "Are you telling me the truth?"

"I thought we'd already established that I've never lied to you. Do you think I'd start now?"

"No, but, I mean—" A wonderful rush of excitement flowed over Jessica. "He loves me?"

Kate laughed even more. "It's pretty obvious to everyone but you two that you're perfect for each other. You need each other in a bigger way than any two people I've ever seen. Whether you go back to regular ranching or run a resort, you'll do fine so long as you do it together."

"He loves me," Jessica repeated. "And he loves Ryan." She looked up at Kate and saw the happiness in the older woman's eyes. There was no doubting the words she spoke. Devon loved her.

Chapter 10

L ooks like it's gonna blow up a snow," Buck said, coming into the house. "I don't like the taste of the air. Wouldn't be surprised to see it shape up to be a bad one."

"Are we prepared for such a thing?" Kate asked.

"I'm having the boys bring up wood from the shed. We'll stack it high against the back of the house. That way, if we have a blizzard like the one the year Jessie was born, we won't have far to go for fuel."

"What about the hands?" Jessica asked, easily realizing the seriousness of the moment.

"They usually ride the storms out in the bunkhouse. We run a rope from there to the barns, and that way, they can keep an eye on the horses and milk cows."

Jessica nodded. "If it gets too bad, let's bring them up to the house. Better to use fuel to heat one place than two."

Buck and Kate exchanged a quick glance and smiled approvingly. "You sound more like your father each day," Kate told her.

Jessica laughed. "I would have thought that an insult at one time. Now, I take it as the compliment you intend it to be."

"I'll bring up extra fuel for the lanterns, and if you ladies think of anything else we need, you let me know," Buck said, heading back for the door. He opened it and looked outside. "Snow's already started," he announced.

"Then we'd best get busy," Kate told Jessica.

Ryan came into the kitchen about that time. His cheeks were flushed, and his eyes appeared rather glassy. Jessica immediately realized he'd been unusually quiet that morning. Picking up her son, Jessica could feel the heat radiating from his tiny body.

"Ryan's sick," she told Kate. "He has a fever."

Kate came to Jessica and held out her arms, but Jessica felt all her feelings of overprotection and inadequacy surface. "I'll take care of him," she said more harshly than she'd intended.

Kate nodded as if understanding. "I only wanted to see how high his fever was."

"You can tell by a touch?" Jessica asked, still clinging tightly to Ryan.

"You can when you've dealt with as many sick boys as I have. Remember, I've nursed the bunk hands, my own sons, Gus, and Buck, even Devon. You get a feel for it after a time." Kate put her hand to Ryan's head. "Feels pretty high. We'd best get him to bed and see what we can do to bring that fever down. Do you see any rashes on his body?"

"Rashes?" Jessica asked in a panicky voice.

Kate nodded. "I heard some of the Newcome kids were down with the measles."

"Measles!" Jessica's voice squeaked out the word. "He just can't have measles."

"Well only time will tell. Let's get him to bed, and we'll work on it from there. Why don't you put him in the bed in our room? That way you won't have to run up and down the stairs all the time, and it'll be warmer here by the kitchen. If you like, you can sleep there, and Buck and I will take one of the upstairs rooms."

"Thanks, Kate." Jessica looked down at Ryan, who had put his head on her shoulder. It was so uncharacteristic of the boy that Jessica thought she might start to cry. She bit her lower lip and, knowing nothing else to do, began to pray.

⁓

The blizzard blew in with the full force Buck had expected and then some. Icy pellets of rain came first, coating everything with a thick layer of ice. Then sleetlike snow stormed across the hills, and visibility became impossible.

Jessica thought very little about the storm, except to occasionally worry about Devon. She had far too much with which to concern herself by keeping on top of Ryan's needs and easily relegated everything else to Buck and Kate.

By the second day of the storm, Ryan bore the telltale signs of measles. Tiny red splotchy dots covered his stomach and groin, and his fever refused to abate. Jessica found herself so weary she could hardly keep her eyes open, yet when Kate offered to relieve her, Jessica refused.

"You aren't doing yourself or Ryan any good," Kate told her. "I don't know why you can't see the sense in letting others help you." Kate's tone revealed the offense she took at Jessica's actions.

"I'm sorry, Kate. I didn't mean to make you feel bad. It's just that. . . well. . .he's mine, and it's my responsibility to see him through this."

"But if you kill yourself trying to nurse him back to health, what good will it do? I swear, the way you act, you'd think I was trying to steal your glory."

"What?" Jessica questioned, struggling to clear the cobwebs from her sleepy mind. "What glory is there in a sick child?"

"None that I know of," Kate replied. "But you seem to think there's some reason to keep anyone else from getting too close to that boy."

Jessica slumped into a chair and nodded. "I just can't lose him. He's so important to me. I don't want to lose him to you or Devon or sickness."

"Why would you lose him to anyone? Ryan knows you're his mother, and he loves you. Well, as much as any two year old can love. Jessica," Kate said, reaching out to touch the younger woman's shoulder, "you've been like a daughter to me. I always wanted to have a daughter, and I would have happily raised you for Gus. Let me offer you a bit of motherly advice."

Jessica looked up and nodded.

"Don't let fear be the glue that binds your relationship with Ryan. Fear is a poor substitute for love."

"But you know about the past. You know what Essie did when I lived in New York."

"Yes, but I don't see Essie around here. It's just you and me, and I'm not about to steal your child away from you. Don't you see, Jessica? The more you smother Ryan with protectiveness and isolate him from being able to love anyone but you, the more hollow and useless your relationship. He'll run the first chance he gets, just to give himself some breathing room."

"I know you're right. God's been working on this very issue with me. I guess I just let fear control me sometimes."

"Sometimes?" Kate questioned with a grin.

"All right, so fear and I are no strangers," Jessica said, smiling. "Kate, would you please watch Ryan while I get some sleep?"

Kate nodded and patted Jessica once again. "I would be happy to help."

Jessica nodded, made her way to the bed, and fell across it, not even bothering to undress.

Father, she prayed, *please heal my son. You know how much I love him and how lost I would be without him. I'm begging You not to take him from me.*

She felt welcome drowsiness engulf her. Devon's face came to mind and, with it, the thought that she needed to pray for him. *Watch over him, Father,* she added. *Please bring him home to Windridge.*

The snow let up, but not the wind, which kept the effects of the blizzard going on for days. The blowing snow blinded them from even seeing the top of Windridge. Jessica saw notable improvements in Ryan's health and forced herself to accept Kate's involvement in nursing him. It wasn't that she didn't dearly love Kate, but the fact was, Jessica still needed to let go of her possessive nature when it came to the boy.

Sitting at her father's desk in the library, Jessica thought back on the things Devon, Kate, and Buck had told her over the course of her time at Windridge.

"Folks need folks out here," Buck had once said. *"It fast becomes a matter of survival."* His point had been made in talking to her about selling property to Joe Riley. He needed a spring in order to assure himself of having water for his cattle and his land. Jessica could easily see that what Buck said made perfect sense. They were so isolated out here in the middle of the Flint Hills that to be anything other than neighborly could prove fatal.

She stared into the fireplace and watched the flames lick greedily at the dry wood. Kate had said, *"It's better to rely on folks than to die on folks."* This was kind of an unspoken code of Kate's. *"The prairie is no place for pride,"* Kate had added. *"Pride not only goeth before destruction, it is the thing that stirs up strife and causes heartache."*

Jessica knew it was true. Her own pride had nearly caused her to alienate Kate's affections. That was something she could never have abided. Kate was like a mother to her in so many ways that Aunt Harriet had never been. Aunt Harriet had raised her, but Aunt Harriet had never loved her the way Kate did.

Devon came to mind when Jessica thought about love. She loved him so much that it hurt to think about what tragedies might have befallen him. She planned to have Buck go into town and wire the livestock yards in Kansas City. They would have records of the cattle transactions and just possibly those records would include the name of the hotel where Devon was staying. It was Jessica's hope that they might learn something about Devon's whereabouts by starting down this path.

But the blizzard had put an end to that thought, and Buck felt certain more snow was coming their way. She felt her enthusiasm slip another notch. Life on the prairie was very hard—there could be no doubt about that—and it was quickly becoming apparent that Jessica could either accept that she could do nothing on her own, or she could perish.

"Don't be so sure you don't need anyone," Devon had told her once. It had startled her to have him read her so easily. She smiled when she thought of the halfhearted protest she'd offered him. She could still see the laughter in his eyes and the amusement in his voice when she'd told him he didn't know anything about her feelings.

"I may not know you or your feelings," he'd countered, *"but I know pride when I see it. Pride used to be a bosom companion of mine, so I feel pretty certain when I see him. Just remember, pride isn't the kind to stick around and help when matters get tough."*

Jessica chuckled at the memory. *He's so right,* she thought. *Pride only offers seclusion and a false sense of security. I have to let go of my pride and allow people to help me when I need it and to help others when they have needs. Otherwise, Ryan and I will never survive life at Windridge.*

"It's been two weeks," Devon heard someone say. His mind was lost in a haze of darkness, but from time to time someone spoke words that made a little sense. He strained to understand the words—fought to find the source of the words.

"His vital signs are good, but the fact that he's still not regained consciousness worries me."

"Any word on the man's identity?" came another male voice.

"None. We really should send someone around to contact the businesses in the area where he was found."

Devon floated on air and wondered why everyone seemed so concerned. Who was this person they couldn't identify, and what were vital signs?

"His injuries were extensive," the man continued, "but the bones seem to be healing just fine, and the swelling has gone down in his face. It's probably that blow to the back of the head that keeps him unconscious."

From somewhere in his thoughts, Devon began to realize they were talking about him. It startled him at first, but then it seemed quite logical. The next realization he had was of being in extreme pain. Something wasn't right. Somewhere in his body, someone was causing him a great deal of torment.

These thoughts came and went from time to time, but to Devon they seemed to transpire in the course of just a few hours. It wasn't until he heard one of the disembodied voices announce that if he didn't regain consciousness soon, he would die, that Devon began a long hard fight to find his way through the mire of blackness.

"Did you have a nice Christmas?" someone questioned.

"A very nice one, sir," came the feminine voice in response.

Devon thought for a moment the voice belonged to someone he knew, but the thought was so fleeting that he couldn't force it to stay long enough to interpret it.

"The New Year's ball was superb," the woman continued. "I'd never been to anything so lovely."

"Yes, my wife loves the occasion. Of course, it's also her birthday," the man responded.

Birthday. Devon thought about the word for a moment. Someone he knew had a birthday on New Year's Eve. Without realizing what he was doing, Devon opened his eyes and said, "Birthday."

His eyes refused to focus for several minutes, but when they did, Devon could see the startled faces of the man and woman who stood at his bedside.

"So, you finally decided to join the world of the living," the man said in a stern voice that was clearly mingled with excitement.

"Where am I?" Devon asked, his voice gravelly.

"You're in the hospital. Have been for nearly a month," the man replied. "I'm Dr. Casper, and you are?"

He waited for Devon's response with a look of anticipation. The woman, too, looked down at him in an expectant manner. Devon stared blankly at them, trading glances first with the woman and then with the man.

"Did you understand my question?" the doctor asked. "I need to know who you are."

"I don't know," Devon replied with a hideous sinking feeling. He shook his head, feeling the dull pain that crossed from one side of his skull to the other. "I don't know who I am."

Chapter 11

The weeks that followed left Devon depressed and frustrated. His injuries were quick enough to heal, so why not his mind?

"How does that leg feel?" the doctor questioned as Devon hobbled around the room like a trained monkey.

"It's sore, but I've had worse."

"How do you know?" the doctor asked curiously. "Are you starting to remember something more?"

Devon shrugged. "I remember little pieces of things. I remember a room with a stone fireplace. I remember riding a horse out on the open range." He hobbled back to bed and sunk onto the edge of the mattress. "But I don't remember anything important."

"Those things are all important, Mr. Smith," the doctor told him.

"Don't call me Smith," Devon replied angrily. "Not unless you have proof that that's who I am."

"We have to call you something," the doctor replied. "Now, raise that arm for me."

Devon lifted his left arm and grimaced. Apparently his assailants had hit him repeatedly and kicked him as well. He had suffered busted ribs, a broken ankle, and a dislocated shoulder. His left arm had been continuously pounded, the doctor believed by boot heels, as had his face.

"It still works. Just not as well," Devon told the doctor.

"I'm sure in time it will all heal properly. Are you in as much pain today as you were yesterday?"

Devon shook his head. "No." He glanced up to find one of the nurses coming down the ward with a well-dressed man at her side.

"Dr. Casper, this man believes he knows our patient."

Devon perked up at this and studied the man for a moment. Was he a friend? A brother? Some other family member?

"Yes," the man said enthusiastically. "This is the man I've been searching for. He didn't have a beard when he stayed with us, but he's the same man. He's a guest, or was a guest, at our hotel. I'm so happy to have found you, Mr. Carter."

"Carter?" Devon tried the name. Carter. Yes, Carter sounded right.

"The assault this man received left him without much of a memory," Dr. Casper told the hotelman.

"No wonder you failed to return," the man said sympathetically. "When I heard about the poor man who'd been beaten in the alley not far from the hotel, I thought, perhaps this is Devon Carter. I knew you wouldn't leave without retrieving your things. After all, you left quite a bit of money in my safe."

Devon nodded. Yes, he remembered having a good amount of money. He closed his eyes and pictured himself handing it over to the man who now stood at his side. "I remember you."

"Good," the doctor said enthusiastically. "Seeing something familiar often triggers memory." He turned to the hotelman. "Did you bring any of his things?"

"No, but I can have them brought here immediately."

"Then do so," the doctor instructed. "Mr. Carter will need all the help he can get in order to remember who he is."

Nearly half an hour later, a boy appeared with saddlebags, two brown paper packages, and a large envelope. The man from the hotel stood at his side as though standing guard. "We have your things, Mr. Carter."

Devon nodded. It felt so good just to know his own name that knowing anything else would be purely extra. He took hold of the saddlebags and noted the carved initials *D.C.* He ran his fingers over the indentation, remembering vaguely the day he'd carved the marker on the bags. Reaching into one side, Devon pulled out his shaving gear and studied it for a moment. It seemed familiar, but nothing that offered him any real memory. Next, he took out an extra shirt and pair of socks. Nothing came to mind with those articles, so he quickly reached into the other side of the bag.

Here, he found receipts all dated from the middle of December. Some of the receipts were for furniture, and others were for homey things like lamps, curtain rods, material, dishes, and such. The kind of things a wife would have need and desire of. Did he have a wife? The same face kept coming to mind. At first she had appeared only in a hazy outline, but as time went on, the warmth of her smile and the sincerity in her dark eyes became clearer in his memory. Was this the image of his wife?

"Do you remember these things?" the doctor questioned.

"Somewhat," Devon replied.

"This," the man from the hotel said, "is the money you left with us."

Devon took the envelope and looked inside. There was a great deal of money, and it immediately triggered a thought. The money was intended for a special use. The money belonged to her. The woman in his mind. Perhaps it was a dowry. Maybe they were setting up house, and this money had come from her.

"Why don't you unwrap these packages? My nurse will be glad to rewrap them afterward, but perhaps they will trigger some memory."

Devon nodded and gently stripped away the paper on the first package. Toy soldiers. Devon felt mounting frustration at not being able to remember. Then to his surprise, the image of another face came to mind. It was that of a child. The fuzzy brown hair of the boy seemed to draw Devon's attention first. There was something important about this child. Then a horrible feeling washed over Devon. Was he not only a husband but a father as well?

"Here, try this one," the doctor said, helping to pull the paper from the other package. A jewelry box was revealed as the paper fell away. Devon stared at the box, feeling sure that he should remember it but having no real understanding of why. Had he bought this as a gift for the woman in his dreams? Had he left a family somewhere to worry and fret over his well-being? What if they were in danger because of his absence? What if they needed the supplies and goods he had procured?

"No," he muttered, handing the things over to the nurse. He stuffed the receipts and money into the saddlebag, then turned to the hotel-man. "I don't suppose I gave you an address?"

"No sir, but you said you were from Kansas. You came to sell cattle."

Devon drew his legs up onto the bed and fell back against the pillow. "I think I need to rest," he told them all. He felt angry and frustrated. He had hoped that with the recognition of his own name, he might instantly remember everything else that he needed to know.

"Thanks for bringing my things," he told the hotelman. The man smiled and prodded the kid to follow him from the room. The nurse and doctor agreed that rest was the best solution and finally left Devon alone.

He stared at the ceiling for a while, then rolled onto his side and stared down the corridor of beds. Several men moaned and called out for help. Others slept peacefully, and a few read. But all of them had their minds. All of them knew their name and recognized their own things.

Sleep finally overtook Devon, and although he passed the time fit-fully, he actually felt better when he awoke. The light had faded outside, leaving little doubt that dusk was upon them. This time of day made Devon melancholy. He longed to be home—wherever home might be.

He thought of the dark-haired woman in his dreams. Thought of the child whose laughing face warmed his heart. He loved these people; he felt certain of that. They were important to him in a way he couldn't figure out, but he knew without a doubt they were keys to his past.

Supper came, and although Devon had figured nothing good could come of the meal, he found himself actually enjoying the beef stew. It wasn't as good as Kate's, but. . .

Kate? Was that the dark-haired woman's name?

Devon stared at the stew and forced an image. He was sitting in a stylish dining room. The dark-haired woman and little boy were sitting beside him, but there was also someone else in the picture. An older woman's face beamed a smile at him. She pushed up wire-rimmed glasses and asked if he'd like more stew. *Kate. Katie!* He actually remembered her.

This triggered other thoughts, and soon Devon found himself overwhelmed with people and events. Still, he couldn't remember the brown-haired woman's name, nor that of the child. Nor could he remember where he lived and where he might find the others.

"I've brought another visitor," Dr. Casper said as he approached Devon's bed.

The supper had grown cold, but Devon didn't care. "I've been remembering some things."

The doctor smiled. "Good! That's very good. This gentleman called for you at the hotel, and he knows quite a bit about your home. We thought you might remember him as well."

Devon looked at the man and nodded. "Yes, he does seem familiar."

"I am Mr. Whitehead. You ordered a large number of chairs and two bedsteads from my company. You also ordered several nightstands and dressers." The man chuckled. "You look a bit different what with the beard. You had the mustache, but the beard is new."

Devon nodded and smirked a grin. "Nobody seems to offer me a shave around here. You say I ordered furniture? I do seem to remember something along those lines, but did I say why I needed so much?"

"You were ordering them for your place in Kansas. You are planning a resort ranch at a place called Windridge."

The word *Windridge* triggered everything. Suddenly it was as if the floodgates to his mind had opened. He realized exactly who he was and who she was. "Jessica." He breathed the name and sighed.

Then, startling both the doctor and Mr. Whitehead, Devon exclaimed, "What day is this?"

"February 3," the doctor replied.

Devon rubbed his bearded face. "Get me a razor and some soap. I have to get home. I should have been there months ago."

The doctor smiled. "Are you certain you feel up to leaving us?"

Devon nodded. "I'm positive. Just get me my things. Oh, and I need to send a telegram." No doubt everyone would be worried sick by now. Especially Jessica.

"Well, it seems as though this is all working out rather well," Dr.

Casper said. "I wouldn't have given you odds on pulling through that beating, but you're one tough man, Mr. Carter."

"I don't know about how tough I am, but I'm definitely a man with a purpose, and that gives a guy strength, even when all hope is lost."

When they left him to dress, Devon felt the overwhelming urge to get down on his knees and thank God for supplying him with the answers he'd been so desperately seeking. Stiff and sore from his inactivity, Devon ignored the pain and knelt beside his bed.

Thank You, Father, he prayed, feeling hot tears come to his eyes. *I was so lost, and I despaired of ever being found. But You knew where I was all the time. You knew what I needed, and You brought it to me. I pray with a heart of thanksgiving for all that You've done to rescue me from the hopelessness. Please keep Jessica and everyone at Windridge in Your care. Help them not to worry, and help me to get home to them quickly. Amen.*

⤴

Jessica awoke with a start. She went first to Ryan's bed and found the boy sleeping peacefully. All signs of the measles were gone, but he was still rather weak, and Jessica worried over him.

She watched him sleep peacefully and thanked God for His mercy.

"I've learned so much here at Windridge," she murmured. "Things I never expected to learn."

She thought of the diary her father had kept and went to take it up from the special place she'd given it on her fireplace mantel. Lighting a lamp, she sat down to reread the final entry in the journal. She continued to come back to this one entry, because while the rest of the book was written to her mother, this entry was written to her:

My beloved Jessica,

I can only pray that you will someday forgive me for sending you away. I have always loved you, will die loving you, but I know I am unworthy of your love. I've tried to help out where I could—tried to be there for you when you would let me, which, although it didn't happen often, happened just enough to give me some satisfaction.

Please know this, I never blamed you for your mother's

passing. People live, and people die, and that's just the way things are. Only God chooses the timing for those things. Only God can give life, as He did in the form of my beautiful child, and only God can take life, as He did with your mother.

I'm sorry I can't leave you a legacy of memories spent here at Windridge, but I hope you'll stay on. I hope you'll come to love this house as much as your mother did. I hope, too, that you'll be good to Katie and Buck and Devon Carter. You don't know any of them very well, but they're good people, and I know they will care very deeply for you. When you think of me, Jessica, I hope it will be with something other than hatred and anger. Maybe one day you will actually think of me as I used to be when your mother was alive. Hopeful, happy, looking forward to the future and all that it had to offer.

Your Father

Jessica sighed and closed the book to cradle it against her breast. She felt warmed and comforted by its words. Now if only Devon would come home. If only they could have some word from him. Some hope that he was all right.

Getting up, Jessica walked to the window and looked across the snowy prairie. "Come home to me, Devon," she whispered against the frosty glass. "Please come home to Windridge."

Chapter 12

Warm southerly winds blew in and melted the snows on Windridge. The land went from white to dull brown practically overnight. Jessica marveled at the change. She could actually go outside without a coat, although Kate told her the warmth was deceptive. But Jessica didn't care. The heat of the sun felt good upon her face, and the warm winds blowing across the land would dry the ground and insure her ability to get to town again.

Jessica didn't allow herself to be concerned with what she would do once she actually got to town. She hadn't a clue as to how she would go about searching for Devon, but she knew the key would be in communication. She would start by telegraphing anyone who might have some idea of Devon's whereabouts.

Bundling Ryan up, Jessica decided a walk to the top of the ridge would be in order. The land was still rather soggy, but Jessica carefully picked her way up the hill while Ryan chattered about the things he saw.

"Bword," he cried out, pointing to a robin sitting on the fence post.

"Yes, that's a good sign," Jessica told her son.

"I want bword," Ryan said, trying to squirm out of her hold.

"No. Now stop it," Jessica reprimanded. "We're going up here to see if we can find Devon."

"Dadon," Ryan repeated.

Jessica smiled. No matter how much Ryan's language improved, Devon's name still came out sounding like some form of *Daddy*.

"Dadon comin'," Ryan said enthusiastically.

"Soon, I hope." Jessica wondered if she'd made a mistake by telling the boy they were looking for Devon. Now he would be constantly chattering about Devon, always asking where he was and when he'd come home. The measles had forced all of them to focus their attention on something other than Devon's absence, and even though Ryan had cried for Devon on more than one occasion, he seemed to accept that the man was gone from his life. At least temporarily. Now Jessica realized she'd probably stirred up the child's anticipation all over again.

"Dadon comin' to me," Ryan told her, patting his hand against her face.

Jessica kissed his fingers and laughed. "I pray he comes home soon." She trudged up the final few feet of the ridge, realizing as she did how much Ryan had grown since the last time she'd carried him up the hillside.

"Oh Ryan," she said rather breathlessly, "you're getting so big."

"Wyan get big," he said, raising his arms high in the air. "Dadon comin' to me."

Jessica shook her head and grinned at the boy's enthusiasm. *Let him have his moment,* she thought. *It can't hurt to be hopeful.* Jessica stared out across the Flint Hills and felt the longing in her heart grow stronger. He was out there somewhere.

"I don't know where you are," she whispered, her skirts bellowing out behind her as the wind whipped at them. She knew she couldn't keep Ryan outside for much longer and had just started to turn back down the hill when she spotted a wagon emerge from behind a hill.

Ryan saw the object as well and started clapping his hands. "Dadon comin'!"

Jessica felt her heart skip a beat as yet another wagon followed the first and then another. Four wagons in all, laden with crates and covered boxes, made their way toward Windridge. Then Jessica caught the outline of the two men in the lead wagon.

"Devon," she whispered, feeling absolutely confident that the man beside the driver of the wagon was her beloved Devon.

"Come on, Ryan, we have to get you back in the house."

"I want Dadon," Ryan protested as Jessica nearly ran down the hill.

Because the grass still held moisture, she slipped and nearly fell. "I've got to calm myself down," she said aloud and forced herself to walk more carefully.

Seeing the wagons come ever closer, Jessica forgot about taking Ryan inside. She forgot about everything but getting to Devon. She started walking down the dirt road, her pace picking up as the wagons rounded the final bend. She tightened her grip on Ryan. *Devon's home!* It was all she could think of.

He apparently saw her, because the wagon stopped long enough for Devon to jump down from the seat. He waved the driver on and walked toward them with a bit of a limp. *He was hurt!* she thought, and all sensibility left her mind. She began to run, mindless of Ryan, mindless of the drivers passing by in their wagons.

"Oh Devon!" she exclaimed. His face registered surprise as she crossed the final distance and threw herself into his arms. "Oh Devon, I thought you were never coming home." Then without thought, she kissed him. At first it was just a peck on the cheek, then another and another, and finally her lips met his and stopped. All rational thought had fled, and she kissed him passionately. Pulling away, Jessica suddenly realized by the look on Devon's face that she'd made a grave mistake.

Her enthusiasm waned, in spite of the fact that Ryan was now clapping and shouting Devon's name over and over. She did nothing for a moment, her gaze fixed on Devon. She searched his eyes for some sign of acceptance, but he only stared back at her as if trying to figure out who she was and why she'd just kissed him.

Thrusting Ryan into Devon's arms, Jessica turned and ran back to the house. He didn't even call after her. Jessica felt her face grow hot with humiliation. Kate must have been wrong about his feelings for her. She must have misunderstood Buck, or Buck had misunderstood Devon.

Jessica wanted to die. Wanted to crawl under a rock and never be seen again. What a spectacle she'd just made of herself. Running out there to Devon as though he was her long lost love.

But, she thought, *he is* my *love.* She might not be his, but he was her own heart's love. And deep down inside, Jessica knew she would never love another. If he couldn't return that love, then she would live the rest of her life alone. The thought terrified her.

"Is that Devon?" Kate exclaimed, stepping out the front door.

"Yes," Jessica barely managed to say. She rushed past, mindless of the shocked expression on the older woman's face. She couldn't stand and explain her humiliating actions to Kate. No, let Devon tell Kate how poorly she'd conducted herself.

Jessica stayed out of sight until suppertime. Kate had brought Ryan to the nursery for his nap, and although Jessica was just in the adjoining room, she didn't open the doors to speak to the woman; Kate, thankfully, didn't knock and ask her to.

She felt guilty for having neglected Ryan, but in truth her emotions were so raw and foreign that Jessica knew it would have been impossible to deal with anyone.

"I don't know what to do," she whispered, pressing her face against the cool pane of the window. "I made a fool of myself, and now I have to face them all at supper."

She heard Kate ring the supper bell, something the woman had come up with in order to call guests to meals. The tradition had been started early, all in order to see how and if it would work. The bell pealed out loud and clear, and Jessica cringed. She would have to go down. There was no other way.

She splashed water on her face and checked her appearance. She'd changed out of the skirt and blouse she'd worn earlier. The hem of that skirt had been laden with mud and grass, and the blouse had clung to her from perspiration. Now she studied her reflection and realized that the peach-colored gown made her look quite striking. The muttonleg sleeves made her shoulders look slightly wider, which accented her tiny waist. The gown was cut in a very simple style, with a rounded neckline and basque waist. The peach material had been trimmed in cream-colored lace and cording, and with Jessica's brunette hair, the effect was quite stunning.

She bit her lip and shook her head. It didn't matter. She had dressed for him, but it wouldn't matter. His feelings had obviously changed while he'd been away from Windridge. She would have to accept this fact and deal with her broken heart.

"Mama! Mama come!" Ryan called out to her from the nursery.

Jessica smiled and opened the door. "Yes, Mama is coming."

By the time they made their way into the dining room, the others had already congregated. Jessica hated making an entrance where everyone could stare at her, but she knew there was no other choice. She swept into the room, Ryan in her arms, and made her way to the table determined that no one would think anything was wrong.

"Here we are. So sorry for the delay," she announced, putting Ryan in his chair and taking her own place at the foot of the table.

"I thought perhaps you'd fallen asleep," Kate said, allowing Buck to help her into her chair.

Jessica could feel Devon's gaze upon her, but she refused to look at him. "Yes, well, I did rest for a time. Thank you for seeing to Ryan."

"Oh, I didn't see to him except to put him down for his nap. Devon wouldn't hear of it. He insisted that they had a lot of catching up to do."

Jessica could feel her cheeks grow warm. "Well, then, thank you." She refused to say his name. It was almost more than she could stand. Being so near to him yet knowing that he was put off at her behavior was too much to bear.

They blessed the meal, with Buck giving thanks for Devon's safe return. Then Kate started the conversation, asking Devon to explain his long absence.

"As I was telling Buck and Kate earlier," Devon began, "everything went pretty well the first couple weeks. I had no trouble selling the cattle and arranging for most everything we had on our list."

Our list. The words sounded pleasant, but Jessica knew she could take no comfort in them. Devon merely thought of Windridge as being partly his own because her father had instilled that belief in the man. How could she blame him for his concerns about the ranch and what would become of it?

"They hit me hard and of course—"

"What?" Jessica nearly shouted, and for the first time her gaze met his. "Who hit you?"

Devon grinned. "I was just telling you that I got myself mugged in Kansas City. A couple fellows waylaid me in the alley not far from the hotel. Thankfully, the money was secured in the hotel safe, and those thugs only managed to get about five dollars. But they hit me hard on the back of the head, then proceeded to beat me. They thought they'd killed me, and why not? I was unconscious and bloodied up pretty good."

Jessica could only stare at him. Her throat tightened as if a band had been tightly wrapped around her neck.

"By leaving me for dead, they did me a favor. Someone found me and hauled me off to the hospital. I was in a coma for about three weeks."

"A coma." Jessica barely breathed the words.

Devon nodded. Ryan began calling for something to eat, and Devon reached over to hand the boy a piece of bread without stopping his story. "When I woke up, I hurt like all get out, but the worst of it was that I couldn't remember a thing."

"Nothing?" Jessica questioned.

His eyes seemed to darken as they locked with hers. "Nothing. I didn't know who I was or where I was from. I only knew the pain and misery of my condition. I couldn't even tell the police what had happened."

"But God was watching over you," Kate chimed in. "We've been praying for you. When you didn't turn up by Christmas, we all had a feeling something wasn't quite right."

"Especially given that you didn't even bother to send a telegram," Buck added.

Devon pulled a wrinkled piece of paper from his pocket. It was clearly a telegram, and he unfolded it and held it up. "I found this waiting at the telegraph office. I sent this as soon as I had my memory back. Seems you people have been impossible to get to because of the snow."

Buck laughed. "That we were, but you could have let us know sooner."

"I know. I should have, but I kept thinking that I'd be coming home any day. Then one week's delay turned into two and so on, and then they mugged me, and well, now you know the story."

"But what happened to help you regain your memory?" Jessica asked.

"A fellow from the hotel came around to see me. He'd heard about the mugging, and since I never returned for the money in the safe, he thought it might be me. He brought some of my things, and little bits of memory started coming back. Then one of the vendors with whom I'd set up a purchase order for chairs came to the hotel when I never came back around to see him. He learned about my situation and came to see me at the hospital, and he was able to help me put together the rest of the mystery."

"What an awful time, Devon," Kate said shaking her head. "I just don't know how a fellow could manage without his memories."

"It was hard. I knew there was so much waiting for me, but I just couldn't force it to come to mind."

Jessica shook her head. "How very awful."

"Well, it's behind us now. I have a bit of limp from a broken ankle, and my ribs still hurt me a bit, but my hard head kept them from doing me in."

Buck laughed. "As many times as you've been thrown from one green horse or another, I'd say that head of yours has held up pretty well."

They all laughed at this. All but Jessica. She pretended to busy herself with preparing Ryan's food. The boy was growing bored with bread, and it was clear he felt himself entitled to something more. She thanked God silently for bringing Devon home to them. She couldn't imagine why such a thing had been necessary to endure, yet Kate had assured her that all things happened for a purpose. As if reading her mind, Devon spoke up again.

"Being laid up like that made me realize just how much I still wanted to accomplish. It made me realize how important some things were and how unimportant other things were."

"How so, Devon?" Kate asked, ladling him a large portion of the beef stew he'd specifically requested for supper.

"I realized it doesn't much matter what direction we go with

Windridge so long as we're happy and doing what God would have us do. What does matter is that we honor God and care for one another. Everything else is just icing on the cake."

"Cake. Wyan want cake!"

Devon laughed and rubbed the boy's head. "I do believe this boy grew some hair while I was gone." Ryan squealed and clapped his hands as if acknowledging his own accomplishments.

Jessica thought about what Devon had said long after the supper meal was over and Ryan had been put to bed. She had thought to just stay in her room, but at the sound of the bell ringing downstairs, she figured Kate had forgotten something and was using the signal to keep from having to trudge up a flight of steps to get her answer.

With a sigh, Jessica went down the back stairs to the kitchen and found Devon leaning casually against the wall at the bottom of the stairs—bell in hand, grin on his face.

"I wondered if this would really work. Kate said it would, but I just didn't believe her."

Jessica began to tremble. She froze on the step and waited to see what he would do or say next. His smile broadened as he set the bell aside. "I thought maybe you'd take a walk with me. Kate says she'll listen for Ryan, so why don't you grab up your coat and come out to the ridge with me?"

Jessica felt her mouth go dry. "I don't know if that's such a good idea."

Devon laughed and reached up to pull her down the last few steps. "Well I do. The country air seems to have a remarkable effect on you."

Jessica's face grew hot. Was he implying what she thought he was? She didn't get a chance to ask because he moved her toward the back door with such speed that she had no time to protest.

He pulled her work coat from the peg and helped her on with it. Then he took up his own coat, which he'd draped haphazardly atop the butter churn. "Come on."

He half dragged her up the hill, not saying a word as they made their way to the top. Jessica felt the warmth of his fingers intertwined with her own. It felt wonderful to have him so near. But how could she ever explain her actions from earlier in the day? No doubt he wanted to discuss her boldness, and he probably wanted to upbraid her for it, given the fact that he was taking her away from the house and other listening ears.

She bit at her lower lip and tried to think of how she would justify herself. She'd simply tell him she was overcome with joy. Which was true. Then, she'd make it clear the kiss meant nothing. Which was not true.

Devon slowed down as they neared the top and nearly swung her in a circle as they came to stand atop the ridge. "Now," he said without wasting any time. "I'd like an explanation."

"An explanation?" Jessica questioned, barely able to look him in the eye. "For what?"

The full moon overhead revealed the amusement in his expression. "All the time you've been here at Windridge, Jessica Albright, you've either been putting me in my place, arguing with me about how things would be, or calling me the hired help. You've berated me for my interference with Ryan, refusing to let him get too close for fear I might steal him away from you, and you've hidden yourself away anytime things got too uncomfortable."

Jessica said nothing. Everything he'd related was true. It hardly seemed productive to deny it.

"Then," he said, his voice lowering, "I return home from an experience that nearly sent me to my maker, and you greet me like I'm your long lost husband. And that, my dear Jessica, is what I want an explanation for."

Jessica took a deep breath. Her moment of truth had come. But she couldn't tell him the truth, not given the way he'd reacted to her. Or could she? Maybe if she was honest, he'd realize the merit in accepting her love. Maybe he'd even come to love her the way Kate presumed he already did.

The air had grown chilly, and Jessica shivered. She refused to give in to her fears. Her entire life had been a pattern of running away from painful situations, and while she'd not instigated the first time when her father had sent her from Windridge, she had certainly allowed many of the other situations.

"Well?" Devon prodded.

His expression was unreadable. Where earlier Devon had smiled with amusement and seemed quite entertained by her nervousness, Jessica could find nothing in his face to reveal how he really felt. She would have to swallow her pride and admit her feelings or lie to him.

"I suppose you do deserve an explanation," she began slowly. "I can best explain by telling you some of the things that happened to me while you were gone. First, Gertrude Jenkins showed up."

"Yes, I remember passing her on the way down the drive."

"Well, she came and we were introduced, and your name came up." She paused and looked away. Why couldn't this just be simple? *Because you're making it harder than it has to be,* Jessica's heart told her.

She held up her hand. "None of that is important. The truth is, I love you." She turned to see what his reaction might be. "It terrifies me in a way I can't even begin to explain, but that's the truth, and I thought from something Kate had told me that you might be given to feeling the same way. Then when I saw you coming home, I just forgot myself and let my heart take over. I'm sorry."

"Truly?"

She shook her head in confusion. "Truly what?"

"You're truly sorry? Sorry you let your heart guide you? Sorry you threw yourself into my arms and kissed me?" He stepped closer and reached his hand up to touch her cheek.

Jessica felt her breath quicken. "No."

"No?" he questioned, the tiniest grin causing his mustache to rise.

Jessica lifted her chin ever so slightly. "No, I'm not sorry. I'm powerfully embarrassed, but I'm not sorry."

"Why are you embarrassed?"

"Because I made a fool of myself," Jessica replied. "Something I seem to do quite a bit when you're around."

This made Devon laugh. "If this is you being a fool, then I like it, and I wouldn't have you change a single thing. But I don't think this is foolish."

"No?" It was Jessica's turn to question.

He moved his face closer to hers, and she knew without a doubt he would kiss her. Could it be, her mind reeled, that he did return her feelings? Was it possible he loved her?

"You never gave me much of a chance to speak to you on the matter," he whispered, his breath warm on her face. "I don't think being in love is foolish. Especially when both people feel the same way."

She felt her eyes grow wide. "Truly?" She found herself repeating the very word he'd used earlier. "You love me?"

"I do," he murmured. "And I'd like to respond to your earlier greeting."

His lips closed upon hers, and his arms pulled her tightly into his embrace. Jessica's knees grew weak. She embraced the overwhelming joy that flooded her heart and soul. It seemed impossible that Devon was standing there, saying the things he was saying, kissing her as he was kissing her, but it also seemed so right. Jessica thought it felt perfect, as if they were meant for each other.

Devon kissed her lips, then let his kisses trail up her cheek to her eyebrow and then to her forehead. Jessica sighed and put her head against his shoulder.

"You know, you seem to make a habit of kissing men you aren't engaged to," he whispered.

Jessica laughed and pulled away. "Then maybe you'd better rectify the situation."

He smiled. "I'd be happy to." He pulled out a ring from his pocket. "This belonged to my grandmother. It's the same one I gave to Jane and the same one she brought back to me. But it's special to me, and I hope you'll overlook her involvement with it. This ring was worn by my grandmother for some fifty-seven years of marriage. She adored my grandfather, and he adored her. I want that kind of marriage, Jess. I want that for us. Will you accept this ring and my proposal of marriage?"

Tears coursed down Jessica's face. She took the ring and slipped it on her finger. It fit perfectly, the little carved gold band glittering in the moonlight. "The past is gone, but this ring will be a reminder to us both of what true love can endure and accomplish. I've prayed for this, asked God to send me the kind of man who could be a father to my son, as well as a husband to me." She looked up from the ring to meet Devon's passionate gaze. "Yes, I'll marry you."

Epilogue

June 1892

R yan danced circles around his parents. Devon and Jessica Carter laughed to see the spectacle the small boy was creating.

"People comin' to see me," he said happily. "Dey comin' now."

"Yes, son," Devon said, scooping the boy up into his arms. "Buck is bringing us a whole bunch of people." He rubbed the thick dark curls that covered Ryan's head.

"I hope we aren't making a mistake," Jessica said, nervously twisting her hands. She'd been married less than two months to Devon, and now they were opening Windridge as a resort ranch. "I mean, maybe you were right. Maybe we should never have let this thing get this far."

Devon eyed her with a raised brow and laughed. "Now you're willing to listen to me?"

Jessica shook her head. "Oh Devon, did we make the wrong decision?" She could see the stage approaching and knew that within a few minutes, total strangers would descend on their steps.

"Remember why you thought to do this in the first place?"

Jessica nodded. "I thought it would make a quiet respite."

"Not only that, but you saw it as the perfect opportunity to share God with other folks."

"But what if they don't like it here?"

Devon shrugged. "What if they don't? We have the partnership intact with the Rocking W, and it'll only be another year or so before we're completely solvent."

"Maybe we shouldn't have taken on all those cattle," Jessica said. "I mean you had to hire all those hands, and now we've got these people coming and—"

Devon put his finger to her lips, and Ryan leaned over to follow suit by placing his pudgy hand against her mouth. "Mama, peoples comin' to see me."

Jessica pulled back and smiled. "All right. I get your point. We can't do anything about it now. The guests are already here."

"Exactly. Let's give it a try. We've got a full summer ahead of us with plenty of folks who want to see what a dude ranch is all about. Let's just wait and see what happens. We might both be so happy to be done with it by the end of summer that we'll never even want to consider doing this another year."

"I suppose you're right," Jessica replied.

"I've no doubt people will find this place a blessing," Devon said. "I know I have."

Jessica sighed. "So have I."

Buck approached with the stage-styled carriage and brought the horses to a stop not ten feet from the front walk.

"Well, they're here," Devon said, shifting Ryan in his arms.

"Peoples here, Mama!" Ryan called and clapped his hands.

Jessica laughed at his enthusiasm. Through the open windows of the carriage, Jessica could hear animated conversation between the passengers. She couldn't make out the words, but knew that soon enough she'd probably hear plenty from her guests. Just then, Buck scrambled down from the driver's seat and positioned the stepping platform for the passengers. The door opened, and to Jessica's surprise the passengers poured out arguing— bickering over something that Jessica couldn't quite make out.

"Well, here are your people," Devon said, leaning close to whisper. "Looks like they could use a good dose of peace and quiet."

She nodded. "I suppose we'd better welcome them before they kill each other."

She stepped forward and rang a triangular bell that hung at the edge of the porch. The metallic ring caused everyone to fall into silence and give her their full attention.

Jessica gave them what she hoped was her friendliest smile. "Good afternoon. I'm Jessica Carter, and this is my husband, Devon, and son, Ryan. We'd like to welcome you to the house on Windridge."

Tracie Peterson, bestselling, award-winning author of over ninety fiction titles and three non-fiction books, lives and writes in Belgrade, Montana. As a Christian, wife, mother, writer, editor, and speaker (in that order), Tracie finds her slate quite full.

Published in magazines and Sunday school take home papers, as well as a columnist for a Christian newspaper, Tracie now focuses her attention on novels. After signing her first contract with Barbour Publishing in 1992, her novel, *A Place To Belong*, appeared in 1993 and the rest is history. She has over twenty-six titles with Heartsong Presents' book club (many of which have been repackaged) and stories in six separate anthologies from Barbour. From Bethany House Publishing, Tracie has multiple historical three-book series as well as many stand-alone contemporary women's fiction stories and two non-fiction titles. Other titles include two historical series co-written with Judith Pella, one historical series co-written with James Scott Bell, and multiple historical series co-written with Judith Miller.

Lucy's Quilt

by Joyce Livingston

Enjoy Your
Bonus Story

Chapter 1

Dove City, Kansas, 1862

"Hello, Mrs. Martin." Stone Piper removed his hat as he entered the lobby of Dove City's only hotel. A large but crudely built structure on Main Street, it sat a few doors down from the general store. "Beautiful morning, isn't it?"

Juliette Baker Martin looked up from the ledger and smiled. "Yes, Mr. Piper, a beautiful morning indeed. Much too pretty to be working inside. What brings you to town on a day like this?"

The man fumbled around in his shirt pocket, pulled out a small white hanky, and held it out to her. "I—ah—wanted you—I thought you—"

She eyed him suspiciously as she lowered her pen, closed the ledger, and rose with a slightly guarded smile. She couldn't help but notice his weathered hand as she took the hanky from him. The finely woven threads seemed out of place balanced on his calloused fingers. "Wherever did you get such a lovely handkerchief?" Upon closer inspection, she noted the lace edge was a bit worn, but the intricate embroidery remained in perfect condition. His delicate gift and his gangly frame seemed incongruous.

"It belonged to Lucy, my wife," he stated simply.

His gaze met hers, and she thought it quite sad. Her heart went out to him. She knew she'd never be able to get over the grief of losing her own beloved husband. The pain was ever present. Certainly, Mr. Piper was feeling the same kind of pain.

"I've—I've been going through some of her things. Should've done it long ago. I—ah—thought you might like to have it. You being such a lady and all..." His voice trailed off as if he had no idea how to finish his sentence.

She felt a sympathetic smile work at her lips as she unfolded the pristine cloth square and allowed her fingers to trace its delicate surface. "Lucy? What a pretty name."

Juliette knew he was at least fifteen years older than she. A friend of her father's, he was a widower and had two small sons living with his sister in Missouri. But according to her father, the man rarely talked about his past.

She smiled at the wrinkles in his shirt and the torn knee on his trousers. *He may be better off than most of us, but his clothing certainly doesn't show it.* It was obvious the man never shirked when it came to hard work and physical labor. The ladies in her sewing circle had said his spread was quite grand by Dove City standards, though she'd never seen it for herself. It wouldn't be proper for a woman of her status to visit a man's home unless accompanied by her parents.

Interested in Stone Piper or not, she had to admit her curiosity about Carson Creek Ranch. It sounded like the place of her dreams. A fine house, acres of timber, and the Neosho River flowing through it. No doubt, Mr. Piper had several fine horses. One day she was going to have a place like his, with her own fine horse to ride. Maybe two horses—one for her, another for Andrew. How or when she didn't know.

Looking back on her life, she wondered what would have happened if she hadn't married so young? Or had little Andrew when she was barely nineteen? What if she'd been single when she'd come west with her family instead of a widow with an infant to care for and support? Would her life have been so different? So hard?

"Ma'am?" His eyes lowered as his fingers moved nervously around the brim of his hat.

She felt a flush rise to her cheeks as she realized her mind had wandered far away from their conversation. "You—you were telling me about your wife? Lucy?"

"Yes, Lucy. She was as pretty as her name," he said proudly with a wistful smile that brought crinkles to his ruddy cheeks. "I should've gone through her things long ago, but—" He swallowed hard. "But I just couldn't bring myself to do it."

She was embarrassed. How rude he must have thought her to let her mind wander like that when he spoke of such personal things.

"You—you must have loved her deeply," Juliette stammered as she refolded the handkerchief and returned it to the thoughtful man. Until now, she hadn't noticed how tall he was or how kind his deep-set blue eyes seemed. "Thank you, Mr. Piper, but—"

"Stone," he interjected quickly, then cleared his throat. "Call me Stone. Everyone does." He leaned against the counter with a friendly smile, the sadness she'd detected now replaced with warmth.

"Stone," she echoed nervously, feeling unworthy to be the recipient of such a personal gift. Her gaze locked with his as once more she extended the handkerchief toward him. "I can't accept something like this. Your daughters may someday want—"

"Don't have no daughters and don't rightly think there's any in my future. Only have sons." He held up a flattened palm between them. "Please, Mrs. Martin. Keep it. Lovely things should belong to a lovely lady."

Juliette felt another flush rush to her cheeks as she twisted the simple gold wedding band on her left hand. No one had called her *lovely* in a long time. Not since David—

"It'd be my pleasure, ma'am, if you'd keep it."

When she met his earnest gaze, he was smiling convincingly. "Well—if you're sure you want me to have it. I hate to see you let something this lovely out of your family—"

He glanced quickly around the lobby, then leaned forward as if to share a secret. With a mischievous smile that seemed out of character for a man of his size, he whispered, "Oh, but I'm not intending to let it out of the family."

She frowned. "I don't understand, Mr. Pi—Stone."

To her surprise, he took her hand in his and gave it a slight squeeze. "I'm gonna ask your father, him being my friend, if it'd be alright for you and me to get married."

Juliette caught her breath sharply, dazed by his declaration. Could he be teasing? *Surely he isn't serious.* She had no idea how she should respond. "Ma–married?" she echoed as she stared up into eyes the color of the sky.

He gave her hand another squeeze, then turned to take his leave. "Not now, but soon. Don't let any other man claim you."

Smitten speechless, Juliette watched him go, then dropped onto the horsehair sofa near the hotel's fireplace, her knees suddenly unable to hold her weight, the dainty handkerchief still clutched in her hand. Had she heard Stone Piper right? Had he said he wanted to marry her? Whatever could he have meant by such a ridiculous remark? What an odd thing to say.

~

"When I get married, I'm going to marry a rich man," Caroline declared as she whirled about the room, holding baby Steven in her outstretched arms as the baby squealed with delight. "I'm going to have a big house with beautiful furniture, and—"

"While you're dreaming, little sister, dream up a rich man for me too," Juliette taunted with a grin that she knew made her dimples evident. If she dared put any stock in Mr. Piper's declaration, she wouldn't be needing any of her sister's dreams—not that she intended to take him up on his proposal. "I'll take a house, too. Only much bigger. With lots of land and trees and a river running through it, and—"

Caroline laughed aloud, her chocolate-brown eyes twinkling. "Whoa! Why don't you ask for the moon and the stars, too? Come on, big sister, you'd better plan on settling for much less. You'll never find a man who can give you all of those things."

Juliette grabbed up her baby sister and rose quickly with a royal tilt of her chin. She whirled around the room in the same dizzying pattern as Caroline. "Maybe we can be neighbors and ride around in fine carriages, our babies on our laps, while other women do our work. That'd be mighty fine. Don't you agree?"

Caroline stopped laughing and appeared wounded. "Now you're making fun of me."

Juliette grew serious as she stopped twirling and stood staring at her. "Not fun of you, Caroline. It's just that our dreams will most likely not become a reality. Life here on the prairie is hard for most folks. Very few came with an abundance of money in their pockets. We've been fortunate to live in this fine hotel. If our father hadn't been an educated man, he would've never gotten the job as hotel manager. We can thank the good Lord for that."

"I know," Caroline agreed thoughtfully. "But I'm keeping hold of my dreams. Someday—well, who knows what'll happen?"

Juliette glanced up the stairway. "Where's that sister of ours? We could use Molly's help with these tired babies."

"Molly's helping Mother change the beds. I told her to come down when she's finished, but you know how forgetful eight year olds can be. She's probably playing with her doll."

Juliette balanced her baby sister precariously on one hip and pulled aside the lace panel curtain covering the hotel's front window. It was nearly opaque with Kansas dust.

"I checked on Andrew. He's still asleep." Reuben leaned over the stair's railing, crunching on an apple.

"Thanks," Juliette said as she smiled at him. "Let me know when that son of mine wakes up."

Reuben nodded before heading back up the stairs, taking two steps at a time.

Caroline hoisted her crying sibling to her shoulder and moved behind Juliette for a better look. "What's all the shouting?"

Juliette cocked her head and listened. "I don't know, but something is wrong. I can sense it. Think you can take care of the twins by yourself for a few minutes? I'll go find out."

Caroline nodded. "I think what they both need is a good nap, but go ahead. I'll manage. Hopefully, Molly will come and help me."

Juliette gathered her skirts about her and hurried through the hotel lobby and onto the street, which had suddenly become as quiet as a watering pond on a still day in June. The few Dove City citizens who were out and about stood motionless, their gaze fixed on the end of Main Street. She hurried to join old Mrs. Pickford, jostling the woman's ribbon-trimmed bonnet in the process. "What is it, Bertha?" Juliette

157

asked as she placed a hand on the older woman's shoulder.

A worried frown twisted Bertha's wrinkled face as she answered with one word. "Kaws."

"The Kansa Indians?" Juliette asked quickly, remembering how her father had told her *Kaws* was the white man's term for the tribe. It wasn't unusual for Indians to be in the area. Whatever caused the woman's concern? She edged forward for a better look.

"Go back inside," a stern voice ordered somewhere behind her. She recognized it immediately without having to turn. It was her father. She knew better than to challenge his bidding, but she was concerned for the safety of her family. She continued to stare down Main Street at the approaching band of Indians, maybe one hundred strong, who were riding into town, all painted, feathered, and equipped for war. A chill of fear coursed through her body and caused a shudder. She'd never seen the Indians in war paint, and the sight frightened her.

"Now," her father ordered, and this time his tone was harsh as his long fingers dug into her shoulders. He spun her around. "Send Reuben out. We may need him."

She backed away slowly. Would her father never realize his eldest daughter had grown up? She was no longer a child but a woman. A mother with the responsibilities of an infant son, and part of that responsibility was to keep him safe. How could she keep him safe if she didn't know what was going on?

"Now, child," he commanded, his voice unwavering as he stared her down. "You heard me."

She nodded before taking a final glance at the cloud of dust filtering up around the hooves of the horses that came to a sudden halt in front of the general store. Muttering to herself about the inequities of life, she hurried obediently back into the hotel.

"Kaws," she explained with a frown of concern as she entered, snatching up her baby sister. "I'm scared, Caroline, and I know Father is, too. It looks like they're on the warpath."

Caroline's hand flew to her mouth, and she let out a loud gasp. "But why?"

The lace curtains parted again as Juliette peered out, her nose pressed against the glass, Stella wrapped securely in her arms.

"Which one of you girls wants to change Andrew's diaper? He don't smell so good." Reuben held the giggling infant at arm's length and turned his head away.

Juliette wrinkled her nose, quickly placed her baby sister onto the pallet, and reached toward her tiny son, the offensive-smelling baby she loved more than life itself. In all the excitement, she'd nearly forgotten her father's request. "Reuben," she informed her younger brother quickly, "you'd better hurry outside. Father wants you. The Kaws are wearing war paint."

Reuben rushed toward the lobby door. "You girls stay in here where it's safe," he called back over his shoulder.

"You girls stay in here where it's safe," Juliette mimicked as she stooped to scoop her gurgling son out in his crib. "It's not fair, Caroline. I'm scared, and I want to know what's going on."

Her sister's eyes widened as she pointed a finger in Juliette's direction. "You'd better not let Father hear you talk like that."

"I'm nineteen years old," Juliette retorted with a lift of her chin and a shake of her head. "I should be able to go out onto the porch if I want to. I'm concerned about my son. How can I keep him safe if I don't even know what's happening out there?"

"As long as you're living under our father's roof, he'll expect you to do as he says." Caroline shifted Steven to her hip and moved to the window.

"It's not that I want to defy Father, Caroline. But I'm a mother now. It's my responsibility to keep my child safe, and I'm worried about you and mother and our brothers and sisters." Juliette clasped her fingers around her baby's thick ankles, lifted his plump legs, and placed a clean square of cloth under his bottom. "Someday, when I get married and have my own home, I'll be able to do as I please." As if on cue, Stone Piper's unexpected words flooded her mind. *"I'm gonna ask your father, him being my friend, if it'd be alright for you and me to get married."*

Caroline turned from the window and placed Stella on the pallet beside Steven. "Another husband? What man would want to take on a woman with a six-month-old baby?"

"Plenty of men," Juliette responded quickly, tempted to tell Caroline of the morning's strange experience with the wealthy rancher. "I could've found one by now if I hadn't been so busy helping with this hotel and taking care of Andrew." She leaned toward the baby and planted a kiss on the tip of his tiny, pert nose. She loved caring for him and knew she was a good mother, but raising a baby in her father's home, in the midst of a large family with twin babies, was not an easy task. She'd much prefer to be on her own, but the meager salary she earned at her father's hotel ruled out that possibility.

Although the sisters couldn't see what was going on outside, they could hear it. The sound of nagging horses and agitated voices rose to peak level.

"I'm going out there just for a minute," Juliette announced as she handed her son to her sister. "Think you can keep an eye on the three of them? They're a pretty big handful. We need to know what's going on out there, and since no one has seen fit to come and tell us—"

Caroline reached out and clasped her hand around Juliette's wrist. "But Father said—"

Juliette pulled away and placed Andrew in the crib she'd bought to keep in the lobby so he could be near her when she worked. "I'm only going to have a quick look. Can I trust you to keep a close watch on my son?"

Caroline nodded. "You know you can."

Juliette moved through the lobby and out the door, doing a quick search of the area. Her attention went to the Indian's leader and Thomas Ward, whom she recognized immediately. Mr. Ward was a bachelor and the owner of the general store. He and Blue Feather were having a heated exchange of words.

She pressed herself against the clapboard siding on the hotel front and moved a bit closer, clutching her skirts.

"You'd better get back inside, Juliette." It was Harrison Rogers, the young man who had accompanied the Baker family on their trip to

Kansas from Ohio, and he was standing behind her.

"Mind your business, Harrison," she retorted with a cold stare and a shrug. Harrison was a nice young man and overly protective of her sometimes, even though they were nearly the same age. She was sure he was sweet on her, despite the fact that she was a widow with an infant to care for. He'd paid an inordinate amount of attention to her on the trail. But when and if she married again, it would be to a rich man—not to a mere boy seeking his fortune in this new land, no matter how nice he was.

"I heard your pa tell you to stay inside." His hand moved to the small of her back as he gave her a gentle shove in the direction of the hotel.

Her hands flew to her hips, and she stepped away from him. "If you tell Father, I'll—"

His hand caught her wrist, and his eyes twinkled mischievously as he leaned into her face. "You'll what? Kiss me?"

With a lifted brow and a coy smile—just coy enough to keep him obliged to her—she answered, "Kiss you? No, but I might be persuaded to do one of your chores for you. If you don't tattle on me. I need to see what's happening, Harrison. I have a son to worry about and need to keep him safe. You do understand, don't you?"

Harrison gave her a quick wink. "All right, just be careful and promise me you'll go back inside if any trouble starts."

She nodded. He was a nice boy but much too young, and he had nothing to offer her but himself and poverty, and she wanted neither. Maybe he'd be a good husband for Caroline, but not for her. "I promise."

Harrison gave her a grin of acceptance, then headed down to join some of the other boys his age who had gathered across the street from the confrontation.

Her heart clenched with sadness. How she wished David could have lived to see the Kansas prairie. He'd wanted so much to come to this territory. Too bad he'd never had that opportunity. Although at times she seemed ungrateful, she knew if it were not for her parents' willingness to take on the responsibility of a widowed daughter with a new baby, she would've been left behind with her father's sister. For that, she'd always be grateful. Life with her stern, maiden aunt would have been intolerable. If only there were some way she could repay her parents for all they'd done for her and her son.

As the voices of the Indian leader and Thomas Ward rose to an angry pitch, she strained to keep up with the words hastily being shouted by the interpreter.

"You sent for these two horses, which my boys stole from a Mexican trader," he told them as he translated the leader's words to the crowd. "You sent word that we must not only give up the horses, but we must turn over to you the two men who stole the horses, that your people might punish them." The leader's bony finger pointed menacingly toward the white man as he spoke.

Thomas Ward stood motionless and waited as he listened to what Mr. Claude Egan said as he acted as interpreter.

"The horses you can have, but the men you cannot have without a fight," Mr. Egan interpreted to the assembled group with exaggerated motions. "That's what he said."

"Who is he?" a woman asked a man standing beside her. "Is he the chief?"

He shrugged. "If you ask me, he's nuthin' but a troublemaker."

Juliette shuddered. It was common knowledge the Indians were not happy with the land settlement they'd been given by the government, and their discontent seemed to grow stronger with each passing day. Although the Indians were basically friendly, they would occasionally steal the settlers' horses and whatever else they could get their hands on if they thought they could do so without detection. The stealing of another man's horses was not taken lightly. A man could be hanged for such a crime.

Although she knew she should be heading back inside the hotel, she lingered long enough to see Thomas Ward's reaction to the Indian's statement. It appeared Mr. Ward was controlling himself as best he could. She'd heard he'd had many dealings with the Indians, and he seemed to know better than anyone how to handle them. But since the Indians had apparently come prepared to have a showdown, it appeared they had the advantage. Fear gripped her heart as she thought of her son, so young, so innocent, so undeserving of what might happen if an agreement couldn't be reached.

For some time, Mr. Ward stood silently, making no comment to Blue Feather's statement as the crowd waited for his response.

Juliette crossed her arms over her chest protectively and hunched her shoulders. What if the Indians decide to attack? There were so few men living in Dove City. Most of the men of the area were either farmers or ranchers and only came to town when they needed to make a purchase, have horses shod, or to attend church or a funeral. Some came to spend their time and hard-earned money in the noisy saloon.

She and the other onlookers stared in fear as Blue Feather and his followers began to taunt and insult the settlers.

Through the interpreter, she heard the Indian leader tell Thomas Ward and the others they had no business meddling with things that did not concern them. *Not concern us? When we're trying to live peaceably with the Kaw Indians? Of course we're concerned,* she reasoned uneasily.

Mr. Ward continued to listen, his fists clenched at his sides as if he were struggling for control, as everyone watched for his reaction to the Indian's accusing words. He turned slowly to his clerk, who was cowering beside him, his face a sickly pallor, and loudly instructed him to bring two revolvers from his store.

Juliette and the others who remained watched spellbound, their hearts filled with fear as the clerk arrived with the guns and handed them to Thomas Ward one at a time. Slowly, he glanced around at the small crowd of citizens as if to assure them he was doing the right thing. His glance roved back to the Indians, now menacingly scattered about the area. Then back to Blue Feather. Everyone held their breath as he slowly lifted the two guns.

Boom! Boom! He fired two shots into the air as he glared at the leader, his eyes fixed on the man's painted face.

"Why'd he do that?" the woman asked as she buried her face in her companion's chest.

Juliette wondered the same thing. *What is his purpose? There's no way Mr. Ward can take on that large band of Indians with only two revolvers.*

"I'm sure it was to scare the Indians and show them he means business," the man explained as he stroked his wife's shoulder reassuringly. "But the main reason was to warn the settlers to get armed and be ready for whatever might occur."

Of course, Juliette thought as she searched the crowd for her father. *He did it to alert the settlers who aren't here. Word of the shots will spread rapidly, and men will drop whatever they're doing and come to help. I should have realized Mr. Ward would never do anything to jeopardize our lives.*

"Are they going to attack us?" the woman asked, her teary eyes filled with fright.

"Umm, I think they're only trying to outfox Ward," the man explained, never taking his gaze from the scene.

One of the warriors moved quickly to the front of the crowd, allowing his horse to trample those in his path. He lifted his bow in the air and let out a war cry that chilled Juliette's bones. It appeared he was taking it upon himself to lead his red brothers into battle, disregarding Blue Feather and his followers. As his horse whinnied and stood on its hind legs, the man ordered in his native tongue with Claude Egan translating, "Ward is shooting at us. Shoot him!"

With fear etched on their faces, the crowd of frantic men and women began rushing past Juliette as they struggled to escape the threat. She knew she should leave, but she was frozen to the spot, needing to know what happened. Once more, she pressed herself against the building, her eyes wide with terror, her heart thundering against her chest, her attention riveted on Thomas Ward. But to her amazement, he simply shrugged, turned his back on the aggressors, and moved into his store, shutting the door securely behind him.

Her glance flitted quickly toward where her father had been standing with Reuben, but they were nowhere in sight. Although she was relieved, she was also concerned. Her father knew almost nothing of the ways of the Indians or how they conducted their wars. He'd never been called upon during their time in Ohio to bear arms against anyone. He was a kind and gentle man with peaceful ways. Though he'd owned several guns, she'd never seen him use them. Yet, she knew if it became necessary, her father would take up arms and do all he could to protect his family. *Oh Father, where are you?*

It was then she spotted them. Harrison had joined them, and the three had moved up directly behind where Mr. Ward had been standing. She was even more concerned for their safety. There was a fourth man she could barely make out in the swirling dust from the horses' hooves. It was Stone Piper, and she found herself concerned for his safety as well.

Some of the young bloods among the Indian band, those who seemed more restless than the others and eager to do battle, fired their guns. Charles Stark, the owner of the hotel her father managed, received a well-aimed arrow in the lower part of his neck.

Juliette gasped and watched in horror as the bleeding man twisted and fell to the ground. Never had she seen death happen so quickly. Her stomach lurched, and she thought she was going to be sick.

Another man she recognized as Mr. Morgan tried to cross the street. He was hit by one of the Indian's bullets, fell close to Mr. Stark, and lay motionless in a widening circle of his own blood.

Everything happened so fast. Shouted threats. Arrows. Gunshots. Screaming Indians. Horses rearing. People fleeing for their very lives. Never would she have believed this sort of confrontation possible in the quiet, friendly town they'd settled in only months before. She wanted to run to Mr. Morgan in the street to see if he was still alive, if he could be helped. But that was impossible. As she neared the safety of the hotel and pushed her way toward the doorway, she breathed a quick prayer of thanks. But as she was about to enter, Juliette turned to listen as she heard the terrified voice of the interpreter.

He was calling out loudly to the Indians in a vengeful tone that resonated through the emptying street as he pointed his long, slender finger at Blue Feather. "Your people have killed one man, maybe two. Get out of this town. Now!"

Blue Feather lifted his spear, and with a shout that echoed against the buildings, he led the band back up Main Street, leaving enough dust behind to choke the breath out of those still standing in the street.

"What? Tell me!" Caroline screamed as Juliette appeared in the doorway. "Did someone die?"

All strength drained from Juliette's body as she snatched her precious Andrew from his sleeping place, her eyes widened from the deaths she'd just witnessed. As she cradled her son to her breast, she lifted a tear-stained face to her sister. "Oh Caroline, what's to become of us?"

Chapter 2

Juliette and Caroline kept vigil at the window. Three long hours passed before their father and Reuben returned to the hotel lobby. Their faces told the story. Things did not look good.

"John, what happened to you? We were so worried!" Juliette's mother made her way to her husband and rested her head on his chest. "Juliette said Charles Stark was shot."

Her father sent a quick, accusing glare at Juliette, and she knew he would have preferred to tell his frail wife about Charles Stark's death himself.

"His death was quick. He didn't suffer." He cradled his wife's head in his big hand and stroked her cheek with the pad of his thumb. "We'll all miss him."

Her mother began to weep. "He has such a lovely family. How will they ever get along without him?"

"I don't know. Charles was a good man."

"What about the other man, Father?" Caroline asked.

"I don't know about the other man."

"Where have you been all this time? Surely you weren't out in the street when all this happened, were you?" her mother asked as she lifted her face and lovingly wiped a smear of dirt from his cheek. "The children and I were—"

"I know. I never meant to worry you. I should've sent word back with Juliette." He sent a frown Juliette's way, and she knew he'd seen her in the street after he'd ordered her back inside.

"Reuben and Harrison and I were with Deputy Piper and the other men. After the Indians left, we checked out the high ground south of Elm Creek, where the tribe had been camped."

"Did you find them?" Caroline asked. "Were they still wearing their war paint?"

"No, we didn't find them. We're assembling a council to determine what to do next. There weren't enough men in town to offer much resistance. I'm afraid the Indians knew it. We must thank God they left without causing further death or damage."

Juliette watched as her father once again forced a confident smile. "A call has gone out to those who live around here as well as the neighboring counties. We've asked all who can to hasten to Dove City as soon as possible." He swallowed hard, then added, "Prepared to fight."

Tears rolled down her mother's cheeks as she grasped his shirt. "Oh John. No, not you. You're not a soldier. You must stay here at the hotel with us. We need you."

He lowered his head, his eyes focused on his wife. "The vote was unanimous. As men, we must protect our families."

Her mother drew in a deep breath and burst into tears as the rest of the family stood by silently, sickened by their father's words. "Oh John. No. Not war."

He nodded as he once again began to stroke his wife's hair. "War seems inevitable. The sheriff's taking care of some trouble over at Heaton. But Deputy Piper is a good man, and the Indians seem to respect him. He'll lead us, and Egan is coming along as our interpreter. They're good, honest men, and both have had experience in dealing with the Indians. They don't want war any more than the rest of us. But Mary, we have to make a stand."

Her grasp on his shirt tightened. "If you wait until tomorrow, more of the men can join you, and it won't be so dangerous. Please, John. Wait."

Lovingly, he pried her fingers away and pulled her into the shelter of his arms. "We can't wait, Mary," he said resolutely, his chin held high. "They might attack. Both Thomas Ward and Egan agree with Stone Piper."

Juliette stepped around the pallet and caught hold of her father's arm. "But why, Father? You said the Indians were gone."

"From what Deputy Piper said, we need to go out to scout their move. Perhaps they've only gone as far as Dry Bed Creek. That's too close for the comfort of the good people of Dove City."

With a heavy sigh, her mother leaned forward and took Stella from Caroline's arms.

Juliette watched as her father smiled, then chucked the baby under her chin as he continued, his face sobering. "The council believes if the Kaws are allowed to go unpunished for the outrage they've committed, there'll be no safety for any of us."

"You're going to follow them?" her mother asked as she hugged her baby, tears again trickling down her cheeks.

He didn't have to tell them. The answer was written on his weary face. "Pray for me, Mary. Please, pray for me like you've never prayed. If we've ever needed God's help, it's now."

∽

"I've never been to war before," John Baker confided to Stone as they rode along. The heavy dust their horses kicked up dried their throats. "I'm not sure if I could shoot a man, even if he was a renegade Indian."

Stone shifted his weight in the well-worn saddle, his gaze intent on the trail stretching out before him. "Oh, you'd shoot him all right, John, if you had to. If it was your life or his or if he meant harm to one of your loved ones." He shielded his eyes and peered off in the distance toward a heavy clump of trees that could easily hide a warring band of Indians.

"Could you do it?"

Stone pushed his hat off his brow and wiped the sweat from his forehead. "Only if I had to." A bird sounded a mournful cry, and both men turned in its direction, listening carefully before resuming their conversation. They feared the whistle might not be a bird's, but an Indian's. A pair of rabbits leaped from their hiding place in the tall grass and scurried across the trail in front of them. "I pray to God I won't be faced with that decision."

They rode along in silence, the drumming of forty sets of horses' hooves beating down the prairie grasses the only sound. None of the riders seemed to have much to say as each kept his eyes trained dead ahead toward Dry Bed Creek, which lay off in the distance beyond the dense grove of trees.

Stone took in a deep breath of the warm morning air. "Those redskins could be watching us right now."

"You know the Indians better than I do." John shrugged and tightened the grip on his reins.

He didn't want to say anything to John, but he was concerned about the womenfolk and children they'd left behind in Dove City. Undoubtedly, the Indians knew their number and could, if they were of a mind to, send some braves back into town to— He didn't even want to think what they might do. "Long enough to know you can't trust most of these Indians. I can't say that I blame them much."

"Oh?" John's brows rose in question.

"Not the way the government handled the land acquisitions. The Indians think they got a raw deal. Sometimes I'm inclined to agree with them."

John frowned. "But does that give them the right to take what they want? Even kill?"

Stone shook his head and spat on the ground. "Course not. But those Kaws didn't want to come here in the first place. They'd have rather stayed near Topeka, along the Kansas River. It was the government's idea to bring them to Dove City, even promised the Indians the choice land along the upper valley of the Neosho River, where the tall timber grows."

"You'd have thought they'd have been happy with that," John reasoned aloud. "Good land and abundant water. What more could they ask?"

"Oh, that's what they were promised but not what they got. Too many problems with some messed up survey, and a lot of the settlers homesteaded on Indian lands by mistake." Stone ordered a halt. The troop of inexperienced would-be soldiers stopped abruptly. Everyone peered off into the distance at the approaching band of riders.

Stone glanced over his shoulder as his hand moved instinctively to the holster mounted at his side. "Kaws. Keep your peace, men," he called out to his troops. "We don't want to anger them."

Forty men sat straddling their horses as fear shone in forty sets of eyes.

The Indians began to circle them, posting themselves to the best advantage—tantalizing the men, goading them, and beckoning them to come on and fight.

"I'd like to shoot that miserable—" one of the riders positioned next to Stone told him under his breath just loud enough for those closest to him to hear.

Stone remained motionless but cautioned, "Don't even think it. They want us to start something. These Indians have been trained from boyhood to fight. We wouldn't stand a chance. One move from us, and it's all over. Keep your peace, man. Keep your peace."

The man settled himself back into his saddle and said nothing more. Apparently Stone's message had brought him to his senses.

"Are we going to just sit here and wait for them to kill us?" John asked nervously, his eyes trained on the circling renegades.

Stone whispered to his interpreter, "Egan, I think we'd better send someone out to talk to the Indians and try to reason with them to avert further bloodshed. Looks to me like we're at their mercy."

Mr. Egan listened intently. "I agree with you. Getting them stirred up won't help anything. Perhaps talking will. Let me have a try. I'll ask for a peaceful settlement of this dispute and let them know that a war between our two factions will mean loss to both sides. I'll tell them, if that happens, the government will certainly step in and take measures of its own."

Stone nodded. "Do it."

Egan slowly rode toward the Indian who appeared to be in charge, and the two talked in hushed tones.

"It's not working. They're not backing off," John muttered as his fingers clutched the reins.

"True. But they're not making any warlike moves either," Stone reminded him. "That's a good sign. Let's hope our man can convince them nothing good can come to them by attacking us."

Taking his gaze off the pair for only a second, Stone singled out two of the younger men. "Ride back to Dove City as quickly as your horses can carry you, and tell the others of what's happening. Tell them we need reinforcements as soon as possible. Our negotiations here seem to be at a standstill."

Without a questioning word, the two men rode off.

"All we can do is wait," Stone whispered. "Wait and pray."

⌐

"I wish I were there." Juliette's fist banged against the counter. "I hate being left behind and not knowing what's happening, especially when it could be affecting our very lives."

"But you're a woman. You know what they could do to you—"

"Not if I had my gun," Juliette responded resolutely with narrowed eyes and a defiant tilt of her chin. "I'd do whatever was necessary to protect my son and the rest of my family."

"Your gun? You don't have a gun," her sister reminded her. "You've never even shot a gun, have you?"

Someone stormed into the hotel and announced the Kaw mission had been opened as a temporary shelter for those families waiting for their husbands and fathers to return.

"Now, what were you saying about having a gun?" Caroline asked as many of the hotel's overflow of occupants headed out the door.

"I don't have a gun, Caroline. If I were a boy, I'd have a gun."

Caroline shook her head.

⌐

The troop of forty men grew to nearly two hundred as groups of armed men on horseback rode out from Dove City and Clacker County to join the others. With their addition, confidence grew among the settlers.

"I think we should try to talk to them again, Egan," Stone advised as he made his way up to their interpreter's side.

"I agree." Egan brought his horse closer to Stone's and tugged on the reins. "I'm hopeful I can get through to them. I know the Indians personally. I've had their children in school. Surely they know we're a peaceful people, and we're trying to avoid any more bloodshed."

Stone put a hand on the man's shoulder. "You do know the risk,

Egan? They could kill you just like that." He snapped his fingers for emphasis. "Since we're still outnumbered, we'd be hard-pressed to do much about it. But I have faith in you. I know those Indians look up to you. I think you're the only one who can negotiate with them effectively."

Egan pulled his hat lower on his brow. "I'll do my best."

There was a space of about two hundred yards between where the white men halted and where the Kansa Indians had taken up their position. Stone knew, from the Indians' vantage point, they could see more reinforcements arriving on the settlers' side. He hoped they would be dissuaded from taking any action they'd all regret later. *God, I know I have no right to ask this, but if You hear me, make them listen to reason. We don't want war.*

The settlers formed a consolidated line as Egan made his move to speak to Blue Feather a second time. Each man stood ready to advance at the first indication of treachery. Mr. Egan was met by the chief, and the two men talked in low tones.

The entire troop watched with heightened interest as the chief called together his key men into a guarded circle, where they spoke. He then relayed their decision to Egan, who hurried back to Stone and the others.

"They'll surrender the Indian who shot Morgan but not the one who shot Stark. They say they are not sure which man wounded him."

"Do you believe him?" Stone asked.

"No," came Egan's quick reply. "I think what they're doing is trying to save their young brave. I'm sure he's the one who shot Stark, but he serves on the council and appears to be of great value to the tribe."

Stone stroked his beard thoughtfully. "I think we're all in agreement here, Mr. Egan. Tell the chief we're not interested in such an arrangement. We'll accept nothing short of a surrender of the two Indians."

A hush fell over both the Indians and settlers as Egan spoke with Blue Feather. Within minutes, he was back with a new offer. "They say they'll pay us eight hundred dollars and forty ponies as satisfaction for the shooting of Stark, but I said no."

"And well you should have," Stone stated in quick response as his narrowed eyes surveyed the vast number of horses and riders who had gathered on his side. His troops now numbered over four hundred, and he was sure more were on their way. "We will take nothing less than the surrender of those two Indians."

Dread ran through the settlers as the young brave suddenly appeared before them, armed and prepared to fight, still wearing his war paint. As he spiraled his arm into the air and shouted to the others, Mr. Egan interpreted in a high-fevered pitch so all could hear. "He says, since they've decided to surrender him, thereby sanctioning his death, he'll sell his life as dearly as possible. If necessary, he'll kill his own chief, then the white man who demanded his surrender!"

Nodding, Stone signaled for his men to make ready but to hold their fire.

Although the brave's fiery speech seemed to stir up the other young braves, it appeared to have no obvious effect on the tribal elders, who held their silence. Yet, they seemed hesitant to give the man up.

Stone's hand moved to grip the saddle horn. He watched as Mr. Egan squared his shoulders and, once again, spoke to Blue Feather.

"Now what?" John asked, his penetrating look trained on the Indian chief and Egan.

Stone's gaze hardened. "Knowing Egan, I'm sure he's still trying to work something out. All we can do now is wait."

The settlers watched impatiently, still hoping for a resolution to the volatile situation. In a matter of minutes, Mr. Egan returned. "Their offer has increased to one thousand dollars and the horses." He removed his hat and slapped it against his leg, then shook his head wearily. "I told them they have committed an outrage upon the settlers and shed the blood of two innocent people. Unless both are given up, our men are determined to fight."

Hating to say the words but knowing they had to be said, Stone nodded. "You were right to tell them that. As much as we hate war, we are prepared to do battle if it becomes necessary. I'm sure they understand our position. What else did you tell them?"

"Sir, I told them if both Indians are not surrendered by the time I return to my people and count to twenty, the consequences rest upon them. I told them when I set my stick upon the ground, they will know I have finished my count."

Stone saluted Claude Egan and instructed, "Then go, Mr. Egan. Take your stick and count. When you have finished counting, set it upon the ground as you've said. We're ready."

"Lord, help us. They're not conceding," John declared loudly.

Stone could sense the fear in his voice and was sure John was preparing to die. He reached across and clamped his hand around his friend's arm. "Have faith. It's not over yet. But if we must do battle, let me lead the way. You're important to your family. Mine cares nothing about me."

John shook his head with a grateful smile. "Thanks, Stone. But I'll do my part in defending our families and friends. If you make it and I don't—" He hesitated and gulped. "Promise you'll tell my family I love them and I died to keep them safe."

Stone tightened his grip on the man's arm. "I will, John. I promise; but we're both going to make it, do you hear?"

All eyes focused on the courageous mediator as he slowly walked to the halfway mark, then loudly counted to twenty before placing the stick on the ground.

The silence was deafening. Even the birds stopped their singing as three hundred Indians and at least five hundred settlers sat on their horses, anticipating each other's next move.

Suddenly, in a loud, clear voice, the chief yelled out, "We're ready to give up the two guilty men."

A sigh of relief washed across the line as Mr. Egan quickly interpreted the Indian's words. Men smiled at one another and relaxed their grips on their weapons a bit.

"God has answered our prayer, Stone," John cried out as he heard the words of the chief. "We aren't going to have to fight."

Stone leaned forward on his horse and stroked the animal's mane. "I know, John. I know."

Minutes later, the guilty pair were brought forth, bound, and delivered to Deputy Piper.

"What happens now?" John asked Stone.

"They'll be put on their horses and ride back to town behind us. Probably go to trial."

"And death?"

Stone nodded. "Yes. Death."

⟳

"Any word yet?" Juliette asked as she picked up little Steven and hugged him. "It's been hours since our father left. I pray to God he's all right."

Caroline led her mother to the worn sofa and asked two ladies to scoot over so she could sit down between them.

"Having those twins on the trail is what ruined her health," Juliette told her sister, taking her aside so no one else could hear. "Father should never have allowed her to come to Kansas with us. The trip was too hard for her. He should've left her behind and gone back for her later."

Caroline backed off in surprise, cupping her hand to her mouth before replying. "Left her behind? You know she'd never stand for that. Father and Mother have rarely been separated since the day of their wedding."

"If you ask me, I think the idea of bringing a woman with child on such a long journey was stupid," Juliette said in a whisper as she brushed the dust from her skirt and straightened her bodice. "Especially one in bad health."

"But he didn't ask you," Caroline reminded her in a snit. "Look at you. Andrew was born not long before we left Ohio. Do you think Father should have left you behind?"

"Of course not," Juliette answered indignantly, finding it hard to keep her voice down. "That's different. I'm only thinking of our mother, Caroline. It makes me sad to see her feeling so poorly all the time."

One of the ladies, an elderly woman named Ethel Benningfield, moved from the sofa and made her way toward them. Her gaze concentrated on Juliette. "Dear," she began with a friendly smile, "please don't talk that way about your parents. I'm sure if your father had any doubt about bringing your mother along, he wouldn't have made the trip at all."

Surprised by the woman's words, Juliette simply stared at her.

"I know you mean well, but one should never criticize her parents' actions—especially someone with parents like yours. You're lucky to have them both with you. I lost mine in a fire when I was only nine."

"I–I'm so sorry," Juliette stammered, thinking back over what she'd said. "That must have been very difficult for you."

The woman touched Juliette's wrist as she smiled up into her eyes. "You have no idea how difficult. God has given you girls wonderful, godly parents. Love them while you still have them, and support them in everything they do. They always have your best interests at heart." With that, the woman turned and walked away.

"I didn't think anyone could hear us," Juliette whispered to Caroline. "But she's right. I should never have criticized Father for bringing Mother along. My mouth is always getting me in trouble."

One of the wives who'd moved outside earlier burst into the lobby. "They're coming! There's a terrible cloud of dust on the horizon."

Everyone hurried outside, hoping to see their loved ones returning. Juliette and Caroline followed close behind, carrying their siblings.

"Father has to be all right," Caroline said as she shielded her eyes from the afternoon sun. "It would kill Mother if anything happened to him."

"When I marry again, I'm going to be strong for my husband. I'm going to ride by his side as an equal. I won't let him leave me behind."

"Ha," her sister retorted. "You're just looking for trouble, Juliette. If Father heard you talk—"

"Well, I am," she broke in. "My husband will be proud to have a strong woman for a wife."

Caroline laughed aloud. "What husband? I haven't seen any men pursuing you lately, Mrs. Martin—rich or poor."

Juliette tucked an errant curl behind her ear. "That's because you haven't noticed. Only today," she bragged, "a man told me he was going to marry me."

"Who?"

Now she had her sister's full attention. "I'm not telling."

Caroline smirked. "Because you've made him up, that's why."

Juliette lifted her chin arrogantly. "Did not. He's a real man and a handsome one, too, I might add. And he has a beard."

Her sister moved closer. "Who, Juliette? Who? If he was real, you'd tell me his name."

"I'm not telling. It's our secret—his and mine."

Caroline cocked her head and looked dubious. "You wouldn't lie to me, would you?"

"Of course not. I don't lie. I can't stand people who lie."

"Then tell me who he is."

"Only when we're ready to announce our engagement."

Caroline's eyes grew bright with anticipation. "You mean you've accepted?"

Juliette thought for a minute. As usual, she'd said more than she'd intended. It was a nasty habit of hers, making more of something than it really was. Well, she'd backed herself into a corner, and her sister was waiting for an answer. She drew a deep breath, and deciding how much she could say without telling one of those lies she hated so much, she looked directly into her sister's eyes. "Not yet. I'm still thinking about it."

Chapter 3

Stone tugged his hat low on his brow with a relieved grin as he and John rode ahead of his men. "Well, things certainly look better now than they did this morning."

The look on John's face grew serious. "Better in some ways. Worse in others."

Stone's brow creased. "Worse? I don't understand."

"I may not have a job."

"Oh?" Stone responded. "Why'd you say that?"

John pulled off his hat and swatted at the sweat bee buzzing around his face. "Charles Stark owned the hotel. With him gone now, I have no idea what his family will do with it. His wife is too old to run the place, and his children have no interest in it. That's why he hired me. If I lose my job at the hotel, we won't even have a roof over our heads."

"You and your family can stay with me until you line something up. You're always welcome in my home. I've got plenty of room, even for your large family."

"And three squalling infants?"

Stone grinned. "Even them."

The group rode victoriously into town and stopped in front of the general store, filling the street to overflowing with relieved faces and renewed spirits. Women and children moved in to hug their husbands, fathers, and brothers and for a better look at the two Indian braves tied onto their horses.

"Hang them!" a voice shouted from the back of the crowd. "They killed Charley and Mr. Morgan. They deserve to die!"

The crowd took up the chant. "Hang them. Hang them."

Thomas Ward stepped out from his store and lifted his hand for silence. "Without a trial? You want these men hanged?"

"They didn't give Charley Stark a trial, and he hadn't done nothing to them," one of the older men called out as he shook a fist in the air. "I say hang them. Here and now."

"He's right," called out another. "Hang them."

Again the crowd took up the chant. "Hang them. Hang them."

Thomas Ward raised his arms in defeat as he called out loudly, "Then let their blood be on your hands!"

A pair of nooses were readied at an old cottonwood tree next to the bridge. The crowd, chanting and shouting, followed as the two men's horses were led to the spot.

In final protest, Thomas Ward stepped up onto a stump where all could see him and shouted to the crowd, "Should these men be hanged without a court? Or an attorney? Or without a judge to hear their case? Is that what you say?"

"There is no case," Mr. Stark's widow shouted. "They killed my husband, a good man. Now they deserve to die." Several of the younger men led the violators' horses beneath the nooses and slipped the loops over the Indians' heads as the shouts of the crowd spurred them on. Thomas Ward scanned the crowd again. "These men shed the blood of two white men who did them no injury, and justice demands they should suffer death. Is that what ye say?"

"Yes. Yes. Yes!" came the unanimous cry from the people.

Mr. Ward raised a fist into the air. "Then, so be it."

A hush of anticipation fell over the assembled throng. Mothers covered the eyes of impressionable children, and husbands wrapped their arms about sensitive wives. The certainty of impending death hung heavily in the air as every adult focused on the men whose demise was only seconds away.

Juliette felt a strong arm about her shoulders. It was Stone. At that moment, she needed the strength of a good man. About to witness her first hanging, the fiery independence she normally felt had been replaced with little-girl fear. As she felt his arms tighten around her, she leaned into him for support.

The robust crowd, who had earlier been so vocal, remained silent as they beheld death in the making. The same men who'd placed the nooses about the Indians' necks slapped the rumps of the Kaws' mounts. They took off in a run, leaving the braves dangling from the tree at the end of their ropes.

Life was a precious commodity. Everyone present had just been witness to the end of two young braves' existence. Their lives had been traded for the lives of Charles Stark and Mr. Morgan. Justice had been done.

"This is a sad day for Dove City," Stone whispered in Juliette's ear. "A sad day, indeed. One death is avenged with another, and the chain goes on. Where, oh where, will it all end?"

⌒

The day dawned gray, cool, and cloudy. It was as though nature itself mourned for the men who had died so needlessly at the Indians' hands.

Nearly all of Dove City's citizens attended the funeral of Charles Stark.

Juliette clutched Andrew tightly and tried not to cry as she agonized over the grief on Charles Stark's widow's and children's faces. Just being there among Mr. Stark's family and friends made her think of David and his funeral only a few short months before. "Your daddy loved you," she whispered as Andrew's pudgy fingers played at her lips.

"Anyone sitting here?"

Taken aback, she looked up into the clear blue eyes of her father's friend. Although she would have preferred the seat remain vacant, she shook her head. "No, no one."

Stone sat down beside her. "Then if it's all right with you, I'll be taking this seat."

He balanced his hat on one knee and whispered softly as he leaned toward her ever so slightly, "He was a good man."

"I know."

"Too bad about his death."

"Yes, it is." Filled with sudden, unexpected emotion, Juliette pulled a hanky from her bag and dabbed at her eyes.

"Should've been me."

She turned quickly and lifted her face to his. "What? What did you say?"

He swallowed hard as deep furrows formed on his forehead. "Been better if it'd been me instead of Stark."

Her eyes grew wide. Surely she'd misunderstood. "Why would you ever say such a thing?"

He let out a deep sigh. "Stark has people who'll miss him. No one would miss me."

Juliette found herself without words and simply stared at the man seated beside her.

"Seems God always takes the best for Himself and leaves the rest of us to mourn."

Before she could respond, Pastor Tyson stepped up and the service began. Men blinked and women wept as the scripture was read and the pastor spoke. After his message, several folks, including Stone and her father, said kind words about the man they'd come to bury. After that, Emma Fritz sang "Amazing Grace." There was not a dry eye in the huge room. By the time the final words were spoken, a heavy rain began to fall and lightning split the sky.

"You girls get the buggy and take your mother on home," John Baker told his daughters. "I'm afraid this has been too much for her."

"Can't Caroline and Molly take her, Father? I want to go on to the cemetery," Juliette explained as she stepped away from him. It was as though going to the cemetery would put an end to her grieving for David. She'd been so numb at his funeral, she could barely remember a word that had been said. Now, despite the tumultuous storm outside, she felt drawn to Lone Tree Cemetery. Perhaps there she could say the good-bye she felt she'd never said to David and have the peace she so desperately sought.

"I don't think it's a good—"

"I need to go, Father," Juliette interrupted with deep conviction. "Please."

"Then let Caroline take the baby back with her," her father advised as he reached for Andrew.

"No." Juliette turned away, clutching her baby tightly. "I want him there with me. He needs to be there when I—"

Her father reached for Andrew again. "He's much too heavy for you to carry for so long. Let me have him."

She twisted to one side, avoiding his grasp. "Don't you see, Father? Andrew is all I have left of David. I want him near me. I'm his mother. I know he's just a baby, but—"

She felt a strong hand on her shoulder. "I'll help her with the baby, John. Don't worry about her. I'll see she gets home all right."

The kindness in Stone Piper's eyes and his consideration of her feelings touched her deeply. Was he the only one who understood the ache in her heart?

He instructed her to wait until he could bring the buggy around to the front. Juliette watched as he strode out the door and wondered at his strange comment that it should have been him who died, instead. That no one would miss him. Whatever would cause a good man like Stone Piper to make such a foolish statement? He seemed to have a habit of making comments she didn't understand.

When Stone returned, he bolted off the seat and up the steps with an open umbrella. Taking Andrew in one arm, he escorted Juliette to his buggy.

The rain had lessened somewhat by the time he halted his team. He offered his hand to help her down, and they joined the other mourners around the grave. She felt faint as her eyes fixed on the gaping hole and the mound of dirt surrounding it. She barely remembered David's funeral. Had there been a mound of dirt like that beside his grave? Had it been sunny? Or rainy? She couldn't remember. All she could remember was that her beloved husband left her that day, put into the ground like a faded flower.

"Maybe I'd best take you on home, Juliette. Perhaps your father was right," Stone whispered as his grip tightened about her.

She managed to rein in her emotions and, with a quaver in her voice she hoped went undetected, answered, "No, I want to stay. I owe it to the Stark family."

"Death is never easy for those left behind."

His words cut through her being. They both knew the meaning of those words. Each had lost their spouse, just like the Widow Stark. "No," she muttered softly as her eyes filled with tears. "It's never easy."

By the time the graveside service ended and mourners were making their way toward their wagons, the rain had stopped and the clouds were dissipating.

When they arrived at the hotel, Stone jumped down from his seat, hurried around to Juliette's side, and took the sleeping infant from her arms. He handed him to Caroline, who'd come out of the hotel to greet them. Instead of offering a hand as he'd done at the cemetery, he reached up and lifted Juliette down from the seat. For a brief moment, their eyes met. To her surprise, Juliette felt as though she'd known this man all her life, and she knew she could trust him. He'd never do her any harm.

"Thank you, Mr. Piper," she said sweetly, fully appreciating the efforts he'd made on her behalf.

"Stone."

Despite the ruddy complexion on his suntanned face, she caught a glimpse of a slight blush as he fingered the brim of his hat.

"Remember? You're supposed to call me Stone."

"Of course, Stone. Thank you."

"Glad you like the hanky, ma'am."

"Hanky?"

He reached up to the seat where she'd just ridden and picked up the soggy hanky she'd used to dab at her swollen eyes. The one he'd given her the day he'd said he was going to marry her. The one that had belonged to his wife.

"Oh," she said, embarrassed that she hadn't remembered she'd brought it. "Yes, I do like it. I carry it often. Thank you."

"I'm glad. I wanted you to have it."

"I'm honored you gave it to me."

He moved away, nearly getting his big feet tangled in the process. "My pleasure, ma'am."

On impulse, Juliette stood on her tiptoe and gently brushed a kiss across his cheek.

"Ah—thank you," he stammered as he continued to back away. "Gi–give my best to your family. I hope your mother gets to feeling better real soon. Guess I'll be going now."

Juliette smiled as she watched him climb onto the buggy and ride off down the muddy street. *What a nice man Stone Piper is. What a shame his wife died so young. He must've been a fine husband.*

She laughed aloud as she remembered his comment about marrying her. *Surely he didn't mean what he said.*

ᔐ

"Good morning, Mrs. Stark. What a nice surprise." Juliette rushed to assist the pale widow as she entered The Great Plains Inn. "I've been meaning to call on you—"

The kindly lady lowered herself onto the horsehair sofa with great effort. "You needn't explain, dear. I know how hard it is to call on someone who's lost a loved one. It's difficult to find the right words. As a widow, you probably understand more than most what I'm going through."

Juliette knelt at her side and wrapped her arms about the trembling woman. "I do know, Mrs. Stark. If it hadn't been for my wonderful family, I'd never have made it. I'm sure your family is there for you, too."

The woman nodded. "Yes, my daughters have been with me constantly since Charles—" She gulped uneasily.

"I'm sure they'll continue to take good care of you," Juliette assured her confidently. "Families take care of their own."

"They try to—"

"I'll tell Mother you're here. I know she'll want to see you," Juliette offered, rising. She sensed Mrs. Stark's need to talk but felt inadequate to deal with the subject of Mr. Stark's death.

The woman quickly grasped her wrist. "No, Juliette. It's not your mother I've come to see. It's your father."

"Father? Really?"

"Yes, I need to speak with him. It's very important."

"I'm here, Mrs. Stark." Her father stepped into the lobby with a gentle smile toward the woman. "I've been expecting to hear from you. I'm assuming this is about the hotel. Am I correct?"

"I'm sorry, John. I wish there was some other way, but I must sell the hotel as quickly as I can." Her face brightened a bit. "Perhaps you could buy it."

Father shook his head. "I could try to get a loan, but the bank requires collateral. I have none."

"I hope you'll be able to raise the money, John. If the bank wants a reference, I'll be happy to tell them what a wonderful manager you've been." She appeared thoughtful. "Or perhaps someone else would give you a loan. One of the local ranchers, maybe?"

"Hmm, I can't really think of anyone with that kind of money who would part with it without adequate collateral."

"Just a thought." Mrs. Stark adjusted her hat and slowly walked toward the door. "Believe me, this is the only way."

He nodded with a forced smile. "I'm sure it is. I'll do what I can."

"I'll wait to hear from you before I take any further steps. Good day, John. I do hope Mary begins to feel better soon. Please convey my good wishes to her."

"I will, and thank you for coming. Good day."

Juliette found it hard to even say good-bye to the woman. She watched as her father lowered himself onto the sofa. "Father? Are you all right?"

Slowly, he lifted his worried face, his misty-eyed gaze pinned on her. "For the first time in my life, I feel totally helpless; but your mother can't know, Juliette. I'm depending on you. We can't let her discover the hopelessness of our situation. Tomorrow I'll go to the banker, and if I don't get any help there, I'll begin looking for another job. I have no experience in farming or ranching, but I'm able-bodied and I can learn. I'm just not sure anyone will want to take the time to teach me."

"You've never let this family down, Father. If you lose the hotel, Caroline and Reuben and I will find other jobs elsewhere. We may not make much, but whatever we earn will help until you find employment."

He lifted his face proudly, his shoulders now squared. "My children work to support my family? Never. Helping here at the hotel is quite enough."

"But Father— "

"No. I won't hear of it. The day John Baker's children have to support his family will be his last day on earth. Do you hear me, Juliette? I'll die first."

Shocked by his statement, she gasped. She'd never heard such words from her normally soft-spoken, peaceful father. "But, if you can't get—"

"If I can't get the loan, I'll feed swine, dig wells, clean stables—any job I can get. But I won't lean on my children."

"But—"

John's fingers circled her wrist, and she winced. "That's quite enough, Juliette. Now go check on Andrew while I see to your mother. I don't want to hear another word of such foolishness."

She pulled away from his grasp, rubbing at the place. "Yes, Father. I'm sorry. I never meant it as an insult. You've been a wonderful father to me and treated me far better than I deserve. I just wanted to help ease the burden around here. I owe it to you."

"You owe me nothing but respect, daughter, and I have to earn that." John's face softened as he took Juliette's wrist and gently stroked the area with the pad of his thumb. "I'm sorry, honey. I didn't mean to be so rough. Taking care of my own flesh and blood is important to me. Trust me, all right?"

Juliette watched her father slowly climb the stairs as if each step were cumbersome. His normally straight body was hunched over, and she wanted to cry.

⌒

"Good morning, John. What are you doing at the bank so early?"

John turned to see Stone tying his horse's reins to the railing. "Didn't expect to see you in town."

"It's America's fault. That housekeeper of mine had a long list of supplies, and Moses couldn't come. I told her I'd ride in, take care of some business, and pick up her needs." He walked up to John and gave him a friendly slap on the back. "You don't look so good. What's wrong?"

John shook his head. "Had some trouble sleeping last night, that's all. Mary isn't doing very well. I'm worried about her."

"She has looked pale lately. I just thought she'd overdone. Taking care of those twins has got to be hard work."

"Those two are a handful all right, but Juliette and Caroline are a big help. And Molly, too. But I'm afraid it's more than overdoing. She hasn't been well since we left Ohio. I guess we need to have Doc take a look at her."

"Probably a good idea. Well, I'd best be tending to my chores. I sure don't want to upset America by making her wait on her flour and sugar." Stone added with a grin, "You know how women can be when they're out of supplies. Good cooks are hard to find. I have to pamper that woman."

"As if she'd ever leave you. You brought her all the way from Kentucky, and you treat her like a queen—probably better than most men treat their wives. But you're lucky to have America and Moses. Those two are as loyal as they come."

Stone gave his friend a grin and a tip of his hat. "That they are. See you later."

~

Stone finished his shopping and was putting the supplies in the wagon when the door to the bank opened. John appeared, his face drained of all color.

"John? What's wrong?"

John leaned his back against the stone building, his shoulders hunched, his chin resting on his chest.

Stone hurried to him. "What is it? Are you sick?"

John didn't answer. He just stared at his feet in silence.

"Speak to me. Do I need to go get Doc?"

"I'm—fine," a weak voice responded.

"Let me walk you to the hotel," Stone offered as he forced his arm around John's shoulders.

"No. Not the hotel. Not now." This time John's voice was firm. "I can't face my family right now."

"All right. Then let me help you into my wagon, and we'll go somewhere we can talk."

Stone led him to the wagon and assisted him onto the seat, then drove out of town, reining up under a large sycamore tree. "Gonna tell me about it?"

John let out a moan as his hands covered his face. "They said no, Stone. I don't know what I'm going to do."

"Who said no? What are you talking about?"

"The bank. They refused to give me a loan. Mrs. Stark is going to sell the hotel. She thought I'd be the logical person to buy it. I explained I had very little money and no collateral, but she suggested I go to the bank for a loan."

"That's what you were doing when I saw you there earlier?"

John nodded.

"They turned you down?" Stone's eyes widened. "Just like that? Knowing the fine way you've managed the hotel?"

"Didn't seem to matter to them. Collateral—that's what they want, and I don't have any." With a mocking laugh, John pulled out his empty pockets.

"So, what are you going to do?"

"What *can* I do? Look for a job."

Stone frowned. "I don't mean to pry, John, but what skills do you have?"

"You know me well enough to know the answer to that one. None."

"What can I do to help you? I'll do anything."

John removed his hat and scratched his head. "Can't think of a thing. If I do, you'll be the first to know. But I appreciate your offer. Your friendship means a lot."

"Remember when we were riding out to meet the Kaws? You said you might lose your job over Stark's death?"

"Uh huh, I remember. What about it?"

"Remember what I said?" Stone grabbed the man's shoulder and stared straight into his eyes. "I said, 'Your family would be welcome to stay with me as long as necessary.' "

John grinned. "And I said, 'Even with three squalling infants?' Remember?"

The two men laughed together.

"Exactly. I meant it, John. Come and stay with me for as long as necessary. I'd welcome the company."

John's face grew somber. "As much as I appreciate the offer, Stone, I could never accept it. I'm an independent man, always have been. I would never take advantage of you." He climbed down from the wagon. "But, thanks. You're a good friend."

"Well, my door is open." Stone tugged on the reins and headed the horses back toward his ranch. "I think I'd better get these supplies to America, or I may have to come and live with you."

⟿

Juliette watched her father pace the floor from her place behind the counter. It'd been two weeks since the bank had rejected his request for a loan. She knew he'd checked out every job possibility in the area, and nothing seemed promising. Their situation was growing more critical each day. "I'm worried about Mother," she finally said. "I think she needs to see Doc Meeker."

"I know, but we can't take her. Not now."

"Can't? Why?"

He sank onto a chair, lowered his head into his hands, and rested his elbows on his knees. "We don't have money to pay Doc."

Juliette rushed to her father's side and put her arms about his shoulders. "Really?"

He lifted a weary gaze. "You're the only one I can talk to, Juliette. Since the bank turned down our loan, we can't buy the hotel. Our savings are nearly gone. Mrs. Stark has only given me to the end of the month. After that, we won't even have a roof over our heads."

Juliette gasped. She had no idea things were this bad. "What can I do to help? I'll do anything. Just name it." She felt her father's shoulders rise and fall, and she knew he was crying. She'd never seen him cry.

"I don't know. I just don't know. I'm all out of answers. I thought sure the Lord would provide a way. He's always taken care of us before. Where is He now?"

"Caroline and I are strong, Father. We've already told you we could get jobs. Maybe Thomas Ward would hire me to work in his store, and Reuben is able-bodied. He could—"

A frown blanketed John's face. "My daughter, work as a clerk in that store? Never. Too many ruffians go in there to buy supplies. Besides, with your mother's bad health, I need you here."

"But Father—"

"No, Juliette. That's my final word on the subject," he said so loudly she was afraid her mother would hear.

A knock sounded on the door. "Pretty late at night for folks to be out." John dabbed at his eyes, then nodded toward Juliette. "You go on to bed. I'll register whoever it is."

⌒

"Evening, John. I know it's nearly eleven, but I've been thinking about you and your situation." Stone moved uneasily into the room. "I don't mean to pry, but I'm wondering if you've come up with a solution yet. You know—about buying the hotel."

John slowly seated himself, then leaned back and locked his hands behind his head with a deep sigh. "I not only can't get a loan, I can't even find a job."

Stone pulled a chair up next to him. "I've been thinking. I—I guess I could give you the money."

"*Give* me the money? You know I'd never let you do that. We're friends, but you've only known me a few months. You'd be crazy to do such a foolish thing."

"Then I'll loan it to you. You can pay me interest."

John shook his head. "I have no collateral to offer you, nothing to secure the loan. No, Stone. I won't take charity, and that's exactly what it would be."

After an interminable silence, Stone spoke again. "Well then, I could buy the hotel, and you could run it for me."

John narrowed his eyes. "You, a rancher, buy the hotel? Don't be ridiculous. You're a better businessman than that. Besides, that wouldn't be any different than giving me the money outright or a loan without collateral!"

"All right, you won't let me give you the money, and you won't let me buy the hotel and let you run it." Stone twisted nervously in the chair, its wobbly legs creaking beneath his weight. "I—ah—may have another solution. One I've been thinking about ever since you got turned down at the bank. I hope you'll be interested."

Now he had John's full attention.

"Of course, I'm interested. I'm desperate. Tell me. What's your solution?"

"Your dilemma could provide an answer for both of us."

John straightened in his seat. "What, Stone? Tell me."

"I'll loan you the money to buy the hotel, interest free—if you get Juliette to marry me."

Chapter 4

John jumped to his feet. "What did you say?"

"I said, get Juliette to marry me. It's a good solution for both of us, John. Hear me out."

John frowned. "I'm listening, but I don't like what I'm hearing. You want me to use my daughter as collateral?"

"Sit down," Stone demanded in a firm voice.

With a scowl, his friend sat down but kept his gaze pinned on Stone's face.

"I've—I've been thinking about your problem." Stone slowly lowered himself onto the sofa beside the distraught man. "I have a problem, too. One I've never discussed with you."

John's scowl turned into a frown. "You have a problem? What has that got to do with asking Juliette to marry you? And how would that solve *my* problem?"

"Patience, John. Let me explain. As you know, I have two sons. They've been living with my sister in St. Joseph since—" He paused and swallowed hard. "Since Lucy—died. I'd like to bring them home. I've been putting it off because I felt incapable of being both mother and father to such young boys. I've even considered hiring a nanny—you know, someone to live in and care for my children and look after the house. But folks would talk, me being a widower."

"But you have America. Couldn't she—"

Stone laughed. "America? Do you realize how old America is? She's far too old to care for two rowdy boys. I need someone with a lot of spunk to look after my children, be a substitute mother, and handle things on the ranch like a wife would."

"Why don't you just marry one of the local women?" John asked with a shrug. "I can think of a dozen who would be happy to be your wife and live on your fine ranch."

Stone shot him an amused grin. " 'Cause I can't think of any of them I'd want to live with. That's important to me."

"But you said I should get Juliette to marry you. I don't understand. What does my daughter have to do with all of this?"

"She's the right age, she's bright, and she needs a home for her and her son. It'd be a marriage of convenience for both of us—a business arrangement. We could even draw up papers. It wouldn't be proper for me to hire a woman to come and live with me on the ranch, but no one would give it a second thought if I married her. I don't want a real wife."

"I don't—"

"Think about it. I could give your daughter the kind of life you want her to have. All she'd have to do in return is be a mother to my sons and take care of my home. That's it. And I'd give you the money to buy the hotel."

John stroked his face and stared off in space. "What about—"

"I wouldn't expect her to perform wifely duties, if that's what you're worried about. I'm not interested in her in that way. But I need help with my sons, and you need money. The end of the month is only a few days away."

"Even if I'd agree, she wouldn't do it, Stone. She's independent, that one. She has her mind set on marrying some fellow who'll whisk her off her feet like her first husband did. I know she won't settle for less. Besides, you're nearly twice her age. I doubt she thinks of you as marrying material."

"She would if she knew it would save the hotel for her family. That daughter of yours is loyal to you, John. She's told me time and time again how much she appreciated you allowing her to come along to Kansas. I think if you asked her, she just might do it. It'd be a good thing for that boy of hers, too. She might do it for his sake."

John stared at the floor and rubbed at his chin. "I—I don't know. If she married you, it'd be for life."

"Look, John. I aim to take care of her and her son as long as I'm around this old earth. It's a good arrangement for all of us, and I'd be a good daddy to Andrew. You know how I love kids. If she ever wanted to leave me, I'd let her go."

John appeared thoughtful. "Would be good for her and her son, I have to admit."

"I want a fine Christian woman to raise my sons, and she's that kind of person."

John straightened. "You've talked to her about this?"

"Not exactly. I told her I was gonna ask for her hand in marriage someday. That's all."

John seemed surprised by his statement. "How did she respond? She never said a word about it to me."

Stone grinned. "I don't think she believed me."

John leaned back into the sofa and stretched out his legs. "I need time to think. This has come as quite a surprise."

"Take whatever time you need." Stone rose and headed for the door. "It's the best solution for everyone. All you have to do now is convince your daughter."

"I'm afraid Juliette won't take to this idea too kindly."

Stone pulled on his hat and stepped through the open doorway. "Then we'll have to convince her, won't we?"

＜〜〜

"You wanted to speak to me, Father?" Juliette asked as she came into the room.

After several anxious moments, John turned to his daughter. "You know the trouble I've been having. Financially."

She nodded with anticipation. "Yes, I know. Have you found someone to give you a loan?"

"Not exactly. But I have been offered a valid solution."

She clapped her hands. "Oh Father. I knew you'd come through for us. What is your solution? Have you found a new job?"

John's heart pounded. "You're the solution, Juliette."

Huge inquisitive eyes lifted to his. "Me? How? You know I'll do anything I can to help. Just tell me."

"I—I know you'd like to find a fine man and marry again. Your son needs a father in his life, and—"

"Father? Tell me. What's your solution?"

"I—I don't think you'll want to know."

"Of course I want to know. Andrew and I are a part of this family. Now tell me."

"Juliette—" John closed his eyes, took a deep breath, and blurted it out. "I need you to marry Stone Piper."

Juliette stared at her father, her face reflecting her shock. "What did you say? Surely I didn't hear you right."

John blinked, then pressed his lips together in a straight line. "I—I said I need you to marry Stone Piper," he repeated.

"But why, Father? Why would you ask such a thing? Just a few minutes ago, we were talking about David and the importance of real love in our lives. I don't understand."

"I didn't want to ask you, but—" John pulled her to him and cradled her in his arms. "It's the only way, daughter. Trust me. The only way."

"I'm confused." She lifted misty eyes to his. "The only way to what? Tell me. I don't know what you're talking about."

John breathed in a whiff of air to clear his head, then let it out slowly. He had to make her understand. "Remember when Stone came to me last night?"

She nodded.

"Since he's my friend, I'd confided in him about my financial difficulties. He'd offered to take our family into his home until I could get a job and we'd find a place of our own."

"But—what has that got to do with me—and marriage?"

"Patience, daughter, I'm getting to that. It isn't easy for a man to talk to his daughter about his inability to provide for his family." He breathed in another gasp and continued. "I told Stone I appreciated his offer, but it would only be a temporary answer to a major problem. He came up with an idea that would help both of us."

"Marry me? How would that solve anything? And why would he want to marry me?"

He brushed the hair from Juliette's troubled face. "Yes, he wants to marry you. But," he hurried on to say, "it would be a marriage in name only. What he really needs is someone to be a mother to his boys and run his household. There would be no—"

"No love?"

"Right, no—ah, love. It would be a simple business agreement between the two of you. In exchange, Stone will provide for every need you and Andrew will ever have. Just think of it, Juliette: You'll live in a fine house, wear fine clothes, have all the things you've always wanted. You and your son would want for nothing. What a wonderful opportunity this would be for the two of you."

She pushed away and stared into his face. "But Father, I don't understand. Why would you want me to do such a thing? You know I don't love him. What about all the talks you and I have had about love?"

He struggled with the words. "Be—because, if you marry Stone, he'll give me the money to buy the hotel, interest free."

Juliette backed off quickly. "You'd sell my life like this? Marry me to a man I don't love? To buy a hotel?"

He reached for her, but she screamed at him and shoved him away. "Never did I think my own father could be so cruel. I want no part of this plan of yours!" She gave him a cold stare. "Or did Stone come up with this idea?"

He touched her hand, but she pulled it away.

"Leave me alone. Don't even touch me! I won't do this! I won't! Do you hear me? I refuse to marry Stone Piper! I don't love him, and I will not marry him—no matter what!"

"It's okay, daughter. Somehow I'll work things out. I had no right to ask this of you. It wasn't fair. Can you forgive your thoughtless old father?"

She curled up in the corner of the sofa and buried her face in her hands.

John sat down beside her, stroking her hair. "Please, Juliette? Please forgive me?" he begged softly. He'd never felt so low, so discouraged.

Here he'd told his children he'd never allow them to help him support his family, and what was he doing? Asking his lovely daughter, his own flesh and blood, to give up her life to keep him from losing the hotel. "I'm so sorry. I wouldn't blame you if you hated me."

She lifted a tear-stained face. "I could never hate you, Father, and I do forgive you. I know how hard all of this has been on you, and I ask *your* forgiveness. I had no right to scream at you like that, under any conditions. But please, don't ask this of me. It's—it's too much."

She went on, "Think back to when David and I came to you, saying we wanted to get married. You lectured us about the importance of the marriage vows. How can you ask me to ignore those vows and marry someone as a business arrangement?"

"What's wrong? Juliette. Are you sick?" Caroline asked with a glance toward their father as she entered the lobby.

Juliette shook her head and placed her hand on her abdomen. "No—I—something just upset me."

John stared at Caroline for a moment. Then, after flashing a quick glance toward Juliette, he motioned for her to join them. "I have a problem, Caroline. Juliette and I have been discussing it. I hadn't planned to tell you—not yet, anyway. But you're eighteen now, and after thinking it over, I've decided you're old enough to handle it."

Without taking her gaze from her father, Caroline sat down by Juliette. "What is it, Father?"

"Mrs. Stark has put the hotel up for sale and—"

Caroline brightened. "We're buying it? The hotel is going to be ours?"

"No. I wish that were true. I've tried to buy it, but I can't raise the money. It appears we may be moving soon."

"But if you don't have the hotel, what will—?"

"I don't know what I'll do for employment, but I don't want you to worry about it. Don't say anything about this to the other children, and please don't discuss it with your mother. She has enough on her mind already. I just felt you should know." He rose and gave them each a smile.

"But, if you—"

He held up a hand. "That's all for now, Caroline. Now go check on your mother and see if she needs any help."

⌒

The clock chimed nine times as her father entered the hotel that night. Juliette was waiting at the door. "Where've you been? Mother has been sick with worry."

"Walking, mostly. I needed time to think. You haven't said anything to your mother or anyone about marrying Stone, have you?"

She shook her head. "No, I haven't. I was afraid you were going to tell Caroline this morning when you told her about the hotel."

"No, that part is between you and me and Stone. I've been chastising myself all day for entertaining such a foolish notion."

"It's not you I'm mad at, Father. It's Stone. How could he be so insensitive? To even offer such a thing to you was cruel, and to think he calls himself your friend."

He slipped the pad of his finger beneath her chin and lifted her face to his. "Don't say that, Juliette. Stone is a good friend. He only wanted to help. That's all. He never intended to cause any trouble. I'm sure of it."

"If he's such a good friend, he should just give you the money."

"He offered, but I refused. That's when he came up with this plan."

"The plan for you to sell me to him?" she asked indignantly.

Father flinched. "No, I'd never sell you to anyone. Please don't ever think that of me. That was never in my mind."

"Isn't that what you intended to do? Marry me off to him so he'd give you the money you need?" Her tone was once again accusatory.

"Oh no, child! You don't understand! Stone wants to bring his sons home to live with him. Unfortunately, in addition to running his ranch, his duties as deputy take him away from home for days at a time. America is too old to care for little boys. Stone needs someone younger to live in, care for them, and manage his household. Someone who can be with his children all the time."

"If he has that much money, why doesn't he just hire someone?"

"He could hire one of the local women, but he's too proper to have an unmarried woman living under his roof. Besides, a married woman would need to spend time with her family. He has his fine reputation to consider, so he came up with this idea. If you married him, he'd have someone to be a mother to his children and manage his house. You'd have everything you could ever want, and I'd have the money to buy the hotel and provide for my family. Really, Juliette, it's not as bad an idea as it seems. You and your son would have a wonderful life."

She listened but was not convinced.

"Please, don't be upset with Stone. If you're upset with anyone, let it be me. I'm the one who asked it of you—not him."

"Well—maybe you're right. But I won't blame you, Father. I know how hard this has been on you. I wish I could help, but you must understand, I cannot marry a man I don't love. I'd be miserable!"

John grabbed her hands and cupped them in his. "Please, let's forget I ever asked you to do such an unforgivable thing."

She stood on tiptoe and kissed her father's cheek. "But I will work at the general store, if it'll help."

"No, and that's final."

⌒

The air was brisk in the quiet town of Dove City as Stone rode in on Blackie that night. Most folks had gone to bed, their lamps extinguished; but the lamp in the lobby of The Great Plains Inn burned brightly, and Stone knew his friend was toiling over the hotel's bookwork. He gave a slight tap on the windowpane and waited.

John opened the door and let him in. "I spoke with Juliette, and it didn't go well."

"She said no?" Stone pulled off his hat and sat down.

"She said a firm no. She was furious with both of us."

Stone leaned back and balanced his hat on his knee. "You explained it all to her?"

"Everything we'd discussed."

He rose and stuffed his hat onto his head. "Well, I guess that answers that. But don't forget my offer for your family to stay with me as long as necessary."

"I spoke with Robert Marquette at the bank this morning, and I'm sure you can guess what he said."

"Another no?"

"Another firm no. Almost as firm as Juliette's. I'd hoped he'd reconsider, but he said he couldn't take a chance on me without collateral."

Stone's brow creased. "What're you going to do?"

"I don't know. I just don't know. I've reached the end of my options."

Stone laid a hand on the man's shoulder. "I meant what I said. Your family is welcome at my house."

"Thanks, I may have to take you up on your offer."

"I'm still willing to give you the money."

John shook his head sadly. "You're a successful businessman, Stone. You didn't get that way by behaving foolishly. There'd be nothing in it for you. I couldn't let you do it."

"My offer still stands." Stone tipped his hat and rode away into the night with a heavy heart.

⌐

Stone rose early the next morning. Each Sunday, he made a practice of arriving at the saloon ahead of the churchgoers to cover up the bars and arrange the chairs. Since Mr. Ward allowed the saloon to be used for public functions, church was one of them. It wasn't that Stone was a pillar of the church. He wasn't. But he'd attended services for so long, sometimes he felt like it. He rarely read his Bible and hardly ever prayed, though he bowed his head when others did. But he liked being around people who were good Christians. They were fine people with high moral standards, and he could trust them. He knew folks in the community took it for granted he was one of them, though he'd never outright claimed it.

He was just putting the last chair in place when the Baker family arrived. As the two men shook hands, Stone nodded a good morning to Mary Baker, then turned to Juliette. "Good morning."

She gave him a cold, emotionless stare and said nothing.

"You're looking beautiful this morning." He watched for a reaction to his compliment but didn't see one.

She moved past him and went to sit with her family in their regular place. He waited until the music began, then slipped into the empty chair beside her. When she made no effort to share her hymnal with him, he slid closer and took the corner of the book in his hand. Although she ignored him, he sang with his usual robustness, harmonizing occasionally with her lovely soprano voice. By the end of the service, he noticed she'd seemed to relax some, and he decided to chance speaking with her.

"Nice day for a drive in the country, don't you think?"

"Drive?" She eyed him suspiciously.

"I thought maybe you'd do me the honor of taking a ride with me this afternoon."

Furrows creased her brow. "I think not."

"Please, Juliette. I know your father talked to you about me. Give me a chance to explain my side of things."

"No need for explanations. My answer is no. Plain and simple, no. I want nothing to do with you." She tried to move away from him, but he slipped his hand under her elbow and firmly led her off to one side.

"I have to make you understand. I don't want there to be any hard feelings between us. Although we've only known each other for a few months now, your father is my friend." He glanced around, then continued, his voice even softer. "I want you to come and see my place. You've never been there."

She pulled away slightly, tugging from his grasp. "Why would I want to do that?"

"I've offered my home to your family if Mrs. Stark sells the hotel. I've tried to convince John there's plenty of room for everyone, but he's a proud man and very stubborn." He wanted to add, *Almost as stubborn as you!*

She relaxed a bit and seemed to be considering their housing dilemma.

"Come on, say yes. You can bring Andrew and Caroline. It's a beautiful day. I know you'd enjoy the ride."

She appeared to be giving it some thought. "That's the only reason you want me to come? Not to talk about marriage?"

"That's the only reason." Stone almost felt he should cross his fingers behind his back. That truly was the reason for his invitation, but he hoped when she saw his spread, she might decide to take him up on his offer, after all.

"Father told Caroline about the hotel, but he didn't tell either of us about your offer of housing. If she comes with me, I'll have to tell her, you know."

"I'm sure that'd be fine with your father, but perhaps you'd better get his approval first."

"I could ask him, but I don't want her to know about—"

"I know. I won't tell her."

"I guess it wouldn't hurt for us to see your place."

"You'll come?"

"If it's all right with Father."

"I'll come for you about three. You won't be sorry."

"I'd better not be." She shook a finger in his face. "This better not be a trick."

Stone crossed his fingers behind his back. "It's not."

∽

"You ladies comfortable back there?" Stone asked with a congenial smile, swiveling in his seat as the horses ambled up the dusty road. Juliette had refused his offer to ride up front with him, opting to sit in back with Caroline.

They'd barely reached the outskirts of town when Andrew began to fuss. Juliette knew her baby would not be satisfied until he was fed. Yet, how could she nurse him? Here in the buggy, with Mr. Piper sitting so close? She could feel a flush rise to her cheeks, just thinking about what she was about to do.

"Mr. Piper, I'm sorry, but my baby is hungry, and I must see to his needs. Would you—could you—please—face the front—for a little while?"

He sat up straight and squared his shoulders. "Ah, yes—certainly. Of course."

They rode along in silence as Andrew suckled beneath Juliette's shawl. When he finished, she handed him to Caroline. Once her clothing had been adjusted and put back into place, she leaned forward a bit. "Thank you, Mr. Piper."

He gave her a nod but kept his eyes on the road.

"Are you warm enough back there?" he asked finally. "I want you ladies to enjoy your ride."

"Thank you, Mr. Piper. We are. Are we getting near your place?" Caroline asked, craning her neck.

He turned in the seat to face his three passengers. "Actually, we've been on my place since before we crossed the bridge. The house is still up there a ways ahead of us."

Caroline scanned the area. "This land is all yours?"

"Sure is. A mighty lot to keep up."

"But you do have help, right?" she asked, obviously impressed with the magnitude of what she was seeing.

Stone let out a hearty laugh. "Lots of help. I could never take care of all of this by myself."

"Could you hire our father to work for you?"

"Wish I could, Miss Caroline, but my work is seasonal. Your pa needs something he can work at every day."

"Oh, I see." She seemed disappointed.

"See over there through the trees? The Neosho River runs across my land. Makes a good swimming hole in the summer and provides water for my stock.

"Look, you can barely see the roof of my house. And over that way are the barns. Down there is the cabin where America and Moses live."

"Your slaves?" Caroline asked with big eyes as she glanced in the direction of the old couple's cabin.

"Slaves? No!" Stone stated emphatically. "They're friends who happen to work for me."

"I heard Mrs. Marquette say they're your slaves."

"No, Caroline. Those two are as free as you or I."

"Then why would Mrs. Marquette say such a thing?" Juliette asked.

"The story probably got all messed up. My father did buy Moses and America, and they *were* his slaves. But my father died a long time ago. The first thing I did after I claimed his property was to set them free."

"If they're free, why are they still with you?"

"It's their choice, Caroline. They wanted to come to Kansas, and since I'd never known life without them, I wanted them here with me. I made it perfectly clear to them that they were no longer slaves of the Piper family. They were my employees, and as employees, they were free to come and go at any time."

Caroline smiled. "Oh, that's so wonderful. What a nice man you are, Mr. Piper."

"Tell that to your sister. I don't think she agrees."

Juliette lowered her gaze and avoided his eyes. "I do think you're a nice man, Stone. It's just that I—"

He reached back and cupped his hand over hers. "I know. You don't have to explain."

The buggy slowly rounded a curve in the road, and Stone's house could be seen in the distance. "We're nearly there," he explained as he gave the reins a gentle flip.

"Oh, my, I've never seen such a huge house," Caroline exclaimed as they moved up the lane. "Do you live here alone?"

Stone nodded. "All alone, but I have two sons living in St. Joseph. I plan to bring them home as soon—" He cast a quick glance at Juliette. "As soon as it's possible."

"Oh Juliette. This is the kind of house we were wishing for, remember?"

Juliette gave her sister a frown. "I don't know what you're talking about."

"Yes you do. We said maybe we could both marry rich men and ride around in fancy buggies while other women did our work for us. Surely you remember. We were standing in the hotel lobby. You were saying—"

"I said I don't remember, Caroline. Please, let's not discuss this now."

Stone grinned to himself. *So, Juliette was talking about marrying a rich man. Could that have been after I gave her Lucy's handkerchief and told her I planned to marry her?*

Caroline let out a sigh. "If you say so."

Time to change the subject. He didn't want Juliette to be upset about anything. He wanted her mind to be on the advantages he could give her if she married him. He made a large circle around the outbuildings, passed by America and Moses' cabin, then turned into the circle drive in front of the spacious house. "Here we are."

He leaped from the buggy and rushed around to assist his guests. After handing Andrew to Caroline, his fingers circled Juliette's waist, and he slowly lifted her down. His eyes never left her lovely face. "There you go, little lady."

She gave him a demure smile that made him grin, and he tipped his hat. *Maybe she isn't as mad at me as I thought.*

"Juliette, look at this place. It's the biggest house I've ever seen! Bigger'n any in Ohio." Caroline spun around, looking in all directions. "Wouldn't you like to live here?"

"Yes," Stone asked with a wink as he took Andrew from Caroline and ushered Juliette up the steps of the wraparound porch. "Wouldn't you like to live here, Juliette?"

With a quick snap of her head, she turned to face him, hostility in her eyes. "For a few weeks maybe. No longer."

"I could live here forever!" Caroline said as she hurried up the steps ahead of them.

America met them at the door, wearing a freshly laundered apron. "Juliette. Caroline. This is America."

America gave them each a nod, then slipped a brown finger into the sleeping baby's chubby hand. "Would you like to lay him down?"

Juliette leaned toward her and whispered, "I nursed him on the way. It's time for his nap, so he'll probably stay asleep for an hour or so."

America pointed to a small daybed in the far corner. "He should be comfortable there. Push that chair up close so he won't roll off."

The three watched as Juliette carefully placed her son on the daybed and tucked the blanket about his shoulders. "Thank you, America," Juliette said as she moved back across the room.

Caroline stared openmouthed at the oversized room, then turned to America. "Mr. Piper said you used to be a slave."

Juliette's hand reached out to cover her sister's mouth.

"It's okay," Stone advised with a laugh. "I don't think America minds talking about it, do you, America?"

"No, I don't mind." She turned to their inquisitive guest. "I used to be Stone's pa's slave, but never Stone's. He freed me and Moses the day he got everything."

Caroline turned to her sister. "Isn't that nice, Juliette? Isn't Stone the nicest man you ever met?"

"Yes, very nice," Juliette agreed sullenly.

"Stone asked me to cook up his favorite little cakes and some tea. Would ya like some?" the old woman asked.

"Of course they would," Stone answered for them, "as soon as I've shown them the rest of the house."

"Why did you ever build such a big house, Mr. Piper?" Caroline asked as they moved through a hallway and into the master bedroom.

"For my wife," he explained proudly. "Lucy wanted a showy house with fine furniture. I built it just like she wanted it."

"Caroline, don't ask so many questions," Juliette cautioned with a warning frown. "You're being rude."

"It's all right. I don't mind answering. That's why I invited you here today. I wanted us to get to know each other better." Turning to Caroline, he went on. "She died. My Lucy died not long after my second son's birth."

"Oh, that's terrible!" Caroline returned with a frown as she put a consoling hand on the man's arm. "I'm so sorry."

"So am I," Stone agreed. "I loved her very much. Life hasn't meant much to me since she's been gone."

"Why don't your boys live with you?" Caroline asked.

Again her sister gave her a warning frown.

"I want them to, but boys their age need a woman to take care of them. Since I haven't found that woman—" He shot another glance toward Juliette. "Since I haven't found that woman, they've stayed in St. Joseph with my sister."

Caroline nodded toward America. "Couldn't she take care of them?"

"Stone won't let me," America answered as she scurried toward the kitchen.

"She's an *old* woman," Stone added with a hearty laugh. "Too old for two rowdy boys. I couldn't ask that of her."

"You could hire someone who wasn't that old," Caroline continued.

"Wouldn't look right for a woman to be living out here on the ranch with a widower." Stone turned toward Juliette, and this time she was looking directly at him.

"Couldn't you find a wife?" Caroline asked with a glance toward her sister, as if she expected Juliette to silence her once more.

He reared back with a vigorous laugh. "I thought I'd found one, but she said no."

"She must be crazy!" Caroline sat down in a well-padded chair, testing the cushion's plumpness. "Can you imagine it, Juliette? Some woman would say no to all of this?"

"Yes, crazy," Juliette answered softly with a piercing glare toward her host.

"Juliette, would you look at this bedroom?" Caroline followed close at Stone's heels. "This is your bedroom, Mr. Piper?"

Stone nodded. "Like it? Lucy fixed it this way."

Caroline leaned over the bed and ran her fingers across the delicate quilt. "I wish I had a bed like this."

They moved on to the room across the hall, a smaller room but quite nice, filled with ladylike furniture. Everything with lace. Even the pillowcases had lace edges. A beautiful quilt with appliquéd flowers covered the bed. "Lucy made that quilt," Stone explained. "She liked to do handwork."

"It's lovely," Juliette admitted with admiration as her fingers traced the swirling green vines that connected the flowers. "You must have loved her very much."

"I did," he conceded. "No one will ever take her place."

"Not even the lady who said *no* when you asked her to marry you?" Caroline asked as she bent to look at a delicate glass vase on the table beside the bed.

"Not even her," he told her with another wink to her sister. "Let me show you the other bedroom on this floor. It's the room I'm going to fix up for—" He paused. "Whoever takes care of my boys."

As they made their way down the hall, Caroline clasped her hand on the knob of a closed door near Stone's bedroom. "Whose room is this?"

Stone quickly moved to the door and placed his back against it. "Storeroom. I—I have things in there that—"

"It's none of our business," Juliette stated sharply as she tugged at her sister's sleeve.

"It's all right," Stone said, interceding. "It's nothing important, Caroline. Really. Just a storeroom. I'm sure you wouldn't want to see it. Let me show you the other bedroom." He ushered them into the smallest of the rooms. "Not much to see in here. Mostly I just use it as a place to keep my books, though I don't have much time to read." He moved back into the hall. "Let's go upstairs."

Caroline's eyes widened. "You have a bedroom upstairs, too?"

Stone's booming laugh filled the house. "Caroline, I have three bedrooms upstairs. That's why I told your father I have plenty of room for your family to come and stay with me."

Caroline climbed the stairs, keeping a full step ahead of their long-legged host.

"Only if Father doesn't buy the hotel or get a job," Juliette explained quickly.

They toured the upstairs bedrooms, then made their way into the kitchen to enjoy the cakes and tea America had prepared. "Look who woke up!" America said, holding Andrew in her arms.

"Hi, precious." Juliette reached out to take him. "Did you have a good nap?"

"He sure looks like it." Stone pointed toward Andrew's smiling face. "You're a happy baby."

America placed the platter on the table. "I hope you like these."

"America is the best cook in the world," Stone commented as he moved to her side and planted a kiss on the little round bun of hair secured to the top of her head.

She grinned. "That man is just used to my cookin'. He don't know no better."

Caroline moved quickly to the table, pulled out a chair, and seated herself. But Juliette waited until Stone pulled her chair out for her in true gentlemanly fashion.

Once they were gathered around the table, America filled their cups with freshly brewed tea.

"This is good," Caroline commented as she bit into one of the tasty cakes. "Do you fix these for Stone often?"

"I've fixed these cakes for Stone since he was two years old," America said with a kindly look toward her employer. "They're his favorites."

Everyone laughed when Andrew's chubby hand reached for a cake as America handed the platter to Juliette.

After they'd finished their tea and cakes, Stone motioned for them to follow him. "I nearly forgot to show you the special room I built on for Lucy. It was her favorite."

He led them through a small door off the kitchen. In the middle of the cozy room sat a large wooden tub. On a table nestled next to it, a row of candles lay in a delicate china dish, along with a tiny bar of French soap molded into the shape of a flower.

"This was your wife's bath?" Juliette asked incredulously as her eyes scanned the intimate little room set into an alcove. "Her very own bath?"

"Only hers."

Juliette stared at the small stack of towels lying beside the rosebud-trimmed china washbowl and pitcher. "This is so nice."

"This smells wonderful," Caroline commented as she picked up the sweetly scented bar of soap and touched it to her cheek. "Wouldn't you like to have a room like this, Juliette?"

Juliette flashed an uncomfortable glance toward Stone, then quickly turned away as their eyes met. "Of course. What woman wouldn't?"

Stone took a quick step up behind her and whispered in her ear. "It could be yours, Juliette. All of this could be yours, if you'd just say yes."

Chapter 5

Juliette moved away quickly. Obviously, no matter how appealing his house seemed or how much money he may have in the bank, she could not, and would not, even entertain the thought of marrying him.

He wished he'd kept his suggestion to himself. He hadn't meant to offend her. He'd simply wanted her to see the advantages for everyone concerned if she'd marry him.

Juliette gazed out the window, turning her back on him.

Stone wanted to follow her to apologize, but Caroline kept going on about Lucy's bath and asking him all sorts of questions.

Finally, he pulled a folded paper from his pocket and moved back to the kitchen table. "Now this is the way I figured we could house the Baker family."

At first, Juliette continued to stare off in space as if she had no interest in his plan. But as he pointed to each square on the chart and talked about where each family member would be housed, she couldn't help but listen. She asked Caroline to change Andrew's diaper, then joined Stone at the table.

"And I thought this small room on the first floor at the end of the hall would be good for you and Andrew, Juliette. There's a nice feather bed in there. That way, you won't have any stairs to climb with that heavy boy in your arms. Is that suitable for you?"

"Ah—yes, ah—anything would be fine if Father doesn't find a job by the end of the month. But I'm sure he will."

Stone checked to make sure Caroline couldn't hear as his face grew solemn. "The end of the month is nearly here. Even if he were to find a job tomorrow, he would most likely not get paid for two weeks. From what John has told me, his money is nearly gone," he said in a near whisper.

"I know. He told me, too," she confessed meekly.

"Plans need to be made now."

"I told him, if we have to move, I could go work in Mr. Ward's store," Juliette inserted. "I might not make much money, but whatever I made, he could have."

Stone reared back with a frown. "Do you honestly think your father would allow you to work in that store? A fine young lady like you has no business dealing with the men who go in there for supplies."

"Women go in there, too, and if I want to work at that store, Father would have to allow it," she answered with an indignant tilt of her chin. "I *am* an adult."

"Well, that's between you and John. If we were honest, I think we both know what his decision would be."

"I'm ready to go home now," Juliette announced as Caroline came back into the room. She grabbed up her cape, snatched Andrew from her sister's arms, and headed out the door. "You have a fine house, Mr. Piper. But hopefully, Father will work something out and refuse your offer."

Stone turned to Caroline. "Stay here with America. Give me a few minutes to speak with your sister."

Caroline nodded.

He found Juliette standing on the porch, attempting to wrap her cape about her shoulders and hold Andrew at the same time. He stepped forward and took the baby from her arms as he motioned toward a bent willow bench. "Please, Juliette. I didn't mean to offend you. Sit down and let's talk. I want you to understand my position in all of this."

She crossed her arms and turned away from him.

"Please?"

Slowly, she moved to the bench and seated herself. Stone sat down beside her with the baby contentedly snuggled up in the crook of his arm. "Look. Your father and I haven't known each other for very long, but he's my friend. I'd do anything to help him through this hard time. I even offered to give him the money to buy the hotel outright. But he refused to take it."

Her gaze lifted to meet his. "You offered to give him the money? Really?"

"Yes. As his friend, I wanted to help. But he wouldn't take it."

"That's when you came up with this ridiculous marriage idea?"

He thoughtfully smoothed at the baby's hair before answering. "Actually, I came up with the marriage idea several months ago. I've wanted to bring my boys home for such a long time. I think you can understand that. Being separated from them all these years has been hard on them and on me."

She smiled at her baby, and he smiled back. "Then why didn't you?"

"Who would take care of them? I'm outside working my ranch from before the sun comes up most days, and what days I'm not, I'm repairing barns and tools, helping other ranchers, or performing my duties as deputy. Those boys need someone to be with them all the time. America's too old to care for two growing, energetic boys. I couldn't ask that of her."

"You could hire someone."

"I've thought of that many times. But who would I hire? One of the local women with a family of her own to tend to? Someone who would go home at the end of the day?"

She grew thoughtful. "Carrie Sullivan could probably do it. She's not much over twenty and would be good to your boys."

"Carrie Sullivan is a single woman. Do you think it would look proper for someone like that to live in my house?"

Her gaze lowered. "No, I guess not."

"Now you're beginning to see my problem. I don't want a nanny and a housekeeper for my sons. They deserve more than that."

She looked up into his eyes. "Then what do you want, Stone?"

He grinned. "You. You're the perfect solution."

"Me?" She jumped to her feet and snatched the nearly sleeping baby from his arms, her face flushed and angry. "I'm the answer for you, maybe, and perhaps for Father. But I won't be anyone's solution, Mr. Piper. I'm not a slave you can buy and sell at your whim."

He rose awkwardly, knowing he'd used the wrong words. Again. "I did not buy America or Moses. You know that. I would never attempt to buy another human being."

She rushed down the steps toward the buggy, nearly tripping on the last step, with Stone at her heels. "Never? You just did, Mr. Piper. You tried to buy me!"

"No, that was not my intention! Why can't you understand my motives?" Frustrated, he stood on the bottom step, his arms dangling limply at his sides. It'd been years since he'd argued with a woman, and he found himself speechless and inadequate.

"Oh, I understand your motives all right," she quipped angrily as she struggled to put the baby into the buggy's seat and climb up herself without assistance. "Your motives are very clear. You need a mother for your boys, and you're willing to buy one. Well, let me tell you, Stone Piper: You will not buy this woman. Juliette Baker Martin is not for sale."

"But—"

Andrew began to cry at the top of his lungs, nearly drowning out their conversation. "But—nothing, Mr. Piper. Now, if you'd be so kind, I'd like to go home. All this bargaining is giving me a headache." With that she squared her shoulders, lifted her chin, and stared straight ahead, ignoring his pleas.

"Caroline," Stone called out loudly. "You can come out now. Your sister is ready to go home."

Silence permeated the air all the way back into town. No one seemed to have anything to say.

Occasionally, Stone would sneak a peek at the girls. Each time, he'd wish he'd been more diplomatic in his approach of the marriage subject. *You're a fool,* he told himself as the buggy rolled toward town, *to even think that lovely young woman would consider spending the best and most productive years of her life with you, taking care of your children, when she could have her pick of men.*

He circled the buggy around and came to a stop near the hotel's door. He hurried to assist Juliette, but she refused his hand and lowered herself to the ground before reaching for her baby. He followed the three of them into the hotel where John was waiting.

John greeted them warmly. "What did you think of Stone's place, girls?"

Still wide-eyed, Caroline was the first to answer. "Oh Father, it is so pretty. I've never seen such a fine house."

He turned to Juliette. "What did you think?"

Stone pulled his hat from his head and rotated its brim nervously between his fingers with a sheepish grin toward her. "There's plenty of room for the Baker family, right?"

She moved toward the stairs. "Yes, I guess so, but not for me. I'm sure Andrew and I can find a place with one of the members of our church."

"Want me to change Andrew's diaper?" Caroline asked, reaching out toward the smiling baby. "I'm going upstairs."

Juliette gave her an appreciative grin. "Would you mind?"

Caroline took Andrew and cuddled him in her arms. "Not a bit."

As soon as she'd reached the top of the stairs, John stepped out and took hold of Juliette's arm. "You and Andrew aren't going anywhere. We're a family. Where one goes, we all go. That includes the two of you."

Ignoring their guest, she turned to face him, her eyes burning their way into his. "But you'd let me go and marry a man I don't love? Move away from my family so you can keep your precious hotel? I think not, Father." She pulled away and followed her sister up the stairs. "You'll have to excuse me. I have to feed my son."

Stone bowed his head in defeat. "Sorry, John. Guess I didn't handle things too well."

"Not your fault. You tried. She's right though. I guess I *am* willing to sell her to keep the hotel."

"No, that's not true. None of us wants to put Juliette's happiness on the line. You want the best for her, and so do I. I could give her the kind of life she's always wanted." He let his shoulders slump. "Oh, I know I'm not the kind of man she wants for a husband, but I'd be good to her, John. I'd give her anything she wants. . .except love. I can't give her that.

My heart still belongs to Lucy. But your daughter would never want for anything."

John put his hand on Stone's shoulder. "I know that. You're a good man."

"That daughter of yours is as stubborn as they come. Did you know she's planning on getting a job at Mr. Ward's store?"

"So she says, but I say no. I forbid it."

"She's an adult. What could you do to stop her? Women are doing strange things nowadays."

"I know, and that's what worries me. But if I can't provide for her and Andrew, what say do I have?"

"None, it appears. But she respects you, John. She'd never do anything to embarrass you or her family."

"I'm counting on that. I finally told Reuben about our financial condition. I hate to keep things from the family. By the way, thanks for bringing the girls home."

"You do know I'll give you the money, even if Juliette refuses to marry me, don't you?"

John nodded. "Yes, I know. But I can't take it—not without you getting something in return."

⤳

Juliette stood at the top of the stairs, listening. How could her father and Stone expect her to marry a man she didn't love? David had been the love of her life, but their time together had been so short. Surely somewhere she could find another man who would love her as David had—a man who could sweep her off her feet and make her spine tingle at his touch. One she could give herself to wholeheartedly.

She listened as her father and her suitor discussed the money her father needed. She marveled at Stone's generosity when he offered to give them his hard-earned money. Not many men would do such an unselfish thing. He'd be a good catch for any woman. If only she loved him.

⤳

Stone jammed his hat on his head, then untied the horses from the hitching post and climbed into the wagon. "Women!" he said aloud as he whipped the reins and headed toward the ranch.

"Juliette, Caroline. Wake up!" Her father's voice pierced the darkened room. "Your mother needs you!"

Juliette sat up and rubbed at her eyes. "What time is it?"

"Nearly four. Hurry!"

She grabbed her robe and wrapped it around her, pulled the coverlet over her sleeping baby, and hurried down the narrow hall to her parents' room. Her father was bending over the bed, hovering over her mother. "What's wrong with her?"

"She started feeling poorly right after you girls left with Stone yesterday afternoon. I didn't tell you last night."

"Did you call Doc Meeker?"

He shook his head and whispered his response. "No, I wanted to, but she didn't want me to call him. I think she knew we didn't have the money to pay him. I shouldn't have listened to her."

"Go get him," Juliette ordered as she bent over the bed and stroked her mother's fevered brow.

John nodded and disappeared.

The two girls kept vigil and prayed over their mother until John returned with Doc Meeker.

"How long has she been like this?"

"She had a bad spell yesterday afternoon. She started vomiting, and she's been having terrible headaches," John explained as he rubbed the pad of his thumb over his wife's frail hand. "She hasn't felt well since the twins were born."

"Why didn't you send someone for me?"

"I—ah. She— We—we didn't have the money to pay you."

The doctor stopped his examination and stared at John. "This is your wife's health we're talking about. I'm a doctor, not a banker. She seems very weak. I hate to tell you this, but the best thing you could do for her is send her somewhere where she can have constant bed rest for a few weeks. I think the woman's problem is exhaustion."

John rubbed at his temples and nodded. "It's my fault. If I'd had any idea she was carrying twins, I would never have left Ohio. Her other births had been such easy ones; neither of us expected this last time to be any different."

"Picking up and moving such a long way, tending to the needs of her family, then having the babies—" Doc paused. "I think all of it has taken a toll on her, John. Look how thin she's become. She's nothing but skin and bones."

"She isn't going to die, is she?" Juliette blurted out.

The doctor spun around to face her. "No, Juliette. But if she doesn't get away from the responsibilities and pressures of her life here at the hotel, I doubt she's going to get any better. This woman needs rest. Uninterrupted rest."

"But how—"

Doc Meeker lifted a hand. "I know what your family has been going through, but it's Mary's life we're talking about here, and—"

"Mary's aunts live about fifty miles away. They've been wanting her to come for a visit." John wiped at his eyes with his sleeve. "Do you think she could stand the trip?"

"Yes, if you make sure she can lie down most of the way," Doc advised. "The sooner you can take her there, the better."

"Since Mary is nursing the twins, we'll have to take them with us, but I'm sure her aunts will be able to handle them."

"Maybe you could send one of the girls along to help out," Doc suggested.

John smiled. "Good idea. I'll send Molly along. She's only eight, but she's a good helper and the twins love her."

"Just so long as Mary gets the rest she needs. That's the important thing," Doc added.

John nodded. "Fine. I'm sure Caroline and Juliette can help us pack. We'll leave as soon as we can get ready."

"What's to become of us?" Caroline asked her sister as the buggy disappeared. "First the hotel. Now this."

"Good question," Reuben stated as he echoed his sister's fears. "Father's already been at his wit's end."

Juliette let out a deep sigh and squished her eyes shut tightly. "The

Baker family needs a miracle."

By ten o'clock Juliette had risen, fed Andrew, dressed him, turned his care over to Caroline, and was walking down Main Street toward the Stark home. She'd never begged before, but if begging would help, she'd do it.

Mrs. Stark answered the door almost immediately.

Juliette moved past her into the well-furnished parlor. "I've come to ask for more time to buy the hotel."

The woman began to shake her head. "I'm sorry, dear. I simply can't do it. There is someone ready to buy it in case your father doesn't come up with the money. I need to get this settled."

"No, you can't sell it to someone else. He needs that hotel!"

"I'm sorry, dear, but this buyer is willing to give me more money than your father had offered. I'm afraid I have no choice but to sell it to him."

"But Mrs. Stark, my mother is sick. My father just left to take her fifty miles away to the home of two of her aunts, where she can rest and get the care she needs. You know how poorly she's felt since we arrived in Dove City. He can't possibly be back in time to come up with the money by your deadline!"

"I'm sorry to hear about your mother, but I must think of myself and my own family."

Juliette jumped to her feet. "You've given him to the end of the month. He had your word on it. His time isn't up yet."

"The end of the month is only a few days away. I'm sorry. That's all the time I can give him."

Furious at the woman, she turned and rushed out into the morning air.

With a small bundle tucked under one arm and an apology in his heart, Stone mounted Blackie and headed for town.

As he passed the Stark house on Main Street, the door burst open and Juliette came bustling out. He called to her, but she didn't seem to hear. Leaping off Blackie, he quickly tied him to a hitching post and hurried after her.

He caught up to her nearly a half a block farther, and to his surprise, she literally flung herself into his arms. He pulled her close, unsure of the reason for his good fortune.

"Oh Stone, Mother had a bad spell when we were at your house. You know how thin she is. She hasn't been well since the twins were born. Doc Meeker said he thinks she needs rest to get well. She needs to get away from the busy demands of her everyday life. Away from us." She buried her head in his chest, deep sobs wracking her body. "I think the worry about Father's job has been too much for her. She's exhausted. She hasn't been eating or sleeping, she's—"

"What's your father going to do? Where would she go?"

"Some of Mother's relatives live about fifty miles away. They've been wanting Mother to come for a visit. They're both widows and don't have children at home, so it will be peaceful and quiet there. Father fixed up a bed in his buggy. They left early this morning."

"Oh Juliette, I'm so sorry. If only I'd known. How's your father taking it? What did Doc say?"

"Father took it pretty hard, but he was brave for Mother. We're all worried. She looked so pale—"

He wrapped his arms tightly about her, wishing he could do something to make things better. "I want to help. What can I do?"

She lifted misty eyes to his. "Marry me!"

Chapter 6

Stone grasped Juliette's shoulders and stared at her delicate, tear-stained face in disbelief. "Mar—marry you? I—is that what you said?" *Is God answering my prayer already?*

Her body trembled, and she pursed her lips before answering. "Yes—that's exactly what I said."

He held her at arm's length. "Why were you at Mrs. Stark's house?"

She hung her head. "Begging for more time."

"And she refused, I take it?"

"Worse than that. She said she had another buyer ready to sign the contract for more money than Father was going to give her."

"So that's why you've had a change of heart. You've decided to marry me so your father can buy the hotel."

She bit her lower lip and avoided his eyes. "Yes, if you'll still have me."

Stone grew sullen. "I told your father I'd give him the money. Talk him into taking it, and you won't have to marry me."

"He won't take it. Please, Stone. Father won't be home for several days. By then, it'll be past the end of the month and too late. But you could close the sale yourself and take the money to Mrs. Stark." She lifted her gaze until it met his. "I promise I'll marry you, and I'll be a good wife."

"I—I don't know," he said hesitantly as he eyed her. "I think we're all asking too much of you. Especially me."

She lifted her hand and stroked his cheek. "No, Stone. Not you. I see that now. Your motives are pure. You've asked so little in return. It is me who's been selfish. You've not only offered me a fine home for my son and myself and all that goes with it, but you're making it possible for my family to keep the hotel. I'm asking for *your* forgiveness."

He leaned away in surprise. "My forgiveness? There's nothing to forgive. I was coming to apologize to you and ask for *your* forgiveness!"

"I'll be a good mother to your boys, and I'll run your house the best I can. I know I'll never be as good at it as your Lucy, but I'll try. Please, Stone. Marry me!"

"You'll do just fine," he assured her as he lifted her hand to his lips and kissed it. "I want you to know I'll never expect—" He fumbled around for the words.

She laughed through her tears. "I know—and I trust you."

He stood proudly, his head held high. "I'll go to the bank now and have Marquette draw up the papers. I'll sign them on John's behalf and have the money transferred to Mrs. Stark's account. By the time your father gets back home, your family will own the hotel."

Juliette's hands covered her face as she wept. "I'm so grateful, Stone. Father said you were a good man, and you are." Slowly, she looked up into his eyes. "When shall we be married?"

He gave her a victorious grin. "As soon as your mother is able to come to the wedding."

She smiled, asking through her tears, "Do you want a small wedding? With just our families?"

"Nope. Want a big one. Let's invite everyone in the community. I want to do it up right."

"Of course, your sister and your sons will come in time for the wedding, won't they?"

The corners of his mouth turned up, causing crinkly lines to form by his eyes. "Yep, I can hardly wait for them to meet my bride."

"I'm excited about meeting them, too. I'm sure they're fine boys. They're yours."

He reared back with a laugh. "Can't take credit for their upbringing, but I'm sure my sister is doing a fine job. You know I'll be a good father to Andrew, don't you? I love that boy already."

Her hand quickly covered her mouth. "Andrew! I almost forgot. I left Caroline taking care of the children, and Reuben is working at the front desk by himself. He needs to do his chores. I have to get home."

He reached for her hand. "I'll walk you there."

"But—" She gestured toward Blackie, still tied up to the post.

"He's got nothing better to do. He'll wait."

After Stone had seen Juliette safely back to the hotel, he walked to where he had hitched Blackie to the post. After making sure the gelding was still secured properly, he walked down the street to the bank.

Robert Marquette greeted him with a handshake as he entered. "What can I do for you today?"

"I need you to draw up a contract for me, Robert," he answered, towering over the man.

The bank president motioned toward his big oak desk. "Gonna buy some more land, are you, Stone?"

"You might say that."

Mr. Marquette pulled some papers from a drawer, then dipped his pen in the inkwell. "I hope you have the legal description."

"Nope, but I'm sure you do. I want the papers drawn up in John Baker's name. He's buying The Great Plains Inn."

Mr. Marquette quit smiling. "I turned down his request for a loan, Stone. He has no collateral."

"He doesn't need collateral, Robert. He has the money. Right here in your bank."

The man shook his head sadly. "No, I'm afraid you're wrong. I'm afraid John Baker would be hard-pressed to come up with enough to buy a new sofa for the inn, let alone purchase the building."

Stone pointed to the paper. "The contract, Robert. Write it up, or would you rather I take John's business elsewhere?"

The man hesitated. "This seems like a waste of time, since I haven't seen John's money."

"You want to see the money?" Stone stood to his feet and pounded a fist on the man's desk, his patience wearing thin. "Then go into your vault and pull it out of my account. I'm covering it for John!"

The banker leaned back in his chair and stared at him. "You're covering it? All of it? Do you realize how much money we're talking about here? John has absolutely no collateral."

Stone stared the man down. "Do you realize it's my money and I can spend it any way I choose?"

"You're sure about this?" the man prodded with concern.

Stone sat back down. "If I wasn't sure, would I be here asking you for a contract?" He pointed to the pen. "Write."

$\backsim$

Juliette sat in front of the window, staring into space. *Well, I've done it. I've committed my life to Stone Piper.* She lowered her head and closed her eyes. *Oh God, am I doing the right thing? I need Your assurance. Please, give me some sort of sign. This is not at all what I expected from life. I want to do Your will. Guide me, please. Draw me close to You.*

"Juliette! Are you up there?" Caroline called to her from the lobby. "Someone is here to see you."

She wiped at her eyes and smoothed her hair, then checked her sleeping baby before heading down the stairs.

"Got something for you," Stone said with a big smile that all but covered his ruddy face. "Here."

Juliette moved toward him. "For me? What?"

He continued to grin. "Actually, I have two things for you. This morning when I rode into town, I was bringing you this." He handed her the china dish containing several bars of the delicate French soap from Lucy's bath. "As a peace offering. But when I heard about your mother, I forgot to give it to you."

Juliette took one of the sweetly scented bars and held it to her nose, breathing in the wonderful fragrance. "What a lovely gift. How thoughtful of you. Thank you." She felt herself blushing.

"I have another gift for you," Stone said, beaming at her, a broad smile covering his face. "You're going to like this one, too."

"Oh Stone. Two gifts in one day. You're spoiling me."

He gave her a sly wink. "I intend to keep spoiling you. You *and* Andrew." He pulled a folded paper from his jacket pocket and handed it to her. "Here's your other surprise."

She carefully unfolded the legal-looking paper and began to read while Stone looked on. When she reached the end, tears exploded from her eyes. "Oh!"

"What is it, Juliette? Why are you crying?" Caroline asked as she hurried into the room. "What have you done to upset my sister?"

"I'm not upset, I'm happy!" Juliette grabbed Caroline's arms and swung her about the room. "Stone purchased this hotel for our father! Mrs. Stark has already signed the bill of sale!"

"You did. You've bought the hotel? Oh Mr. Piper, I love you. You're an angel!" Caroline said happily.

Juliette laughed with amusement. "Careful there, little sister. You're making Mr. Piper blush."

"I've been called a lot of things, but never an angel."

"Well, you're our angel." Caroline grinned as she climbed the stairs. "Wait'll Father and Mother get home and hear about this!"

"You can keep thinking that, if you want to!" he called out with a chuckle before turning to Juliette. "I'd best be going. If you need anything before your father gets back, just send Reuben, and I'll come running. I mean that, Juliette." He bent and whispered in her ear, "You're my family now."

"You're my family, too."

"You and I'll get together soon to discuss our plans. That is, if you're still willing to go through with our marriage."

"Of course I am! Can you have supper with us tomorrow night?" she offered. "I'm fixing bean soup, and I'm pretty good at it."

"Bean soup, eh? That's one of my favorites. With cornbread?"

"With cornbread."

"I'll be here." He stepped away, nearly stumbling over a chair. "About six?"

"Six is fine." Juliette watched him go. In a matter of hours, Stone had managed to turn the Baker family's life around. Hers, as well. He was quite a man. She was sure he'd make a fine husband.

If only she loved him.

⌒

Reuben stepped out from behind the counter in the hotel lobby and extended his hand. "Juliette said you were coming for supper. We're having bean soup. It's one of the few dishes my sister can cook."

Stone smiled as he removed his hat and hung it on a peg. "With cornbread, right?"

Reuben shrugged. "Yeah, I guess so. She's been scurrying around all afternoon, setting and resetting the table. You'd think a general was comin' to eat with us." He led the way through the hall and into the kitchen with Stone at his heels.

"Oh! You're early." Juliette quickly untied the apron from about her waist and began fidgeting with her hair. "I look a mess."

"You look fine to me."

"Well, make yourself at home. Dinner will be ready soon. Reuben, take him into the lobby where he can be more comfortable."

Stone pointed to a chair near the stove. "Can't I just sit there and watch? Hmm, that cornbread smells mighty good."

Juliette spun around quickly and grabbed at the stove's door. "The cornbread! I nearly forgot. Do you think it's too done?" she asked as she extended the hot pan toward him.

He looked at the heavily blackened edges with a lifted brow. "Naw. Just the way I like it. Well done."

"I wanted it to be perfect," she groaned with a scowl as she placed the hot pan on an iron trivet. "But it's ruined."

"Looks perfect to me."

"You're just saying that because you're a gentleman."

Stone took her hand in his. "I'm saying it because you fixed it for me, and I'm grateful. I'm sure it'll be fine. Don't fret yourself about it." He sniffed at the air. "Beans smell good."

She turned away and lifted the lid on the big pot. "They do smell good, don't they?"

Stone moved up beside her, took the long-handled spoon, and began to stir. "Ah, we may have a problem. These beans are kinda stuck to the bottom of the pot. Fire must be a mite hot." He lifted the spoon from the boiling mass and gazed at a wad of burnt beans.

She ran from the room with a shriek, her head in her hands.

Stone pulled the pot from the fire and dropped into the chair.

A few minutes later she returned, wearing a wan smile. "Well, do you still want to marry me, or is the wedding off?"

He touched the tip of her nose. "I didn't ask to marry you because of your cooking capabilities. I have America for that."

"Sorry about the beans and cornbread."

He picked up his plate and carried it to the table, where she'd put the hot pan. After carefully cutting a piece of cornbread from the area where it was blackest, he topped it with a massive scoop of the burnt beans. "America burns them all the time," he quipped with a broad smile. "They're exactly like I like them."

She reached for her own plate. "Liar."

"What about the rest of the family? Aren't they going to eat supper with us?"

"Not tonight. Caroline fed them earlier. I thought we needed a chance to talk—just the two of us. There are decisions to be made and things to discuss."

Stone took a forkful of beans and cornbread and ate them as though they were the best beans he'd ever tasted.

Juliette watched, then took a bite of her own. "They're awful!"

"I wouldn't exactly say awful."

"Well, I would!" She grabbed his plate and scraped the contents into a small tub of food scraps. "I'll fix you a sandwich."

He watched as she sliced the bread and topped it with thick wedges of smoked pork, glad he wasn't going to have to eat that big plate of beans to appease her.

He took her hand in his when she brought the sandwiches to the table. Since he attended church regularly, he was sure she'd expect him to pray. "I think we need to get our relationship off to a proper start by thanking God for this food."

She bowed her head.

"Thank You, God, for this food—" He sneaked a peak at his companion, then added, "and for Juliette's willingness to share it with me. And all the other blessings You've poured out upon us. We bring Mary to Your attention and ask that You will make her well soon so she can attend our wedding. And—ah—I thank You that Juliette has agreed to become my wife. Amen."

She lifted misty eyes to his. "Amen," she echoed. "That was so sweet of you, to pray for my mother."

After they'd finished their meal and the table had been cleared, Stone asked, "How soon do you want to announce our engagement?"

"As soon as we're sure Mother is going to be all right."

For the next hour, the pair discussed their wedding plans, with Stone agreeing with everything Juliette said.

"Well," he began awkwardly when they'd finished, "thanks for supper. I'd best be gettin' on home. Guess I won't see you again until Sunday. That is, unless you need me for something, with your mother and father gone."

"I have plenty to do here, and hopefully we won't be needing you. But if we do, I'll send Reuben."

"Then Sunday it is," he said with a tip of his hat as he backed out the door, nearly bumping into two incoming hotel guests. "At church. Save me a seat."

⌒

Four days later, looking weary and tired, John Baker arrived home without Mary.

"How is she, Father?" Juliette asked with a worried frown.

"Better, I think. She went right to bed when we got there. She was tired from the trip, of course, but I think Doc was right. She needs uninterrupted rest. I wish I could've stayed with her, but I wanted to check on you children. How have things been going?"

"Mr. Piper—"

Juliette's hand clamped over Caroline's mouth. "It's my secret. Let me tell him."

Her younger sister stopped talking, despite the fact that she looked as though she was about to burst with the good news.

"I think you'd better sit down, Father. It's about the hotel."

John lowered himself onto the horsehair sofa and cupped his face with his hands. "Things look mighty bleak, and I apologize to you girls. I never thought I'd see the day I wouldn't be able to provide for my family. But it seems it's come to that. I can't even offer—"

Juliette dropped to her knees before him, pulled his hands from his face, and took them both in hers. "Father, you don't have to worry anymore. The hotel is yours! We won't have to move after all, and we've had every room rented since you left. I've been—"

John lifted his face and stared at his eldest daughter. "What are you talking about? What do you mean, the hotel is mine?"

She placed her hand over his affectionately. "The hotel belongs to you. Stone took care of it at the bank. The bill of sale has been signed, and your name is recorded as its sole owner!"

"Stone did that?" His face took on a deep frown. "But how? And why?" John closed his eyes and allowed his shoulders to slump. "He talked you into marrying him, didn't he? Because of me."

Juliette shook her head vigorously. "No! That's not the way it was! It was my decision!"

John squinted. "Oh daughter. No one should have to marry someone they don't love to save their family. He should never have forced this upon you."

Juliette pulled her hanky from her sleeve and wiped at her father's eyes. "Don't blame Stone. It *was* my decision. He did it for you, for all of us, and he's going to be a father to my baby. We'll never want for anything. It's going to be wonderful!"

"But can you honestly say you love him, Juliette? You said you'd never marry a man you didn't love. Remember?"

She hesitated.

"Juliette, I've asked you a question."

"I—ah—I once heard that love isn't always a funny feeling in the pit of your stomach when the other person is around. It's an act of will. And Father, if any person deserves to be loved, it's Stone Piper. I'm hopeful I can learn to love him in time."

John took a deep breath and exhaled it slowly. "Is that going to be enough for you? This is a lifetime commitment."

"I can't honestly say. But I know Stone is a wonderful man. I've only recently realized it. And I have Andrew to consider. Marrying Stone will give my son things and opportunities I could never give him. What more could I ask of a man?"

"You could ask for love, like you had with David," he reminded her softly.

"A love like that may only come around once in a lifetime. All I could ever want is right in front of me, being handed to me by one of the finest, most thoughtful men in the community. Dare I wait to see if love happens in my life again?"

"You've resigned yourself to this, daughter?"

"Yes, Father, I have. Stone and I are going to be married."

"You should've seen the supper she fixed for him while you were gone," Reuben cut in with an outright laugh as he came through the front door. "Burned both the beans *and* the cornbread. That man's crazy to marry her."

John's somber face took on a smile. "She burned them? Really?"

Juliette allowed a snicker to escape her lips. "Burned them something awful. I had to fix us sandwiches."

"But he still wants to marry her. Can you believe that?"

Juliette swatted at her brother. "Be quiet."

⁓

The night was still. Stone tossed and turned, unable to fall asleep despite the hard work he'd done all day. Deep in his bones, he felt an uneasiness that couldn't be explained. Even thoughts of his upcoming marriage and bringing his boys home couldn't soothe his restlessness.

Was that the sound of horses' hooves off in the distance? He sat up in bed and listened intently as the sound grew louder. *Who could be coming to Carson Creek Ranch this time of night? Well, whoever it is, I'll be ready for them.*

He pulled on his pants and shirt, grabbed his jacket and his rifle, and stepped out onto the porch as a band of men on horseback appeared in the faint streams of moonlight fanning their way across the yard. He squinted in the darkness, unable to make out the riders, his hand tightening on his trusty rifle.

"Halt!"

He immediately recognized Zach Nance's voice as the band came to a stop, the dust whipping up in a cloud about the horses' hooves. "What's wrong, Nance? What are you doing here this time of night?"

"Clint Norton rode into town and said a band of outlaws are robbing and torching settlers' homes up the creek from you. They've already burnt down Homer Bailey's place. We've got to stop them."

"Where's the sheriff? He know about this?"

Zach Nance shook his head. "He's taking care of trouble somewhere else. That's why we came for you."

"Give me a second." He rushed back into the house, pulled a second rifle and a revolver from a shelf, and filled a saddlebag with ammunition before grabbing his leather vest from the peg.

Moses had heard the commotion and saddled Blackie by the time Stone rushed into the barn. "Take care of things, Moses," he shouted as he mounted the big horse. "Don't take any chances if those men come by here. Keep your gun handy."

Stone joined the men who'd already assembled when the alarm went out, and they moved toward the creek with Stone in the lead. "Anyone seriously hurt?"

"I'm afraid so. Bailey's dead. Don't know about his wife. Clint was pretty shaken up and didn't have many details. He was lucky to get away undetected."

Stone nodded. "What is it with men who think they can ride in and take the belongings good folks have worked a lifetime for?"

"Human nature, I guess."

"Sinful nature, I'd call it," Stone said with disgust. "Just like the Bible says."

"Couldn't agree more," a familiar voice sounded as one of the riders rode up to join the two men.

"John, that you?" Stone guided Blackie nearer the man. "I didn't know you were back. How's Mary?"

"Better."

They rode the rest of the way in silence until they neared the Mac-Gregor house.

Stone turned toward his troops, lifted a hand, and tugged on the reins of his horse. "Gentlemen, we're getting close to where the outlaws were last spotted. When we get there, I think we'd best separate. Zach, you take four of the men and circle around to the north. I'll take four, and we'll ride along next to the creek. John, you come with me. You other three men go to the west with Jake Murdock. Everybody else, stay here on the south side. I'll give all of you time to get into your positions. Then, when you see me ride in, come at them from all four sides. Let's try to surprise them."

He cleared his throat and looked around at his ragtag group of volunteers. None of them knew much about fighting a gang of cutthroats, but he knew each one would do his very best. He just hoped no one would be injured. . .or worse yet, killed.

"From what Clint Norton told us, they're riding from north to south. He said they've already hit the Baileys', the Carters', and the Baxters' places. All three were on fire, and from the smell of things, so is the MacGregor house. We have no idea where any of the families are or if they're even alive. Keep an eye out for them; they may have escaped on foot and be in the woods somewhere."

"Smoke's getting stronger, Deputy Piper," Jake Murdock shouted from behind him.

"I know. We're getting close. Be careful. These outlaws are desperate and incredibly stupid to think they can get away with something like this. They'll probably shoot at anything that moves. More than likely, they've been drinking, and their brains aren't functioning too well. I don't want to have to take any of you men back to your family strapped across your horse's back. If the gang is still there, take cover. Don't be an open target."

His men nodded solemnly.

When Zach Nance and the other men broke off and headed toward the north, Stone and his group headed east, staying close to the edge of the creek. John rode directly behind him. The smoke became strong enough to gag them. As they rounded the top of a slight mound, they could see flames shooting into the sky.

Stone turned and told his men, "The family may still be in the house! Watch for them!"

In the north, he could see Zach Nance and those who rode with him. Jake Murdock and his men were to the west. Everyone was in place. He gave the signal, and they rode in.

It was difficult, despite the light from the burning home, to distinguish which men were theirs and which were the outlaws. Stone spotted Mrs. MacGregor and her three children huddled behind a broken-down wagon. "John, take them into the woods where they'll be safe! And stay with them!"

John shouted back, "I'll take them, but I'm coming back!"

"That's an order, Mr. Baker! I'll cover you. Go!"

Covering John, Stone watched until he was sure the MacGregor family was safely deposited in the woods, then rode in to Zach Nance's side as bullets whizzed through the air. "We found MacGregor's family! But he wasn't with them! Have you seen him yet?" he shouted above the noise.

"We think he's still inside, but I haven't been able to get near the house," the man shouted back. "They must've tied him up or taken him! I'm sure he'd have come out on his own by now!"

Stone blinked hard. "That, or he's dead. I'm going in after him."

"No!" Nance shouted with a wave of his hand. "It's not safe. You'll never make it! There're more of these guys than we thought!"

"Cover me!" Stone shouted back as he rode Blackie straight across the yard toward the burning cabin. As he leaped from the horse's back, he slapped him across the rump to send him on his way, then threw himself into the doorway of the burning house.

"MacGregor, are you here? Where are you?" he called out.

Nothing.

"MacGregor, can you hear me?" he shouted even louder, intent on finding the man.

Still, no answer.

Stone dropped to the floor and began to crawl around, searching with his hands through the smoke and flames. He was just about to give up when he heard a slight moan. Moving quickly toward the sound, he found Calvin MacGregor. His hands were tied behind his back, a deep gash crossed his arm, and he was nearly to the point of unconsciousness. "Hang on! I'll get you out of here!"

Stone cut the ropes and dragged the man to the door, then whistled for Blackie. The obedient horse darted back across the yard. "Good boy, Blackie!" He lifted the man and draped him across the saddle, hoping he'd stay put. Then, once more, he slapped the horse's rump. Stone took off toward the trees as a shot whizzed by his face, narrowly missing him. A second shot crackled and whizzed past him, this time grazing his forehead and causing him to lose hold of his gun as he dove for the shelter of the woodpile.

As Stone wiped away the blood from his face, he heard someone calling for help on the opposite side of the woodpile. John and one of the outlaws were struggling. The man had a headlock on John, with the tip of his knife pressing against John's throat.

Stone leaped into the air and thrust his body across the man, forcing him to release his hold on John.

"Get out of here!" Stone shouted at John as he fought to get the upper hand.

John hesitated. "It's my battle!"

"Go! That's an order!"

With Stone's attention momentarily diverted, the man seized the moment and rammed the knife's point deep into Stone's shoulder. Excruciating pain exploded in Stone's body. Blood gushed forth like an untamed river and soaked his shirt.

As the man scurried away, a second member of the gang flung himself on Stone, pinning him to the ground. In pain, but with anger as his catalyst, Stone wrapped his good arm tightly about the man's neck and squeezed, remembering what had happened to Bailey and the others.

"That's the man who shot and killed Homer Bailey!" John screamed out over the fracas. "He bragged about it!"

Stone stared at his assailant, then tightened his grip on the man's throat even more until he began to gasp for air.

As they struggled, the outlaw was able to pull one arm free. He poked his fat finger into Stone's eye. For a brief moment, Stone lessened his grip long enough for the outlaw to become the aggressor as the two wrestled on the ground.

He and the man were evenly matched, Stone realized all too quickly. With the wound in his shoulder, he feared he might end up the loser. But to him, losing his own life was better than losing John's. John's family needed him. Calling upon every ounce of strength he had left, Stone flipped the man over on his side and lay on top of him, hoping to be able to get in one good punch that would render the man helpless.

But as quick as a bolt of lightning, his assailant pulled a revolver from beneath his belt and pointed it at Stone's gut. "Die, fool!"

Stone froze. Could he possibly move fast enough to get control of the gun before the man pulled the trigger? Or would this be the end of him? If he did nothing, the man would shoot him. He had nothing to lose. He had to take a final chance. Stone grabbed the gun's barrel. By sheer force and a will to live, he worked to turn it away from himself.

Boom!

The gun went off.

One man fell limply to the ground.

Dead.

Stone lay pinned to the cool ground, the outlaw draped across him. With one final burst of energy, he shoved the man's heavy body off and struggled to his feet, his head spinning.

"I've got you." John tugged Stone's good arm around his neck and dragged him to the safety of the trees where the MacGregor family huddled together. He placed Stone on the ground and tended to his wounded shoulder as best he could. "I need to get you to Doc Meeker. That knife went in pretty deep, and your head doesn't look much better."

"Can't go," Stone muttered almost incoherently as he fought against John's restraint and tried to stand. "Need to get my gu—" He fell back against his friend's chest.

"Hold your fire!" Zach Nance's voice boomed out loudly enough for everyone to hear. "We got them!"

Everything went silent except for the crackling sounds of the burning remains of the MacGregor home. The outlaws' robbing and killing spree had come to an end.

"It's over," John said with a deep sigh of relief as he leaned over Stone. "I'll look for your gun, then we can go home."

Stone sucked in a gasp of air. With great effort, he grasped at John's sleeve and again tried to pull himself up. "He's—he's dead, isn't he?"

"Yes, but he's the one who pulled the trigger. You were only defending yourself. He would've killed you."

"I—never—never wanted him to die," Stone whispered faintly just before he lost consciousness.

⌒

Juliette sat up in bed, wakened by the sound of horses' hooves thundering down Main Street. She grabbed her robe and ran down the stairs. By the time she reached the street, Zach Nance and some of the other men were pulling the outlaws off their horses, their hands tied behind their backs. Mr. Nance was shouting angrily at them and shoving them toward the general store. "Get Ward," he told the man called Smith. "We'll hold them in his store until we can get them to the calaboose."

She scoured the crowd for her father. At first, she couldn't spot him. Then she caught sight of him pulling a man from a horse, and the man's shirt was soaked with blood.

Her father's frightened voice echoed through the street. "Juliette, come quickly! Stone's been knifed!"

Juliette rushed to her father's side and assisted him in lowering Stone from Blackie's back. "Is he—"

"No, but he needs help. Go get Doc Meeker. Quick!"

"I'm here."

Juliette turned to find Doc Meeker, bag in hand, rushing to their side. "I heard the group riding into town and thought I might be needed. How bad is he?"

"Pretty bad, I'm afraid," John admitted as he pulled a big handkerchief from his pocket and wiped at Stone's brow. "Got knifed in the shoulder, and he's got a head wound, too. The guy was aiming to kill him. He's lost a lot of blood."

"Can we get him into the hotel? I need light and water."

"Certainly." John motioned to Juliette. "Go on ahead, girl. Light the lamps and put some water on to boil."

As much as she hated to leave Stone, she did as she was told. By the time she'd lit the lamps, several of the men were carrying him into the kitchen and placing him on the table. She hurriedly put the water on, then rushed to his side. "Will he be all right?"

"Don't know yet," Doc admitted as he lifted the edge of the bloody shirt from Stone's shoulder. "He's a pretty tough fellow."

She hurried to check on the water, then rushed back to his side. It frightened her to see Stone lying so still.

"I could use some clean rags," Doc was saying.

"I'll get them." Caroline moved quickly from her place on the stairway. "You stay with him, Juliette. He needs you."

Juliette nodded toward her sister appreciatively. She wanted to stay by his side. *Oh dear God. I've lost one husband already. Not Stone, too. Please spare him.*

Stone stirred slightly, opened wide the eye that wasn't nearly swollen shut from the gash, and stared at the ceiling.

Doc shook him gently. "Stone, it's Doc. Can you hear me?"

No response.

"Stone, look at me. You've been knifed. Do you remember?"

He gave a slight nod.

"You've lost a lot of blood, and you're probably feeling quite dizzy, am I right?"

The eye blinked several times.

"How many fingers am I holding up?"

Again the eye blinked, then a feeble voice answered, "Three, Doc. Plus your thumb."

Doc laughed. "I'd say he's going to be all right, just pretty weak for a few days, and we'll have to watch that wound."

Juliette cradled her throat with her hand and muffled a nervous laugh. Stone was going to recover.

Caroline entered with the rags Doc had requested.

"You suppose that water is hot by now?" Doc took the rags and began tearing them into strips.

"Yes, I'll get it." Juliette hurried over to the stove and returned with a pot of bubbling water, which she placed on the table beside Doc.

"Thanks. I'll need some assistance getting this bloody shirt off him. I've got to get that wound cleaned up."

Both Juliette and her father moved in to help. She tugged on the sleeve while John steadied Stone's arm and Doc cut the shirt off his shoulder. Although Stone didn't make a sound, she knew he had to be in terrible pain, being shifted around like that.

"Take a rag and wash the blood off as close to his wound as you can, Juliette," Doc ordered as he rummaged through his bag.

She dipped a rag into the hot water, carefully wrung out the cloth, and tested the temperature before touching it to Stone's skin. He gave her a slight smile as she leaned over him and began to wipe away the blood. She'd never seen him without a shirt before. Although she'd been sure he would have well-developed muscles from his work as a rancher, she was surprised at the beauty of his physique and the even, golden color of his skin—no doubt from years of working out in the sun. She hadn't touched a man's skin like this since she'd lost David. It felt strange. Intimate. And although her father, Doc, and Caroline were in the room, she felt as if the two of them were sharing a private moment. As she gazed on this man of strength, she knew she would be safe living under his roof. He would do whatever was necessary to protect her and her baby, always.

Juliette grimaced each time the needle entered Stone's flesh as Doc stitched up the wound. Finally, after applying a thick, dark salve and bandaging the shoulder, Doc closed his bag. "I've done all I can do for him. He'll need to keep that sling on for a few days, and I'd prefer he stay at the hotel tonight. If he's doing all right, he can go back to his ranch tomorrow afternoon. Right now let's set him on the parlor sofa. That work, John?"

"Of course. I wouldn't have it any other way. And thanks, Doc. I owe this man my life."

"A lot of folks in this town could probably say the same thing." The two men worked to take their weakened friend to the sofa to rest. Doc picked up his bag. "Guess I won't have to worry about you, Stone. I can see you're in good hands," he said with a smile as he gestured toward Juliette. "I know you're in terrible pain. Have John fix you a toddy. That'll help."

John laughed. "Stone Piper, drink brandy? He won't touch it."

"If he hurts bad enough, he might," Doc answered with a grin.

Stone gave a slight flinch. "No, th—thanks. I'll tough it out."

"Suit yourself. That laudanum I gave you should help. I put a bottle on the table."

Stone lifted a hand toward Doc. "Isn't that stuff opium?"

"Oh, so you know your medicines, do you?"

Stone wrinkled his nose. "Think I'll pass on that, too. Heard bad things about men having trouble giving that stuff up once they got on it."

Doc laughed. "Well, if you need it, it's there. Good night."

John closed the door and walked back to the sofa. "I'll sit up with him, daughter. Go on to bed."

Juliette scooted closer to the sofa and put a hand on Stone's good shoulder. "Have you forgotten, Father? Stone is going to be my husband. I'll take care of him. Go on to bed. You need your sleep. I'll call you if I need you."

"But I—"

"You heard her, John," Stone inserted with a moan. "Juliette'll take care of me."

John shrugged, waved good night, and headed up the stairs.

Juliette lowered the lamp and pulled a chair up close beside the sofa. "Are you warm enough?"

"Yes. Don't worry about me."

"But you must hurt awfully bad. Will you be able to sleep?"

"I—I could, if I knew you were upstairs sleeping in your bed instead of down here watching over me," he whispered with effort.

She scooted her chair even closer. "I have no intention of leaving. I'm staying right beside you. You might need something."

"Like what? What could I need?"

She thought a moment. "Another blanket. Maybe a glass of water."

He gave a slight groan as he attempted to shift his position. "Or a soothing hand on my brow?"

"Even that."

He closed his eyes and relaxed a bit. "If I were Andrew, would you sing me a lullaby?"

"Possibly, if you were having trouble going to sleep."

"I'm having trouble."

"Well, let me see—" She leaned forward and began to sing very softly. "Sleep little baby, shut your eyes. Morning will come by and by. Angels will guard and care for you. Nobody loves you like I do."

"After you sing to him, what do you do?" he asked in barely audible words.

She stared at the man she knew had to be in dreadful pain as he lay unbelievably still on the sofa. "I cover him and kiss him good night."

His breathing settled into a rhythmic pattern, and once again, she was sure he had drifted off.

"I'm waiting," he said in a low murmur, "for my kiss."

"Thank you, Stone. For everything," she whispered softly before bending to plant a slight kiss on the cheek of this unselfish man. As she did, she remembered the testimonies she'd heard of his heroism, and she was suddenly overcome by deep emotion and a thankful heart. Dove City's residents thought of him as a hero, and now so did she.

"You're my hero, too," she said in a voice so soft she doubted he'd be able to hear it.

He opened one eye. "Your hero, huh? I kinda like the sound of that."

Chapter 7

Juliette dozed off during the night but woke each time Stone's breathing grew uneven, he moaned, or he'd shift his position. Although she couldn't make out the time on the wall clock in the semidarkness of the room, she knew it would soon be dawn.

Suddenly, Stone grabbed at her wrist and began making sounds like those of a whimpering child. She took his hand in hers and realized he was not awake but dreaming. He mumbled something almost incoherently at first, then the words became clearer. "Lucy, Lucy. I won't, I won't. Lucy—"

Juliette shook him gently, fearing he was having a nightmare about Lucy's death. "It's me. Juliette. You're dreaming."

He stopped thrashing about, and his body grew still as his eyes opened wide. "Di–did I say anything?" he whispered as he held tightly to her hand.

"Nothing I could understand," she answered, not wanting to upset him. "You're probably running a fever, that's all."

"You've been here at my side all night, haven't you?"

She stroked the good side of his forehead gently. "Yes. How are you feeling? How's the shoulder?"

He moved slightly. "Uggh. Sore."

"Your head looked pretty nasty, too. How did that injury happen?"

Stone cringed as he lowered his shoulder back onto the pillow. "Shot grazed my head after I came out of MacGregor's cabin."

Fear coursed through her veins at the thought. "A shot came that close to your head? Oh Stone. You could have been killed!"

"Yes, he could have," her father added as he came in with a fresh glass of water. "Three times. Once by that shot. The second time by the man who knifed him. Then when that gun went off, it could've hit

Stone as easily as it did its owner."

Amazed, she turned quickly back toward Stone. "What happened to that man?"

Her father answered for him. "He died."

Juliette let out a loud gasp. "I didn't know. Oh Stone. I had no idea what you went through. He died? How awful you must feel."

"Juliette, that man tried to kill him," her father inserted quickly in his defense. "It was him or Stone. Stone tried to get the gun away from him, but the man pulled the trigger during their scuffle. There was nothing Stone could do. It wasn't his fault."

"Oh, I wasn't blaming Stone, I just—"

Stone clamped his eyes shut and gnawed at his lip. "I didn't mean for him to die. It just happened. I wish I could've prevented it. Maybe captured him instead of—"

"But you couldn't," Father interjected. "I witnessed the whole thing. The man's death was unavoidable. He pulled the trigger, not you."

Stone's fingers touched the cloth covering his shoulder. "But it happened nonetheless. His blood is on my hands."

"That's not so. Don't even think it!" John replied sharply. "If it weren't for you, even more lives would've been lost. Ask anyone who was there last night. Ask Zach Nance. Ask MacGregor. Ask me!"

"They all said you were a hero," Juliette added proudly. "I heard them."

"Don't feel much like a hero."

"Well, you are one." John placed the glass on the table. "I'm taking over now, Juliette. Go upstairs and get some sleep. Stone is my responsibility now."

"No, he's mine. I'll take—"

"Do what your father says, Juliette. Andrew will be waking up before long. You'll need to be rested. Go on up to bed."

Reluctantly, she nodded. "Oh, all right, but first I need to check the covering on your wound." She carefully removed the clean dressing Doc Meeker had placed on his shoulder. It was only slightly damp with blood and the watery substance that had seeped from his wound. The sight of his stitched-up flesh made her light-headed, but she wouldn't let on.

"How's it look?" he asked through gritted teeth.

She knew he'd never admit to how much pain he was in. "Well, I'm not exactly sure how it should look, but I can tell it needs a clean wrapping. I'll try not to hurt you."

"You won't hurt me," he assured her as his fists clenched at his sides.

Juliette held her breath as she pulled the cloth from the cut, which, in her opinion, was looking quite nasty. She dabbed the area around the wound with a dampened cloth, wiping it as clean as possible without removing the salve or hurting him, then applied a fresh one. "There, that should hold until Doc Meeker comes by. I'm sure he'll do a much better job." She straightened the comforter and tucked it around his body.

"But he's not as pretty as you are," he said, flinching and letting out his breath. "Thanks. Now do as your father says. Get some sleep."

"Well, if you're sure—"

"I'm sure." He reached out a hand and touched hers. "I wouldn't have made it through the night without you. Thanks."

Juliette felt herself blushing. "I didn't do anything."

"You were here. That's what counts."

She patted his good shoulder, kissed her father's cheek, and headed up the stairs with a backward glance toward the sofa. *Yes, he's going to make a fine husband.*

⤳

Stone shifted his position with a groan and turned toward John. "You never told me about Mary, other than she was getting better."

"I'll be bringing her back home soon, I hope," John said with a slight smile curling at his lips. "Maybe in another couple weeks. If she continues to improve, she'll be home in plenty of time for your wedding."

Stone smiled back. "Oh, so you've heard."

"I heard. Juliette told me all about it. The last things I expected to be told when I came home were that the bill of sale for the hotel had my name on it and that my daughter was making wedding plans. How can I ever thank you?"

"You just did. Besides, I'm getting a wife out of this deal."

John's smile disappeared, and his face became somber. "You shouldn't have done it. You know she doesn't love you—not like a woman should love the man she intends to marry."

"I know," Stone conceded with a sigh. "She's a fine woman, but I don't love her either. Never will—not in that way. I promised Lucy I'd never love another woman, and I intend to keep my promise."

"So—you won't—ah—"

Stone smiled. "No, I won't consummate the marriage. You don't have to worry about that. Juliette and I have an agreement. We understand each other. We're going to get along just fine. I promise you, John; I'll take care of her and that son of hers as if they were my own."

"You still gonna be my friend now that I'm gonna be your father-in-law?"

"Of course," Stone assured him. "Just don't go pushing me around."

"I have one question: She'd made it perfectly clear she was not going to marry you. How'd you get her to go through with it?"

Stone grinned. "I didn't. She asked *me* to marry her."

⁓

Stone was wide-awake, propped up on a pillow against the arm of the sofa, when Juliette and Andrew came down the stairs about nine. "Well, there's my little man," he said when he saw Andrew cuddled in her arms. "You didn't keep your mother awake, did you?"

Juliette handed the baby to her father and hurried to Stone's side. "Did you make it through the rest of the night all right?"

"Even without the brandy," her father said with a chuckle. "Although I know he was in more pain than he'd let on. This is one tough man."

Despite Stone's objection, she pulled back the bandage from his shoulder with a gasp. "It's still bleeding a bit. You'd better let me put on a fresh dressing."

"Not necessary. Really. Doc'll do it later."

She ignored him and set about removing the soiled cloths.

He cringed and his eyes widened.

"You are hurting. Oh Stone—"

"A bit," he confessed as he shifted slightly. "Guess a certain amount of pain goes with the territory. It's better'n being dead, I reckon."

"Don't say that." She gave him a slight slap on his good shoulder. "From what Father and Mr. Nance said, you could've easily died last night, several different times."

"They were exaggerating."

Father stepped forward. "No, Stone. We weren't. You're lucky to be alive. So are we. If it weren't for you—"

"If I hadn't stepped in, you would have handled that man without me."

"That's not so! He was nearly twice my size. I didn't have a chance. It'd have been me you'd have been burying, not him."

Stone shrugged his good shoulder. "Well, I guess that's something we'll never know. I say you would've handled him without me." His face took on a look of defeat. "At least you didn't cause a man to die."

Her father shook his head. "How many times do I have to tell you? *He* was the one who pulled the trigger, not you. The gun was in *his* hand. You can't blame yourself for his death. If he and the rest of those no-good men hadn't been out robbing, killing, and setting homes on fire, you'd have been out at your ranch, safe and sound. They brought it upon themselves. Think about what they did to those families."

"I'm not so sure—"

"Well, I am," Father stated firmly. "Now, let's have no more of this foolish talk."

"Is that cut on your head paining you much?" Juliette asked as she finished taking care of his shoulder.

Stone's hand rose to the spot. "Naw, I'd forgotten all about it."

The front door of the hotel opened. Two adults and three children stepped inside.

"Well, good morning, MacGregor family. You're out and about early." Her father moved to shake Mr. MacGregor's hand. "Welcome."

The entire family nodded, then moved directly to stand before the wounded man on the sofa.

"Heard you was spending the night here at the hotel, Stone," Mr. MacGregor began. "Me and the missus and my children want to thank you for what you did for us."

Mrs. MacGregor dropped to her knees in front of Stone, tears bursting from her eyes as she looked at him. "Our home can be replaced, but if you hadn't gone into that burning house, Calvin wouldn't be here."

Calvin knelt down and put an arm about her shoulders, his own eyes misting over. "If you hadn't drawn attention to yourself while John led my family to the safety of the trees, I might've—"

Stone blushed and turned his head away. "Aw, come on, you two. Stop it. You know you'd have done the same thing—"

Mr. MacGregor shook his head. "Stone, don't try to act like what you did was nothing. You're a hero, not only to our family but to the entire community."

Juliette listened to the grateful family from her place next to Stone. Hearing of his bravery from the McGregors made the danger seem even more real than it had sounded the night before. He *was* a hero.

"Not one word," Stone cautioned Juliette when they were alone. "I don't want to hear anymore about that hero stuff."

She went back to her task of cleaning his wound and putting fresh padding on the area where the bowie knife had done its work and on his head. "But you are— "

He held a palm up toward her. "I said, no more!"

"No more what?" Doc Meeker asked as he pushed open the door and made his way to his patient's side.

"That hero stuff. I don't like it and I don't deserve it," Stone explained as Doc pulled up a chair and sat down beside him.

"Oh, I see. You're a bit modest, eh?"

Juliette stepped back with a slight snicker as she let Doc take over. "Modest? Stone?"

"Well, you'd better get used to the title. Seems everyone I've met on the street this morning is calling you a hero." Doc pulled the cloth off the deep wound. "Looks pretty good, considering."

"Considering?" Juliette repeated as she leaned in for a better look.

"Considering the man was out to kill him instead of wound him," Doc reminded both of them as he inspected the wound.

Hearing Doc's words suddenly made her sick to her stomach. The wound *was* meant to kill Stone. If he hadn't been able to overpower the man, like her father had said— A tremor coursed through her body, and her knees felt weak.

Stone flinched as Doc poured a solution of some kind onto a cloth and applied it to his shoulder.

"Burn a bit?"

"Whew! What is that stuff? Liquid fire?"

Doc let out a chuckle. "Almost, but it'll help start the healing. If I let you go home today, you have to promise me you'll have America dab some of that on each time she changes the bandages. I mean *each* time, not just once in a while. Understand? Wouldn't hurt to put some on that cut on your head, too, if you're man enough to take it."

"You mean I can go home now?" Stone asked with an anxious look toward the woman who'd been taking care of him.

Doc nodded. "Yep. No better place to rest and recover than in your own bed."

⤚

Reuben tugged on the reins, and the buggy came to a stop in front of Stone's home. America opened the door wide and motioned to Juliette. "Hurry on in here! That wind's mighty chilly. We don't want that baby takin' no cold."

Juliette hurried in and found Stone sitting in a chair by the wood-stove, looking much more fit than she'd expected.

He grinned and held out his hand. "Thought you'd never get here."

"I'm here now." She took off her cape, pulled the blanket off Andrew, and slipped into a chair beside the man she was going to marry. "How are you? How's the shoulder? Are you feeling any better? Let me see your head."

He held up his hand. "Whoa, woman. One question at a time. I'm doing just fine. And, yes, I'm feeling much better, especially now that you're here. He pushed the hair back off his forehead with his good hand. "The bullet only grazed my head. See? It's healing nicely." He reached out and took Andrew's pudgy hand in his. "And how is this little man? He's really growing, isn't he?" He let loose of Andrew's hand and reached for hers. "How are you? I've missed you."

She allowed a weary sigh to escape her lips. "I'm doing all right, I guess. With Mother gone, it's been pretty difficult at the hotel these past few days. I never realized how much she did. Father is so lonely without her."

"Does he have any idea when she'll be ready to come home?"

She poured a fresh glass of water and handed it to him. "Yes, he does, and it's good news. While Gordon Haynes was in Conner's Corner visiting his aunt, he looked in on Mother. She said to tell Father she was feeling rested and much better. Her aunts and Molly have been taking care of the twins for her, and she's ready to come home anytime he can come and get her."

"Does this mean—"

She nodded, her face aglow with joy as she thought of their upcoming marriage. "Yes, we can set a date for our wedding. When shall it be?"

He grinned and shrugged, wincing a bit. "I'm ready. How soon can *you* be ready?"

She thought for a moment. "One month. Is that too soon?"

"Not for me. How about you?"

"Where shall we have it? If we have it on a Sunday afternoon, we could have it at the saloon."

"The saloon will be too small if we invite as many folks as we said." He thought for a moment. "How about the mission?"

She clapped her hands together as her smile broadened. "Oh, what a good idea! That'll be a lovely place for a wedding. Maybe four weeks from this Saturday? In the early afternoon?"

"Perfect." He squeezed her hand. "I'll write my sister and tell her to have the boys here by then."

"Oh, I do hope they'll be able to come early. I'm so anxious to meet them."

"You're going to be my wife now. I want you to purchase anything you want on my account at Thomas Ward's store. That means anything, Juliette." He grinned sheepishly. "From shoes for Andrew to any personal items you need for yourself. Get anything you need to make our wedding the biggest and best Dove City has ever seen."

"And you'll wear a black coat and a pleated white shirt?"

"If you want me to, I will."

"And Caroline will be my bridesmaid."

"Of course, John will walk you down the aisle."

"Let's have cake and cider at our reception."

"We'll invite everyone we know." He braced his arm on the chair back with a groan. "But promise me one thing, Juliette."

"Of course. What?"

"Since you haven't been a widow very long, I understand why you have to wear those dark dresses; but do you think maybe your wedding dress could be that pretty mauve color? Or maybe dark blue?"

She smiled at his request. "I think that's a reasonable request. Which do you prefer?"

"Green."

She threw back her head with a giggle. "Green? I thought you said mauve or dark blue."

"I like green better. I just didn't know if it was proper."

"How about dark green? About the color of the oak leaves?"

He grinned. "That'd be nice."

"Then green it is. I like green, too."

"Juliette?"

"Yes."

"Why don't you have that dressmaker, Lettie Farnes, make your wedding dress? I've heard tell she does good work. Maybe have her make you a couple of new dresses to wear around the house after we're married. Something more colorful than those black and gray things you've been wearing."

She gave him a mischievous smile. "You don't like my black and gray dresses?"

"Ah—sure I do," he said, obviously fumbling for words. "You look pretty in them, but I think it'd be nice for the boys to see you in color. That's all. What do you think?"

She laughed. "I think you're absolutely right. I'll drop by and talk it over with Lettie as soon as we announce our engagement."

"You've made me so happy, Juliette. I know my—ouch!"

"Stone! You're hurting. Why didn't you tell me?"

America pointed her finger at her boss as she came in from the kitchen. "Ya better stretch yourself out on that daybed for a while. I'm gonna go put some extra pillows on it so you'll be comfortable."

"Yes, Stone, please do as America says," Juliette told him with great concern. Then, smiling, she added, "I'd hate to have to help you down the aisle at our wedding."

"Whatever you ladies say." Wincing again, he struggled to his feet. "I've gotta get this wing of mine healed so I can carry you across the threshold." He reached for his bride-to-be's hand. "I can hardly wait for you to move in. It's going to be nice having you and the baby here in this house. I've been so lonely since—"

"Since Lucy died? That's the way I felt when I lost David. Especially when I'd go to bed at night. At times, I thought I'd die from the loneliness."

He took on a serious expression. "We're going to be a family soon. But I want you to know, once you're moved in, you can be assured of your privacy. I will never come into your room uninvited. As we've agreed, we won't—"

She put a finger to his lips. "I understand, and it's good to know you don't expect me to—" She gulped awkwardly. "Either."

"This is going to be your home as well as mine, you know. I want you to make any changes you'd like. Anywhere, except—"

She frowned. "Except where?"

"Never mind."

She confronted him directly. "No, let it out. I want to know exactly what you were about to say. No secrets."

He sucked in a deep breath. "Except the room I keep locked."

"That storeroom?" She could tell he was uncomfortable talking about it. Why would an old storeroom be such a problem?

"Yes, the storeroom. I don't want you going in there."

"But you said it was filled with things you should probably throw away. Maybe I can help you clean it out."

He grabbed her tightly by the wrist, and she pulled back in surprise. "No. Stay out of that room. Don't ever go in there."

"I won't!" she agreed, wondering why the mere mention of a simple storage room would make this peaceful man behave in such a strange, aggressive way.

He released his grip and leaned back against the pillow, his hand covering his eyes. "I'm sorry. I don't know what got into me. I must be more unnerved by my injuries than I thought. I didn't mean to upset you."

"I'm—I'm not upset. Just surprised," she explained, masking her concern. "I didn't know the old storage room was that important to you. I'll keep my distance from it, if that'll keep you happy."

Stone extended his hand. "Don't be mad at me, please."

"I'm not, honest I'm not. With all you've gone through—"

"That doesn't give me the right to take it out on you. There's never an excuse for anger, especially when the other person has done nothing to provoke that anger."

"Really, I understand." She took his hand in hers and gave it a slight squeeze. "I've got to be going now. I promised Caroline I'd help with supper."

He went from a frown to a grin. "Four weeks from Saturday?"

"Yes," she said as she gazed into his tired eyes. "Four weeks from Saturday."

"Can we announce our engagement at church this Sunday?"

"Yes, let's, if you feel like going. Everyone will be surprised."

"They're going to wonder how an old geezer like me could snag such a beautiful young woman."

Juliette felt a flush rise to her cheeks at his compliment. "Let them wonder. It'll be our secret."

"Does that mean you don't want me to tell them *you* asked *me* to marry *you*?"

～

The time passed quickly as Juliette bustled about each day, preparing for their wedding. Finally the big day arrived.

"Wake up, sleepyhead. It's your wedding day." Caroline giggled as she pulled the covers off her sister.

Juliette sat up with a start. She'd lain awake most of the night worrying about last-minute details, going over them one by one in her mind until she felt completely worn out. "What time is it?"

"Nearly eight," Caroline answered with a shake of her finger as she turned and moved into the hall. "You'd better hurry if you plan to make it to your wedding on time."

Juliette whizzed through the morning, packing a few final things for their move to Stone's, spending time with each of her siblings, and saying her good-byes. She knelt at her mother's side just before going to her room to dress for her wedding. "I want you to know how much I love you, Mother. What a wonderful example you and Father have been to me. While Stone and I are not marrying because we love each other, I do plan to use your example to create a happy home for our new family."

"Then listen carefully, Juliette. What you're about to hear is the most important advice I can give you." Her mother kissed her cheek, then wrapped Juliette in her frail arms. "Love God with all your heart and keep His commandments. Put God first in your life, your husband second, your children next, and yourself last."

Startled by her words, Juliette pulled back and stared into her mother's big brown eyes. "Put Stone above Andrew? When I don't love him?"

Her mother nodded. "Yes, put him above Andrew. He's going to be your husband, Juliette. In some countries, parents pick their children' spouses. Couples learn to love each other after they're married. You can do the same thing, if you try. If you really want to. Stone is a good man, one of the best. See that you honor him."

Juliette thought long and hard about her mother's words as she readied herself for her walk down the aisle. The advice sounded good, but would she be able to do it?

⁓

John and his prospective son-in-law stood at the front of the great room in the mission house.

"Nervous?" John asked as he pulled out his timepiece for the fifth time.

"Me? Nervous?" Stone fingered at the tight, black string tie. "Think she'll go through with it? She won't back out?"

John shook his head. "Not a chance. The two of us had quite a talk last night. She's determined to marry you. By the way, you're looking good in that black suit and white pleated shirt. Never seen your hair slicked down like that."

"Think Juliette will like it?"

"She'd better. She's gonna be stuck with you for a lifetime. Your sister get here all right?"

Stone smiled as he nodded. "Yes, late yesterday. I can't believe how my boys have grown. Gonna take them awhile to get used to having their old dad around again."

"Well, don't worry about it. Between the two of you and Andrew, they'll soon warm up and be calling your place home." He checked his timepiece again. "In five minutes, I'm going to walk my daughter down the aisle. Think you can make it on your own, or do you need Reuben to hold you up?"

Stone offered a nervous chuckle. "Never fear, John. I can make it. You know I'll be good to your daughter, don't you?"

John shook his friend's hand. "I'm counting on it. May God be with you both."

⁓

Juliette blinked back tears of happiness as the double doors at the back of the big room opened and the pianist began to play. She glanced down at her dress, smiling at the lovely color—green, the color of oak leaves— as she held on to the arm of her beaming father. It was her wedding day, and she was happier than she'd ever expected she could be.

How generous Stone had been when he'd told her to purchase anything she'd need to make their wedding the biggest and best Dove City had ever seen. She moved slowly down the aisle, passing chairs filled with family and friends, her gaze fixed on her husband-to-be. Her heart pounded loudly within her, so loudly she was sure those seated nearest the aisle could hear it. But she didn't care. This was her wedding day.

The sight of so many people and the sounds of the music from the piano made her giddy. She wanted to laugh out loud, to tell everyone how happy she was. *Could I actually be falling in love with this man like my mother said?*

As she approached the first row of chairs, she pulled away from her father's grasp, bent, and kissed her mother's cheek. "I love you, Mother," she whispered before smiling at her precious Andrew, who was tugging at his grandmother's beads.

Her mother smiled up at her. "I love you, Juliette, my baby girl, my dear one. God be with you. And don't forget what I said."

Juliette proudly took her father's arm. Again, the two of them proceeded down the aisle to stand beside Stone, with her father between them and Caroline at her side.

Pastor Tyson opened his Bible and the ceremony began. "Who gives this woman to be married to this man?"

Father took Juliette's hand and placed it in Stone's. "Her mother and I do."

~

Stone wrapped his fingers around Juliette's delicate hand and grasped it tightly as he gazed into her eyes, but it was not Juliette he was seeing. It was Lucy. His heart broke, and he found himself pressing back tears as he remembered a wedding of seven long years ago.

After the pastor read from the Bible and explained what God's Word had to say about marriage, he challenged the couple to live for each other and for Christ. But Stone's thoughts had wandered to another time, another place.

"Stone?" Pastor Tyson whispered. "Are you listening?"

Stone straightened and took a deep, cleansing breath. "Yes, sorry. I–I'm listening."

⌒

Juliette watched as Stone seemed to have a battle going on within himself as he struggled for words. She wondered if he was having doubts or experiencing the same last-minute jitters that had plagued her all day. But the smile he sent her way and the squeeze she felt on her hand assured her nothing was wrong.

"Do you, Juliette Baker Martin, take Stone Jason Piper to be your lawfully wedded husband?"

She turned to the man standing beside her, so handsome in his black coat and white shirt, with his hair slicked down the way she liked it. "I do."

"Do you, Stone Jason Piper, take Juliette Baker Martin to be your lawfully wedded wife?"

Stone paused.

Juliette felt herself gasp. What if he didn't answer? Or said no?

Pastor Tyson seemed agitated by his delay. "Stone? Do you?"

She watched as Stone took a deep breath, then let it out slowly as he stared into her eyes, almost as if he didn't see her at all.

She squeezed his hand and waited as a lump rose in her throat. Was their marriage going to be over even before it began?

"I, ah—I do," he whispered softly.

"Speak up, Stone. I think your friends and family would like to hear you." Pastor Tyson smiled nervously toward their audience.

Stone blinked, then opened his eyes wide. "I do!" he stated firmly. "I do take this woman as my wife."

Juliette breathed out a quick sigh, as did the pastor.

Pastor Tyson placed his hand over theirs as they cupped them over the family Bible. "By the power of God, and in His sight, I now pronounce you husband and wife. What God hath joined together, let not man put asunder. You may kiss the bride."

The newly united couple stood gaping awkwardly at one another.

Stone glanced around with a nervous expression, his free hand fidgeting with his string tie. Finally he bent and gently kissed Juliette's cheek.

"You're married now. Kiss your bride properly," Pastor Tyson whispered with a grin.

Juliette lifted her face toward Stone's. She realized, if Stone took the pastor's instructions to heart, this would be the first time he'd ever kissed her.

Stone turned to Pastor Tyson, his face flushed, and whispered back, "I'd prefer giving Juliette our first kiss as husband and wife in private, if it's all the same to you."

Pastor Tyson nodded his agreement, signaled the pianist, and the "Wedding March" began.

Stone grabbed his wife's hand, and they bolted back up the aisle and through the double doors.

"Sorry," he whispered after they'd reached the privacy of the foyer. "I just couldn't bring myself to kiss you in front of all those people. It just—well, you know. We've—I've—I've never kissed you before. Somehow it didn't seem proper to have our first kiss in front of an audience."

She smiled. "I know. It felt that way for me, too."

"None of them, except your family, know why we really got married. I'd just as soon keep it that way, if that's agreeable."

She managed to whisper a quick yes as the many well-wishers crowded into the foyer to congratulate the happy couple.

When all hands had been shaken and everyone had gathered around them, Juliette climbed up to the fifth step of the lovely oak stairway, turned, and tossed her bouquet over her shoulder. It fell into Caroline's hands.

Stone laughed as he whispered in her ear, "Ah, Caroline caught your bouquet. One of these days, maybe you'll have some little nieces around to pamper."

Juliette sent a quick glance over the crowd. "Which reminds me. Where is your sister? I haven't met her or your boys yet. I've been looking for them."

He quit smiling. "She had a headache. I sent her and the boys on home with Moses. You'll meet them later."

His reaction upset her, although she didn't know why. It did seem odd that he wouldn't at least introduce his children and his sister to her before sending them away; but if his sister hadn't been feeling well and the boys were tired and cranky from their trip, she'd just have to wait. There'd be plenty of time for that later. For now, they'd enjoy the company of their neighbors and friends.

"Got yourself a beautiful woman for a bride, you ugly old man," Doc Meeker teased as he shook their hands. "Don't strain that shoulder on your wedding night."

Juliette flashed a look of surprise at Stone.

"Don't worry about that, Doc. I've married me a lady. I intend to treat her as such."

She appreciated his evasive answer and gave him a look of approval.

"Well, I'd say Juliette got herself a fine gentleman. You leave this nice young couple alone now, do you hear me?" Mrs. Meeker told her husband as she pushed him toward the refreshment table.

"Sorry," Stone whispered in his bride's ear.

"It's all right. They meant well," she mumbled back as she turned to greet their next guest with a smile.

"I'm so happy for you and Stone," Ethel Benningfield told her as she smiled back. Then, leaning forward, she whispered, "I've been watching you since that day we spoke in the lobby of your parents' hotel. You've blossomed into a fine Christian woman. I can see the change in you, and I'm sure our Lord is pleased."

Juliette's heart was touched by her words. "He's brought our family through some real trials lately, but I've become much closer to Him through it all. Without God to turn to, I don't think any of us could have made it. But He answered our prayers. Mother is feeling much better. Father was able to purchase the hotel—"

"And you're marrying a fine, upstanding Christian man. My, but God has been good to you. Just keep your eyes on Him, and you two will do fine."

Juliette bent and kissed the woman's cheek. "I want you to know I appreciated your advice about my parents. Because of you, I'm learning to think twice before speaking." She leaned close so no one else could hear, then whispered in the woman's ear. "I still have trouble with my mouth. Words still seem to slip out when they shouldn't. Please pray for me. At times, I still have trouble with my temper, too."

"I have been praying for you and will continue to do so." Ethel reached out and gave Juliette's hand a squeeze. "If you ever need someone to talk to, dear, I'm always available."

Juliette watched as the woman walked away, remembering their prior conversation. Somehow, to her, it almost seemed that conversation had been a turning point in her life.

By three o'clock the cake and cider on the reception table had been enjoyed, and America and Caroline started cleaning up the wedding mess.

Juliette handed Stone the valise with the few remaining things she'd need in her new home. She'd prepared them before leaving her father's house this morning. The rest of her belongings, along with Andrew's, had been taken to Carson Creek Ranch the day before. They were waiting for her in the room she'd occupy. "I'm ready."

"Where's Andrew?"

"Father will bring him out later. He was getting cranky."

Stone took her hand, and they headed for their buggy, which Moses had left parked by the door. The crowd of well-wishers cheered wildly when Juliette and Stone stepped hand in hand out of the mission.

After he waved, Stone gently lifted his new bride into the buggy, then climbed in beside her and took the reins.

Juliette snuggled close beside him, thinking that was what all new brides would do. But she didn't feel like a new bride. She felt like a traitor. They were deceiving all their friends.

Stone seemed to feel the same way. He leaned awkwardly toward her before whipping the reins and starting the horses toward home. "Guess we've gone and done it, Juliette."

"Yes, I suppose we have. Are you sorry?"

He leaned toward her, planting a kiss on her forehead. "Not one bit."

"Neither am I."

There was no one to greet them when they reached the ranch. America had stayed behind to help Caroline clean up and put the mission house back in order. Moses had gone back after her. Juliette had been sure Alice, Stone's sister, would meet them at the door with open arms, but she didn't.

Her new husband assisted her as she exited the buggy, then whisked her up in his arms and held her close.

"Are you sure you should be doing this? With your shoulder?" she asked, genuinely concerned, knowing lifting her must be causing him a great deal of pain.

"I may not be the husband you wanted, Juliette, but I am going to carry you over the threshold like a proper husband would."

She wrapped her arms about his neck. "Just be careful, please. I wouldn't want you to hurt yourself because of me."

"I'm almost as good as new. Let me worry about that." He climbed the steps easily and pushed open the door before ceremoniously stepping across the threshold and depositing her on the other side. There, sitting on three chairs lined up in a row, were Alice, his oldest son, Eric, and a darling boy with tightly curled dark hair who had to be Will.

Juliette hurried to them, her hands extended. "Hello! I've been so eager to meet you. I'm Juliette. You must be Will. Eric, you look just as I thought you would. And you have to be Stone's wonderful sister, Alice."

The woman reached out her hand with a warm smile. "Hello, Juliette. It's nice to meet you, too. Stone has told me so much about you and your wonderful family."

The older boy, Eric, stood. "Nice to meet you, Miss—"

Juliette hurried to his rescue. "Why don't you call me Juliette for now? Would that be all right with you?"

The child smiled, obviously relieved. "Uh huh."

She tousled the smaller boy's curly hair. "Will, you have no idea how excited I've been to meet you. I have a son, too, only he's not as big as you are. I think you two will get along just fine. He'll be here before long, and you can get acquainted."

The boy didn't say a word, just stared at her with big, blue eyes topped with long curly lashes like his father's.

"Sorry I didn't get to meet you before the wedding, but we were a mite tired when we got in yesterday," Alice told her.

Juliette pulled up a chair and sat down beside the woman. "I was looking forward to meeting you. I'd hoped we could spend some time together before the wedding. I have so many questions for you because I want to make the boys feel at home. I want to know about their favorite foods, what games they like—all sorts of things like that. I hope you're going to stay long enough to tell me everything before you have to go back to St. Joseph."

Alice gestured toward the two boys. "Those are fine children—obedient, thoughtful, and very responsible. Eric looks after Will—"

Stone stepped in, breaking into her sentence before she could finish it. "She has to go back tomorrow. I've arranged transportation for her."

"Oh no!" Juliette grabbed Alice's hand. "You can't leave so soon. I'm sure it would be much better for the boys if you were able to stay a few weeks—at least until they get used to me and their new surroundings."

"Impossible," Stone answered for his sister. "She has to get back to St. Joseph."

"But since you're not feeling well—" Juliette began.

Alice seemed confused. "Me, not feeling well? I'm fit as a fiddle. Whatever gave you that idea?"

"Your headache? The reason you couldn't stay for the reception. Is it gone now?"

Alice looked surprised. "I don't know what you're talking about. I haven't had a headache in years."

"She was tired from the trip. I guess I just supposed she had a headache," Stone explained awkwardly.

"Well, I didn't! I feel fine. I brought the boys back to the ranch before the reception because Stone wanted me to."

Juliette flashed a questioning look toward her husband, which he ignored as he extended his hand toward her.

"Come with me, Juliette. I want you to see what America and I have done to your room, and I'm sure you'll want to get out of that wedding gown and into something more comfortable."

Juliette refused his hand and stepped away from him. "I'd rather visit with Alice since she's leaving so soon."

"Come, Juliette," he said in a firm voice that irritated her. He was her new husband, but he had no right to make her decisions for her. "I said I want to show you your room. Now."

She offered Alice a feeble smile, then followed him down the hallway. As soon as she was sure they were far enough away that his sister couldn't hear them, she turned to him with a glare. "Don't you ever do that to me again! I don't appreciate being ordered around."

"I—I only wanted to show you your room. Don't you like it?" He gestured around the newly arranged room. "America put your things in the chest, and I moved this rocker in so you could rock Andrew."

"Stone, this is all well and good, and I appreciate it. But what I'm interested in right now is spending time with your sister and your boys before Father brings Andrew." She pushed him toward the door. "Now, give me some privacy, I want to change my clothes."

He moved awkwardly out the door, gently closing it behind him.

Within a matter of minutes, she was back in the living room, dressed in a calico frock. "Now, let's visit," she told their houseguests. She turned to the oldest boy. "Eric, tell me about your trip. Did you see any buffalo on the way?"

His eyes filled with enthusiasm. "Yes ma'am, a lot of them. Some coyotes, too."

She leaned over and took Will's hand. "Did you see any buffalo or coyotes?"

The boy just stared at her.

"Will, did you see any buffalo?" she asked again, this time impatiently dropping to one knee in front of the lad.

Again, he simply stared at her without answering.

Alice shot a sudden look at Stone that Juliette couldn't interpret.

"Will," she said firmly, looking directly into the boy's face. "Did you see any buffalo?"

"He can't hear you, Juliette," Stone finally said, coming to stand by the boy. 'He's nearly deaf."

Chapter 8

Juliette felt faint. "Deaf?"

"Yes," Stone confessed in a nearly inaudible voice.

"How—how long has he been deaf?"

He shut his eyes, letting out a long sigh. "Si–since birth."

Juliette rose and beat her fists on his chest. "And you didn't tell me? Is this why Alice and the boys didn't arrive until just before the wedding? So I wouldn't know about this until after we were married?"

"I—I was afraid you wouldn't marry me."

"Because of Will's deafness? I'm not that kind of person!"

"I'm sure he thought he'd lose you, Juliette," Alice interceded in her brother's behalf. "Most women wouldn't want to take on a child with a hearing problem."

Stone nodded as if echoing his sister's comment. "Alice is right. That's exactly what I thought."

Alice stood and motioned to the boys to come to her. "Why don't I take the boys in the kitchen. I'm sure America can find something for them—a glass of milk or something."

Juliette searched her heart as she watched them go. The last thing she'd want to do was hurt those innocent little boys. Toning her voice down a bit, she continued. "I would've wanted some answers from you, Stone, and from Alice, since she's the one who has been caring for him. But I think I would have said yes. After all, you accepted Andrew and me with very little knowledge about us."

"I—ah, couldn't take that chance, Juliette. Before I could bring them home, I had to know I had a woman committed to help me with my boys. I knew I'd have a difficult time convincing any woman to take on the added responsibility of a deaf child."

What she wanted to do was scream at him; but for the sake of his children, she restrained herself and kept her voice on an even keel. "So you decided to trick me into it by keeping this a secret until after I'd married you? What kind of a man would do that? Are there any other surprises I should know about?"

"I didn't—"

"That's absolutely right. You didn't do right by me, Stone Piper!" She fell down onto the chair with a thud, frowning and crossing her arms. "Do you honestly think it was fair? To lie to me?"

"I didn't exactly lie, I—"

"No, you just didn't tell me the truth! Is that supposed to make it better?"

"I'm sure he meant no harm, Juliette," Alice said, coming back into the room again. "He's wanted to bring his sons home for such a long time. Perhaps he—"

"No harm? Of course he meant no harm—no harm to himself! But what did he do to me? While he goes off to work in his fields, he expects me to perform miracles with his deaf son."

He shook his head. "I—didn't see it that way. Exactly."

"Well, that's the way it is. Exactly."

He reached for her hand. She drew it away. "Does this mean that—"

"That I'm walking out? Even before our marriage starts? I should! I'd have every right!" Juliette thought about the sweet face of the innocent, motherless boy she'd met only minutes before. His questioning eyes had broken her heart. He'd seemed so lost and in need of love. Her mind went to her baby. *If Andrew had been born deaf, I would never have turned my back on him.*

Alice remained silent.

Stone stood gaping, a look of defeat on his face. "I'll drive you back to the hotel, if you want."

She turned to the man with fire in her voice and tears in her eyes. "I'm so glad Will can't hear this conversation. He deserves so much more than this. I have no intention of running away and turning my back on him. That child needs love and a mother, and I intend to give him both."

Stone smiled gratefully, his eyes filling with tears. "I can't thank—"

"You're right!" she retorted sharply. "You can't thank me enough, because I don't want thanks. I want cooperation. Treat me like an adult, Stone. I may be young, but I am not a child and will not be treated as such." She rose, her hands on her hips. "And no more ordering me around. Do you hear me? I refuse to take orders. If you want me to do something, ask. If I decide to do it, I will. But don't order me to do it unless you want a rebellious woman on your hands. Now," she said, brushing her hands together and taking charge of the awkward situation. "Go get your boys and take them for a walk. Show them the horses or something. Just keep them busy while Alice and I have a woman-to-woman discussion."

"But I—"

"Stone."

"Yes, Juliette. Whatever you say."

Once he and the boys were out of the house, Juliette turned to her sister-in-law. "Now, I want to hear all about the boys—especially Will, and don't hold anything back. Tell me everything."

At the first hint of dawn, Juliette climbed out of bed, careful not to wake her sleeping baby. She pulled her robe about her, then hurried down the hall to see if the woodstove needed another log added before Alice and the boys came down for breakfast. Only a few remaining embers penetrated the darkness, casting a dim glow. As she moved toward the stove, she tripped and nearly fell over something on the floor. It was something big and furry, and it was alive!

She let out a bloodcurdling scream and backed away in fear as she felt it move to stand beside her, its thick fur brushing against her leg.

Stone came running in, still in his nightshirt. "Help me!" she shouted as she grabbed for a nearby chair to defend herself.

He flung an arm about her waist and pulled her into his arms, lifting her flailing feet off the floor. She hugged his neck tightly, still screaming at the top of her lungs. "Get it out of here!"

"Kentucky, go," he said as he opened the door and let the would-be monster out into the cool morning air.

"Kentucky?" she repeated, still trembling with fear. "Who is Kentucky? *What* is Kentucky?"

Andrew wailed from his cradle. Eric tugged at his aunt's nightgown, his face buried in the folds.

"Everybody quiet down," Stone shouted above the maddening noise. "It's only Kentucky, my dog. He's perfectly harmless."

Juliette shoved him away from her. "A dog? You let him in the house?"

"Of course," Stone admitted with a grin that upset her even more. "He always sleeps in the house."

"Not anymore, he doesn't!" she stated flatly. "Not as long as I live here."

"But he's a good watchdog, and—"

"I don't care if he packs a gun, he is not sleeping in this house! Nor is he coming in here at any other time. Is that clear, Stone Piper?"

"Yes, Juliette. But a boy should have—"

"A boy should have a dog—outside! Not in the house. Dogs are smelly and unclean, and they shed. I refuse to have dog hair in my food. He's your dog. Keep him outside with you. I have no reason to get acquainted with him." With that she whipped around and went to take care of Andrew.

As she moved away, she heard Alice say, "You'd better listen to her, Stone. That woman is the right one for those boys. She's young, and she's got spunk and spirit. It's going to take all of that to mother these two boys—not to mention the patience it'll require to live with you. Be kind to her."

Juliette had difficulty getting back to sleep, knowing she'd behaved badly in front of her new family by causing such a scene. *I have to apologize,* she decided after much tossing and turning. *But there is no way I'm going to be able to live here with that big dog running in and out of this house.*

⏜

For the next several weeks, Juliette added her own personal touches to their home while getting acquainted with Stone's boys. She saw very little of her husband. He spent most of his time outside, catching up on the tasks he'd neglected during his recovery. Some days, he donned his badge as Clacker County's deputy to fill in when the sheriff was absent.

Will was warming up a bit more each day. He loved playing with Andrew, and Andrew loved being around both Will and Eric. She found it easy to love Stone's boys. Their aunt Alice had done a good job raising them in their parent's absence. Andrew cooed to his new father each time he came into the house. He seemed to be accepting Stone's presence in his life.

Although Stone came in to have a quick lunch with them most every day, he rarely came into the house in the afternoon. Sometimes, rather than go into her room to nurse Andrew when the boys were upstairs taking their nap, Juliette would sit in Stone's chair in front of the fireplace, nursing her baby under the blanket, singing a lullaby to him as he suckled.

⌒

Stone searched the house for Juliette. Finally noticing her door open, he realized she was probably in her room, putting Andrew down for a nap. He stepped into the room quietly. Then he stood transfixed.

The sight was too beautiful.

Lucy had never nursed their boys. She'd never wanted to. Although he'd wished she would have, he'd never pressed the issue.

He leaned slightly forward, wanting to get closer, to become a part of something so sweet and innocent. In his exuberance, he knocked a cup from the table, and it crashed to the floor, clanging loudly.

Juliette screamed and swept a shawl to cover herself.

Andrew, frightened by his mother's reaction and the crashing of the cup, began to howl.

Wide-eyed and consumed with guilt, Stone simply stared at her, not knowing what to say.

"You've been watching me!" Juliette yelled accusingly, clutching her baby tightly to her as she glared at him.

Eric came running down the stairs. Frightened and crying, he leapt into his father's arms.

"Now see what you've done?" she shrieked at him above her crying baby.

"I'm—I'm sorry. I didn't mean—"

"Whatever were you thinking?"

"I only wanted to—"

"To watch me? To spy on me? Have you forgotten our agreement?"

Stone hugged his son, then moved toward the door. "I won't let it happen again. Please forgive me. I would never—"

"Never?" She harrumphed. "You just did!"

He moved out the door without another word and quickly closed it behind him.

Soon things were back to normal. She and America worked on curtains for the boys' rooms, then prepared supper.

But Stone didn't come in at suppertime.

By bedtime, he still hadn't come into the house.

Juliette fed Andrew, tucked him in, pulled her cape about her shoulders, and lit a lamp. She was worried that something might have happened to her distraught husband.

She made her way to the barn and found him. He was in Blackie's stall, brushing the big horse. "Are you all right? I was concerned when you didn't come in for supper."

"I'm fine," he said quietly, keeping his back to her as he continued his brushing. "Don't fret about me."

"But I am concerned," she told him as she laid a hand on his shoulder. "Come on in. I'll warm up your supper. It's chilly out here in the barn."

"I—I figured I'd sleep out here tonight." He turned toward her. "I didn't think you'd want me in the house."

She stared at him. In the dim light of the lamp, she could detect an air of sadness on his wearied face. "This is *your* home, Stone. Of course I want you in the house."

"But—I broke my promise."

She moved a little closer to him. "You didn't do anything wrong. Not really."

"The minute I realized you were feeding Andrew, I should have gone back outside. But—but you were so beautiful, nursing your baby and singing to him. Once I'd entered the room and seen—"

"I should have shut my door. I realize that now. You scared me, that's all. I didn't know you'd come in the house. If I'd known, I would never have screamed like that."

"I should have coughed or something, I guess."

She touched his face with her fingertips. "You're forgiven. Now, come on in the house and have some supper."

She reached out her hand, and he took it. Holding the lamp ahead of them, she led him to the house.

~

The next evening, after Eric and Will had been tucked in for the night, Juliette took Andrew into her room to ready him for bed. Once she'd dressed him and settled herself in the small rocking chair, she covered herself with a blanket and began to feed her baby. She knew Stone was sitting in front of the fireplace. Normally, she would have shut the door, but this night she didn't.

Adjusting the blanket, she called out loudly enough for him to hear, "Stone, come in here, please."

He hurried to see what she wanted, but when he reached the door, he turned his head and drew back. "I've—I've done it again. I'm sorry. I'm really sorry."

She reached a hand out to him. "No, I called you. Come to me."

Surprised, he walked toward her, his gaze going everywhere but to the blanket.

"I've thought a lot about yesterday," she began as she motioned for him to be seated in the chair across from her. "You *are* my husband, even though we've vowed not to share a marriage bed. There's no reason you shouldn't share in the joy I have in nursing my baby as long as I use a blanket. You can stay if you want to."

He leaned forward slightly. "Oh Juliette, do you mean it? It's really all right if I stay?"

"Of course I don't mind. Especially since you told me Lucy never nursed the boys. The two of you missed out on a wonderful experience. I love feeding my baby. It's a miracle from God that I not only gave him birth but can also give him the nourishment he needs."

Slowly, Stone leaned back in the chair and began to listen to the little noises coming from under the blanket as the baby nursed. "It is a miracle," he agreed in awe.

"You're always welcome in the room, Stone. Whenever I nurse my baby, we'll share the experience of this miracle together, as husband and wife."

A tear formed and trailed down his face. "Thank you, Juliette. You've made me very happy. I've missed out on so much, with my boys living in Missouri."

From beneath the blanket, Andrew gave a big sigh as he turned loose of his mother's breast.

"That's a beautiful sound," her husband said softly, turning his face away so Juliette had time to remove the blanket from the baby's face and adjust her clothing. "He's a lucky boy to have you as his mother."

"He is lucky. You've become the father he lost."

"I'll be a good father to him, Juliette. That's a promise."

~

Long after Stone had gone to his room, Juliette lay in her bed, thinking. She had seen a softer, more caring side of this self-sufficient man—one she hadn't known existed. She liked what she'd seen.

She woke several hours later, stirred by a scraping noise she didn't recognize. Had Stone let Kentucky in the house again?

But as she listened, she became aware that the noise had a rhythm to it. No dog would make a sound like that, and it was coming from the other side of the wall. From the next room.

The locked room.

She crawled out of bed, pulled her door open quietly, and padded down the hall as the rhythmic sound continued. Careful not to make any noise, she felt the door's handle in search of the oversized padlock.

It was gone.

She stood there in the darkness, wondering who or what could be in that mysterious room. An intruder, maybe?

Should she awaken Stone?

Deciding that would be the logical thing to do, she moved down the hall to his room. To her surprise, his door stood wide open. In the moonlight that shone through his window, she could see his bed.

His empty bed.

It had to be Stone. But why? What could he be doing in there at this time of night?

She started to call out his name, but remembering how firm he'd been about her staying away from that room, decided against it. Perhaps he'd explain himself in the morning.

She padded back to bed and tried to get back to sleep, but the constant sound seemed to magnify in the darkness.

Eventually, the sound ceased. She heard the door open and close, the sound of the padlock being put back in place, then her husband's bedroom door being closed.

Why was her husband so adamant about keeping her out of there? What could possibly be of that much importance to him? And why did he go in there long after he thought the rest of the household had bedded down for the night?

Of one thing she was certain. That room held more than storage items. *Someday,* she told herself, *even though I know I told him I'd stay out of there, Stone is going to forget to lock that door. And if he does, I just might have myself a quick peek. After all, what could it hurt? I am his wife now. There shouldn't be any secrets between us, should there?*

⌒

Stone being in the room while Juliette nursed Andrew soon became a nightly ritual in the Piper household. It was a precious time for both of them, a time for them to be together, alone, to share in conversation and wonderment. It also had become a ritual for Stone to lean over and kiss the sleeping baby after Juliette placed him in the crib, just before saying good night to her.

For her birthday, Stone gave her a beautiful gelding she named Diamond because of the unusual marking across his nose. She and Stone spent many pleasant hours together, riding through the pasture and down by the river. She enjoyed their many conversations and the way Stone treated her like an intelligent woman as they discussed his ranching business.

Through her tutelage, Eric could now read the simplest of words. She'd been working with Will, too, and he had become her shadow. Things were going well in the Piper household.

One afternoon during a hard rain, at his wife's insistence, Stone decided to take a few hours off and spend them with his family.

"Stone, look into Will's eyes and, very slowly, with an exaggerated movement of your mouth, say, 'I love you.'"

Stone frowned. "Why?"

"Go head. Do it."

He pulled the boy onto his lap. "I—love—you."

A gigantic smile broke across the child's face. Then, in his strange, high-pitched voice, he answered, "Ah—wuv—ooh, da da."

Stone began to weep openly. "It's a miracle!" he shouted as he leapt to his feet and began whirling his son about the room. "You can talk. You can actually talk!"

"It's a beginning," Juliette said with pride. "We're working on it every day. Soon, there'll be more."

Tears flowed down his cheeks unashamedly. "I'm sorry to admit it, but at times, Will didn't seem like a real person to me. He was off in his own dream world, and I couldn't penetrate it. But you've gotten through to him. How did you do it, Juliette? What's your secret?"

She beamed as he lowered his son to the floor and sat down beside her. "Love. It's that simple, Stone. That boy needed the love of people who cared for him. Between the two of us, we're giving it to him."

Stone slipped an arm about her waist, pulled her close to him, and pressed her head against his chest. "Having you here has changed our lives, Juliette. How can I ever repay you?"

"Seeing my husband and our boys happy and secure is all the payment I'll ever need. Being your wife has changed my life, too." She offered a slight chuckle. "Oh, I'll admit I had doubts our arrangement would work, but I'm quite happy living here on Carson Creek Ranch and being Mrs. Stone Piper. You're a fine husband."

He tightened his grip and kissed the top of her head before nestling his face in her hair. "I'm glad you're my wife."

～

"Today is a very special day."

Juliette stopped sweeping and leaned the broom against the wall. "Someone's birthday?"

Stone shook his head. "Nope. Not a birthday."

She brushed aside a lock of hair and frowned. "What, then?"

"Woman, it's our third-month anniversary! Did you forget?"

"Three months? How can that be? How the time has flown!"

"Well," he began, taking her hand in his and drawing her close, "I didn't forget. I've planned something special."

Before she could respond, the door opened, and her sister burst in. "Are the boys ready to go? Father is waiting in the buggy."

Juliette's brows lifted, and her eyes widened. "The boys ready? What're you talking about, Caroline? What's going on here?"

"She's here to take the boys into town for the afternoon so we can go on a picnic together down by the river. Just the two of us. America is already preparing our basket."

"Come on, boys," Caroline instructed Eric and Will as she wrapped Andrew in his blanket. "Grandfather is waiting for us." She grabbed the bag America had prepared and headed out the door. She called over her shoulder, "We'll bring them back in a couple of hours. Have fun!"

Minutes later, as the couple walked across the meadow holding hands, laughing and talking like old married folks, Kentucky ran up behind them and began jumping onto his master's legs.

"Does Kentucky have to come?" Juliette came to a halt, her arms crossed over her chest.

"He won't bother us, he's—"

"Stone, please! You know how I feel about dogs."

"Go, Kentucky," he told the excited dog as the friendly animal circled around him, barking and nipping at his heels. "Go home."

She stood on tiptoe and kissed his cheek. "I'm truly happy. Aren't you?"

"You know I am." He wrapped his arms about her and gazed into her eyes. "Are you ever sorry you married me?"

She braced her hands against his chest and looked up at him, her expression becoming solemn. "Of course I'm not sorry. I love being married to you. I love your children. But I have to admit—sometimes, when I'm all alone in that empty bed at night, I miss the closeness I had with David. There's nothing as comforting as cuddling up in bed next to the man you love."

Quickly donning a smile, she pushed away and ran in the direction of the river. "But I knew that would never happen again when I decided to become Mrs. Stone Piper. I've resolved not to let it bother me."

He hurried to catch up with her, the picnic basket swinging in his hand. By the time he caught her, she'd already reached the river and was sitting on the tattered quilt America sent along. He sat down beside her and watched as she began to pull things from the basket.

"I'm—I'm sorry, Juliette," he told her, hanging his head. "I know I can never take David's place. You're young and so beautiful. You could've had your pick of men. Handsome, witty men. Single men, without the burden of children to care for. I should never have forced you into this arrangement."

"Forced? You think I was forced into it?" she quipped with a mischievous laugh as she pulled the last of the food from the basket. "No one forces me into anything. You, of all people, should know how stubborn I am. You could never have put this ring on my finger, Stone Piper, if I hadn't been in agreement."

"But—"

"Look, it's our anniversary. Let's forget such foolishness and have some fun. This is our day, and I aim to enjoy it." She touched her finger to the tip of his nose with a giggle. "Don't be such an old worrier."

He took her hand in his as he gave her a broad smile. "You win! But remember this, Juliette: If being married to me ever becomes too much for you, I'll let you go."

"You'll never get rid of me, Stone. I'm here to stay." She broke from his grasp, leapt to her feet, and ran along the river's edge. Twisting and motioning for him to follow, she teased, "Bet you can't catch me!"

Stone rose quickly and took off after her. When he caught her, he held her tight as she struggled to free herself.

When all her energy had been spent, she relaxed in his arms. Then, she leaned into him and looked up into his eyes. It took all her resolve to keep from kissing him and telling him how important he had become to her. Just the touch of his hand made her giddy. Was this love?

"I'm hungry," he finally said, releasing her from his grasp. "How about you?"

Straightening her frock, she headed toward the quilt they'd left spread on the ground. "Me, too."

But even as they enjoyed their food, Juliette couldn't get her mind off Kentucky and the look of disappointment on Stone's face when he'd sent the dog away. *As usual, I've been unreasonable, putting my own needs above those of my husband's. It wouldn't have hurt one bit if that dog had come along with us.*

Lord, forgive me and, please, make me more like You.

~

The next afternoon, after Stone had gone back to the barn and the older boys were taking their naps, Juliette carried Andrew to a grassy spot outside and let him lie on a blanket while she went back into the house to get her basket of laundry. By the time she'd hung the wash on the line, he was fast asleep. *I'll just leave him here while I go grab a few more things to wash. He should be fine. I'll only be gone a few minutes.*

With one final glance toward her child, she carried her empty basket into the house and gathered a few of the baby's small garments.

Suddenly, Kentucky began barking loudly. "That dog! He must be near Andrew!" she said with disgust, as she dropped a tiny gown, grabbed the broom from behind the door, and ran outside.

She was right. The big dog was near Andrew. And he was snarling and baring his teeth. But not at the baby. At a wolf!

Juliette knew she could never run the vicious wolf off with a broom. Hoping Kentucky would be able to hold him at bay, she ran back into the house and pulled Stone's revolver from its hiding place. When she reached the porch, she lifted the gun into the air and fired.

Boom!

The wolf took off across the field.

She fired a second shot. *Boom!*

Quickly, she placed the gun on the railing and rushed toward her screaming baby, who had already begun to crawl off the pallet. After grabbing Andrew, she ran into the house and slammed the door behind her. Her mind raced with thoughts of what might have happened if Kentucky hadn't been there.

Eric was standing in the middle of the room crying, wakened from a sound sleep. She looked around for Will, then realized his sleep probably hadn't been interrupted. He may not even have heard the shots.

With her baby in her arms, she took Eric's hand, led him to the rocking chair, and tried to calm them both.

The door burst open, and Stone came running in with Kentucky in his arms. The dog wasn't moving. "What happened? I heard the gunshot and came running. I found Kentucky—"

Juliette gasped. The dog was bleeding profusely, his blood flowing over his master. "Is—is he—dead?"

"No, he's still alive, but he's very weak. He's lost a lot of blood." Stone knelt and lowered Kentucky onto the small rug in front of the fireplace. "Why did you shoot him, Juliette? He's done nothing to you," he asked sadly as he stroked the dog's back.

"Me, shoot him? I didn't shoot him! He saved Andrew's life! I fired at the wolf!" she screamed in defense of her actions. "If it weren't for him, Andrew might have been killed!"

"I—I didn't know." Stone dipped a rag in the pail of water heating on the woodstove and began to wipe at the dog's wounds. "He's alive—but barely."

Juliette placed Andrew on the pallet and fell to her knees beside him. She began to cry as she stared at the blood-soaked fur. "He has to live. Oh Stone, make Kentucky live. Please."

"I don't know. That wolf really did a job on him. Juliette." He paused and swallowed hard. "He's missing an eye."

"An eye?" She crumpled into a ball on the floor, her face cupped in her hands. "It's all my fault. If I hadn't left Andrew in the yard. If only I'd—"

His arm wrapped tightly about her. "You did the right thing."

Her tears flowed profusely. "That brave dog! If only I hadn't been so cruel to him. If I'd—"

He stood and pulled her up with him. "I've got to get him to Doc Meeker. He'll know what to do. Stay here with the boys. I'll be back as soon as I can."

"But I want to help—"

"Then pray. Be prepared—Kentucky might not make it. From the looks of things, his wounds are pretty deep, and with that eye gone— well, we'll just have to wait and see."

Juliette placed Andrew's blanket over the bleeding dog. "Wrap him in this, Stone. He'll need to be kept warm."

Carefully, he wrapped the blanket about the animal's limp body. "But this is Andrew's blanket."

Her tear-filled eyes met his. "Without Kentucky, there might not be an Andrew."

⤿

Stone returned four long hours later with Kentucky wrapped in the blood-soaked blanket. "Doc did everything for him he could. All we can do now is take care of him, pray, and hope he makes it."

The two took turns keeping vigil over the injured dog for three days and nights. Praying over him. Urging him to drink and eat. Encouraging him to get better. On the fourth day, during Juliette's watch, Kentucky lifted his head.

She hollered for Stone, then bent and kissed the dog between his drooping ears. "Oh Kentucky, Kentucky. You're a hero, too."

"This dog a hero?" Stone teased as he hurried to her side. "Is this the same dog who was banished from the house? The dog who wasn't allowed to go on picnics with us?"

She leaned into her husband and rested her head on his shoulder. "If only I'd known what a fine dog he is. The only dog I ever got close to was our neighbor's dog in Ohio. He bit my hand when I was three." She held up her hand and showed him a nearly invisible, jagged scar. "I've never forgotten. I've always been terribly afraid of dogs."

"I guess you know now, Kentucky would never hurt anyone."

She stroked the dog's back lovingly. "Yes, I know. And, Kentucky," she said pulling her hair away from her face and leaning close to the dog's ear. "This is your home, too. Come in anytime you want. You can even sleep in my room."

Stone reared back with a loud burst of laughter. "Now I'd say that's quite a concession. What can *I* do to get into your good graces like Kentucky?"

She smiled up at him. "You already are."

"Well, I'd say your loving care is what's going to put that dog back on his feet, if anything will."

"Is he really going to be all right?"

As if on cue, Kentucky tried to stand. Stone lowered him back onto the rug. "Looks like it to me."

∽

Within weeks, Kentucky was running about the yard during the day and spending his nights curled up at the foot of Juliette's bed. Still not used to maneuvering around with only one eye, he would bump into things occasionally. Although the sight tore at the hearts of the adults, the boys would laugh at his awkwardness.

∽

"I have to make a trip to Topeka tomorrow," Stone announced one afternoon several weeks later, "to take a look at some cattle one of their local men will be selling. Will you and the children be all right while I'm gone?"

"We'll be fine," she assured him. "Don't worry about us."

He crossed the room and pulled his valise from a shelf. "I'll leave first thing in the morning, but don't get up."

Stone pulled Juliette into his arms and planted a kiss on her forehead. "I'll be back in a few days. If you need anything, send Moses into town."

She waited until he was asleep, then lit her lamp and wrote him a note. Quietly, after rubbing one of the sweet-smelling bars of soap across the page, she slipped it into his valise.

Chapter 9

He frowned, picked up the little paper, and carefully unfolded it, noting a sweet, sweet fragrance that reminded him of the wife he'd left behind in Dove City.

Dearest Stone,
I wanted to tell you how much I enjoy being your wife and a
mother to Eric and Will. But I find it's hard to put it into
words. If I had my pick of husbands, I'd choose you. I feel privi-
leged to bear the name, Mrs. Stone Piper. I'll miss you. Hurry
home to us.

All my love,
Juliette.

Stone rubbed at his tired eyes and reread her note. Especially the signature line. Smiling, he sat down on the side of the bed, tugged off a boot, and wiggled his toes. *Hmm, all my love, huh?*

The smile quickly changed to a frown as the second boot hit the floor with a kerplunk. *Most likely she's just happy to have a nice place for her and her son to live.* This time, he lifted the paper to his nose and breathed in the pleasant aroma. *I've sure got me a fine woman. Beautiful, too.*

After refolding the note and slipping it back into his valise, he climbed into bed, crossed his arms behind his head, and lay staring at the ceiling. *I promised her I'd leave her alone, and I meant it. I aim to keep my promise.*

With a grunt, he flipped over onto his side and tugged the covers over his head. *Sometimes, I want to grab that woman and kiss her like she's never been kissed.*

Eventually he drifted off to sleep with dreams of a lovely young woman standing on her tiptoes, planting a good-bye kiss on his lips.

Since it was still much too early to begin preparing breakfast, Juliette decided to wash out the shirt Stone had worn the day before he left. As usual, she found his room immaculate. She pulled the shirt from its peg, knowing he'd be pleased to find it freshly laundered when he returned. She was about to dunk it into the wash water when she felt something hard in the pocket. A key. A large key. Like one that would fit a padlock.

Her heart raced. Could it be a key for one of the boarded-up areas in the barn? Maybe it was the key to the padlock on the mysterious room.

Remembering Stone's admonition, she slipped it into her apron pocket, fully planning to place it on the floor, just under the edge of his bed, after she'd finished washing his shirt. He'd think it had fallen out of his pocket when he'd hung it on the peg and never suspect she'd found it.

Perhaps it is the key to a padlock out in the barn and not the key to the mysterious room, after all, she kept telling herself. The key seemed to grow heavier and heavier in her pocket with each passing moment.

If the key *was* the key for the padlock on the mysterious room, what would one tiny peek hurt? Stone would never even have to know. *He told me to stay out of that room!* her heart said. But the little voice inside her head answered back, *Go ahead. Look. He is your husband. There shouldn't be any secrets between the two of you. As his wife, you have every right to know what's in that room.*

She stood gazing at the key. *Why? Why would Stone want to keep me out of there? It doesn't make any sense.*

Slipping the key back into her pocket, she hurried outside to hang his shirt on the line. The longer the key remained in her pocket, the more curious she became. It nagged at her, goading her to try it in the padlock.

Finally, once the boys were down for their afternoon naps, she crept down the hall to the locked room.

With trembling hands, she lifted the heavy padlock and inserted the key. "Forgive me, Stone," she whimpered softly, "but I have to try it."

She counted to three, giving herself time to change her mind. Knowing, if the key fit and she used it, she'd not only be invading her husband's privacy but disobeying his orders.

She gave it a turn.

The padlock opened.

Still trembling, and feeling like an intruder, she removed the lock and warily pushed open the door, intending to take a quick peek, then close and lock it. Her mind was filled with all sorts of things she thought she might find in there. Tools. Packing crates. Old clothes. Musty-smelling books. Cobwebs. Spiders.

But none of those things were what greeted her as she hesitantly pushed open the door.

Instead, she found a room with sunlight flowing in through expensive, imported lace curtains. The room was filled with French furniture—an ornate chest of drawers, a carved bed headboard, and an upholstered rocker. Her breath caught in her throat. *The rocker. Of course! That's the rhythmic creaking sound I've been hearing during the night. Stone has been rocking in that rocker. But why?*

She stood in the doorway, trying to convince herself to walk away, but she couldn't. Tiptoeing carefully, knowing she shouldn't be touching anything but unable to resist, she opened drawers, peeked in boxes, sorted through stacks of linens, and quickly scanned each area of the lovely room. Although she found many items she would like to have for herself, she left everything in its place. It had to have been Lucy's room!

She held a lovely silk-fringed scarf to her cheek, reveling in its softness. Had Stone kept all these things locked away, thinking she would be jealous of his dead wife if she saw them? That she would be unable to live with Lucy's things around her as a constant reminder of the woman he'd said he'd loved more than life itself?

After folding the scarf and putting it carefully back into its place, she lifted a heavily embellished lace camisole and held it to her bosom. *What a lady Lucy must have been. No wonder Stone has never been able to get her out of his mind.* She caught sight of her reflection in the tiny mirror hanging above a delicately carved dressing table. *Each time Stone looks at me he must be thinking about Lucy! Is that why, at times, he seems moody and distant?*

Being careful to refold the camisole into its original shape, she placed it alongside the scarf, still awed by its beauty. She'd never owned lovely silky things like Lucy's. A tear rolled down her cheek as she remembered the pristine white hanky Stone had given her. She couldn't help smiling at the dear, awkward way he'd presented it to her.

Deciding she'd seen more than enough, she started for the door. But on her way, she caught sight of a beautiful carved chest, quite large by most standards, which stood in the far corner.

She paused long enough to lift the lid, carefully working her way through its contents. Each piece she found in the chest was even lovelier than the piece before it. *What fine things Lucy had,* she marveled as she fingered a delicate, beaded silk purse, trying to imagine where the woman would carry such a costly thing. It seemed Stone's first wife had had nothing but the finest of everything.

Next, she found a large silk drawstring bag containing at least a dozen beautiful handmade Christmas ornaments, many with beads and bangles sewn onto them. She wondered about the Christmas trees Lucy must have decorated with Stone's help. *How sad she died so young, when she had so much for which to live.*

She lifted several layers of intricately embroidered pillowcases and table scarves, but something on the bottom caught her attention. There, neatly stacked together and tied with a red silk ribbon, she found twelve beautifully hand-pieced flower basket quilt blocks. In the corner of each one, someone had embroidered the name, Lucy Piper. Probably Lucy herself. *She must have died before she finished this magnificent quilt,* Juliette thought sadly as she examined each block and its perfect, tiny stitches.

She placed the blocks back into their corner of the chest, alongside the folds of fabric already cut for the backing and the sashing of the quilt. But as her fingers touched the wonderful blocks, an idea occurred to her. *I'll finish the quilt for Stone for Christmas! That'll show my husband I'm not offended by having Lucy's things around me.*

She glanced around, taking in the many crystal vases, fancy pillows, framed pictures, and such. *Stone's boys deserve to see the things their mother held dear. Wouldn't it be nice if, because of my finishing the quilt for Stone and letting him know I don't mind having Lucy's things around, he would open this room and allow the children to see and enjoy their mother's belongings?*

She removed the fabric and the blocks, holding them close to her as she began to dance about the room. *What a delicious idea. He'll be so pleased. I can just imagine the look on his face on Christmas Day when I present him with Lucy's quilt.*

She hurriedly put the rest of the things back into the chest, closing the lid with a satisfied smile. *This is going to be so much fun. My stitches may not be as perfect as Lucy's, but I'm sure Stone will never notice. He'll be so happy to see the finished quilt.*

She hurried into her room, slipped her treasure into a box beneath her bed, then rushed to close the door and secure it with the padlock before placing the key on the floor in his room.

⟨⟩

Three days later, Stone walked into his house, hoping he'd be met with the same kind of kiss as his good-bye kiss. But all he got from his wife was a smile and a look that told him she had something on her mind she wasn't about to share with him.

⟨⟩

With discontent among the local Indians and many land disputes, Stone, Zach Nance, and the others found themselves spending much of their time keeping peace between the Indians and the landowners. Juliette hated his being gone so much of the time. While she couldn't understand why he felt responsible to ride with the men every time the sheriff was out of town or something happened, it did give her time to work on the quilt.

And although Stone kept close-mouthed about much of what he did, her father kept her well informed of her husband's heroism, bravery, and talents as a tactful negotiator.

Two days before Christmas, Stone brought home a tree he'd cut from their pasture. The smell of freshly cut pine filled the house as Juliette and the children made crude ornaments from popcorn, paper, twigs, and string. All the time they were making them, she thought about the lovely ornaments in the trunk in Lucy's room, wondering why Stone didn't get them for their tree.

She and America set about making gingerbread cookies, poking holes in some of them, and threading ribbons through the holes so the miniature gingerbread men could be hung on the tree. Even little Will kept repeating in his strange, high-pitched voice, "Twee. Twee. Twee."

Stone would laugh loudly as his son repeated the word over and over, then he'd pull Will onto his lap and place the child's hands on his throat. "Christmas. Say Christmas."

With a smile that touched his father's heart, Will responded. "Kwis—mass. Aa Kwis-mass."

Stone's eyes filled with tears as he hugged the boy. "Hearing you speak is the most wonderful Christmas present a father could have. Oh Juliette, you've done wonders with my son. I'm so grateful."

Once the boys were settled down for the night and the house turned quiet, the couple sat on the floor in front of the tree. Stone leaned against a chair and pulled Juliette close to him. "We have quite a family, don't we?"

She nodded and snuggled back into his arms contentedly.

"So, if you could have your pick of husbands, you would pick me?"

She sighed and pulled his arms closer about her. "Uh huh."

"You still mean it?"

"I wrote it, didn't I?"

"Sometimes folks say what they think other folks want to hear."

"Is that what you think I did?"

"I hope not. I'd like to think you meant it."

"I did."

The next two days were busy as Juliette put the last few stitches in the quilt by lamplight, long after Stone had gone to bed. When it came time for them to open their gifts, the quilt had been finished, folded, and placed in a lovely box her mother had given her, ready to be presented to her husband.

⤴

"Christmas is a special time," Stone began Christmas morning as he pulled out his big Bible and gathered his precious family around him. "It's when we celebrate the birth of the baby Jesus." He opened it to the second chapter of Luke and read the Christmas story. He prayed and asked God to bless each one present and draw each member of their little family close to Him and to one another.

The children unwrapped their gifts, then spent most of the day playing with the few toys Stone had either made for them or purchased in Topeka. Later that evening, Juliette clapped her hands to get their sons' attention. "Time for cider and cookies, then off to bed. You boys have had quite a busy day."

"I have a present for you," Stone said with a grin, once the children had been tucked in for the night.

She smiled demurely. "A Christmas present for me?"

He took her hand and led her to his room. Her heart pounded. Was he going to ask her to share his bed? Lately he'd certainly shown signs of caring deeply for her. She wondered how she should respond if he did. Should she seem surprised? Resist his advances? Remind him again of their vows? Or fall into his arms and hope he showered her with kisses? After all, they *were* married. It would be perfectly proper for them to share his bed.

"Close your eyes," he told her as they were about to enter his room. "Open them."

There, in the middle of the room, stood a beautiful hand-carved chest much like the one she'd seen in Lucy's room with flowers, birds, and trees adorning it.

"I made it for you. I hope you like it."

She bent low and ran her fingers over the delicate carving, overcome by his magnificent gift. "But when did you do this?"

"I worked nights, after you'd gone to bed. Other times I'd get up in the early morning darkness and go to the barn to work on it. I wanted to make something special for you, something with my own hands."

"Oh Stone. I love it. Thank you." She crossed the room and threw her arms about his neck.

His lips met hers and, for the first time, she felt the ghost of Lucy was no longer standing between them as his kisses trailed down her neck. It was as if suddenly his pent-up emotions had been released. As quickly as he'd pulled her to him, he pushed her away. "I'm sorry. I should never have done that."

Disappointed but excited about the gift she had for him, she grabbed his hand and tugged him back to the living room. "Sit here. I'll be right back."

She hurried into her room and pulled the box from beneath her bed, then rushed back to him, her heart pounding with anticipation. "Here, this is for you."

"Aw, you didn't have to get me a present."

"Open it." She seated herself beside him and waited expectantly.

He untied the ribbon, removed the lid, and lifted the quilt from the box. But the appreciation and joy she'd expected to find on his face were not there. Instead, his face twisted with anger and took on a look of shock.

"You've been in Lucy's room!" The sound of his infuriated voice echoed through the house.

He shouted at her with such wrath, it frightened her, and she pulled away from him. Her heart was broken by his outrageous response, and she feared he'd wake the children.

"What right did you have to go in there after I told you to stay out!"

"I only—"

"I had a padlock on that door! That room belonged to Lucy!" He moved about the room, knocking chairs over, brushing things off tables, kicking at anything in sight. "I forbade you to go into that room, and you disobeyed me!"

She stood and faced him squarely, needing him to understand her motives. "I'm your wife now! Me! Juliette! Not Lucy! Must everything be a shrine to her?"

"You're only a substitute." He clutched the quilt in his arms, grabbed his jacket from the hook, and rushed out the door, slamming it behind him.

Juliette stared at the door. What had she done that had been so awful? She'd only wanted to make him happy.

She waited up for him until after midnight, then went into her room to think. She could no longer live with this man. He'd offered to let her go. Perhaps she should accept his offer. *But what'll become of Will? And Eric? Will they have to go back to St. Joseph? And what about Andrew and me? Will I be able to find work that pays enough to support the two of us?*

She crawled into her bed and wept most of the night, crying out to God for wisdom. She loved this man.

⁓

Stone didn't come back in the house until noon the next day. He'd spent the night in the barn, warring with himself about the gamut of emotions he'd been experiencing since Juliette had come into his life. On one hand, he'd been sulking about her blatant disregard for his orders. On the other, he'd battled with the overwhelming desire to rush back into the house, take her in his arms, apologize, and make her truly, completely his—despite what he'd promised her.

"I'm glad you're back. We have to talk," Juliette told him after they'd finished their lunch. "Tonight, after the chores are done."

He nodded, keeping his face expressionless. "Fine."

As he made his way back to the barn, Zach Nance rode into the yard and hurriedly dismounted. "Stone," he said, trying to catch his breath. "The brothers of the man who died at the MacGregor place have been in town, bragging they're gonna kill you to avenge their brother's death. They also said their gang is gonna rob some of the banks in the area."

"Got any idea which banks?"

The man nodded. "I'm afraid so. A rider came into town just before I left. He said they've already hit the Gordon City bank this morning.

He overheard one of the men say the Bartonville bank was gonna be next."

"Let me get my guns." Stone ran to the barn, gathered up what he'd need, and returned riding Blackie. "Let's go."

"Aren't you going to tell Juliette you're leaving?"

Stone shook his head. "She'll find out soon enough, not that she cares. Let's go. Maybe we can intercept them before they get to Bartonville."

~

Juliette watched from the window. What had Zach Nance said to Stone? Why had they ridden off so fast? Well, if he'd wanted her to know, he would have told her. Obviously, he no longer thought of her as an important part of his life.

She told America to take the rest of the day off and went about tidying up the house. She took down the Christmas tree and the few decorations she'd placed throughout their home.

Several times during the long night, Juliette tiptoed down the hall to see if her husband had slipped in undetected. The empty bed confirmed her suspicions. If only she'd heard his conversation with Mr. Nance, she might have had a clue as to his whereabouts.

By noon the next day, worry had replaced her concern. She spent the afternoon packing up the things that belonged to her and Andrew and placing them in the buggy in preparation for moving back to the hotel. She'd just carried the last box to the buggy when a man she'd seen her husband speaking with in town several weeks earlier came riding into the yard looking for Stone.

"I'm sorry, my husband isn't here. I'm not sure when he'll be back," she told the man, embarrassed at her lack of knowledge.

"Actually, I've come to warn Deputy Piper," the out-of-breath man said hurriedly. "In the saloon last night, I overheard one of the Dighton boys saying they were going to find Stone and kill him to avenge their brother's death. I'm sure they meant it. The deputy needs to know so he can be on his guard. Those men mean business. Tell him to be careful!"

Juliette thanked him, then watched as he rode out of the yard. *I've got to let Stone know!*

Forgetting all about leaving for the hotel, she raced to the barn, screaming at Moses to help her saddle up Diamond. After grabbing a shawl, one of Stone's heaviest jackets, and a woolen scarf from a hook by the door, she shouted out orders to Moses, telling him to have America stay with the children until she returned and to keep their guns handy. She waved, then rode out in search of her husband.

～

Stone and his band of volunteers spent the rest of the day search-ing the area near Gordon City. The entire night, they hovered in the graveyard next to the bank in Bartonville. If the band of outlaws hit the place, as they'd said they were going to, he and his men would be ready for them.

The bank opened at ten as usual. Other than the few regular cus-tomers who showed up, there didn't seem to be much activity.

"Think they've outfoxed us?" Stone finally asked Zach Nance several hours later. "Maybe they started that rumor to throw us off the trail. You think they might have lured us out of town so they could hit our bank in Dove City?"

"Don't know." Mr. Nance stretched first one arm, then the other as he arched his back. "There sure isn't anything going on around here. I think we'd better head for home. That way, if we are needed, we'll be a whole lot closer than we are now."

Stone signaled the group of men, and they rode back toward town. When they reached the cutoff to Carson Creek Ranch, he saluted and headed Blackie toward home. "Let me know if you need me, and I'll come running."

But as he turned Blackie into the yard, Moses came rushing out of the house, his arms flailing about wildly. "Juliette's gone!"

Stone let out a sorrowful sigh. *So she couldn't even wait for us to have our talk. She's already left me.*

"She rode off on Diamond lookin' for you!" Moses cried out. "The Dighton brothers said they was gonna kill you!"

Stone's heart sank. He reined up and leaped off Blackie. "Where are the children?"

Moses bent to catch his breath. "With America."

Stone pounded his palm against his forehead. "I should never have left her like I did!" Reminding Moses to keep himself armed, he rode out on Blackie in search of his wife.

~

Juliette maneuvered Diamond through the trees along the river's edge, snagging her clothing, catching her long hair on the branches and brambles until exhaustion overtook her and she could go no farther. Why hadn't she found Stone? Perhaps he hadn't even come this way. Perhaps she'd been going in circles. Disgusted by her lack of tracking skills and growing more concerned over her husband, she began to cry. *Why did I come out here all alone? Did I actually think I could find Stone?*

The sudden hoot of an owl sent shivers down her back.

Lord God, she pled as her tears flowed freely. *Protect me, please. You know how afraid I am. Most of all, protect my husband. His children need him.* She wiped at her tears. *I—I need him. I love him so much. I have to tell him.*

Thinking she heard voices off in the distance, she paused to listen. The voices weren't those of Stone and his men, but the voices of the band of outlaws! Maybe they had a lookout. Maybe two or three, and she'd be discovered! Terrified, she scrambled off Diamond and cautiously led him through the dense trees. She tried to be quiet, yet put as much distance as possible between her and her potential captors without attracting their attention. *Those men would like nothing better than to find Deputy Stone Piper's wife alone in the woods and at their mercy.* She trembled at the thought.

Mounting Diamond again when she reached an open area, she rode for what seemed like hours until the late afternoon turned into evening. She constantly listened for sounds of riders, keeping an eye on the sky and the rapidly approaching storm. She was hopelessly lost and had no idea which direction she should go to reach the ranch.

Suddenly, a bolt of lightning split the sky and thunder rumbled overhead, spooking Diamond. The horse reared, throwing her to the ground before taking off through the trees and disappearing into the darkness.

Excruciating pain consumed her body. Sure her arm had been broken in her fall, Juliette lay crying on the ground, her head bleeding from where she'd hit it on a rock. "Oh Stone, Stone, where are you?" she whispered as she cradled her aching arm close to her body. She was afraid if she called out, the outlaws might hear her. "I need you!"

The rain began to fall, as thunder growled fiercely and lightning flashed across the night sky. *I have to find shelter,* she told herself as she struggled to her feet. After much searching, she discovered a huge, fallen tree with a rotting cavern in its side just big enough to hold her. Feeling woozy from the bump on her head and clutching her arm tightly to her, she bent low and worked her body into the elongated opening. "I–I'm so co–cold. I'm not sure I can ma–make it through the ni–night," she mumbled through chattering teeth, working to pull Stone's wet jacket close about her to ward off the brisk night air. *Stone will never find me here, but I can't stay out in the storm all night.*

After pulling a few leaves and brush about her to fend off the cold, Juliette closed her eyes and tried to sleep. But sleep wouldn't come. *I was stupid to have ridden out here by myself! It was a crazy thing to do. I should've gone into town and tried to find Thomas Ward. But I had to come! I was so worried about Stone. What if that man found him?*

Suddenly, she felt something touch her side—something furry. She froze with fear, remembering the look on the wolf's face as he'd bared his teeth in her yard that day. *Oh God,* she prayed, holding her breath and trying hard not to move. *Have I escaped those men only to be eaten alive by some wild animal? What will become of my baby without me there to care for him? Help me!*

A single flash of lightning made her worst fears a reality. An animal of some kind was creeping low across the ground, circling her, and she knew her life was about to come to an end. She closed her eyes and held her breath. *Oh God, please don't let me die! Not now! Not yet! Not this way!*

Instead of attacking her, the animal began licking her face! Her heart pounded furiously, and she tried to back away, but the stump prevented it. As another flash of lightning split the sky, she caught sight of the gentle, one-eyed face of Kentucky.

"Oh Kentucky, you dear, sweet dog," she told him as she wrapped her good arm about him. "You followed me!"

Kentucky licked at her wounds, then settled down beside her, sharing the warmth of his body. She praised God for answering her prayer and sending the big dog to comfort her and keep her warm.

"You're almost as good as an angel."

~

"Not much use looking for her in this darkness. Let's go. Maybe Juliette's already back home waiting for us." Faint with feelings of discouragement and defeat, Stone turned Blackie around and headed for the ranch.

"Sorry, Stone, I ain't seen Juliette," Moses told him as he rode into the yard. "She never came home."

Shaking the rain off his hat, Stone turned and rode out of the yard again. "She'll freeze out there. I've got to find her!"

Hours later, he dismounted Blackie, tied his reins to a sapling, and fell on the ground, striking it with his fists. "God," he called out, confident the God of heaven would hear his cries. "I've sinned against You something awful, and I've sinned against others. There's been so much unrighteousness in my life. More'n most folks would believe."

He swallowed at the lump in his throat as tears of repentance flowed down his cheeks. "Only You know what a fake I've been—pretending to be this fine, upstanding Christian man, when deep inside, I was nothing but a lying scoundrel. The Bible says You are faithful and just to forgive our sins. I'm begging You to forgive mine. I'm accepting Christ as my Savior. Cleanse me, Lord. Come into my heart. Come into my life. Take over, God. I'm Yours now. My life is in Your hands now."

As he lay in the rain, communing with God, a sweet peace came over him. He knew God had heard and answered his plea. With a new-found faith, he began to pray again.

"God, I've done wrong to the finest woman I've ever known. Don't let her suffer because of me. She's got a little boy who needs her." He paused and lifted his eyes heavenward. The rain fell upon his face and his shoulders, soaking his jacket. "I need her. I—I—love her. Watch over her, please. Bring her back to me. Give me another chance to do right by her. I promise I'll tell her everything."

He stood and listened to the night, hoping for a sound that would lead him to his wife. But the only sounds he heard were those of the whining of the wind as it whipped through the trees and the thunder rolling about overhead.

The storm finally over, the sky began to lighten somewhat as Stone sat crouched beside Blackie. He'd searched the entire night. *Juliette, sweet, sweet Juliette, where are you? If only I would've told you how much I love you!*

He stared at the sky as streaks of red, pink, and blue lifted themselves above the horizon. *She always loved the sunrise,* he reminded himself as the splendor of the new day dawned before him.

Wearily, he rose and mounted his horse. "Which way now, Blackie?" he asked, stroking the horse's mane. As he turned to take one last look at the sunrise, something caught his eye. Something moved by a huge fallen log several yards ahead of him. It looked like a wolf or a coyote. He couldn't be sure.

Curious, he slowly edged Blackie closer. It *was* an animal of some sort, all right, and it almost looked like his big dog. He blinked and looked again. It *was* his big dog! *But why would Kentucky be out here in the woods? Did he follow me?*

He called to him, but the normally obedient dog didn't come. He just sat there, staring at his master. "Kentucky, come here," Stone ordered firmly, but the dog ignored his command, turned, and walked away from him, disappearing behind the huge fallen log. Fearing the dog might be injured, Stone quickly dismounted and rushed toward the log as Kentucky pawed at the ground and began to whine.

Stone stooped to see what the dog had been digging at, and there, tucked into the rotted-out area of the fallen tree, he found his precious Juliette.

"Oh Stone. I knew you'd come," she said in a mere whisper. "I've been asking God to send you."

"God led me to you, my beloved." As he squatted and leaned close to her, the sight that greeted him made his stomach lurch. He barely recognized his wife. A huge knot distorted her forehead, and she was covered with blood. He gently kissed her wounded face. "My darling, I've searched for you all night."

"I'm fi–fine," she whispered through chattering teeth, so softly he could barely hear her. "Th–thanks to Ke–Kentucky."

He tried to pull her from the log, but she winced in pain. "M–my a–arm. It—it's br–broken."

"Oh Juliette, if it weren't for me—"

She gave a slight shake of her head. "No, d–don't s–say it," she whispered. "N–not your f–fault."

"I've got to get you to Doc Meeker. That nasty cut on your head and your broken arm both need attention." New energy filled his body as he tenderly scooped his wife from the log's crude opening, lifted her in his arms, and kissed her face. God had answered his prayers. He'd kept her safe. Even with her injuries, she was still the most beautiful woman he'd ever seen—far lovelier than Lucy had ever been.

Lifting his face to God, he called out loudly, "I praise You, God, for answering my prayers and leading me to my dear wife. Forgive me for ever doubting You!"

Turning to Kentucky, he asked, "Gonna make it, boy?"

The big dog barked, then began ambling along behind them as they rode toward town to find Doc Meeker.

⁓

"She'll be fine, Stone. Just make sure she gets plenty of rest. She's been through quite an ordeal," Doc said. "You take good care of her, you hear me?"

Stone nodded as he carefully gathered his wife up and lovingly placed her in the buggy John had brought for him to take Juliette home. "I will, Doc. She's precious to me."

Juliette's sound arm circled her husband's neck as he carried her up the steps and into their home.

"Da-da," Andrew called out in his baby voice as he reached his arms toward them.

"Looks like my son wants me," Stone said with a grin as he tenderly placed his wife on a chair and took the smiling child from America. "Look who I brought home, Andrew. It's your mama."

Eric reached out and touched the heavy layers of cloth that covered the knot on Juliette's forehead. "Does it hurt, Mama?" he asked with a look that tore at her heart.

She slipped an arm around the boy and pulled him close. "It's not as bad as it looks." Noticing Will staring at her, she reached out a hand.

The little boy came running to her and leaped onto her lap. "Ma-ma h–h–hut?"

Juliette bent and kissed the boy's sweet cheek. "Yes, Will. Mama hurt. But she's going to be all right, now that she's home with her three boys." She sent a loving glance toward Stone, who appeared to be trying to mask his tears.

Later that night over a cup of hot tea, Stone told Juliette how he'd prayed in the woods that morning and had asked God to forgive him for his sins and asked Him to save him.

"I'm so glad, Stone. We both needed to get our lives straightened out. God has been so patient with us. Neither one of us deserves His love."

Stone gazed into her lovely face. "I know." Then, he and Juliette held hands, bowed their heads, and thanked the Lord for keeping each of them safe and bringing them home to their family.

⌒

Two days later, after a nourishing supper of potato soup prepared by America, Stone put the boys to bed, then carried his wife into her room. He placed her on her bed and propped her up against a pile of pillows, then sat down beside her, took her free hand in his, and kissed her palm. "If you're up to it, we need to talk."

She gnawed at her lower lip. She'd been dreading this since the moment Stone had angrily stormed out of the house with the quilt under his arm. "Yes, we do."

He gazed into her eyes and blinked several times before speaking. "I need to apologize for my actions on Christmas Day."

She wanted to scream out, *Yes, you need to apologize! I did nothing to deserve your wrath. I only wanted to make you happy!* Instead, she kept her silence.

"I—I haven't been totally honest. When I was out there looking for you and asking God to help me find you, I promised Him I would tell you everything. Even if you hated me for it. There's so much you don't know. I hardly know where to start." He gulped hard. "Maybe I'd better go back to the beginning."

She nodded, knowing as angry as his words might make her, she could never hate him. Nothing could make her hate him. She loved him too much.

"My father, and his father before him, owned huge tobacco plantations. We had a fine house and many servants. All of them were slaves, bought by my father and my grandfather. Even as a small child, I hated watching the slaves working so hard and being mistreated by my father. Although the other wealthy people of Kentucky thought of him as this fine, upstanding man, he wasn't! He was cruel. He used to get drunk and beat my mother. She never told anyone because of the shame she felt, but the slaves and I knew."

Juliette gasped as her hand rose to cover her mouth. "How awful!"

"I used to tell her of my big plans to leave and take her with me, but we both knew it'd never happen—not with my father being so rich and powerful. We'd never get away from him. When he'd beat her, I'd put cold cloths on her bruises, trying to make her feel better. She'd always smile and say it helped, but I doubted it did."

"Didn't your friends and neighbors see her bruises?"

"No, she'd stay in the house until they disappeared, cover them with powder, or make up stories about falling down our staircase. She never told anyone. No one would've believed her anyway. Many times, I heard my father tell his friends she drank heavily, but that wasn't true. She never took a drink. He said that as a cover-up for the way she looked, all bruised and sad."

"Oh, your poor mother. How awful it must've been for her. For both of you."

"Well, one night when I guess I was about sixteen, I found my mother lying on the floor in her room in a pool of blood. My father was standing over her with a heavy candlestick in his hand. He'd been beating her with it. I grabbed it from his hand and hit him once. Real hard. On his head. He clutched his chest and fell across the bed. I didn't know what to do. My mother screamed for me to go get help, but I didn't. I just stood there, almost hoping he wouldn't make it."

Juliette let out a slight moan. "Oh Stone."

"Moses went for help, but by the time someone arrived, Father was already dead. To protect me, Mother told them she'd hit him. But the doctor said the blow hadn't been enough to kill him. He'd died of a heart attack. Still, I knew better. I'd killed him. If I hadn't hit him, he wouldn't have had that spell with his heart. I'm sure of it."

"You were only sixteen at the time?"

"Yes. My mom and I did the best we could to run the place after my father died. She died about five years later—from her illness they said, but I always thought it was from a broken heart. As their only child, I inherited everything: the plantation, my father's business, his bank accounts." He paused. "Everything. I freed all the slaves when my mother died, and I became the legal owner."

"That's when you freed Moses and America?"

He smiled. "Yes. Most of the slaves stayed with me. I improved their housing and gave them an honest wage for their labors. I ran that plantation until about nine years ago. That's when I decided to sell out and come west. I needed a change in my life, a new challenge."

"And America and Moses came with you?"

He shook his head. "Not at first. They stayed behind with the new owner. I brought the few possessions I wanted to keep with me to St. Louis. I made my home there for a year or so. I'd never planned to stay in Missouri. My sights were set on Kansas and the open prairie."

Juliette tilted her head. "What about Alice?"

"Alice? Oh, she's maybe my half-sister. Father just showed up with her one day. He said he thought she might be his daughter and moved her in with us. We never knew her real mother's name, and Father wouldn't tell us. He said he'd been paying some woman to look after her since the day she was born. The woman had died, so he'd brought her home to us. That's another reason my mother died of a broken heart. If the truth were known, some of the slave children were probably my half-brothers and sisters, too."

He sucked in a fresh breath of air and continued. "Alice is five years older than me. When she got old enough to be on her own, she left us and moved to St. Louis to get away from my father. That's one reason I stayed in Missouri—because of her. I'd always loved her, almost as much as if she'd been my real sister."

"Is that where you met Lucy? In St. Louis?"

He rubbed at his chin and stared at the wall as if seeing a vision of his deceased wife. "Yes. I met her at a dance one of my new friends took me to. She was beautiful—the prettiest and wildest girl I'd ever met. She took a shine to me, too. I used to think she really liked me. Looking back, I sometimes wonder if she'd learned about the money I'd banked from the plantation's sale and only tolerated me because of it."

Juliette shifted her position with a frown as pain shot through her arm. "Stone, surely you don't mean that."

"I might've been wrong, but I guess I'll never know for sure. Anyway, I fell for that woman in a big way. She hung all over me. Kissing me and making over me like I was the catch of the century. No woman had ever done that before. In two weeks we were married. Just like that." He snapped his fingers.

"She must've really loved you, to marry you so quickly."

"Well, I know she spent my money like there was no bottom to the barrel. And she never wanted to move west, even though she knew from the beginning that'd been my plan. I promised her a fine house and servants. Finally, she agreed to give it a try. I came on ahead and bought the land and turned it into Carson Creek Ranch.

After I built the house, I brought her here. Since I'd promised her servants, I wrote to America and asked if she and Moses would like to come to Kansas."

Juliette smiled. "Oh, but she had to have been pleased when she saw this fine house. She must've loved moving to Kansas, to the new frontier, and being with her husband again. I'm sure she missed you."

Stone let out a long, deep sigh. "No, she hated it. She complained about everything. The house wasn't formal enough for her. It was too isolated. Too hot. Too cold. Too far from a big city where the elegant parties were held. Nothing I did pleased her."

"But—you loved her," she inserted softly. "You've told me so, many times."

"I did love her—or I thought I did. I remembered watching the way my father treated my mother. I vowed then that I'd never marry a woman I didn't love. And when I did marry, it would be forever. I took my marriage vows seriously."

"I'm sure Lucy did, too."

Andrew stirred in his bed.

"Let me nurse him. I'm sure he'll go right back to sleep," Juliette told him as she smoothed the covers beside her.

Stone bent over the crib and lifted the sleepy baby, placing him at his mother's side. "I'll go after a fresh cup of water while you nurse him."

~

He moved to the other room and sat down in the chair beside the fireplace, cradling his head in his hands. *God, can You ever forgive me for deceiving Juliette? I don't want to hurt this wonderful woman anymore, but she has to know the truth. I need Your help. Give me the right words. I can't put this off any longer.* He rose, plunged the dipper into the pail of water, and filled her cup. *She's been through so much these past few days. Dare I heap any more on her?* With a heavy heart, he moved back into her room with the cup.

She smiled as he came through the door, motioning toward the sleeping baby, a trickle of milk still evident on his rosy little cheek. "Would you put him back in his bed, please?"

He nodded, took Andrew from her side, and carefully laid the sleeping baby in his crib.

As soon as he was seated again, Juliette reached out and cupped his chin with her hand. "Poor Stone, I never realized you'd been through so much."

With a heavy heart filled with guilt, he hung his head. "I don't want sympathy, Juliette. Please know I'm not telling all of this as an excuse for my behavior. I'm telling it because you deserve to know. What I've done is inexcusable."

She shook her head. "Nothing can be that bad. Go on. I'm listening."

He settled himself beside her and began again. "I even took Lucy back to St. Louis several times to purchase some of the fine items you've seen here." He grinned. "Some I didn't know you'd seen."

"I'm sorry. I never meant to—"

He put a finger to her lips. "You did nothing wrong. You only wanted to please me." He paused. "For a while, she seemed happy. But she was soon as discontent as ever, saying her life with me here in Kansas bored her. She constantly threatened to leave me and find another man who would take her back to St. Louis. Then, she began to be sick around the clock, and Doc Meeker said she was with child. That news really upset her. She blamed me and said she'd never fit in her beautiful clothes again because of what I had done to her. She even talked about doing away with the baby."

Juliette gasped. "How could she?"

He shrugged and let out another deep sigh. Telling her all of this was harder than he'd ever expected, but he couldn't stop now.

"I finally talked her out of it. When Eric came into this world and she had a pretty rough delivery, she swore she'd never have another child."

"But she loved Eric, didn't she?"

"Maybe. When he wasn't crying or wet. Then America or I had to take over. Lucy would go into hysterics, run into her room, and lock the door. She wouldn't come out until one of us had put him to sleep."

He stole a glance toward Andrew, sleeping peacefully in his bed, his stubby legs tucked up under his little bottom. "She never even considered nursing him. We lived like that for about three years, I guess. Those years were pretty miserable for both of us."

"But—I always thought you two were so happy! You worshipped that woman!"

"I misled you. My pride wouldn't let me reveal the truth. I don't know how one man could've been so stupid."

He continued. "To keep her from brooding, I took her to St. Joseph or Topeka several times a year to shop for the newest fashions. Sometimes, I think promising her those trips was all that kept our marriage together. She'd hug me, kiss me, and tell me how wonderful I was. Like an idiot, I believed her. When we were visiting in St. Louis, her friends would give grand parties. Lucy would pile curls on her head with those fancy ribbons, and she'd wear low-cut gowns that cost me a small fortune. She'd parade herself back and forth in front of all the men. They'd make over her and whisk her about the dance floor, while all the ladies watched and envied her and her beauty. She loved it."

"If she treated you so badly, why did you put up with it?"

He swallowed hard. He had to answer her question as honestly as he could, no matter how much it hurt him to verbalize the words. "Be—because I saw my father in me. I felt the same hatred and discontent that he felt for my mother. Oh, not for the same reasons. Lucy and my mother were nothing alike. But I knew I had the same power my father had. The same—"

"Same what?" she asked, her eyes wide.

He paused and nibbled at his lip. "The same anger. It scared me. I never wanted to see that anger unleashed. I kept it all buried inside me. I'd turn my back on the jealousy and the things that made me mad. I made myself believe the attentions those men paid her were really compliments for me because I'd been able to convince such a beautiful woman to become my wife. In truth, I deceived myself."

"But you had two children—"

"Oh yes. That was the blow that nearly sent Lucy back to Kentucky. We had—" He bit his lip. *How can I say this?*

"I'm your wife, Stone. You can tell me anything," she whispered softly.

"We were together as husband and wife. Often. It was her way of controlling me. And, to be honest, I never complained."

Her cheeks flushed. "I—I think I understand. You needn't explain."

"Anyway, when Doc Meeker diagnosed her second pregnancy, again she turned on me. She was even more upset than the first time. She considered having the baby taken from her. Although she never admitted it, I'm sure she tried some home remedies her friends had told her about to get rid of the baby. I've always thought that's why Will was born deaf."

Her mouth sprang open. "How awful. I can't imagine any mother wanting to get rid of her baby!"

"I guess I'll never know. Anyway, she insisted I take her back to St. Joseph to have the baby. I got her a nice house, and I asked Alice to look in on her occasionally. I couldn't be gone from the ranch all the time."

"That's when she made the quilt squares?" Juliette asked, prodding gently.

He nodded. "Yes, she always loved doing needlework. She made those twelve blocks, or squares, or whatever you call them. But she never got them put together before she—"

"Before she died?"

"Patience, I'm coming to that. From that first minute when I took Will in my arms, I suspected something might be wrong with his hearing. His cry had a strange sound to it. He didn't sound anything like a normal baby. Lucy wouldn't even talk about it. She wanted to put him up for adoption as soon as possible, saying one child was enough. I wouldn't hear of it. We had terrible arguments. I'd never been so angry in my entire life, other than when my father was beating my mother."

Stone wished he didn't have to tell his whole sordid story, but she had to know. He looked at her beautiful face, now swollen from the bump on her head. If she hadn't been his wife, none of her injuries would have ever happened. He'd bear that guilt the rest of his life.

"Go on, please. I didn't mean to interrupt."

The lump in his throat nearly choked him. "She refused to come back to Dove City. She said she needed time to recuperate, so I hired a nurse for her and one to take care of the boys. She stayed on in St. Joseph while I came back to tend to the ranch. I got several of the men to take over for me and went right back."

"Many women have a hard time adjusting after giving birth. Perhaps she—"

"Actually, that's what I thought at first, but that had nothing to do with it. Will's birth—"

Her eyes widened. "That's when she died of childbirth complications? Like you'd told me?"

He clenched his fists and blinked. "No. I wish I could say she died from childbirth complications, but I can't. That was a lie!"

Chapter 10

A deep frown creased her forehead, and her face turned a ghostly white. "Wh–what do you mean?"

"She *didn't* die soon after Will was born. I lied."

"If she didn't die then, when did she die?" Juliette pressed herself tightly against the pillows, her face convulsing with anger. "Oh Stone! Don't tell me she's still alive! If she is, that means you're still married!"

He reached out to her. "You've got it all wrong. Hear me out!"

She began to beat on him with her good hand. "How could you marry me, knowing your wife is still alive? How could you lie to me like that?"

He grabbed her wrist to fend off her blows. "She didn't die then! She died two years later!" She tried to pull away from him, but he held her fast, determined to tell her everything.

"But why? Why would you lie about such an important thing? It doesn't make any sense. Is anything you've told me the truth?"

"Everything I told you, up to the part about Lucy being upset about having a second baby and wanting to put Will up for adoption, is true."

"Go on."

"From that minute on, when she realized I was not going to agree to give him up, she said she hated me. Lucy actually told me she'd never loved me. It was my money and the lifestyle I could give her she was after. She called me names and refused to live under my roof any longer. I sent the children and their nurse over to my sister's house to stay. I hoped Lucy would feel differently about things once she got over having a second baby, but she didn't. She was moody and hateful. She'd attend parties at night, then sleep until noon the next day. She drank too heavily, and what time she wasn't sleeping or celebrating with her friends, she slept on the sofa with an empty bottle in her hand. Life was miserable for both of us. She constantly brought strange men to our house, and when I tried to send them away, she'd go with them."

Warily, he reached out and cupped her hand. "She'd be gone for days at a time. I had no idea where she was or who she was with. Then, one day, she walked in with this Mexican trader and announced she was tired of being married to me and living her dull, boring life. She was going to Mexico with him. Two hours later, she was gone, and so was a good bit of money from our bank account."

"I never knew. I thought the woman was a saint. I envied her."

"Juliette, I knew the day she walked out with that man, I'd never want her back. I'd rather live the rest of my life alone, raising our two sons by myself, than have her come back to me. She'd shattered every bit of pride I've ever had."

"Didn't you try to stop her?"

"I started to. She *was* my children's mother. I couldn't just let her walk out that way, without knowing how to reach her. I've told you about my anger. At times, I felt like strangling Lucy, I was so furious with her. I reminded myself of my father, and it made me sick. I was afraid if I got near the man, I'd kill him with my bare hands. Then my sons wouldn't have anyone to provide for them. I—I just stood there and watched them go."

"But the padlocked room? Her things? I don't understand."

"I'm getting to that." He turned her hand loose, rose, and began to pace about the room. After pulling his handkerchief from his pocket, he blew his nose loudly.

"I brooded around St. Joseph for a while, but I knew I had to get back to my ranch. I couldn't ask my sister to leave her home and her friends, but I begged her to keep my boys until I could find someone here to care for them. She finally agreed. I was embarrassed and ashamed to admit my wife had walked out on me and my children. I think if it hadn't been for Eric and Will, I might have done away with myself. I didn't want anyone to know the truth, so when I finally came back to Dove City, I invented that lie and told everyone she'd died of complications after Will's birth—even though she was still alive. Since they had no reason to think otherwise, they believed me. I was consumed with guilt when people offered their sympathy. I've never told them any differently."

"What happened to Lucy? Did you ever hear from her again?"

He rubbed at his forehead. "No. Not a word—not even to ask about her children. But about two years later, almost to the day, on one of my few trips to visit my sons, I ran into a friend of hers. She and Lucy had kept in contact with one another. She's the one who told me Lucy had died. Apparently, she came down with an illness in Mexico. She was sick for several months and eventually died. Her Mexican boyfriend had contacted the woman in St. Joseph and told her about Lucy's death. I tried to learn more for our sons' sake, but I was never even able to find out where she died or even the name of the man she left with."

She stared at him as if still trying to comprehend what he was saying. "Then why have you kept her things the way she left them?"

He sucked in another breath and let it out slowly. "I don't have an answer for that, Juliette. I guess because they remind me of happier times. Those first few months, I was captivated by her beauty and her charms. She was the kind of woman men dream about. I was stupid enough to believe she loved me. In truth, all she was doing was using me; but after Will was born and she didn't want him, my anger took over. The same uncontrolled anger I'd seen in my father. I wanted to smash everything she'd ever touched, get rid of everything that reminded me of her. I even wanted to burn the house down."

"I'm glad you didn't. It's the perfect place for your boys."

"My hatred consumed me. She never cared for me. I know that now. It was my money she was after. For a year or so after she died, I kept that room locked and never opened it. I didn't want to touch her things or even see them. Because of her and what she'd done to me, I decided I'd never let a woman get close to me again. I refused to put myself in a position to be hurt again. All I wanted out of life was to bring my boys home."

Juliette wiped at her eyes. "I'm beginning to understand. It must have been a terrible time for you."

"The worst." He smiled at her. "Then I met you. You were from a fine family and seemed to be the perfect mother. I knew from the first day I met you, you were the woman I wanted to raise my boys. I also knew you were too proper to stay in my home and work for me unless I could talk you into marrying me. I brought you that handkerchief just to start up a conversation. I hoped eventually you'd agree, and I could bring my boys back where they belong."

"Then Mr. Stark was killed. Mrs. Stark decided to sell the hotel, and my father needed the money to buy it. Correct?"

"Yes. I'd have given anything to have my boys back home. I know it sounds like a devious plan, but honestly, Juliette, if you wouldn't have agreed to marry me, I would've given John the money."

She lowered her gaze and dabbed at her eyes again. "But you didn't have to, did you? You bought a wife instead."

"Yes," he conceded, "I bought a wife instead—a wife I never intended to love. I'd vowed I'd never love another woman. Not after the way I'd been hurt by Lucy. That's why I wanted a marriage in name only. I was never going to put myself in that position again. I only wanted a fine Christian woman to run my house and be a mother to my boys. I never planned on falling in love with you. Your father needed the money, and you wanted a home for you and your son." He paused, guilt ripping at him, tearing at his heart. "It seemed the best solution for all of us."

She began to weep uncontrollably. "All of us? For you, you mean! The Baker family's needs were just a way for you to gain what you wanted. A business deal! We were just a means to an end. An end to your search for a way to bring Eric and Will to Dove City."

"I *was* concerned about your family!" he nearly shouted at her. Andrew stirred in his bed, and Stone lowered his voice before continuing. "I've never met a finer man than John. I would *never* have let that hotel get away from him. Even if I'd had to buy it and beg him to run it for me. But at that time, I had no idea *you'd* become so important to me!"

"Important to you? Is that what you call it?" She turned her face away as tears trailed down her cheeks and fell onto her gown. "What do you think all those people who've been calling you a hero would think if they knew you'd lied? Not only to me and my family, but to them? What do you suppose God thinks?"

"As their deputy, those folks trusted me. I'm sure they'd hate me for it." He shifted in the chair uncomfortably. "What does God think? He thinks I'm a fool," he answered softly, lowering his face into his hands.

"Please leave," she said, her voice quivering. "Go into Lucy's room. Rock in her chair and remember the times she tossed you aside like an old boot!"

"But Juliette—don't you see? I hated Lucy. That's why I went into that locked room night after night. I knew I was falling in love with you, and I didn't want to! By going in there and sitting in that chair, I reminded myself of the miserable life we'd had together. I had to convince myself taking you as a true wife might be no better than living with her." He hung his head, lacing his fingers together. "How did I know you wouldn't do the same thing to me that Lucy did if I told you I loved you? I've saddled you with a deaf child, just like I did her. How did I know you wouldn't try to take my money and leave me, just like she did?"

She glared at him, her eyes filled with anguish. "I thought you knew me better than that! You trusted me with your children!"

"I thought I knew her! Don't you see? I was afraid! Afraid of loving you! Afraid of losing you!" His voice softened again as he glanced toward the sleeping baby. "I thought I loved Lucy. But now, after being with you, I finally realize what I had with her was not true love. The love I had for Lucy was nothing like my love for you. In fact, if I were honest, I'd probably have to say what I had for her was lust, not love. I wanted to possess her. She was an object to hold up in front of people. There was constant strife between us, right from the beginning. We were never truly happy. Being with you, going on picnics, holding hands over the supper table, sitting on the floor in front of the fireplace, reading our Bible together, watching you with our boys, sitting beside you in church—that's true happiness—the kind of happiness God intended between a husband and a wife."

Juliette struggled to refute what he was saying, but no words came.

She, too, had discovered true happiness by being with him.

"The love I have for you is different—sweet and sincere. Although you are a beautiful woman, I'm not interested in showing you off like an object I've purchased. I want you all to myself. I want to hold you, to shelter and protect you. I want to take you in my arms and shower your face with kisses. And yes, I want to take you to my bed, but only as a way to express my love for you. You're everything to me, Juliette. Can't you see that?"

He leaned his face close to hers, so close he could feel her warm breath on his cheeks. "Look into my eyes, Juliette. You're my wife. I'd lay down my life for you. Can't you see that? Can't you find it in your heart to forgive me?"

She gulped hard. "Th–this has all come as a shock, Stone. Ca–can we talk about this in the morning? I need time to think."

"Of course. But remember the things I've said. I love you, Juliette." With a look of defeat, he rose and slowly walked away.

⤶

She spent a restless evening as the love she felt for Stone battled with the ill feelings she harbored in her heart for his deception. His lies had crushed her. She felt lower than she'd ever felt in her life. Yet, in some ways, her heart sang. He loved her. He really loved her. Wasn't this what she'd wanted all along?

Before she blew out the lamp, she pulled the Bible from her nightstand and held it to her bosom before turning the pages to the love chapter in First Corinthians. She read it silently, with an open heart. *Oh God, I do love Stone. Help me! I want to make the right decision. What is Your will for our lives?*

Early the next morning she heard a slight rap on her door, and her heart began to pound furiously. "Juliette? Are you awake?" She quickly pulled the covers about her. "I—I guess so. Come in."

"I know you're furious with me. You have every right to be, but let me talk. I–I've been awake most of the night, reading my Bible and settling this thing with God. I asked for His forgiveness, and He has forgiven me. I know He has because it says so right in His Word. I've rid myself of the ghosts of my past. As soon as I can get to it, I'm going to take everything out of Lucy's room and give it all away. I know there are some things you'd like to have, but I'd rather buy them for you new than have them around as a reminder of her."

"Stone, I—"

"Shh, let me finish. I need to get these things said. I've wronged you, Juliette, and I've come to apologize." As he moved slowly to the bed and sat down beside her, she could see his eyes were puffy and he'd been crying. "I had no right to lie and deceive you like I did. There's no excuse for what I've done. I—I know I don't deserve it—but I hope, someday, you'll find it in your heart to forgive me. I—I never meant any harm, honest." A tear rolled slowly down his cheek.

"Come here. I have something to say, too." She waited until he'd seated himself, then continued. "When you told me you'd lied about Lucy's death, I—I felt completely devastated. If it hadn't been for Eric and little Will, I would have taken Andrew and gone back to the hotel. But—" She paused, wanting to say just the right words to convey her sincere feelings. "I spent a long time with my Bible last night. God has been speaking to my heart, too. About forgiveness. I—I love your precious boys. While I can't condone all the lying you've done, I can almost see why you did. Experiences that shake our lives and turn them upside down can make us respond in strange ways. I still intend to stay true to my wedding vows. When I made those vows, I made them before God. I feel He would have me stay." Her heart clenched as a slow smile crept across his face.

"You mean it? You'll stay?"

"We're both sinners saved by grace, Stone, and we're still legally married. I'll stay if you want me to. I—I love you, too."

"You do? You really do?" His hand lightly touched hers. "I love you more than life itself."

She felt his fingers tighten over hers.

"With God's help, do you think we can work this out? That you can find it in your heart to forgive me for lying to you? I love you so much, my dearest. God has forgiven me. Do you think you'll ever be able to forgive me?"

She gazed into his eyes, his words of repentance softening the ache in her heart. "I'd strayed away from Him, too. I'd been playing at church. Through all of this, I've discovered I need a closer walk with Him. God has forgiven me, so I must forgive you."

"I'll never lie to you again. I promise I'll do everything in my power to restore your faith in me. I want God to control our lives and be the head of our household."

She reached out and touched his cheek as Andrew stirred in his crib. "I love you, Stone. I think I've always loved you. I was just afraid to admit it. I want to be your wife in every way."

Epilogue

Juliette's arms circled her husband's neck as she gazed into his kind face with adoring eyes. "Do you realize this will be our fourth Christmas together?"

"Sure do." He gave her a broad grin, then nestled his chin in her hair. "I've loved every day of our time together."

"Stone," she began slowly, smoothing back the hair from his forehead, knowing her words might upset him. "I've been thinking about that quilt."

The smile on his face disappeared.

"It's a beautiful quilt. It seems a shame to have it boxed away, out of sight. I think it's time we did something with it."

He frowned. "Like what?"

"I put in many nights of work on that quilt. Probably far more than I should have. I wanted it to be a special gift for you. If you agree, I'd like to remove Lucy's name from those blocks and embroider my own name in those places. After all, I'm the one who put it together, bound it, and did all the hand quilting."

He tilted her chin upward and gazed into her eyes. "You sure you want to do that?"

She stood on tiptoes and kissed his cheek. "Yes, my love, I do. I've forgiven you for what you did to me, and I think it's time we both forgave Lucy, don't you?"

"You're quite a woman, Juliette, and you're right. How could I have expected God to forgive me when I haven't been willing to forgive Lucy?" Stone wrapped his long arms about her waist and pulled her close. "Of course it's all right with me. Anything to make you happy. But—are you sure having that quilt around won't bring back too many unpleasant memories? Perhaps it'd be better if we just gave it away."

"We're so happy together now. We're expecting our first child together. Our boys are growing up. Will is able to communicate with us. My mother's health has improved, and the hotel is doing well. God has blessed us in so many ways. With His help, I'm sure we can put all those bad memories aside. I'd rather think of the joy I felt as I labored on that quilt. Each stitch I added, I added with love for you, my darling. In many ways, our life together is wrapped up in that quilt."

"God has been good to us, hasn't He?"

She nodded. "Far more than we deserve."

"I love you, Juliette Piper."

"I love you, too, dear Stone."

"You're truly a gift from God. If you want the quilt, it's fine with me. Now I realize how much work you'd put into it. I only wish I'd appreciated it at the time. I was a fool to react the way I did when you gave it to me. An utter fool!"

Juliette planted a kiss on her husband's cheek. "Shh, remember? Those bad memories are behind us now." She could feel his loving gaze upon her as she moved to the closet and pulled a box from the top shelf. Her fingers trembled as she removed the lid and lifted out Lucy's quilt.

Joyce Livingston has done many things in her life (in addition to being a wife, mother of six, and grandmother to oodles of grandkids, all of whom She loves dearly). From being a television broadcaster for eighteen years, to lecturing and teaching on quilting and sewing, to writing magazine articles on a variety of subjects. She's danced with Lawrence Welk, ice-skated with a chimpanzee, had bottles broken over her head by stuntmen, interviewed hundreds of celebrities and controversial figures, and many other interesting and unusual things. But now, when she isn't off traveling to wonderful and exotic places as a part-time tour escort, her days are spent sitting in front of her computer, creating stories. Joyce became a widow in 2004. In 2008, she married her Sunday school teacher, Pastor Dale Lewis (who had also lost his spouse), and became a pastor's wife, serving daily with him in his ministry. Four of her books have been named Contemporary Book of the Year in the Heartsong Readers Poll, and she was voted Favorite Author of the Year 3 times. In addition, her Heartsong book, *One Last Christmas*, won the coveted Contemporary Book of the Year award given by The American Christian Fiction Writers organization. In addition to writing for Barbour, Joyce also writes for Love Inspired. Her first venture into a larger women's fiction book is *The Widows' Club*, also published by Barbour Publishing, soon to be followed up with a second book, *Invasion of the Widows' Club*. Joyce feels her writing is a ministry and a calling from God, and hopes readers will be touched and uplifted by what she writes. What's on the horizon for Joyce? More and better books that she hopes will please her readers!

If You Liked This Book, You'll Also Like...

Logan's Lady

Enjoy a classic historical romance set in Colorado from bestselling author Tracie Peterson. Lady Amelia Amhurst, leaves England on holiday to discover the beauty of America in 1875 and discovers a love for the land—and her rugged trail guide. Also includes a bonus—*Along Unfamiliar Paths* from author Amy Rognlie.

Paperback / 978-1-63409-653-9 / $9.99

Journey of the Heart

This classic historical romance set in Texas is from bestselling author DiAnn Mills. Pulled between the Comanche lifestyle she was raised within and her family at Fort Davis, Katie Colter is faced with hard choices for her future. Also includes a bonus—*Song of the Dove* from author Peggy Darty.

Paperback / 978-1-63058-628-7 / $9.99

The Carpenter's Inheritance

You'll enjoy Laurie Alice Eakes' gripping historical romance between an upstart female lawyer and her client, a carpenter with a questionable past. When faced with a choice, will Lucinda Bell choose career over love? Also includes a bonus story, *A Love So Tender* by Tracey V. Bateman.

Paperback / 978-1-60742-580-9 / $9.99